The Reverend's Apprentice

The Reverend's Apprentice

David N. Odhiambo

ARSENAL PULP PRESS | VANCOUVER

THE REVEREND'S APPRENTICE
Copyright © 2008 by David N. Odhiambo

ARSENAL PULP PRESS
Suite 200, 341 Water Street
Vancouver, BC
Canada V6B 1B8
arsenalpulp.com

The publisher gratefully acknowledges the support of the Canada Council for the Arts and the British Columbia Arts Council for its publishing program, and the Government of Canada through the Book Publishing Industry Development Program and the Government of British Columbia through the Book Publishing Tax Credit Program for its publishing activities. David N. Odhiambo would like to thank the Canada Council for all of their support.

Cover design by Information-Office.org
Cover photography by Melodie McDaniel
Editing by Bethanne Grabham

Printed and bound in Canada

Library and Archives Canada Cataloguing in Publication:

Odhiambo, David Nandi, 1965-
	The reverend's apprentice / David N. Odhiambo.

ISBN 978-1-55152-242-5

	I. Title.

PS8579.D54R49 2008   C813'.54   C2008-904096-1

for Mum and Dad.

Volume One

Contents

Principal Characters

JONAH AYOT-KOLOSHA—anti-hero, MFA student, dandy, rake

REVEREND NEHEMIAH AYOT—babu or grandfather, man of God

PHINEAS KOLOSHA—baba or father, wheeler and dealer in matters pursuant to finance

RAHAB AYOT-KOLOSHA—mama or mother, goodly Christian

REVEREND JAMES LEWISHAM TUSKER—the Rev at St Peter's Episcopalian Church, power of attorney over the Ayot-Kolosha fortune, the Rev

MEREDITH TUSKER—the Rev's late and beloved wife

ELISHA TUSKER—the Rev's underemployed son

DOROTHEA TUSKER—Elisha's inner city African American wife with an assortment of shoulder length blonde wigs

HIROKO ISHIGOWA—rival, Babycakes, kinky she-love

INGRID ISHIGOWA—thirteen-year-old sister of Hiroko, prodigy with abnormal attention span

CLEMENTINE "DA STYLUS" PINKSTON—girlfriend, chaste choir member

QUINT C.—Q., friend, soon-to-be published author of *Gangrene & Other Stories* (Dilchester Press)

ELIZA MAY MORTON—friend, bright light, up-and-comer, the future

BINGO "JACKPOT" JEFFERSON—ex-con, freelance laborer, all around hustler

RACHEL DALGLEISH—agent

RITA PETRA-FREUD—neighbor, Ma Petra-Freud, Black Republican

ALISTAIR FREUD—neighbor, Papi Freud, Black Republican

LORETTA TUCCI—Rev's "friend" with a mane of brown Barbie-doll hair and bright red televangelist-wife lipstick

LEROI JOHNSON—toll-booth attendant

MONAY SHOTT—exotic dancer, peroxide oldie with sagging olive skin

KETI—childhood friend, son of watchman

PROFESSOR COLIN ITON—faculty at Dingham University (DU), man of letters

FISH COLEMAN—author of *In the Cut* (best-selling trade paperback)

TAMALA EXETER—TV actress, star of Emmy Award winner, *Switcher*

RAFE CURTIS—TV actor, costar of Emmy Award winner, *Switcher*

LANCE ITBY—celebrity, tycoon hubby of Tamala Exeter

ALICE MARKHAM—the Silver Fox, administrative assistant at DU

CYBIL HARRIS—Bostonian, author of short story published in the *Shipleigh Journal*, former writing resident at Wing Gate Manor

DAVID WINCH—steelworker's son, working on a blook

ROSEMARY LEVY—self-avowed bookworm, the Bookworm, "unapologetically pomo"

RICHARD SPOILS—muttering Canuck from TO

THE SPEILMANS—neighbors, "Spy-Christ killers"

YULIYA—girl-next-door type with chestnut hair and acid-washed jeans

NURSE SHELLEY—on staff at Fred Mullins General, embroiled in scandal with Dr

DR—on staff at Fred Mullins General, embroiled in scandal with Nurse Shelley

THE BLACK COP—a black cop

THE FLYWEIGHT—a "cabbie"

THE CUTTLEWOTS—cat-happy neighbors, paintings of their home

ITO MORITA—fiancé of Hiroko

COMMANDER-IN-CHIEF—guest appearance by his eminence

THE boyCEO—patient at mental cklink

THE STRAIGHT SHOOTER—patient at mental cklink

LADY G—patient at mental cklink

Paralepsis

It has been said that this is a true account of Jonah Ayot-Kolosha's journey from Liwani to Curranvale City, his year as a protégé for his master, Professor Iton, at Dingham University, and his early writings as well as the events that occurred during this youthful juncture. As a matter of course, we at the Dalgleish Agency Inc. deny any claims that the facts herein are in the least bit biographical. The intention to tell Mr Ayot-Kolosha's story as a memoir was part of the original contract with the author, but subsequent events that cannot be commented upon, pending litigation in the case, have made it abundantly clear this story is riddled with libels too great to address in this forum. We refer the interested party to the landmark ruling in the case of *Ayers v. Saltzman* in which a sum of $120,000 was awarded to the Saltzman Literary Agency for "liberties with truth" undertaken by Mr Ayers. While we at the Dalgleish Agency are confident our motion to block the publication of this work will be upheld by the State Courts, as a precautionary measure we deem it necessary to distance ourselves from any and all presumptions of veracity heretofore found between these pages. We refer the interested party to other biographical works on our list at *www.dalgleish.com* that more fully embody the material we proudly make available for your reading enjoyment.

Rachel Dalgleish, Agent
Geneva, NY
May 8/08

BOOK I

In Medias Res

arrfter your bones hve spatially doubled from yr shoulder to yr fingers

u are in hospital and the nurse takes bllod from yor arm. Shesticcks the needl right where the inside of the bicep becomes the tricep. Thereis a headache in the   back where your cranium is. yr foots have an itching feeling in it.

yu think the tall nurse with the mean talk will wrap a bandage around yor trachea and snuff u out. if u go to the toilet, u think the dr will stick you with a knife just like that.

U say yr mind to them that ths is what mkes u afeard.

btU should shut up to powEr. Not a peep. Then they wouldn't talk about that you present with the diagnosis of psykosis.

they give u to   the green paper to sign.

"Don't bother reading that one," the soft-faced nurse sys. "It's just procedure."

Thehospitalpeoples gives moremedication to u and showeded u brochures with pictures of the Center. Drs smile with old folk, paraplegics,   nuthousers.

U rrlly don't remebre your mind.

Y'll see round the clock care," they tell to yu.

"i want to gohome now,. you say

they show to u the green sheet with yr signture which said u am a voluntteer in for days.

"i'm tricked," you reply. "I wastold to me it was procedureand told to me not to read the greane paper."

"sir, They say. Sir you,re paranoid sir. YoU signed sir. It is in black and whte sir. This is serious, for you to be taken frumout to in. yu hve issues from angre,sir"

"get me out of here," u shout . "idon't want to go to the nut-housers." Youdo not know where to turn where they don't not search yor thoghts.

"sir, sir," they say. We may need to operate on your cerebral lobes, 'n' yor crebral fornix. This is serious, sir.

"idon't not want to go to the nuthousers."

they put a needle iNn cartilage iNn your arm. They take yr belt and everything. then say "visiting hours is for eight to nine-thirty o'clock."

You'rre tired from the injection and tired that no one who can listen. Yor tired From everyone that says we hAve our evalua-tion and we choose that iz how we see is the realdeal and what you is is not what it is we want. They say,maybe if you change to us,maybe.

Yor given to bed.

U do not sleep well in this mental c(k)link of the hspital with a reputation for pleasing baby deliveries. On no side is there to turn where there is no pain in it. InsteaD u study many stories, about night. U go to the oTher places and obsess over mistakes, toSSed prettily to the lefvt, lichen and ludicrous.

It is something-thrty in the drk that u get up. U cannot make a walk becuz your hands is tied with ropes and on yor feet is fire.

"Let me get from here." U do not remember your mind. "Let me go NoW."

At yor door is a guaRrd, he calls to men to come and put a new injection in of u. After it, u sleep in the place that when you touch a thing it is not a real thing. ★ ★ ★ ★ ★ ★ ★ ★ ★ ★ ★ ★ ★ ★ ★

★ ★
★ ★ ★ ★ ★ ★ ★ ★ ★ ★ ★ ★ ★ ★ ★ ★ ★ ★ ★ A nurse with the name of
shellie comes to shake you up. Still in yr diaphragmchest is there a
burning there, and you're made captive by ropes to the bed and
a   security guard at yor door.

  Sshe puts pills from a plastic container to your lips,

    you look around the bedroom to nother bed   and one curtain
around it, one bedside table, a closet and a toilet. There are no
windows.

  You am tied on by leather restraints. U are wet in your diaper.
Yor cerebrum is out and in two hemisphrs, andback and forth to
your cerebellum, out and in, back 'n' 4th.

  U cannot track what is your coordinates in spACe-tyme is it.

BOOK II

Anachrony

I

Curranvale City is having a go at Happy Hour on a Saturday
eve. Folk from its segregated hoods as well as those from the
ones that have integrated since the race riots in the late six-
ties buckle down with favored brands of brew

Some sit alone in rheumy light with a bottle in rooms that replay
episode six of *Switcher*[1] on the telly. Others with flutes of bubbly
hover in groups as large as fire marshals will allow while outdoors,
a dim backdrop of stars mark time with imperceptible shifts by
degrees. Down the hatch. Offensive remarks mingle with endear-
ments that loosen the mood, and strangers stamp feet like horny
satyrs pawing their cloven hooves before the fucking. *Salud.* Off
to one side of the drinking, Jonah Ayot-Kolosha sits in a dimly lit
corner of a scuzzy booty club with a pocket full o' cash, and waits
among others beside a scummy main stage infested with ants.

(The plan: Don't be a punk.)[2]

Babycakes is tall in her black nine-inch boots among the vari-
ously colored panties who posture around her. He knocks back
shots of Patron and watches her lean back against a pole in a cus-
tard sarong waiting for the sap who'll slip ducats into her garter.

---

1   A Nielsen ratings behemoth on Tuesday nights from nine to ten o'clock.
The storyline follows a cougar (older woman) in an on-again-off-again
romance with a young up-an-comer (male), liberally using hand-held digital
cameras to create *cinema verité* effects.

2   These lines were cut from the second to last draft.

She waves him over to a seat at the side of the stage, lays a fleece blanket on the floor, and gets to work.

Besieged by red and green light, he watches her lift her sarong, spread her legs, and show him her pussy. In burnt umber skin, a diamond stud winks at her belly button. She mouths along to Outkast's "SpottieOttieDopaliscious," drops her bra, and leans forward to brush her black nipple against the tip of his nose. Off-kilter, he inhales the scent of peaches before she pulls back, sits sideways-longways at the edge of the stage, and lifts her turquoise garter for him to slip a folded bill against her skin. A run of funky trumpet kicks in, she lies on her back, her legs spread-eagled in the air, her fingers teasing open mulberry lips.

"You haven't been in a while?" she says.

"You noticed?"

"No. I'm asking."

"So am I."

"Asking what?"

"If you noticed."

She lifts her garter again. "And I'm asking where you were."

"Which means you noticed."

She smiles. "Well?"

"I went home to take care of my late grandfather's estate."

"Home?"

"Liwani."

"Where?"

"Central Africa. Africa. Across from the Mediterranean, left at the Atlantic."

"I know where Africa is, bonehead."

He slips her a bill.

She gets down on all fours and furiously shakes her rump in his mug before sitting beside him, lifting her garter for another one.

"I bet you thought about me the whole time I was gone," he says.

"Get over yourself."

"No. Really." He stares off into space the way Professor Iton[3] often does. "I'm the swag, and you're like an open parachute drifting in chop toward this bountiful bootay I got going."

"So what you're really saying is how much you wanna hit this." She pats her fanny. "You've got a bad case of the Babycakes. I see it all the time."

"Not at all, babe. I hate you."

"I hate you too, sweetie. But we're talking about what you wanna do with all this here."

"Wrong, again. Don't forget, I have a girlfriend."

"The missionary! It's gotta be exhausting pretending to be something you ain't for her."

"You got that right."

"Aha! I knew it," she exclaims.

"What?"

"You're not getting enough of the kinkies. You're upset. So you need a taste of the Cakes."

"No. That's wrong. It's waaay off."

"Which is it? Wrong or way off?"

"Is there a difference?"

"There sure is, hon. Sure is."

---

3 Winner of the Tolstoievsky Prize for Literature, 1982 and 1999, and Professor of Creative Writing at Dingham University, 1984–present, whose current bedside reading is a first edition copy of the *Satanic Verses* by Salman Rushdie.

Da Stylus wants her first time to be just so. There has to be a Willow tree, a body of water, a full moon, a woolen blanket, condoms with spermicide, breath mints, and it should take place on a weekend. So we drive to Bull Lake and walk through a field used by dogs to shit, nuzzle amongst duck droppings at the roots of a willow, and watch the moon in the water.

"Are you doing okay?" I ask.

"Oh, besides being petrified?" she replies.

"We don't have to do this."

"Yah, riiight."

"You don't want to do this?"

"Of course, I do."

"Yah, riiight."

"Don't be like that."

"I'm not being like anything."

"You're mad."

"Not in the least," I pretend. "It's just ..."

We've been together for eight months, and she's still dragging her feet (even though I followed through on her endless list of detailed demands just to get us to this point—spending quality time, being a quality audience for her various struggles, donating quality gifts at regular intervals, and providing evidence of a desire for a quality relationship with the Heavenly Father).[4]

Fed up, I help her to her feet, pack our supplies, and walk her to the car.

∞

Babycakes kneels in front of Jonah, cups the back of his head, and tugs him forward.

---

4   *The Notebooks*, July 12, 2003. All future references to *The Notebooks* are in regards to the texts made available to the author with the expressed written consent of the Jonah Ayot-Kolosha estate.

He can smell her as her trim tickle-licks him.

"I *don't* have a case of the Babycakes." He slips her a fiver. "I wouldn't do that to my girlfriend."

She pulls away.

"Left at the Atlantic! You really are a bonehead."

She dresses, gathers bills strewn around her, and moves her fleece blanket over to dance for a bearded fuck and his lady friend.

Jonah sits at the side of the stage drinking himself stupid as Babycakes leans in to tug a twenty from lady friend's mouth with her lips. He watches her dip her face into lady friend's cleavage and slurp up another bill; watches while Cakes turns around as lady friend smacks fivers onto the sweaty bare cheeks of her ass.

The bearded fuck wheels a deal on his cell before he sends a phone picture of "the girls" to someone in Anchorage, Alaska. Two songs later, Cakes takes a hold of both of them by the hand and together they disappear into the VIP.

Ebonay, the hustler, jiggling cellulite in a coal teddy as dark as her skin swarms Jonah.

"Wanna private dance, sugar?"

"No." He feels guilty for rejecting one of his own. "Not to-night." But not guilty enough.

She moves on.

What is guilty enough?

On stage, a peroxide oldie with sagging olive skin has her knees gripped tight around the ears of a 300-pound behemoth.

Jonah glances at other dancers—Desiree, Carmela, Natasha—who smile, pull aside their thongs, and play flabby customers who will gamble that if they hit the ATM machine one more time, perhaps they'll finally score. Paunchy accessorized fellas with big-ass rings and fading lookers under either arm sit at side tables that waitresses supply with a steady stream of booze. Across the stage, Natasha, a bundle of bones, slaps a groping customer, gathers up her discarded kit, and stalks off stage.

When the behemoth with his head deep between the peroxide oldie's sagging thighs emerges to show her his empty pockets, she slides over and drapes her legs over Jonah's shoulders, her shaved *punani*[5] a tongue's length away.

"What do they call you, darling?" she asks.

"Jonah."

"I'm Monay," she says. "Monay Shott." She looked like she was pushing forty. Whatever cash she's made in the past has gone up her nose, or toward the reconstruction of her scarred bod. "I see you here all the time." She lifts her garter as he slides in a bill. "It's fuckin expensive to get a sitter," she continues. "Two hundred bucks a night, and my asshole ex won't give me a red cent. Then I heard he got hisself an Escalade. An Escalade! You imagine? I didn't make that baby myself."

Jonah's bored outta his tree as he slips her some ones, and talks hifalutin verbiage to kill the time. Yes, he went home to "interface" with lawyers about "important matters pursuant to my grandfather's estate," and to deal with his late father's investments in stocks[6] that "accrued more than anyone realized." Good Lord! "*De facto*, tedious is too weak a word to describe it." He's not

---

5   A woman's honey pot, coochie, hoo ha, yum yum.

6   During the late 1980s, Jonah's father, Phineas Kolosha, invested with Citadel Inc., an American-based technology company that develops, manufactures, and sells computer and other technology-related products worldwide. He died of an illness when Jonah was eight years old, and did not live to see the huge profits from the investment.

"built for administrative matters of pertinence to finance, being a creative writer by trade," so he turned it over to "someone else with a head for numbers." At least the paperwork is done, and, yup, he's coming "into a fortune" on his twenty-first birthday, "three months from the day after tomorrow which is, in the parlance, rather expeditious."

"Wow!" Monay says. "Don't forget about the little guy who knew you when."

Changing the subject, he asks about Babycakes.

"Dead end, darling," she replies. "Forget her. She's engaged to a fella fighting in Iraq." Monay gets back to how her shoes kill her feet, how her hip's been bugging her, how she wishes the deejay would play Bob Marley,[7] mon. "Wow, an honest to goodness millionaire," she concludes.

"Listen." He gives her a twenty. "Could you tell Babycakes I'd like to buy her a drink?"

"You're shitting me."

"I want to buy her champagne in VIP *posthaste*."

"What about me?"

"Another time."

"Know what?"

"No. What?"

"Fuck you, rich piece—a ... prick!" Monay then rolls over to harass the next customer.

---

7 Tragically, Jonah's father never got to see the great man perform before his own passing, but he left a collection of LPs that his son traded with Bingo for weed that lasted him two months. There's speculation that many events that affected Jonah at this juncture were brought about by his growing affection for the herbal product.

Time to get back to Colby Manor.[8]

It takes Jonah at least an hour before he staggers into the parking lot and walks toward black plastic garbage bags heaped on the sidewalks.

"What about what, fucker?" It's Babycakes in a dark corner of the lot, puffing on weed. "What about what?" She jaws at a fella in a white apron who stands in steam leaking out of a restaurant on the other side of a fence.

"What 'bout you, me, and Benji Franklin here do a whole lotta pokie pokie when you get offa work," he flirts.

She gets shrill. "What about me, Smith, and Wesson here pop a round into an asshole's asshole."

"You threatenin' me?"

"I don't see nobody else on the other side of the fence."

"I know where you dance, doll."

Jonah interrupts them. "What about leaving her alone, son?"

"Says who?"

"Her boy. Ralph 'motherfuggin' Ellison."[9]

"So go fuck yourself," she says.

---

8   Named by Reverend James Tusker after his grandfather, Colby Tusker, the first of the freed Tusker clan to emigrate from Missouri to Kansas City in 1860 before they finally moved to Pennsylvania. One of the Reverend's uncles, Colby Tusker II, played the saxophone with both Dizzy Gillespie and Miles Davis, but quit music to pursue a career in a profession no living relative will talk about before his mysterious death in 1958. Therefore, the Colby as so referred in relation to the Manor is the grandfather, not the disgraced uncle.

9   Alias used by Jonah Ayot-Kolosha on email and other computer mediated activities. This name is based on his admiration for the work of African-American author, Ralph Ellison (1913–94). Quint C. Murdoch speculates that Ellison's novel, *Invisible Man,* is a proto-model for Jonah's manuscript, a theory the reclusive Mr Ayot-Kolosha refuses to comment on.

"Apologies, brah." He backpedals into the steam. "I didn't mean no disrespect."

Babycakes rattles the fence. "I didn't need your help," she snaps at Jonah. "I can take care of myself."

"You're welcome."

"I'm no pussy."

"Don't overdo the gratitude," he teases.

She looks him over, puzzled. "Monay Shott says you wanna go VIP." She stamps out the remainder of her spliff, takes him by the tips of his fingers, and leads the way back to the club. ★ A sudden *ka-pow* of wind sweeps neat piles of browning leaves into a neighborhood of swimming pools where the help will descend at dawn to fish out the drain-clogging buggers. The world from Karachi to Arusha smells of boiled chicken, and Hiroko Ishigowa, a.k.a. Babycakes, and Bingo "Jackpot" Jefferson, the Reverend's contractor, support the ill Jonah Ayot-Kolosha while they walk up a driveway in North Oldeham.

"Niiice," Hiroko says about Colby Manor. "It must cost a bundle."

"'N' a 'alf."

"Yup," Bingo says. "This here is money."

There's sudden pain beneath Jonah's ribs that pinches as he stutter-steps. "Whoa." She steadies him against her hip while Bingo rings the doorbell. The porch light flickers on and a curtain pulls back before the Rev rushes outside to help them get Jonah through the front door.

"Good Lord," he gasps. "Did he have a seizure?"

"I dunno," Bingo says. "I met 'em on the driveway."

"He had a drink," she says. "We were in VIP. He wouldn't stop puking his fucking guts out." The Rev flinches. "I couldn't leave him there, so here he is."

"Where?" He shout-talks. "What?"

"Carnival."

"The Gentleman's Club!"

"On 41st," Bingo says.

"You mean below Collins Avenue?"

"Yah," she replies.

"Over near the Skipman's Circle?"

"Christ Jesus. Do I look like a tour guide? Yah, take a right at the stoplight and a fucking left ..."

Their voices crowd Jonah's overfull cranium.[10]

"'Ellooo. Allooo," he interrupts.

"Hold on, Jonah," the Rev requests. "With all due Respect, are you telling me he was in the Red Light District?"

Hiroko's brow winces as the cleric narrowly avoids banging his side of their patient into a banister.

"Eaaasy," she warns.

"Don't mar-marry soldier boy, Iroko," Jonah pleads. "You, Miss, pleash you mar-marry me."

"I'm right the fuck here, darling," Hiroko replies.

---

10   Original wording in *The Lost Boy*, the first draft of the manuscript, *Medulla Oblongata*.

2

Reverend Tusker abandons work on his farewell sermon,[11] and rifles through the foul-mouthed hussy's handbag

He finds Hiroko's wallet buried among ones and fives rolled in elastic bands. There's more: a photograph of a soldier in combat gear signed, Love, Your Fiancé, condoms, plastic gloves, lubricant. Indignant, he opens an unsealed envelope and reads:

Monay Shott's Bio.[12]
I'm ½ Phillipino and ½ Swedish born and raised in Curran-vale City, PA. I started my career doing magazines such as Boom Titty Boom, the video's that got me started were distributed with Jag Off International. Two years ago I was in New York dancing at "Club Caracha" when I was approached by Torvil Hurston III and ended up shooting my first X-rated video called "Tossed Salad", apparently the scene was hot because not having any future plans of doing any more in the video industry my phone started ringing off the hook and be-fore you knew it there I was sukking and fukking on camera. I was brought up in a Catholic school called "St. Margaret's"

---

11   Documentation of Reverend Tusker's final sermon on December 6, 2003 is available in the archives of the Religious Studies department at Dingham University.

12   From the private collection of Hiroko Ishigowa. Used with permission of the author. No evidence exists to indicate Monay Shott is either of Filipino or Swedish descent. Spelling mistakes and problems with punctuation are contained in the original.

in Curranvale City and wouldn't have dreamed of doing this. Now I would like to go back to my school reunion and just say "Look at me know"!

It's been a very busy year. I got a contract to do my very own toy line which will include a doll and a pussy & butt mold coming out next year. I have my new Cam site at www.damonay.com and will keep you posted in my daily diary of any new projects. This is my favorite thing because I get to be in touch with my fans which some have become very good friends that I IM on a daily basis. Oh, before I forget, for all those people that are afraid to email me thinking that it goes to someone besides me, all of my emails come straight to me and I answer everyone of them even though it may take a day or two. I still like knowing what you have to say as long as you are nice of course. I have a schedule link on my site so you can see me when I'm in your area, make sure you do, we can do a Polaroid or maybe even a lap dance :-)

Mwuah mwuah

The Right Reverend James Lewisham Tusker PhD is justifiably distressed, and it is clear the root of this feeling is grounded in a predilection that is both "Moral and Ethical." He was born in Philadelphia, PA, into "a respected Family" with a history of clergymen that "stretches back to the Revolution." He is a widower who still loves his late wife—Meredith Tusker. He is a dutiful father to Elisha Tusker Esq.—underemployed sales merchant. He serves as a mentor and guardian to Jonah Ayot-Kolosha, and he is considered "a loyal Friend to eminent Persons of considerable Renown and Number." Also, he is a proud Truman-style Democrat in neo-conservative times who owns Colby Manor, his four-bedroom home with a guest room under construction, among

the Petra-Freuds, the Sutters, and the Richardsons. He maintains
a schedule that begins with a robust walk at sunrise with "his
Friend" Loretta Tucci,[13] and his days end right after Channel
Eight's *Ten O'Clock News*. His alma mater is Howard University
wherein he graduated with a doctorate in theology, *and* in his
professional life he's been "a Man who kept Company with the
Go-To Men and Women of God charged with shaping this Era."
He sits in on spiritual matters "privy to the highest Religious
Offices," embraces the four cardinal virtues—justice, fortitude,
prudence, and temperance—and follows "the finest Principles"
embodied in the ten commandments as well as the sermon on
the mount. Also, he's well regarded for considered acts of charity within a 2,400-mile radius, and his daily practice of seeking a
right relation with the OmnipresentOmniscient One leaves him
little patience for those, like Monay Shott, "unpracticed in the Art
of Moral Discipline."

　　This news of a rival comes as a tremendous shock to him. As
Jonah's protector, he harbors hopes for the boy's relationship with
Clementine "Da Stylus" Pinkston, an alto in the choir at his recto-
ry[14] and a fellow African-American with a desire to do missionary
work in Liwani. Although the Pinkstons belong to "a low Income
Bracket" and Clementine's financial circumstances could ultimately
place a burden on Jonah, the Reverend has no doubts in regard
to the goodness of her nature. Biweekly, she treks at least twenty

---

13　Widow and best friend to his late wife.

14　St Peter's Episcopalian, founded in Curranvale City in 1901. Luminar-
ies in attendance over the years include silent acting legend, Isabella Orilla,
quantum physicist, Oskar Koen, Canadian 800m record holder, John "Leeds"
Kipligat, and pioneering bikini model, Ursula Volt.

minutes by foot from her aunt's modest abode in Santori Heights[15] to help him research his sermons, as well as type them for him.

In his estimation, Clementine is "a Saint." She's the only person who mentions his beloved Meredith by name, or takes time on the subject of Elisha and "the Boy's delicate Constitution," and how he's "sensitive like his late Mother." Clementine takes an interest in the robins that descend on the garden in the morning and the squirrels that chase them away at noon. In her presence, he feels as if he isn't receding into irrelevance "like the old Buildings in the Garment District" in which the Rev spent his childhood. Consequently, Jonah's latest errant distraction has Reverend Tusker worried about his hopes for this match. He takes his own heartbeat, checking for irregularities.

Who knows what this common Jezebel is currently doing with Jonah. Who knows what this foul-mouthed hussy will steal from Colby Manor. There is antique jewelry from his mother's side in his bedroom, and its value isn't just sentimental.

Caveat emptor![16]

He opens a manila folder and has a look over the final wording on Jonah's documents for the recently finalized inheritance. Paragraph two, subsection four gives the Reverend power of attorney until such time the boy presents suitable levels of maturity. Relieved, Reverend Tusker gingerly climbs with the documents up carpeted stairs in order to protect his sleeping chambers from that whore.

---

15   Her parents live in DC, so during the school year she lives in Curranvale City with her aunt.

16   Let the buyer beware (Latin).

3

After a furlong of wobbles, they stand in front of the toilet

"Let me at your belt," Hiroko requests.

Jonah stares at aqua blue toilet water.

"It's nothing to be embarrassed about." She clutches the buckle and expertly unhooks the strap.

He giggles.

"Okay," she says. "Put your hand on my shoulder and I'll lower you onto the seat."

He throws one arm around her waist and she bucks him with her hip until he collapses onto the toilet seat.

"I'll wait outside," she says.

Walls teeter inward. Pop. A dog whelps into tangerine moon. Wallpaper welts and his stomach cramps into a knot.

"Iroko!"

His fingers are numb and he can't manipulate the roll of toilet paper. Woozy, he topples to the floor.

Alarmed by the thud, she marches in. "Oh, God." Turns a rigid Jonah onto his side to prevent him from swallowing his tongue, and waits out the convulsions. "Mr Reverend!" she shouts. "Mr Reverend!" The only response is a choir from Harlem singing "Oh, Happy Day."[17] "Great." She wraps toilet paper around her fist

---

17   "Oh, Happy Day" is a hymn written in the mid-eighteenth century by English clergyman Phillip Doddridge. It is also the theme music for the popular nighttime soap opera, *Switcher*, where it is used without irony. Salacious

and Jonah coughs, belly-deep, as she wipes, flushes, and helps him back to his feet.

Once in his bedroom, she lowers him between the sheets and tucks him in.

"That should just about do her," she says.

"No, don't, go, please," he mutters.

She sees tightness around his eyes. She kicks off her boots, squeezes in beside him, and drapes an arm and leg over him.

"Leave oldjier boy, miss," he murmurs.

"Shuuush, bonehead!"

On guard, Reverend Tusker sits on the edge of his four-poster double bed flipping between Christian broadcasts on cable. The forty-eight-inch television rests on a teak antique dresser that he keeps forgetting to ask either one of the two boys to place on a silk cloth from Singapore that belonged to his grandmother. He works the remote while alternating glances out a window over-looking moonlit lattices in Colby Manor's vegetable garden and the television screen displaying a new crop of savvy preachers us-ing PowerPoint presentations and giving out the URLs for glossy websites. *Eheu! Fugaces labantur Anni.*[18]

The Reverend has yet to put up a St Peter's website, and now he may never get an opportunity to do so. In about two weeks,

---

material aside, the show's popularity is in part due to its wholesome messages of sex between couples in committed long-term marriages. It is the favorite Tuesday evening fare for Reverend Tusker and his lady friend, Loretta Tucci. On a personal note, Bolling's Pharmaceuticals is a major advertiser with the program, and the narrative text in no way takes a position over debates about the success or failure of their nationally distributed male enhancement product.

18 Alas! Our fleeting years pass away (Latin). The misspelling of *labuntur* is in the final manuscript.

give or take, he may be driven to step down from the church, whose congregation he grew to unprecedented numbers, because his under-performing son, Elisha, borrowed against money that belonged to the parish. Everything depends on his waning ability to craft a successful *apologia* to appease a restless flock who will vote with an up and down on either yay or nay.

He remembers open air meetings in Hoppa where it was just him, his Bible, and the distinct aftertaste of a rain shower that hung in the roof of his mouth. He stood in front of crowds who had walked through mist and rain in their smartest dress, and he spoke to them of fallen nature and salvation through grace. His friend, Nehemiah, translated his pithy sentences into WaSimbi.[19] He preached extemporaneously and with an inspired clarity. *Tempus fugit.*[20] Indeed, it fled, and continues to do so forthwith as he concentrates on a pastor who uses bullet points to teach alignment of one's will with a God who desires one's worldly coffers be exceedingly filled. On the bottom of the screen scrolls an offer of prayer minutes, a DVD of sermons on the Acts of St Paul,[21] and

---

19   Fourth largest ethnic group in Liwani, population 187,000, migrated from the Lower Nile circa 1300 in search of arable land. A good documentation of this oral history has subsequently been written by cultural scholar Peace Matabele. It is available online for a small fee.

20   Time flees (Latin).

21   St Paul was a Christian convert, missionary to the Gentiles; author of several Epistles in the New Testament. His conversion took place when he was blinded by a bright light on the road to Damascus. Reverend Tusker has theorized in a sermon in April of '98 that the light was the luminous halo of Solar Rex, the Sun God. His research has since made the luminous halo found in Medieval and Renaissance art a trope that can be traced to figures in the Pyramids of Ancient Egypt. In part, these findings laid the groundwork for the unrest among most of his parishioners during the Holy Season of 2002.

an accompanying text with daily meditations for a donated gift of $99.99. If one makes the order today, a complimentary DVD of the Book of John as well as a subscription to the ministry bulletin will accompany the package.

Subsequently, the past month has been marked by a slog through one rough patch after another. His "good Friend," Loretta Tucci, has been his ear in helping to ascertain where the source of his church members' malaise is. He learned that Mrs Krantz, whom he counseled through a death in the family, spoke with Samuel P., whom he counseled through the drama of three wives, about how Elisha's dereliction fell into a pattern that confirmed acquaintances, on second accounting, "set one up to fail." The Torvils wanted to know how this latest breach in the public trust could keep "any Parent optimistic" about protecting their young. The Filberts said they did not see reasons why they shouldn't join cheaters who make "Hammock loads of Cash." Inner circles realigned, a consensus was reached that the Reverend's continued tenure would only confuse the issue of "determining the Way to Truth," and Samuel P. led a group of forty, more or less, to another church.

Reverend Tusker listened to Loretta Tucci's reports in silence, unable to stop a renegotiation of his congregation's relationship with metaphysical reality. Then he began to spend his afternoons shuffling different combinations of dress shirts with black trousers before giving up on the outline of his sermon.

Unable to focus on the TV, Reverend Tusker reaches for a bottle of green pills on the bedside table. He swallows one more than the recommended dose, and forgets what it was like to have the energy to take his daily exercise with a walk around the block. His muscles constantly ache, and he cannot remember what it was like to have the desire to leave this perch on the edge of his bed from which he wages battle against doubts that eat into his power of resolve.

I lie in bed curled next to Hiroko and can hear my own heart pumping lickety split.

Circling within circles—centerless—I listen to the jibber jab-bered, mumbo jumbo of beatific creatures—baller's ballers—cat-erwaul and catcall. There's another cramp closer to my heart, my tongue is a chunk of meat, and I dip below an unknown thresh-old.

I remember geckos slithering from cracks in cement reddened by dust and, against my will, my eyelids close.

I can no longer picture the dead: Gramps, Mama, and Baba long before that, and I recall a more distinct outline … another time zone[22] … dressing quietly for PE class in the locker room next to Hans Hoffman on our first day of secondary school at the Acad-emy.

"What's that on your shoulder?" he asks.

"Nothing." I slip on a yellow t-shirt.

"Did you have smallpox?"

I point to his yellow t-shirt and change the subject. "You must be in Hildegaard House too."

"Just keeping it in the family." We walk out to the hockey pitch together. "My father was House Head a million years ago."

"Brilliant."

It's the start of field hockey season and Mr Derringer's mandate is to whip us into shape with his whistle. We do two laps around

---

22 Liwani, circa 1995.

the chalk-lined pitch, with Hans and me pushing to the front.
Then we lie down on the prickly grass for pushups, situps, and leg
lifts before it's time to sort through a pile of hockey sticks for a
scrimmage.

I get picked for skins.

Reluctantly, I peel off my shirt, and my team captain, the Head
Boy, asks me if I'm a leper, and my teammates laugh. When play
starts, I stay well out of the way on the wing. Occasionally, I pretend to show an interest by jogging in the general vicinity of the
action.

As soon as PE is over, I run to fetch my t-shirt, put it on, then
rush off to my locker.

"Jonah!" Hans shouts.

I ignore him.

I'm anxious among the Ayimbis, the Blacksmiths, and the
Khans. And I won't make up stories that my dead father was the
head of his House. I will not say how he drove a Citroën. Instead,
I retreat to art class, take a can of paint from a cupboard, and
decorate my face with yellow streaks. Then I take a field hockey
stick from the sports shed and return outside.

Hans is alarmed when he sees me. "What's with the war paint?"

I ignore him.

"Jonah!"

He follows me to a small gaggle of smokers.

I rush in.

The trifecta of prefects scatters this way and that, but I manage
to clip the Head Boy, Timothy Wells, on the knee. He falls and
curls into a ball.

I slam the stick into a kidney, into the small of his back.

"Take back what you said," I demand.

"Fuck off."

I hit him in the shoulder.

"Take it back."

"Fuuuck off."

Another blow, then another. "Say it."

It takes Hans plus a scrum of sixth formers to wrest the hockey stick from my hand. Then I'm marched down to the Reverend Father's office.

Gramps is called in.

The Very Reverend Nehemiah Ayot, bless him, is a man who walks with God. He always wears his cleric's collar and never goes anywhere without polished shoes. He sings hymns in a rich baritone and, for a man blessed with a solid reputation, remains humble. Always, he directs glory-be's to the Almighty, he's sharp with the translation of cryptic scripture into a palatable message, and he's generous with his laughter. In effect, it's said by all who meet him that there's a precious loving joy in him.

"I don't belong at this school," I complain.

Gramps shakes his head.

There's so much he doesn't understand about the many ways I lose control. Too often I wash my hands. I stare at myself for hours in the bathroom mirror. I constantly dab an old bottle of Baba's cologne beneath my nostrils to rid them of the stench of dry blood. Endlessly, I search for traces of ants riding up walls. Gramps doesn't understand me at all.

I don't know how we end up in the school's chapel.

"Ready?" Gramps asks.

I kneel in front of him at an altar beneath a wooden crucifix hanging from the wall and shut my eyes as he places his hands on the top of my head.

"Do you renounce Satan and all the spiritual forces of wickedness that rebel against their God?" he recites.

"I renounce them."

"Do you renounce the evil powers of this world which corrupt and destroy the creatures of God?"

"I renounce them."

"Do you renounce all sinful desires that draw you from the love of God?"

"I renounce them."

"Do you turn to Jesus Christ and accept Him as your Savior?"

"I do."

"Do you put your whole trust in His grace and love?"

"I do."

"Do you promise to follow and obey Him as your Lord?"

"I do."

He makes the sign of the cross on my forehead.

I experience a temporary flush, maybe dizziness, and then I'm clear.

He hands me a copy of *Against Heresies.*[23]

"Look at what he has to say about our transformation into children of God through the exercise of free will, then search in your heart for ways to better serve Christ's one Holy, Catholic and Apostolic Church."

My world turns black. ★The last thing you remember is the clumpclump of keys.

---

23   By St Igantius of Antioch (vol I, 180 CE). This book belonged to Reverend Simpkins, the missionary who oversaw Jonah's grandfather's rise as a minister of the Anglican Church in Liwani.

You're strapped to a bed in a foreign room with a stranger who's hIdden behind a curtain thatseparates your beds.

Work it through.

You're in ospital. Okay … a major hiccup.

Don't not dwell.

Pitter patter moves freely in the hallway, screeks skcrape against walls and window, and it is notpossible to tell which noise is to what reality.

Blu Pills take you under.

"Waaakey, waaakey." A nurse shakes your shoulder, her dirty-blond hair tucked neatly inside a baseball cap.

You shriek.

"Take her easy." She waits for you to settle before raising the back of the bed and lifting a cup of hexagonal pills to your dry, chipped lips. As liquids jostle about with chemicals in your system, a Dr enters with a female intern.

"Good morning," he says to the nurse in work voice.

"Dr," she replies.

You watch him turn to the intern. "Nurse Shelley is one of our on-call team leaders." He reaches for the nurse's elbow. "Please stop by my office after your rounds. We'll finish assembling the team for the influenza workshop next week."

You watchthe nurse snatches her arm away. "Here's the deal." Her hands travel to her hips. "I won't be joining you one iota for any more of your malarkey. Not today, not ever."

The Dr addresses his intern. "As you can see, there are a number of on job stressors, but that's all the more reason for a regular in-terface with your attending." You wacth him swivel to face Nurse Shelley. "You. My office. After rounds." Then he marches away without giving you your round-the-clock care.

Nurse Shelley's eyes well up. She dabs at tears with a sleeve, she tightens the drawstring on her scrubs, and with a big harrumph wheels a food cart to your bed.

"I'm fasting," you say.

"An apple a day keeps Nurse Shelley at bay," she smiles placing a tray on your lap, picks up a spoon, dips it into oatmeal, and holds it up to your mouth. "Four. Three. Two. Yum. Tasty, tasty, for the tum."

You stare hard at her wet eyes. "I can't."

She fiercely wipes a tear away. "Okie doke, sweetie." She wheels the cart over to behind the curtain of the other bed.

"Waaaakey, waaaakey, time for breaaaky," she says.

"No, no, no," the man there shouts in response.

"Settle down, Mr Gallagher."

A tray clanks to the floor.

"No. No. No."

"Great. This day is an A-one fuck up," she says.

You watch the curtain open and you watch Nurse Shelley go from the room.

And so yu are an impaled butterfly, and it begins that u consider probabilities to be facts in this room where doors cklose, but do not lock. It's easy to imagine shadows may indeed have flesh, as well, rabbbit ears and horo\scopes may be read for planets in decLine and suns that rise in 5ifth or 6th houses. Tmples and their altars maybe divinedby oRacles for futures as ggood to go as those fore/casted by kola nutz. In this room anythg is possible where dors swing ohpen with the slightest push, alwaYs, and in the h★allways iN-patients march upand dowN without their own heads.★ ★

★ ★ ★ ★ ★ ★ ★ ★ ★ ★ ★ ★ ★ ★ ★ ★ ★ ★ ★ After a gargle and rinse to tame dryness in his throat, Jonah makes his way downstairs to the kitchen.

The Rev sits in flannel jammies at a table covered in legal papers while Hiroko washes plates in the sink.

What's she doing here?

"What time is it?" Jonah asks, shocked to see her.

Hiroko wipes her hands on a dishtowel, then accosts him with a loud and sloppy kiss. When she wraps him in her arms and presses into him, he cringes. "You slept like a baby, sweetheart," she coos.

He's ashamed his gal pal sports black fuck boots and has white knickers peeking from beneath her barely there miniskirt. "I'm having a difficult time remembering when you came ..." He doesn't finish the sentence because of a scratchy uvula.

"We came together, silly fuck," Hiroko reminds him. "You really don't remember?"

The Rev appears startled.

"I hope I didn't have to force you in cuffs," Jonah joshes.

Cumming! Cuffs! She's a succubus.

"No. All that freaky trembling got to me, so I came with you."

"You're the best."

"I aim to please."

"Well, I owe you big time."

She laughs. "I don't take checks, hon."

Freaky trembling! Checks!

The Rev sternly closes a file. "I see you're feeling much better, Son."

"Much," Jonah replies.

It's after nine and the Rev should have taken the green pills, and then read Philosophy in the Middle Ages[24] in bed until the *Ten O' Clock News.* A night without his dead scholars will make for a difficult morning—he'll be upset with the disruption to his routine and he'll be impossible to please.

The Rev gets formal. "You've been a tremendous Help, Miss. But your Services are no longer needed."

"Man, you suddenly got rock hard," Hiroko tells Jonah. "Then all hell broke loose."

"Is that when …"

"Yah."

"And you're okay with it?"

"Oh, yah," Hiroko purrs. "How's your fucking tongue?"

"Sore."

"You really know how to show a girl a good time," she jokes. "We'll have to do it all over again and soon."

"Over again is a redundancy," Jonah teases. "It's either over or again. Not both."

She mimics a talk show host. "I'll take over for two fucking hundred, Mr Ayot-Kolosha."

"Good Lord!" The Rev explodes. "What about your Fiancé?" Hiroko steps back dumbfounded. "Huh?"

"You seem like a smart Girl," he lectures. "Don't you think you're pushing the Envelope on what's Appropriate? Probably not, eh. This sort of Behavior is Par for the Course for a Woman who wears a Bandanna instead of a Blouse."

Both Jonah and Hiroko are confused.

---

24   Hyman, Arthur and Walsh, James J. *Philosophy in the Middle Ages: The Christian Islamic and Jewish Traditions.* Indianapolis: Hackett Publishing Co., 1973. This is the book used extensively by the Reverend to prepare his big sermon (see section on Al Ghazali).

"How I dress is not your business," Hiroko snarls.

"Goodness Gracious. You've got an enlisted Boy waiting for you in 130-degree Iraqi Heat?"[25] he continues.

"RevRev," Jonah interrupts. "Have you taken your meds?"

Hiroko heads toward the door.

Still feeble, Jonah manages to get to the front step before her and nimbly blocks her path.

"Cakes!" he pleads.

"Old man better fucking check hisself," Hiroko screams, tears bristling in her eyes.

The Rev responds with a treatise on taking the long view, and he paraphrases King Solomon on the subject of "a good Woman."[26] Clementine is "Jonah's Friend," and "you, young Lady, could learn a Thing or Two from her" about dutifully keeping her hand on the spindle.

Jonah stands between them, increasingly anxious. All he can think to do is gently lead Hiroko outside as the Rev's bantering continues from the top of the stairs.

Cars no longer roll out of driveways.

"Let's get the fuck outta here," Hiroko finally sputters to Jonah.

"He's not going Anywhere!" the Rev shouts.

"You coming?" she asks with indignation.

"*Noscitur a socio!*"[27]

"Jonah?"

"What about Clementine, Son?"

---

25 Referring to the soldier's duty in the second US-Iraq War (2003–).

26 Proverbs 31.

27 One is known by their companions (Latin).

4

In the nation's capital, tongues wag about possible dirty secrets in the Commander-In-Chief's War, and on a driveway
in North Oldeham, Jonah and Hiroko run from filthy specu-
lations concerning their own

As they rush across the Rev's lawn, they see Papi Freud and wifey,
currently leaving their home. He wears a pink shirt with a pink
silk tie, both items color-coordinated with Ma Petra Freud's hip-
hugging dress.

"We're on our way to a soirée with members of the book club,"
Papi informs them, smiling wide.

"I called to see if you wanted to come," Ma P.F. adds. "But I
didn't hear back from you. Todd Bolling," eldest son of Gareth
Bolling, CEO of Bolling's Pharmaceuticals, "will be with us for
the last time. He just received an appointment to the United Nations, which Alistair here recommended him for."

"This is Hiroko," Jonah responds.

They look through her.

"W.E.B. Dubois was right about the necessity of building a Talented Tenth," Ma P.F. continues. "An erudite fellow like yourself
would be most welcome at our gathering. The Daltons will be
there, and with their recent purchase of the *Curranvale City Times*[28]

---

28 *Curranvale City Times* was founded in 1929 as the *Curranvale City Concord*.
Ownership changes in 1983 led to its acquisition by the Polson Group (a sub-
sidiary of Citadel Inc., the company responsible for the Ayot-Kolosha fortune).

an opportunity could present itself that would most certainly further your writing career."

"I'm sure he's busy with his studies," Papi interjects.

"Oh, don't be a fuss bucket," she admonishes. "We could all use a break from work once in a while, am I right?"

Jonah tries his hand at introductions again. "Hiroko, these are the Freuds."

"Nice to meet you both," Hiroko says, each syllable stated with clarity and precision.

They look past her.

"So, what about it?" Ma P.F. asks buoyantly. "Would you like to come with?"

"Rita!"

"It's fine, Mr Freud," Jonah assures him. "I'd love to, but not tonight. I've got Brontë[29] to read for school tomorrow. It's an efficiently told story, but a lot of pages to get through." He waves a hand the way Professor Iton does when he speaks about the finer contours of the literary enterprise. "Do let me know when the next meeting comes up, and I'll let you know whether I can manage it."

"Purrr-fect," she responds.

After a robust round of good-to-see-yous, the Black Republican[30] power couple move toward the Curranvale City that made

---

29 The likelihood of Professor Iton assigning British author Charlotte Brontë (1816–55) is remote. At the time, anecdotal evidence suggests Jonah was immersed in a smutty volume of *Gargantua and Pantagruel* by François Rabelais.

30 The term "Black Republican" is used to denote those African-Americans who ascribe to the notion of being part of the Party of Abraham Lincoln, and who look to Ronald Reagan as a transformative figure in ushering in the end of Affirmative Action. The term is often considered derogatory, but these uses are not to be ascribed in any way to the author, narrator, or publisher of this work.

Alistair Freud's reputation for his part in the case of *Bolling's Phar-maceuticals v. Jim Dewey* ongoing four plus years. Details among the general public remain sketchy, but in the main the Bollings have been put upon by trial lawyers intent on squeezing a buck with a frivolous suit. In this instance, Jim Dewey, supported by the money of leftie judicial activists, has so far been stymied by the Freud, Leaman, and Collins team. Legal maneuvers germane to the case have prevented the establishment of a precedent that will allow the collection of millions in damages by those who develop rashes upon the orifices, anal or otherwise, due to the uncoerced uses put to a Bollinger manufactured weight-loss pill. Yes, the Freuds hurry toward the circle who can be counted upon to receive them as champions for their cause.

∾

We enter Santori Heights, a blur with no distinctive features; a hodgepodge, a mishmash, and nothing worth mentioning to oth-ers who live elsewhere. It's as if an Etch-a-Sketch has been shaken, and the pattern encroaches on us. Trees are scribbles, apartments ram against sidewalks jammed against narrow roads. Traces of liver-colored stone are hidden by boards and buildings that lean on one another, a line of tumbling dominoes, falling among dust bins, a dump site, zones where trouble clings.

Hiroko's flashy jools are hidden in her handbag (as are her cell and her iPod). I do not tuck in my shirt or wear a tie. Guilt. I'm guilty of thinking that Africa-America isn't safe. Guilty, but not nearly enough.

To the right is a field of rubble-trash overrun by stubbly grass. Onward, in front of rows of burnt-orange brick, older black folk on the sloped sidewalk sit in white plastic chairs and keep an eye on young'uns buried in hoods. They talk of terr'ble trouble to be excised at church services; noxious soot from the exhaust of cars roils and spills into the cantankerous, cankered neighborhood teetering among the mewl of state-of-the-art sound systems that shark through wind. With a shudder, clouds dismantle like slabs of chiseled rock that falter before falling gracefully into the churning, cranky swill.

"I'm not like them," I explain.

"Huh?"

"The Rev. The Freuds. Really, I'm not. Alistair believes the cream rises. I'm for the rights of puppies in equal proportion to those of people. I'm no asshole."

She shrugs as I stare at a busted sidewalk teeming with those returning from shift work at tollbooths, care facilities, or privatized clinks. They talk of trouble while marching past hot, stuffy rooms full of loud men in wide-brimmed chapeaus and equally noisy women with cleavage and bright lip gloss.

"They were rude," I say.

"They've made it."

"Still."

"I'm nobody."

"Nonsense."

"Sure I got my fans, and the cell's blowing up with offers. But, I'm talking on a whole 'nother level. You'll see. In a couple of years I'll have my own line of perfume, and my own clothing label. Those fuckers can kiss my ass. I'll buy their damn property and make 'em pay *me* rent. You'll see."

Stars align with a tangerine moon as we step around coochie in gator boots who roll straight up VIP (and wait for trouble to court

them with dwindling wads of cash). Above it all, a white cross juts
from the shingled rooftop of St John's Baptist storefront church, a
sanctuary from habits of despair practiced by those who no longer
know how to conjure spells that ensure happy ends. Trouble has
this night by the scruff as we slip between bald tires laid out to
block through traffic.

Overhead, warplanes buzz from one base to the next. Pilots
strapped into cockpits will not be troubled by stop-loss, tours of
duty of indeterminate length, as we make a left near a long line of
those with shaggy hair who wait on a free meal. One block west
of the church is a liquor store, and a crew of teens emerges from
it flicking bottle caps. They wear shorts that end above the ankle
and wife-beaters that show off shoulders bruised with tats.[31] Lively
with in-jokes, they are sick of the ways people whom they don't
know sign papers that send them off to a war using language that
says one thing and means the opposite. So tonight they'll convene
at a nightclub, templates of funk knocking them unconscious
as they wait out the hours with hopes of a grabby, grubby fuck.
Speckled light jumps from the tips of their cigarettes, and ashes do
a jig in the air before sparks go humping away at the dark.

A yellow cab grinds to a halt in front of Hiroko and Jonah.
   "Jefferson and 5th," she directs.
   "Get in," the driver replies.

---

31   Tattoos. One story has Jonah placed at a tattoo parlor the morning of his
confinement to the hospital. However, the anonymous source, a convicted py-
romaniac, spends her days talking to herself in the People's Laundromat, where
Jonah works part time.

She clears newspapers from the back seat before they sink into beige leather.

The cabbie looks about thirty. Check. No hardness in his eyes. Check. Flyweight. Check. Harmless. Check. Check.

Relaxed, Hiroko checks her cell for messages. *No one major.* She sets it on vibrate, thinking of how she's hit the jackpot with the heir to a fortune, how she'll move to the Big Apple in a year, how she'll buy a home where she'll piss off stuffy neighbors with loud pool parties on weeknights *and* weekends.

"How are you doing?" she asks again.

"Tired," the cabbie responds.

The question was meant for Jonah. But, what the heck.

"This country is all about work," he continues. "You work. You sleep. You work."

"True dat," Jonah complies.

Hiroko fingers bills wrapped in rubber bands and tucked into the waistband of her pantyhose. She wonders if she'll ever slim down to 115 pounds (there's a snapshot of herself she likes at eighteen). She's gotta be ready, always. A nudie agent who comes to the club pitched her a reality TV series.[32] He's talking six figures, a whole lotta scratch. She's no dunce. She doesn't think money will buy her happiness because she knows from experience that no one is happy all the time. But cash—and loads of it—makes the purchase of comforts possible in decent enough doses. Adrift, she wonders about the bills coming in and the

---

32 No record exists of *Geisha Palace*, the purported reality TV series about a bisexual Asian woman looking for a bisexual lover allegedly pitched to MTV. However, the premise has subsequently appeared as Tila Tequila (MySpace star, b. 1981), and as of this writing a purported suit by Russell Rushton, nudie agent, is in the works.

surgery it'll make possible; *plump up the lips a little, definitely some lipo on the thighs, but no boob job. Those leak.* To her, comfort is a place she once knew with plenty of musky hardbacks to read. It was concrete objects that were hers to do with as she pleased. Put her feet up on them. Use to put her clothes into. Look at them, break them, and do with them as she pleased. But that life, first on Oahu and then in Oldeham Proper, was replaced by one she began to discover like a malignant lump in her lymph nodes. At fourteen, there were bills she discovered were hers to pay. Ones that covered monthly payments for the car that was eventually auctioned away. One that brought cable to the television set, and another that kept the creditors from calling. This discovery metastasized as she thought less about what she wanted and more about what was expected. Occasionally, she pulled herself together long enough to try for something she desired, a job at JC Penney, a career teaching the art from books she had less and less time to read. But she learned that her desires would have to be set aside while she took buses to waitress in restaurants first, then in bars where the tips were better. In and out of diminishing expectations, she couldn't make heads or tails out of whether she ever meant anything she said.

"Sometimes a man's just gotta relieve the stress," the Flyweight confesses.

"Suresure," she hears Jonah mutter.

"So how much for the girl, bro?"

"What?"

"Eighty? One-twenty?"

"Try four grand," Hiroko interrupts. "Four grand plus a twenty percent tip."

"Yah," Jonah adds. "*And* a twenty percent gratuity to the house."

The cabbie whistles.

I'm thirsty, Hiroko thinks, leaning into her prince. ★ ★ ★ ★ ★ ★
★ ★
★ As they make
a sharp left at 15th, a flashing siren pushes up behind them.

"Five-O," the Flyweight slams fists into the steering, then parks
it hard on the side of the road. ★ ★ ★ ★ ★ ★ ★ ★ ★ ★ ★ ★ ★ ★ ★ ★
★ ★
★ ★ ★ ★ ★ ★ ★ ★ ★ ★ ★ ★ ★ ★ ★ ★ ★ ★ Too late, Hiroko sees Jonah
stepping out of the ride.

"Get the fuck back in here," she commands.

The first cop, a brother, approaches with a hand on the pistol at
his waist. "Get back into the car, sir," he demands.

Jonah is polite. "Hello, officer. It's a mighty fine evening,
wouldn't you say?"

"Get back in the car," the officer says.

Jonah offers him a hand to shake. "Jonah Ayot-Kolosha, here.
I'm from Liwani, land of the rare black rhinoceros."

"Now!" the cop barks.

"Get in here, nigga," the Flyweight blurts.

Jonah scrambles back to the car, breathing heavy while the
Black Cop creeps up on the driver's window.

"Put your hands where I can see them," he orders.

Both Hiroko and Jonah place their hands on the head rests on
the seats in front of them.

The Black Cop smiles at the Flyweight. "Ray, Ray. My nigga.
What did the cat drag in?"

The Flyweight gets out of the car, they whisper, and then the
Black Cop shines his flashlight into the back seat.

"Well, well, what have we here?" he says with menace.

"Just hitching a ride, officer," Hiroko contritely responds.

The Black Cop gets sarcastic. "Is that what they're calling prostitution these days."

"They're asking for four grand *plus* a tip," the Flyweight adds.

Jonah and Hiroko both talk fast. No, no. Nothing of the kind. We were joking. Joking!

The Black Cop cuts in. "One at a time, folks. One at a time."

Hiroko explains how Jonah had a seizure, and how she's "taking him back to her spot."

Jonah hiccups. "Hic ... hic."

Both men look them over.

Hiroko is quick to mention that Jonah is "Liwanian royalty," and a "grad student at DU."[33] Then she loses the narrative thread of their counter jibber-jabber sounding like a surround sound of inner chatter. She knows what they think of her. She's put it all out there. Easy, they think, from the right vantage point, to tell that the carpet does match the drapes. Her mind jitterbugs and only stops when she leans—once again—into her prince's shoulder.

"I don't know what his highness does over wherever he comes from," the Black Cop condescends. "But never get out of the car when you're pulled over by the police. Un'erstand?"

"Hic," Jonah responds.

The Flyweight laughs. "I'm from the land of the black rhinoceros."

---

33   Dingham University, a private institution founded by F.R. Dingham, a quadruple threat—blues singer, essayist, lepidopterist, and neurologist. His pioneering work on phantom limbs is taught worldwide.

5

PARENTAL ADVISORY
EXPLICIT CONTENT

Holding Jonah's hand, Hiroko leads him across the hardwood
floor past scarves, sweaters, and overcoats on top of a pile of shoes.
They slalom through library books, newspapers, pizza boxes,
garbage bags, and empty booze and beer bottles scattered around a
love seat repaired with duct tape. "Don't mind the mess," she says,
shyly.

"I hardly noticed," he fudges.

She pulls him through the rustle of multicolored beads that
hang in her bedroom's doorway.

Lights spark, flicker, and go out.

"Perfect!" she exclaims. "A blackout!"

In pitch-darkness, suspended in a spatial time that will be
remembered for a war, she feels her way through hard objects to
locate the drawer with candles in it.

"Sit." She lights a couple and places them on a shelf above her
bed.

Jonah shoves aside clothes and a stack of papers, then he gets
comfy on her mattress.

"I could use a drink," she says, leaving for the kitchen.

Jonah leans back against a poster of the Dalai Lama, squints in
poor light, and sneaks a peak at her pile of papers.

He's not easily moved:

Prepubescent girls with breast implants balance precariously
on stilts, rope burns slit the wrists of bloated infants discarded in
dumpsters, shrapnel is dipped in menses, and checks bounce like
balls down stairs; demons with big dicks drink Americanos in
gated neighborhoods ringed with electric fences, plimsoll lines
are submerged in oil as female deckhands throw thimbles full of
the stuff overboard. All of it captured in a mix of pen and pencil
sketches.[34]

His nostrils whinny and buck.

After slicing the bird's neck, Babu lets it sit in boiling water before plucking its
feathers.

"You act as if the world owes you," he says.

I shrug—misunderstood—and return to quietly plucking feathers.[35]

Hiroko returns with two glasses, a bottle of scotch, a hash pipe,
and a bag of weed. She sparks up and takes a hit as variations on
Beethoven's "da da da daa" seep in from upstairs. Then she hands
the pipe over to Jonah.

"It's too soon," he says.

"Fah sure."

Quietly, she has herself another pull.

"Hiroko."

"Yah."

"Mind if I stretch on the floor?"

"G'head."

He pushes aside CD cases, plops down on the Persian rug, and
stretches his arms above his head before sitting in lotus position.

"Four grand," he chuckles. "Good one."

---

34 Sketches available upon request.

35 *The Notebooks,* January 5, 2001.

"A twenty percent tip to the house was high, though."

"You think?"

"Try more like zero percent."

He flexes biceps. "These guns don't come cheap."

He seems poised like old money. No, not that exactly. More that he comes off like an aristocrat with an accent that was lifted from the Shakespearean stage. Hiroko knows money. She came from money her father lost on cockfighting ventures in the Philippines. Now the guy lives in Santori Heights, drinks, sings rugby songs, and threatens to leave her mother who is sixty percent Hawaiian; distantly related to Duke Kahanamoku,[36] who was a good bud of Elvis.

"Jonah."

"Uh-huh?"

"I'm tense in the shoulders," she says.

"Zhat so?"

"I'm not hinting, if that's what you mean."

"Yah, right."

"Honest to God. But I'm open to kicking up the cut to five percent if you gimme a rub-down."

He cracks his knuckles before joining her on the bed. "Brace yourself." Then goes to town on her back. "The sensation has been described as ice water trickling down the spine. So don't be surprised if you burst into tears."

They get quiet for minutes.

"'How could a woman know that you meant nothing that you

---

36   His full name, Duke Paoa Kahinu Mokoe Hulikohola Kahanamoku, isn't reproduced in full due to concern over pacing of the narrative (note in the margin of the original manuscript).

said: that you only spoke from habit and to be comfortable.'"[37]

"Huh?"

"It's from a short story about a fella on a safari in Africa who's dying of a gangrenous wound. He looks back and sees his past with a series of rich gal pals as a series of the same ole adventures with different people in the same ole places."

"Could you go a little to the left?"

"That's a bit like how I feel around Da Stylus. Like I want to start again with someone else and make an effort in new ways, different ways. But I wonder ... do you think we live the same ole dramas with the people we imagine will be our salvation?"

"Right there. No. You lost it. There. Good. Harder. Too hard. Too hard!"

"Are you listening?"

"Surely. You're talking motivation. We all try for reasons not to lose the momentum to get our asses out to hustle. Some days, you don't know if you've ever progressed. It's like the same day keeps filling with habits you keep hoping to change." She gets quiet again, thinking of how far she is from where she used to be ... on a scholarship at a private high school with the ones who'd made it to financial freedom; the Meyers, the Gillespies, and the Solomons. As in all her classes. Her paintings of disemboweled watermelons selected from a statewide contest to hang for a month in the Curranvale City Contemporary Art Gallery. Her marks even led to staffroom debates over whether her future would be better served in the humanities or in law. Back then, her time wasn't spent on the goal-oriented tasks that would protect her against what hap-

---

37   A quote of a quote by Professor Iton alluding to *The Snows of Kilimanjaro* by Ernest Hemingway.

pened to her folks; the signed affidavits that gave the court power to take away the objects she didn't think she could do without; the house in Oldeham Proper, the cars, the washing machine. "It's what people do. So, don't be a tight ass and dig your thumb in harder."

Jonah isn't so sure. "With all this tension in your shoulder you should try a long steam in the sauna," he finally says. "I tend to find it's a great place to lay around with other towel-less fellas, massaging one another in all the sore spots."

She giggles. "That sounds more like what the women's sauna is s'posed to be like."

"It isn't?"

"Disappointed?"

"Don't ladies slather around squirting lubricants on each other, saying oopsy daisy as they run around with their bouncies bouncing?"

She's self-conscious about her boobs. "Oh, you're one of them guys."

"Those guys," he corrects.

"Into bazoombas with implants."

"Sure, but not in a bad way."

A ringing cell interrupts them.

Hiroko reaches to the floor, picks up the phone, and then rolls her eyes. "Monay! Monay! It ain't a good time." She holds the receiver away from her ear and tunes out a loud spill of fast-paced nattering. "Buh-bye." She hangs up, grabs for the pipe, and lights up again.

"Anything important?" Jonah asks.

"Nah. It's all good."

At a certain point in the fuzziness, the cell rings again.

This time Hiroko talks quickly as he works his thumb into a knot between her spine and a rib.

"I miss you, baby." Boy-Toy digs in. "Ouch." She slaps at Jonah's hand. "Course I do, sweetheart."

∞

the arm on his watch clicks clocks over as they are alone,
away from all noise that isn't the electronica hiroko selects. up
against the portal of her bedroom door, in the jamb among
hanging beads, he works the paint. his fingers fiddle with the
buttons of her blouse. there's buttery light from street lamps,
the moon, while her brassiere drops to the floor, maybe black
or red, and it doesn't matter as he steps back and stares at
her in this light from whatnots. among the clack of beads he
sees the protuberance of a mulberry nipple which he takes
between his thumb and forefinger. hiroko's breath quickens
as they move to the mattress and the ruffled surface of bed
sheets on which he loosens the zipper of her skirt and learns
what fabric she chooses as underwear. yes, quickened breath.
black lace. he doesn't take it off, but moves it aside with the
tip of a forefinger so he can look at the shock of the raven
bush gashed with purple lips that glisten. sticky, sleek. and yes,
in the buttery light from the moon, from the streetlight, from
whatnots he pulls back to peer at hiroko, semi-buck nude,
her small bell-shaped titties. her nether belly a raven-dipped
triangle of hair. she tugs a pillow from behind her head, slides
it behind her back, then leans back, her neck exposed, her eyes
blown open, her mouth puckers as she takes his head in her
small hands and draws him low to tongue taste the saline-

sweet paradox between her thighs. beads chuckle, truly, as he
licks and laps and tastes the borders of freaky scents and as
she trembles in his mouth, the slight hitch of her hips rises up
to meet the cleave of him tonguing deep in her. he will not
forget this funky, gooey, dish of a cunt. nor the way her cocoa
hips lift then drop and the way her nether hair is tangled and
soft and wet and *brune* between his lips. God, yes, and his chin
draws up to a gold ring in her belly button, then he kneels
between her splayed thighs as her fingers unzip, then tussle
with the hardness of his cock and the sticky tip that is hers,
for hiroko and only her. her tiny fingers tug fast, and slow,
whatever she wants, and he reels and whirls and tosses and he
is hers, and her, his busy hummingbird, his wet freaking, fucking angel. she is guttural as she takes him in the buttery light
of the moon and the freaking, fucking headlights of cars that
go by as they fuck, slow, steady, hard, as they just fuck, his dick
in her pussy. he looks in eyes that have given over to a mucky
muddle, glazed as he feels his way forward in the meat of her
purple lips, forward into the hiccup-ed clenching-unclench-
ing snatch that he deep-dicks. fuck me. he slows as he feels the
jut of her pubic bone grind against his own and his waist taps
against the bone at her hips and he murmurs like a goddamn
kook and doesn't want this to end. she says, fuck me, fuck me,
until she knows what it means for him to cum and for him to
know how it is when her mothers quake and she cums before
she is still. he lies on top as she bears his weight and the blend-
ed mess of sheets is clammy beneath her ass. the patter of rain
outside flicks against panes and ledges. her hands start again
wherever, and he wants all of her again, wherever. hardening,
he wants to know all her pleasures and what she desires, even
if it is rank and crazy, busted out and perverse. whatever it is,

he wants it all from hirosita in the buttery light from lamps, or the moon, and or miscellaneous whatnots.[38]

---

38   A copy of an email from Jonah to Hiroko on October 4, 2003.

6

In East Heights, Jonah blinks awake in an orange ray of mote-inflected sunlight that barges between sheet-curtains

Hiroko's bi-amplified speaker system blasts Björk,[39] and fjords rustle in a voice that reminds Jonah of other mornings music played while the early Curranvale City crowd was loaded into buses, or erratically driven cars, and writhed with the rigmarole of the various Americas: rural to urban, Bible thumpers to Godless heathens, right-wing crackpots to left-wing wackos, folk sorted by color and ranked by whatever rep they may or may not have, namby pamby apathetics to hardcore know-it-alls, big-time flash willing to make a fast buck any which way the fajita crumbles.

To do's flap in his grey matter like open cupboards slapping wood to wood in gales of wind. He reminds himself to call Da Stylus. He *will* tell her it's not working between them. He *will* return to the Rev's and get to the bottom of why the guy's been weird about staying in his room of late. He *will* hop to it and get bucked up, just not yet. For now, he draws a blanket to his chin and sticks fingers into his ears, wishing to be Anyplace-Elsewhere-Slickity-Slick: New York-New York, Lala Land, Not This Place-Nowhere C. City.

Getupgetup.

Nothing doing, as he does nothing.

---

39 Björk Guðmundsdóttir (b. 1965)—Icelandic alternative musician who Jonah is said to have spotted at an airport in Zurich on his first trip to the US.

A dull pain travels from his temples to his clogged sinuses. He can hear Hiroko's shower running.

Loosen up, son, Jonah thinks, lying on his back, wiggling his toes and stretching his feet, then working sinew and muscle till he's clenched and relaxed all the way up to his neck.

Amabo, amabas, amabat.[40]

La table takes the feminine, and he remembers when he was dressed in a white robe and baptized with holy water by Gramps at St Andrew's[41] in Hoppa. Back then, he saw himself as a cartoon character who aped the manners and dress of the Europeans. So he worked hard to rid himself of shoddiness by increasing the frequency of his good works. He ladled soup for the children who fled to the chapel at night to escape the murder of the WaSimbi. He didn't curse, nor play cards, and before bed he read a chapter of the Bible from Genesis to Ecclesiastes. He studied articles of faith in Cranmer's Prayer Book, said grace before as well as after meals, and knelt at his bedside to pray both morning and night. He also applied the teachings of St Paul's letters to the Corinthians, so it was generally agreed he was charismatic like his Gramps.

Now Jonah's a skeptical dingbat who failed in his duty to follow his grandfather into the clergy. The woman in whose bed he lies is the flesh he's tracked like game on a reserve. He has debts, lacks the wherewithal to modulate his grudges—against Da Stylus, against Gramps—as translucent spots flicker before his eyes. His earlobes tingle, and he can't force himself out of bed without a redemptive shot of Jim Beam.

---

40 I love, you love, he or she loves (Latin).

41 St Andrew's Anglican Chapel founded by Reverend James Simpkins in 1930.

Sunlight coppers the room while wet-haired Hiroko Ishigowa watches Jonah who is lying on his back with the bed covers pushed down to his ankles, his cock lolling on his pelvis. Outside, a multiethnocolor-of-all-sorts dole out handbills—Gentlemen's Lounge, Jeezus Saves, Happy Hour—the jobs that brought them in having gone high tech, global.

Meters tick something fierce as she shucks her insides with remorse.

They've been together nonstop for two days, far too long to be away from the grind. Especially considering there are only three days left to raise the four hundred to cover the rest of her monthly overhead. He hasn't offered his help despite her many hints. So it looks like she's gotta "high roll it to the six to midnight shift."

Because of prospects with the TV project, she's slacked off with her peep shows on the cam. This means she hasn't drummed up new business in chat rooms or stayed in touch with her fans through email, or updated her daily blog entries to let them know when she'll next be starring online.

"Did you sleep well, daaah-link?" she asks, careful to work the angles.

"Yup."

Her nails trail up his inner thigh and lightly scratch his balls before rising up the base of his sore, hardening cock. He arches his hips, whinnying, as she rubs a forefinger against the drip of cum at its tip.

"Too bad I've got to go to work, huh."

"Stay," Jonah insists.

She kisses his belly. "Are you gonna pay for what I lose for missing work?"

"You serious?"

She laughs. "Course not," she says, and then gets up to massage cream onto her legs, squirt on body spray, and slip into a wife-beater and baggy overalls. "I'll be back late." She's got to be careful with this fan. The heir apparent comes equipped with all the bells and whistles; he goes to DU, he's coming into a huge inheritance. *Mi casa es su casa.*[42] She can't come off like a gold digger. "But if the land line rings, don't answer it."

He grimaces.

"And it's not Ito,[43] if that's what you're thinking." She hedges on the truth because if her man calls she doesn't want Jonah to pick up. "If anything, it'll be Mum, yah." She spackles his face with kisses before "tootaloo." ★ ★ ★ Strapped to metal in a diaper, you're dizzy for a drink. ★ ★ ★ Babycakes makes for the door like a frisky colt on E. She lights a smoke, the edges of her body kick like a pot of boiling porridge, her bootay insisting on all kinds of you-will-be-missed. ★ Early mornings. ★ *I stand in a long line of people outside the hut. I wait with them beside banana trees, afraid to see what death looks like. When I finally reach Mama, her skin is black like charcoal and wrinkled like fraying rope, her knuckles are ashen. Her eyes have begun to cloud over with a grey glaze as she drifts off into the unknown. Teasing. Gentle, with laughter.*

It begins to rain.[44] ★ ★ ★ ★ ★ ★ ★ ★ ★ ★ ★ ★ ★ ★ ★ ★ ★ ★ ★ The hospital bed won't end. ★

---

42   My house is your house (Spanish).

43   Ito Morita is a US Marine in unit -------, stationed at --------, as a --- ------ specialist (notable information classified). Six months earlier his name appeared in the *Curranvale City Times* in connection with a series of interviews conducted for the local paper by an embedded journalist in the field.

44   *The Notebooks,* January 17, 2001.

★ ★ ★ ★ ★ ★ ★ I kneel down beside Hiroko's bed.

Wrong's wrong, I say.

I'm sorry, I say.

Amen, I say.

Feeling no different, I take in a crib that looks like ruined bleachers after a ball game.

I'll appease inner quibbles by performing good deeds.

I make a file of disconnection notices for her cable, cell, and gas bills. I sort overdue credit-card statements and unfilled loan applications before shuffling them into a stack on the kitchen table. I collect laundry strewn like pennies on her bedroom floor, dropping the mother load into a hamper. I gather garbage bags that sit in clumps, clear away newspapers that go back years, and drop the lot into a pile in the alley. What else? After a jolt of caffeine, I rearrange her collection of trendy mags—*Vanity Fair*s and *Harper's* for the coffee table, *Vogues* and *Elles* for the underused rack in the hallway, the *New Yorkers* for the trash.

The telephone rings and goes directly to the machine. No message. Then it rings again, no message, and again, no message, before the damn thing finally stops.

Trouble.

I lose energy. *What if Baby-grrrl leaves everything she touches in worse shape than when she found it?*

I continue to reorganize her in ways that will make our days together easier. I take a brush to the grime ringing the toilet bowl, wipe down her sink as well as her bathtub, and scrub away slime from her shower curtains. It takes a dark hit of Detroit techno to get me picking up library books from the floors—I tally up eighty-plus dollars in unpaid fines—and place them in a duffel bag for their return.

I think back to the post-church brunch where Da Stylus and I first met. We stood in a small group among the Reverend's family and friends gabbing beside a window that looked out onto a cemetery. She told dull stories that made her out to be a heroine, and I listened to the way she jokingly scolded the Reverend with constant reminders to make him wipe the chalice he lifted to parishioner's lips during communion. Even then, I realized without knowing it that she enjoyed playing the role of an amusing hostess, but she hadn't yet learned to convincingly deliver her lines. Yours truly, worldly jackanapes, told myself *she* would change as *we* evolved. But eight months later, I'm the one who tries to measure up to her expectations.

I start moving to the kitchen where I drain stank water from the sink before refilling it. Soapsuds bubble at my wrists as I scrub away trouble to the tuh-ticktick of jacked beats—clean glasses go with the mugs in the cupboards and spit-polished silverware goes into a drawer I line with newspaper.

The friggin phone again!

"Ello ello," I say.

"Who are you?" a girl responds.

"Who are *you*?"

"Tell my sister, Ingrid is coming to stay tomorrow." It's her thirteen-year-old sister.

"It's Ingrid is coming tomorrow to stay."

"What are you, some kind of idiot?"

"No. Are you?"

"I'm Ingrid."

"Got it."

"I-N-G …"

"I know how to spell."

"Buh-bye, then. Jerk."

She hangs up.

I leave the phone off the hook, and get back to the side of me that has chosen Babycakes. ★ ★ ★ ★ ★ ★ ★ ★ ★ ★ ★ ★ ★ ★ ★ ★ ★ ★
★ ★

Dark is grubby.

You screem to gt out.

But you're held firm and pok?d with mre fingers, and mre needles.

You writHe like a nuthouser.

7

**Cam Grrrl hustles, rubbing her chin against a limp slab
of meat inside the fly of a ruin-in-a-wheelchair at the VIP
Lounge, Club Carnival**

The rug chafes her knees as she squirms on cheap synthetic fiber.
She labors to hold on to her apartment, Internet access, stuff.

She looks toward the door at the point in the night when it's
necessary to scram. Scoot. No more dilly-dallying. Just get the
fuck out of the booty club, go home, and curl on her couch with
her pipe.

Fried from sets on the main and back stages, she lifts a tittie near
the wheelchaired-ruin's mouth, and waits while this-guy-who-
came-with-another-guy slurps.

In the gut of a bloated metropolitan center, she gives him a
wan, smoldering look-see, braces her hips against his, and balances
herself by setting her feet wide apart.

Beneath brackish, anxiety-inducing routine, she bobs to the
surface by imagining what the ruin sucking on her tittie imagines.
Eight, seven, six. She imagines what she imagines herself to be
imagining. *Four, three, two.* Her heel thwacks the rubber wheel of
his chair as the pop song lurches to an end.

"That'll be eighty bucks," she says.

"Today is my birthday," he replies.

"You still gotta pay."

"Birth …"

"Day. Got it." She picks up her silk thong. "Where's the fuggin hard-on you came with?"

"She said it was a gift."

"Say what?"

"The girl said it was a gift."

"Which one?"

"We met at the bar."

"Fuck!" She wobbles into her pinkish-purple number. "What's her name? Give me a name."

"Shott."

"Shott!"

Hiroko abandons the wreck and hurries down the hallway.

The clit better have stuck around. ★ ★ ★ ★ ★ ★ ★ ★ ★ ★ ★ ★ ★ ★
★ ★ ★ ★ ★ ★★ ★
★ ★ Oops, no doubt about it, her shoulder blade scuffs against the jacket of the guy who dresses like cash-money.

He mumbles this, that, then introduces himself as B-something-or-other.

"Got to find someone," she responds.

He winks. She pushes on.

For ages, she searches the spot.

Nine-inch heels lean against poles, the open-legged work sheepskin rugs. Hiroko stumbles to the booth with the white teddy before pulling her off the guy who loves a good reaming up the ass.

"Where's Shott?"

"Fuck off," the white teddy says.

Hiroko fucks off.

She has a *tête-à-tête* with one of the tuxedoed boys from upstairs.

"You seen Shott?"

"Get your cunt back to work."

She opens the curtain of the booth where the star-spangled bikini-wearing Pilates instructor is working.

"Shott?"

"What?"

"Where's Monay Shott?"

Star-spangled bikini points to the translucent light that is feeling its way to the front door.

Hiroko catches her breath before stumbling past a forty-something functionary smacking twenties onto shaken ass. She rushes the exit, but tumbles on a stair and lands hip-first, smack dab on dusty concrete.

For fucksakes!

She's been played. Monay's gone.

"You okay?" a stranger asks.

She sits up, more embarrassed than hurt, and stares at white stars gussying up the upper atmosphere.

Her time has been spent watching those who come to her with secrets of an unhappiness no one in their circle is equipped to handle. The accumulation of decisions they've made locks them into arrangements that will take an effort to undo. But hits of caffeine no longer provide the necessary lift as she watches them come to her, or Da Monay, or Desiree. Some once a month. Others when their payments on various lines of credit allow.

She's tired.

8

... When Hiroko's keys click in the lock of her front door, I'm ready

"Let me get your jacket, Cakes." I pull it off her freckled shoulders and hang it in the closet while she gives the hallway a once-over. "You like?"

She stops in the entranceway of a revamped living room and turns ferocious. "You can't just ... fuck, Jonah ... if I wanted it clean I'd have done it myself, yah. I'm not a mental case, *and* I don't need to be fixed."

She lurches, ranting from room to room, and I follow her like a dog on a leash, offering up I didn't mean ... I should have checked ... fiddlefaddle.

Eventually, she slumps onto her bed, quiet as a titmouse.

Tuh-tock, tuh-tock.

I'm not up for this. First, I need a drink. Then I'll be able to manage a thought that doesn't wobble on its axis.

I stand among the beads in the doorway. "In Hoppa, we have an expression." She's damaged, and damages. "If you wait for the food to cool, you'll eat with the visitor." She doesn't respond, so I call an audible. "When I was a kid, I thought my dad had a sleeping sickness. I'd sit at his bedside, try to see him as a healthy person, and worry about him because he never went to church. I kept tidying up his room and scrubbing the smell of blood from his sheets. It was the only thing I knew to do." Tightness fidgets in my larynx. "Anyway, the night he died, I thought, 'He's gone to hell.'" Hiroko studies me. "So, I'm not trying to fix you. I'm no good at fixing anyone."

"Bonehead," she mumbles.

"No argument here."

She crawls over, pulls me onto the bed, lifts the front of my t-shirt, and presses my stomach against hers.

"I need money, hon," she confesses.

"How much?"

She tells a story about being ripped off at the club, then deviates into another one about lending cash to Monay Shott, who hasn't paid her back. "Monay's television was stolen, and she wanted to replace it. I felt bad for her. She has three children, just broke up with her boyfriend, and since she's kinda over-the-hill, she hasn't been doing great business lately. So I tried to be nice. But now she says she won't pay me back for at least two months." She still hasn't told him how much. "I guess that's what you get for trusting people."

"How much?"

"Four hundred."

"Dang!"

"Forget it."

"That's a lot of money. It won't be in three months, but ... dang, girl. Until then, I'm living off embers."

"God! I wish I was dead right now," she says.

"Babe!"

Tuh–tick. I imagine her spiraling off into worst possible scenarios, a future of even dingier apartments with clangy radiators, getting to be an old dancer like Monay Shott, the peroxide junkie who just broke up with her teenage boy toy, who once showed up at the club with a handgun and threatened to put a bullet in a customer's head.

"There's a guy who comes every Tuesday night for one thing," she continues. "He gets in close and stares at my pussy for half an hour. It's creepy and I can't fuckin stand the thought of seeing him tomorrow."

"I'll get you the money," I say.

"When?"

Displacing Ito and prepping to be Hiroko's *numero uno* won't be cheap. I'll have to stay several kind acts ahead of the ticking meter by putting out for drinks and dinners with a movie. I'll need to purchase her day passes to the spa, or give her shopping sprees. There will be tips to pay at Club Carnival: for the doorman, the waitresses, the deejay, and girlfriend's girlfriends. The only way I'm getting her any money is if I get an advance on my household duties from the Rev.

"Tomorrow," I say. "I have some banking to do, but it should be settled by the end of the business day."

"Can we meet on campus around six?" she asks. "I've got Professor Z's class till then."[45]

One of her meaty legs curls around my ass, and I stare at contours around her thick pink mouth.

I'll get the money, I'm certain of it. Going this route is a damn sight better than the short-term pain of a night watching her run a gamut of emotions: pessimism, the waterworks, a tirade followed by a reconciliatory speech, and hugs before she leaves me in the land of awake people filled with anxiety.

I can do this.

---

45   Contemporary Women's Art (MWF 4:30–5:30).

"Oh, yah. Ingrid called. She's coming tomorrow to stay."

"Shit. Something must be happening at home."

"Like?"

"Like, I'll fill you in when I'm not so tired."

We face each other—noses touching, eyes shut tight—stirring only for citrus fruit and toilet breaks as the occasional chirp of cursing pedestrians enters the open window.

She is up at three, like usual. She's in and out of cupboards, looking for sugared biscuits, sugared peanuts, brown sugar to put on a slice of toast. She doesn't want to take care of her kid sister. At least, not when her own life is in such transition. She needs time to get clear about where she is in relation to where she's supposed to be.

Ah, sugared cereal.

9

The family sits on sofas organized around a low, long table surrounded by walls covered in black-and-white family photographs. Food steams in huge tin bowls on the middle of the table

Babu is seated at one end, praying in WaSimbi.

Amen.

Mama brings around a basin full of tepid water. Each of us takes turns dipping our hands in it to give them a quick wash before digging in to the food from the communal dish.

While we eat, Babu makes a speech. He talks about how I'd been circumcised several months before. He talks of pride that his grandson is finally a man; he speaks of responsibilities I'll inherit as the caretaker of the family. He says I'm about to embark on my secondary school studies, and with this comes great responsibility. Then he puts his hand on my shoulder and leads me outside.

Tied to a tree is a grey-haired goat with horns.

"It's for you," he says.

I look to Babu in confusion.

"We'll sacrifice it tomorrow," he says.

The following day, I watch as my goat is brought before me by several men who hold tightly onto its legs and neck. A knife is sharpened against a stone, then one of the men begins to slice its jugular. Blood splashes onto the grass, my goat twitches, then its front legs buckle as it sinks into the sticky grass.

Its eyes bulge in pain, confusion, and fear; I want the end to happen quickly.

After its eyes close and its body stops twitching, I watch as the animal is skinned. A knife cuts a straight line down the goat's belly, and then one of the men peels the skin away from pink flesh. Flies swarm around the blood and attempt to snack on the exposed muscle that thinly covers bone.

It smells of rotten eggs.

Soon, my goat is sliced into pieces that are placed on a steel rack on top of a charcoal barbecue. Then I watch Babu roast the meat over an open fire. [46]

---

46   *The Notebooks*, February 3, 2001.

10

Outside Colby Manor, I run into Ma Petra-Freud

The Black Republican juggles four brown bags stuffed with groceries in her driveway. She must have an international support system to keep her looking so fabulous: an Italian hair stylist, a Korean manicurist, an exfoliater from the Eastern Bloc.

"Need a hand?" I ask.

"How gallant." She pronounces the -ant as -ont, like gall-ont. "I'm glad to see chivalry isn't dead."

She unloads all four bags into my arms, and I stagger into her house with them.

"Do you mind helping put them away?"

"Not at all."

I follow her detailed instructions—the bag with the veggies needs to be close to the fridge, the one with the cans of whoop ass goes under the shelf beside the stove, the toiletries go in the hall closet, and "could you take the meats to the freezer in the basement?"

Done.

Ma Petra-Freud removes a dollar bill from her wallet and hands it to me. "For your troubles."

"No need," I say. "It's the least I can do for the Nefertiti of the Suburbs."

"Oh, my," she giggles. "Well mannered and quite the charmer." She places the bill on the counter. "Quite the opposite of the troublemakers from the Heights."

"Thank you, ma'am."

Better magazines on the matter call the forties the new thirties, and I begin to sense I've overdone it. The Republican is flirting back. But before she can throw her chiffon-stockinged leg up next to the dollar bill on the kitchen counter with an open invitation to explore the right-of-center merchandise, I politely excuse myself.

"I'll walk you to the door," she responds.

On my way out, I notice a wedding photograph on the fireplace and several high school graduation shots of her bespectacled daughter.

The wedding shot showcases the early days of an African-American dynasty. There it is, the day she joined in holy het[47] union with Alistair Freud, solicitor-at-large.

Ma Petra-Freud's gown is of a generic sort, frilly and puffed out like whatever else others wore back when. Alistair Freud stands next to her in a white tux. Smiling in the background, her maid of honor and her bridesmaids—all of whom she's likely known since preschool—who wear powder-blue gowns with matching wrist corsages. Displayed next to the photo are ribbons and cups for horse jumping and tennis. But as far as I can tell, none for skeet shooting or lawn bowling.

Her walls are fixed up with oils of slaves in iron chains, red-capped porters bearing suitcases, and shoddy liquor stores in urban ghettos.

"You've got some wonderful art," I say.

---

47   Heterosexual. From this point on, bi will refer to bisexual, tranny to transvestite, quadruped to those with four legs, and octopussy to those with eight cats.

"It's a start," she replies.

I point to an impressionist painting of a black man. "Who's that one by?"

"It's a copy of Beauford Delaney's self-portrait."[48]

"I've heard of him."

"He made it during a period of exile in Paris toward the end of his life."

"I suppose it took getting away from the States to be able to look at himself with that kind of honesty."

"I never thought of it that way." She's genuinely impressed. "I studied his work when I was at art school back ... oh, a long time ago."

"You paint?"

"Not since Helen."

"Helen?"

"My daughter."

"Shame," I say.

"Not at all," she replies. "Time moves us forward and we become something we didn't necessarily imagine. Something more. So I pick up the brushes once in a while, but I wouldn't call myself a painter."

"I'd love to see your work."

"No, no," she objects. "It's not very good."

"I sincerely doubt that."

---

48 Jonah tells the story of the night he was talking to Professor Iton, and his mentor pointed out how the illuminated night was reflected in a puddle of water. It gave him a new way of thinking about multidimensional reality. Further research shows this is similar to a story James Baldwin tells of an epiphany that came out of a conversation with African-American modernist painter, Beauford Delaney. One must draw one's own conclusion about the coincidence.

After a moment of profoundly silent silence, we say goodbye at the door. "You must come to the next meeting of our book club, dear." Her eyes spark with light. "It'll undo some of the damage the Blackout caused to our image." I don't know what she's talking about. "Believe you me, those hoodlums are niggers, not black folk." I'm uncomfortable and pretend to follow her meaning as she tells of how that night Mr Freud helped set up a barricade of mattresses at the bottom of the street, and how she led "the women's effort to gather all the children into a cozy huddle" in the Cuttlewots' basement. "The community can't keep looking the other way whenever thugs behave like niggers. For Godsakes, we need more educated folk like yourself, persons with leadership potential who are willing to take a principled stand on issues that require good old-fashioned common sense."

It's time to bolt. "I'm expected at home, ma'am."

"Yes, yes. Of course. I've got the Reverend's number. Why don't I get back to you once the dates for our next book club meeting are firmed up?"

"*Fantastique, madame*," I reply.

∞

"Ouch." The kitchen at the Rev's is a hot bed of steaming pans and oil flicking onto Jonah's skin. "Ouchouch." Caked in sweat, he clutches bare bits and charges back and forth from the open fridge to the sliced tomatoes on the cutting board to the bubbling chaos on the stove and the pile of dishes in the sink. When the phone rings, he rushes the receiver with suds dripping from his hands. "Yup!"

"Darling." It's Da Stylus. "Whaazaaa?"

"Can I call you back?"

Jonah doesn't catch her response. He slams down the phone and races to the stove, to the boiling water overflowing from the pot full of potatoes.

Safe.

Once mushrooms and tomatoes have been added to the sautéing onions, he pokes a fork into the apple crumble in the oven before polishing the silverware.

Frig! The phone again!

This one is from a number he doesn't recognize on the call display.

"What?" he snaps.

"Excuse me?"

"Go."

"Is this Reverend Tusker's residence?"

"Not in."

"It's important that I speak with him."

"Name."

"Excuse me?"

"Your name?"

"Mary ..."

"Mary." Jonah hangs up. With one hand he removes the pan of hot oil spitting from the stove element, and with the other he spills a packet of pre-packaged salad into a wooden bowl.

Done.

When the doorbell rings, he's shocked to find Da Stylus waiting for him on the front step. She's rigged out in a plain, yellow cotton dress, and she's just had her hair relaxed into a retro 1950s Wilma Rudolph bob. Gadzooks! All that's missing are bobby socks to go with her flat-soled shoes.

What is she doing here?

They peck on one another's lips before he gestures vaguely toward the kitchen. "I've still got to set the table," he says. "Can you give us a hand?"

He hears her slip out of her sensible shoes before she joins him in the dining room.

"*Mademoiselle*." Jonah hands her white napkins to be put in the ebony napkin rings. "*Merci*."

"Are you avoiding me?" she asks.

"Course not." He's quick to answer. "The past few days have been mad craaazy."

"Sooo, you're not still vexed about the other night?"

"Oh, God no. No."

She'd muttered something about coming over, but he thought that meant in the distant future, like on the weekend.

"I've had so much to do with the writing submission to the workshop," he continues. "You know how that is, going squirrely for the higher cause."

She takes china dishes out from an antique cabinet and places them onto an ivory tablecloth next to the napkins. "I don't mean to be a pest," she says. "The last thing I want to do is distract you from your schoolwork."

"We're good, hon."

"So you're not giving me the cold shoulder?"

He forces a don't-be-silly smile and changes the subject to an exchange of pleasantries about her new hairdo, the Rev's appetite, the color of his stool, and the frequency of his urinations. All the while he watches her, noting how her beauty is of a tragic sort. It's as if she's been banished by it to sit on park benches during the peak of a sunset, unhappily beautiful and alone. It makes her look bored, a little blank, and unable to flourish without sympathy over how much of a burden it all is—being despised by other women for it, suffering the harassment of old perverts as a result of it, never quite getting enough of what is due her because of its curse.

"Did you hear about Leroi Johnson?" she asks.

"Who?"

"He's a fella I know from work," she says. "Got shot by a cop the night of the Blackout on his way back from a shift at the toll booth."

"No!"

"He's dead."

"God, no." Jonah's sorry for her loss. Is she doing alright? Would she like to stay for supper? Not tonight, she replies. She and her aunt are doing their weekly grocery shopping. Out of guilt, he offers to spend time with her tomorrow night. She can't, she's doing her Christian hip hop show on campus radio.[49] However, there's Youth Rollerskating the day after that. Niiice. Direct bus routes are discussed, a meeting place is decided upon—nine o'clock by the skate rental is both practical as well as safe. Informal dress will be worn. A schedule of advance check-in calls is arranged. Once again, he's sorry for her loss. God bless you, Jonah. She nuzzles in his arms; he feels her as excess weight then breaks the embrace to fiddle with the salad.

"Did you hear of the bloke who had a pain beneath his right eye while he drank coffee?" he asks.

"Was it in the paper?"

"No," he replies. "It's one of Elisha's jokes."

She's a wilting thing, life dissipating in glaze that overwhelms

---

49   Dingham University's student-run radio station, 93.7 CKCU FM.

her eyes. "The bloke has pain beneath his right eye every time
he has a coffee, so he goes to a hospital. Problem is, nobody can
find anything wrong with him. 'Well,' the doctor says, 'I'll have
to watch you drink coffee to see if I can figure out the problem.'
Okay, so the guy starts in on another caffeinated beverage, and the
pain returns. 'Ah,' the doctor says, 'I see the problem. You forgot
to take the spoon out of the cup and it's digging in beneath your
eye.'"

Da Stylus scrunches her nose at him—beautiful, bored, and
alone. Thank God the Rev's Buick pulls into the garage.

∞

When we last parted company with Reverend Tusker, he was
in the kitchen at Colby Manor making Jonah choose between
himself and Hiroko. He does not know that he's mistaken her
for Miss Monay Shott, XXX attaché. This circumstance has been
exacerbated by the news of the unfortunate shooting of Leroi
Johnson, Clementine's co-worker. Reverend Tusker can't let this
sort of unexpected tragedy happen to Jonah (whose recent behavior has been most alarming—first, public drunkenness, and then
soliciting the services of that slut). Sadly, Jonah's studies have not
been enough to furnish the boy's mind with the requisite laws to
govern his passions, and the Reverend's concerns about his own
deteriorating health make for a state of some urgency. He has no
choice but to secure a new course.

Forthwith, he phones Mrs Loretta Tucci, and after preliminary
salutations and consultations about their respective health, he
presses forward with the crux of the difficulties ahead. He lays
out the problem with propriety, omitting words such as "Hussy"

and "Slut" in favor of "lost Sheep" and "Delilah." Then he finishes
with a mention of the shooting, and the very real possibility that
Jonah's "Dalliance in the World of Pornographers" will end with
"the Boy dead in a Gutter."

Loretta is a "good Woman" who responds with dexterity on the
subject of a "good, young Woman," one whose "moral Influence
transforms Sons into effective Fathers." Women whose "Beauty
is a Faculty of Character" rather than "bound to the transitory
Nature of physical Features."

"*Donec eris felix, multos numerabis Amiscos. Tempora si fuerint Nubila,
solus erit,*"[50] the Reverend says.

They observe a moment of silence to reflect on this truth.

Suddenly, "Clementine," they both say in unison.

Indeed. How obvious. The solution lies in an artful combina-
tion of carrots and sticks. What Clementine wants most is to do
missionary work in Liwani. However, the road to get there is
complicated by a lack of funds. Jonah is her ticket, so if she agrees
to do her part the Reverend can use his power of attorney to
withhold the inheritance until Jonah commits to an engagement
with her. Also, her tenuous financial straits leave her vulnerable
to a more lucrative circumstance—she works at a toll booth on
the H 12, her parents are both unemployed and unemployable,
and her living situation at her aunt's place is deplorable. She often
talks of gunshots on the corner where both drugs and sex can be
purchased. In more ways than one, Jonah is her way to freedom.

"What an age she's at," Loretta says. "These are years full of
choices colored by the anticipation of what's possible. However,

---

50   As long as you are lucky, you will have many friends; if cloudy times appear, you will be alone (Latin).

what we imagine this future to be is handicapped by our limited ability to think clearly. I wish I'd known that. One can't take for granted that there will eventually be money or that careers one wishes for will materialize." She sniffs, swallows. "My hope is Clementine's sensible enough to realize her youth won't endure, some choices are irreversible, and an offer of this sort isn't to be sniffed at."

"She's a Person of great Sensitivity," he answers. "If an Appeal was couched in such a way as to focus on securing Jonah's Well Being, the infusion of Cash coming her way would rightly seem like the Byproduct of a larger Blessing."

"One hopes," she replies.

For some, the Tusker-Tucci scheme is unfit for a man of the Reverend's office. For others, he is absolved of any wrongdoing by the righteousness of their motives. After all, it was the prodigal's late grandfather who originally suggested the inheritance be used as a motivating tool. Of the latter, there are those who either exonerate the Reverend for an application of a most necessary pedagogical intervention (due in part to the alarming statistics pertinent to wayward black youth). From the former, some find him guilty of a most pervasive liberal bias (due in part to the alarming statistical evidence of the moneyed dilettante investing for tax purposes in all that is goodly).[51]

---

51 For my part, I take no side in the matter. Instead, I draw attention to the interval between Jonah's leaving and the Reverend's response to learning from the prodigal of his imminent return to Colby Manor. I won't belabor the reader with details of this occasion with an excruciating account of Reverend Tusker's routine with his toilette, his passing of wind, his daily prayers, his diet, and so on. Instead, I'll focus on the summation of a visit he pays to Clementine at her aunt's apartment in Santori Heights West in order to lay out the urgency of his case.

After quickly securing an invitation via an email to her Dingham U address, he's lucky to find a parking spot on the street directly in front of her apartment building. Since he wears his cleric's collar, he's emboldened as he passes dismembered metal fences and block after block of dull concrete. He walks a path to an unlocked front door and climbs eight flights of a graffitied stairwell before standing in the smell of urine in front of number eighty-four.

"Welcome." Clementine shows him in.

He's courteous and makes himself comfortable by squeezing into a plastic chair in front of a trunk covered in a crocheted table cloth and between two single beds. While Clementine fixes the Reverend's tea, he takes in the room. There's a radio, but no TV set. There are no curtains, and the walls are decorated with religious memorabilia: crosses and portraits of the Christ at penultimate moments in his life—born in a manger, changing water into wine, riding a donkey on Palm Sunday, and so on. All that is missing is the Last Supper, and of course, the Sermon on the Mount.

Clementine's aunt is out, so it's just the two of them.

Once the kettle has boiled, the choir member pours two cups, drops a tea bag in each one, and then joins the Reverend by sitting on one of the beds.

In sum, he commiserates with her over the recent passing of her co-worker. The loss of potential is noted, and they both say a prayer for the "safe Passage of his Soul to its final Home."

After an appropriate interval, the Reverend tells Clementine of his own narrative concerning "his failing Health," does not mention Jonah's saucy minx, but describes "the emotionally charged Moment" that resulted in a "Promise made to The Right Reverend that his Grandson would be allied with the Right Sort of

Society." At the completion of his monologue, he underscores "how great an Influence Clementine has over Jonah." He mentions the lucrative estate that will provide "a sizable monthly Allowance" to Jonah as well as his concern that "it will be put to Uses with ill Consequences if he doesn't take a Wife who knows the Lord."

Touched by her own close encounter with tragedy, Clementine is moved to tears. It's coming together in an unexpected way, her desire to eliminate the suffering of God's people, and it seems as if she's being moved forward by a larger design.

After the Reverend's gone back and forth over the logistics of the enterprise, he attains her consent in the deployment of the Tusker-Tucci scheme.

"Long day, Rev?" After a brief tussle, a tentative Reverend Tusker lets Jonah pry his briefcase away from him. "Go wash up and we can get started on supper."

"My, my." Crystal sits among china, lit candles, a bowl of salad tossed with an orange vinaigrette and topped with puréed shallots. "I thought you'd decided to leave us for saucier Groves." If only the boy realized he's not at all like those hoodlums from Santori Heights. "Are you here to …" He stops cold, seeing Clementine washing pans in the kitchen sink. "Well, this is a pleasant Surprise."

"Hi, Reverend," she says.

Jonah nervously laughs. "Mary called."

"Oh, Dear!" the Reverend exclaims.

"Is there a problem?" Jonah asks.

"Of course not."

"You sure?" Clementine chimes in.

"Goodness, yes," the Reverend pretends. "Don't be such fuss Buckets. I'm no sulking Achilles, and I don't need Pacification. I just forgot to make a Call this Afternoon. That's it."

The Reverend totters on tired feet to the living room, turns a corner at the doorway, and leans his forehead against the wall. A lump gallumps in his throat; Mary's with the bank and she's readying to send Elisha's bungled business loan to creditors. Once again, the trail of his son's scandal has thrown the Reverend *contra Hostium insidias.*[52]

He drags himself back into the dining room and slumps down at the head of the table, worrying about the potential loss of the house he bought with Meredith.

Enter Jonah bearing food.

The Reverend toughs out a smile. "Is Clementine staying for Supper?"

"She can't," Jonah says. "She has to help her aunt with the groceries."

"Nonsense." He calls her into the dining room. "What's this Hogwash I hear about you leaving us, Dear?"

"I've got places to be," she replies.

"Fiddlesticks," he says. "*Miserere! In Manus!*[53] Join us for Supper. Where Two or more are gathered in His Name—emphasis on the more—so shall He be there."

Da Stylus watches Jonah pour gravy onto a plate of mashed potatoes, baby carrots, turnips, and a medium-rare steak. Glug. More gravy. Glugglug.

---

52   Against the enemy snares (Latin).

53   Have mercy on me! I am in your hands! (Latin)

"Would you do the Honors and say Grace, Son?" the Reverend asks.

They bow their heads. "For what we're about to receive, may the Lord make us truly grateful."

"Amen."

She's jumpy, leaping at wind-induced rattles that give Colby Manor its own voice.

It took every ounce of courage she could muster to show up this evening, but the plan appears to be going smoothly. All that's left is to brace herself for the difficult conversation ahead.

I will go where you ask me to follow, she repeats to herself.

The meal begins with a *post-mortem* of Leroi's death during the Blackout. He was an A student at Curranvale City Community College—Da Stylus knew him, witnessed to him on occasion, but wasn't close to him—and after the observation of a minute-long silence, she asks the Reverend questions about the effect of cold temperatures on his arthritis and as to where he'll vacation this winter. The Reverend is a sweetie. He talks of how uplifting it is to see her again and delves into his latest research into the history of a tram that once rode through North Oldeham prior to World War II.

Boiled carrots are passed around, and then the Reverend introduces the delicate matter of the inheritance. Da Stylus can't focus on the details of his agreement with Jonah's grandfather about the prerequisite of an engagement. Uncertain of Jonah's response to the news that she's the chosen candidate, she searches for the miraculous in the lightbulb reflection that glances off the copper frame of an art piece with hands clasped in prayer.

"... *In foro conscientiae,*[54] I cannot release the Monies into your Charge unless you show Evidence that your Priorities are in Order."

She catches Jonah's eye, looking at him like ... oh, what a kook the Reverend is. Then she makes eye contact with the Reverend and gives him an encouraging nod. However, when the cleric makes an inexplicable left at sacred mathematics, she worries that he's lost his way.

"... consider Universal Principles of Harmony, shall we? 3.14 is a mysterious natural Number that seems to arise out of the basic Structure of the Cosmos." *I will follow you wherever you lead, my Lord,* she prays. "Divide the Circumference of a Circle by its Diameter, and this is what you get. Or, put differently, it's empirical Evidence to support the *a priori* Claim of the Existence of a Divine Plan, an over-Soul. Catch my drift? Draw a diagonal Line from one Corner of a Square to its Opposite, and what do you get? A Hypotenuse that creates two Triangles of equal Size. Magnificent, isn't it? Two Examples of what is both Determined as well as guided by free Will. So, try to think about the Question of your Marriage as a lovely Confluence of these Principles. Or at least, go back and read Al Ghazali's[55] wonderful Essay on this Paradox. I'm fairly certain I made a Photocopy of it for you both. Yes, two Months ago. Or was it three? No matter. The general Point is ..."

When Jonah excuses himself to check on the apple crumble in the oven, the Reverend shoos her after him.

"I can't stand being manipulated," Jonah fumes.

---

54   In a court of conscience (Latin).

55   See footnote 24.

"I understand, darling. He can be a bit wacko sometimes."

"He can't force us to make firm plans about our future," he says. "That's bullshit."

"Jonah!"

"Sorry." She doesn't like it when he curses. "It's just ... I'm embarrassed for *you*." He opens the oven, pulls out the crumble, and places it on top of the stove with a bang. "He's put *you* in an awkward position by not talking to me first."

"I know, sweetheart. I know."

Jonah stabs slices into the dessert. "I should march back in there and tell him what's up."

"Darling, you're right. He's way off base. But you know how important the next sermon is to his immediate future." Jonah dumps apple crumble onto side plates. "Maybe we should humor him, y'know? For now. Just for now. The main thing is getting the inheritance in play. You need the money, and how you get it is immaterial. Let's just go along to get along. In order to be sure you get paid, we can ... and I'm just thinking out loud here ... tell him we're engaged."

"Engaged!"

"Not for real. No! No! Just as a pragmatic step until you get control of your Trust Fund."

"No way."

"Don't be rash, darling," she insists.

Jonah tops off each dessert with whipped cream and, in so doing, slows down long enough to realize that he may have found a way to get Hiroko her money. If he goes along to get along, he'll be in a position to ask the Rev for the cash to buy a couple of rings. Then he'll get some cheapo ones, and give the difference from the loan to Hiroko. Problem solved.

He marches with the plates of crumble into the dining room. Da Stylus follows him closely, clipping his heels from behind.

"By the bye, Jonah, I ran into Mrs Petra-Freud on the way in." Reverend Tusker wipes crumbs from the corner of his mouth with a cloth napkin. "Just between you, me, and the Stove, she's not a happy Camper. She's upset with you for cutting across her Lawn. Please use the Sidewalk, she's sensitive about People walking on her Grass."

"Dope," Jonah replies. "That's coolio."

The Reverend fills his glass with purified water from a jug, his knuckles contracting. "Why do you insist on talking like That?"

"Like what?"

"Like Bingo, Son."

"'Cause it's crunk," Jonah says.

A small riot breaks out in the Reverend's head.

"*O Tempura, O Mores!*"[56] he exclaims.

Uncomfortable around raised voices, Clementine manically chatters. "You're both in the right. Not that either one of you is making an argument *per se*. This crumble is both crunk and delicious, much like Al Ghazali's paradox. In this instance, superlatives are appropriate in both colloquial and standard English." Both men stare at her like she's a visitor from another planet. "Okay." Jonah nods.

They observe another silence until Clementine breaks it. "Jonah, don't you have an announcement for the Reverend?"

"I do?"

"Don't you?" she asks.

"Yesyes," Jonah says. "Da Styl, uh, Clementine and I are getting

---

56   Oh times, oh manners—Cicero (Latin).

hitched."

"Hitched?" the Reverend asks.

"Married." Clementine reaches across the table and strokes Jonah's hand. "No date just yet. We're taking it one step at a time."

"Praise the Lord." The Reverend glances at the art piece with hands clasped in prayer that Meredith purchased at a yard sale in the second month of their marriage. "Brava! *Rara avis in terris, nigroque simillima cygno!*"[57] Unable to contain his excitement, his words plane along surfaces that he no longer has the stomach to plumb for depth. "Marriage. Oh, my, my. We should do formal Meals like this more often. The Unexpected often occurs while Bread is broken." He pours himself more water. "Did I ever tell you about how Meredith and I got engaged? No. Well, we used to hold Wednesday Night Potlucks at the Church. Everyone would come. You know that Singer, what's her Name? The One with the Sister who was in that Movie about the Race-Car Driver? Sherry something. Sheronda? Cheryl?[58] Anyway, her, Loretta, and Meredith would collaborate to ensure the success of our weekly Endeavor. What a Team they were. Their Spreads grew increasingly elaborate as they outdid themselves from Week to Week. One Day it would be Ratatouille, the next it would be Quiche. What an impressive Undertaking. Truly." Jonah stands to put on a kettle for the Reverend's post-meal tea. "So, we're eating a Lemon Pie. Or, I'm eating and Meredith, the Organizer that she was, is seeing to one Detail after the next. She was always excellent with the Tid-bits, I lacked Patience, she was a real Arachne, and the very Op-posite of me." He laughs. "And when I looked up, there she was

---

57 A good woman is as rare as a black swan!—Juvenal, *Satires* (Latin).

58 Sheronda Mosely, sister of Marta Mosely (star of *You Go, Girl 1, 2, &3*).

wearing a polka-dotted blue Apron, bustling back and forth from Room to Room. That was it. That was when I knew I had to find a way to be with this Vision each Day for the rest of my Life. So I asked her to marry me within the Week." The youngsters respond, but he doesn't hear them. "By the bye, Jonah, have you had a chance to read the Article on the Sun Deities I left on your Bed? No? Clementine found it fascinating. Am I right in such a bold Assertion on your behalf, Dear? I'll take that as a Yes. Where was I? *Solar Rex*. Did you know ancient Cultures marked December 25 as the first Day of the solar Year? This was three Days after the shortest Day of the Year. The Sun was at its lowest Point and beginning to move North against the eastern Horizon." The Reverend pats down a jutting clump in his relaxed head of hair. "Now that would be an excellent Time to have the Wedding. March 22. The Day we experience the Equinox, after which the Sun ascends above the celestial Equator for the first Time in the Year. That's ninety Days between the Winter Solstice and the Equinox. That's a ninety-degree shift in the Earth's Orbit around the Sun, the Trajectory of its Zenith above the Meridian Equator. Ninety Degrees times Four equals the Angles of a perfect Square. Ninety times Four equals 360, the Dimension of a complete Circle as well as the Length of the solar Year minus five sacred Holidays. Divide 360 by ninety and you get the Intervals of the Precession of the Equinoxes. March 22 certainly packs quite a Wallop, doesn't it?" He wipes fingers smudged with gravy onto his forehead. "The Sun. The importance of the Sun. Sunday. This is no Accident. Without the Sun there would be no Life, and how much more dramatic a Happenstance than to watch this Miracle of rebirth annually? If you go along with my Recommendation, your Life together will simultaneously track according to the Sun Deity's

Journey through the Sky. You'd be aligned with Numbers that
cyclically emerge naturally. Ones that you'll be reminded of as the
Sun travels North above the Equator, and brings longer Days until
its next transition on the Summer Solstice three Months later." He
can hear Mr Freud pull into his own driveway. "Does that remind
you of Anything? It should. Mary, the Virgin, gave birth to Jesus
Christ, the Son of God, on December 25, the Autumnal Equinox.
Virgo, the Sign associated with this date, marks the Sun's descent
into the shorter Days of the Year. See the connection? Virgo, the
Virgin, drops into the third Trimester, one that ends in the birth
of a Sun on Christmas Day. Fascinating. Christ, the Light of the
World, was a Sun Deity born from Virgo, the Virgin. Loretta has
done additional research and found that the Morning Star, a
Name interchangeably used for Christ as well as the Sun, rose, or
was born on December 25. Follow? Christ, the Sun or Son of the
Virgin, was crucified on March 22, and rose again on the same
Day the Sun rises above the celestial Equator. Take my meaning?
Out of a Period of Darkness came the return of the Light, or the
Sun. Astounding isn't it? What remarkable Symmetry here. Think
about Plato's use of the Cave as a fitting Metaphor. As we emerge
into the Light, illusory Shadows disappear from its Walls and we
begin to see what is real, that the Birth of Knowledge emanates
from Ignorance. And after the 280 Days between the vernal
Equinox and the Winter Solstice, what else do we learn? Yes, that
this Time Frame is also the Length of the Gestation Period of an
Embryo ..."

With Da Stylus gone, Jonah is left alone to listen to the Rev
continue the latest rough outline of his final sermon. He gradually
steers the cleric into his study with a pot of tea, places a blanket
on his legs, and puts the *New York Times* crossword puzzle into

his hands. Then he excuses himself to do the dishes, sweep the kitchen floor, and check to make sure all doors are locked before attempting to work on his writing sample for Professor Iton's workshop.

On the way upstairs, he can hear the Rev telling Loretta Tucci about the engagement over the phone.

Since *l'arriviste*, Monsieur Proust, plastered his bedroom walls with cork board to insulate against noise, Jonah walks into his own facsimilie of the great man's successful methods with a messy placement of tacked blankets on his walls. He sets his alarm clock to beep on the hour (a time when he'll undertake a word count, and try to maintain the rate of production for as long as it takes), taps the window (a new wrinkle in the routine), kisses each one of his fingertips, and sits in front of his computer waiting for his inner guru to pounce.

A sinus headache comes on.

How often has Professor Iton explained, and how often have Jonah and his best bud, Quint C., talked of how the ideal relationship for a writer was the one he had with his work? This couldn't be what they had in mind, excruciating agony that begins in the temple, follows a diagonal line of approximately thirty degrees that cartwheels before sticking a landing in the corner of his left eyeball (opposite the occipital lobe).

Beyond the blankets, cars with improved crash-protection features rampage toward the inner city as Jonah sucks on his teeth.

He can't get his mind to rev up enough to make symmetry out of the pre-linguistic, and the seconds become minutes that encroach on this creature who can't summon the will to choose better, who sits at his desk and toils unproductively in high frequencies of light, livid with the desire to multiply his worth.

Nauseous, he finally regroups by clicking into his email to check his messages.

Doubleclick.

> Hi Baby, My name is Yuliya from St Petersburg, Russia. Do you remember meeting me the last months? I give you hint. I have tattoo on ankle. I cannot forget you, and I find your address from Agency. My English is not of good sort and I look for good man for to have for my life. I remember that maybe you may be this man. Agency tell me I get good job in your city if you give me name, address and these things. They give me ticket in two weeks.
>
> I am hard worker and having teaching certificate. If you look my picture, you see I am not supermodel. I know how mans likes the looks. But if you will still like me, I can leave my village near St Petersburg to do big things in the world, and to meet with you my special friend. I have sister who meet boyfriend in your country. In three months they marry and come for to Russia to see my Mama. My Papa was going away when we were small, so it is struggle for us. But this is not time for sad things. I am happy to meet my special friend again.
>
> Please to reply for I am impatient for you.
>
> xoxoxo
>
> Yuliya

There's an attached jpeg of a girl-next-door type with chestnut hair, standing in front of a wall in acid-washed jeans. It appears she's dressed to face a firing squad, a leather handbag under an arm.

In response:

Hello Yuliya,

For the life of me I don't remember you, but this is probably my fault as I was probably tangled up with assignments at school. So, yes, I'm a student doing a Masters at Dingham University, Pennsylvania (feel free to be impressed), and I don't know what to say to make up for forgetting what must have been a scrumptious-looking ankle.

How about this? I'd like to get to know you a little first. The basics. Like what is in your diet that makes you so darn lovely? Do you like Maxim Gorky's novels? Lenin or Trotsky? The bloated USSR or the slimmed down Russia?

Lets ke i tuch, k.

Ralph Ellison[59]

After sending the quick missive, Jonah logs onto MesoHorny.com to see if Hirosita is drumming up business in the chat room. (He wants to tell her he'll have her money. But not tomorrow since he'll need a couple of days to butter the Reverend's toast.)

No luck.

He toggles over the names of tonight's lineup of Camgirls.

Nope, she isn't working.

He clicks onto Messenger.

Ralph_Ellison (10/18/2003 8:28:04 pm): hi babe
Ralph_Ellison (10/18/2003 8:28:14 pm): r u der bb
Ralph_Ellison (10/18/2003 8:28:21 pm): u der
Ralph_Ellison (10/18/2003 8:30:14 pm): wtf holla when u git this grl lol

---

59 Email exchange from the private collection of Jonah Ayot-Kolosha, donated by the Ayot-Kolosha estate.

Unsettled, Jonah liberates a bottle of Jack that was duct-taped to the back of the dresser, perches on his windowsill, and washes down two aspirin with his meds. Then he surfs Google for information about the death of the toll-booth attendant—Leroi was nineteen, the cop who shot him is suspended pending an internal review; it is alleged that Leroi was among the criminal element who used the Blackout to ransack parts of North Oldeham (random violence took place after word was purported to have quickly spread about an alleged beating of a thief who'd allegedly robbed a pawn shop). Stars are heliocentric spheres that flare and expand as he can hear the Rev in another part of the universe call out for the whereabouts of his reading glasses. ★ ★ ★ ★ ★ ★ ★ ★ ★ ★
★ ★
★ ★ ★ ★ ★ ★ After they find them in the Rev's front pocket, Jonah jots down bullet points for a conversation with Hiroko before calling her from the kitchen phone.

"Z'uuup?" he says into the receiver.

"Who is this?" a girl replies.

"Jonah," he says.

It's Ingrid. "Who?"

"Jonah Ayot-Kolosha. Is Hiroko in?"

"Have you signed the petition for Leroi Johnson?" she asks.

"What petition?"

She's irritated. "Leroi Johnson was murdered. A case of police brutality."

"I know that. Smart aleck."

"It doesn't sound like it, idiot. He's the toll-booth guy from the night of the Blackout."

"Listen, is Hiroko there or not?"

"Do you even know anything about police brutality?"

Thankfully, Hiroko shoves the mouthy brat aside and gets on the line. "Z'uuup?" she says.

"Jeezus! That sister of yours is a piece of work. Have you considered charm school?"

"Go on, baby," Hiroko says. "I'll be with you in a second. Charm school? No. She's protective of me is all."

"She's a smart ass."

Hiroko giggles. "So what can I do you for?"

Topic one: "Do you think the cops who hassled us the other night were involved with Leroi Johnson?"

"Not on the phone."

"Sorry?"

"Not on the phone."

Bugs. Good point. I check my notes, skip topic two, and go with my strength: the literary enterprise. "I'm not getting any writing done." Hiroko's silent. "I mean, I've got all these ideas, good ones I think. Like I plan to add snapshots, or at least one snap in miniature at the top of each page of a story I hope to write. You know, just the same shot of my left butt-cheek. But ..." The lock turns at the front door. "Hold up a sec, Cakes."

Elisha Tusker, son, walks into the kitchen. "Well if it isn't Mr Ayot-Kolosha," he says.

Jonah points to the telephone to let him know he's on the line.

"I'm gonna crash on the couch." Elisha must have got in an argument with Dorothea, his African-American wife who wears an assortment of shoulder-length blond wigs, over the lucrative investment potential of corn as a substitute for fuel, and left his own place in a huff. "Don't mind me."

"Where were we?" Jonah asks Hiroko. "Yes, I've got ..."

Elisha interrupts again. "I heard a good one this aft. Wanna hear it?" Jonah shakes his head; no, never, ever. "A man laying on his deathbed confides to his wife. He says, 'I can't die without telling you the truth.'" Elisha belches, then pops a Rolaid. "I cheated throughout our whole marriage. All those nights when I told you I was working late, I was with other women. His wife takes it in, then replies, 'Why do you think I gave you the poison?'"

"Dude! Phone!"

Elisha rollicks with belly laughter, then burps again before sticking his head into produce in the fridge.

"Sorry about that, Hiroko," Jonah says into the receiver. "Where were we?"

"Did you get the money?" she asks.

"I'll have it for you a little later than planned."

"How late?"

"The evening after tomorrow?"

"Tomorrow evening?"

"No. The evening after that. I lost my bank card and, with my schedule, I won't be able to physically go to the bank for a couple of days."

"Okay."

After a brief pause, she asks what he's up to, as in that evening. Jonah waits for Elisha to clear out of the kitchen before responding. He whispers, eight inches, as in the heft of his manly ding-a-ling. Dang, she replies. In a flash, Jonah goes with a full court press. I'm thinking of trying penis enlargement supplements, but it might be too ... Oooh, Daddy, she replies. Oooh, cousin, he replies. Cousin? she asks. I'm going along with your creepy incestuous theme, he says. No. No. Daddy doesn't mean like father, she says. It's an expression. Like, Oooh, Mama. I know that, he says. But the language is imprecise, a linguistic crime, and I'm using it etymologically. Huh, she replies. Jonah looks at bullet-point number four, talking smut, subsection D. My, my, it's sooo muggy sitting here in this towel, he says. Hold up a second, ahhh, that feels sooo much better without all this scratchy material binding around my waist. Teeheehee. What are *you* wearing? A sarong, she replies. Sweet, he responds. But, wouldn't you be more comfortable if ... here, let me get that with my ding-a-ling.

It's jazizzle izzle, XXX-rated for the next half-hour.

When it's all over, his headache is gone and they've panted their way beyond every rule of decorum considered appropriate to bougie folk.

"Can you be here by nine the day after tomorrow?" she says.

"Sure." He's supposed to meet Da Stylus at the same time for Youth Rollerskating, but he'll come up with a good excuse to jam out of it. "Nine on the dot, Cakes."

"Respeck," she replies.

"Respeck."

Charged up and ready for alone time with his own dirty thoughts, Jonah tiptoes through the dark living room, past Elisha who snores on the couch. Stealthily, he creeps forward, but gets tangled in a bundle of Elisha's clothes piled every which way on the floor. He teeters with trousers wrapped around his feet and, in balancing himself against a dresser, sends a wooden carving of a giraffe crashing to the floor.

"Jonah, is that you?"

Dang!

"Wanna hear another one?" Elisha takes Jonah's no to mean yes, love to. "A wife asks her husband if he's planning to do anything for their anniversary. The husband looks at her and replies, 'Where I'm from, we don't celebrate mistakes.'"

"Tell me, Elisha. Do you even like being married?"

"Yah. I love it. Why?"

"Your jokes seem hostile to the institution."

"Don't shoot the messenger." He burps. "Wanna hear another one?"

"Maybe in the morning." Jonah resents Elisha for the heartache he causes the Rev. "I need at least eight hours of sleep if I'm going to function tomorrow."

On that note, gentle reader, eminent critic, we leave our hero to regroup upstairs gathering paraphernalia—Vaseline, a facecloth, printouts of hot pics from Hiroko's MesoHorny homepage—and we turn the page while he gets down to a sticky task most suited for moments of privacy.

II

Nurse Shelley pops her head into your room, sees the Dr taking your temperature, and pops out again

He's fidgety as he sticks a cold stethoscope to your pecs, then takes your blood pressure. After a pause to jot notes on a chart, he puts his gloved hand all up in your naughty bits.

"I see from your chart you live in North Oldeham," he says.

You nod.

"There was real excitement over there the night of the Black-out," he continues. "Am I right?"

"Blackout, yes."

"The wife and I had our share of problems that evening." He cups a testicle. "Not like yours, mind you. Just troubles. We lost power for most of the evening. Nothing worked. Cellphones. Computers. Not a one. So I'm telling the wife about an article I read in *Nature*. A darn good read too about the species' overde-pendence on technology." He squeezes each ball with a thumb and forefinger. "But she's terribly upset, see. She can't get a hold of the parents who are aged, and the radio's going on about the loot-ing." Dark hairs poke out of his nostrils as well as his ears. "'Your parents live all the way off in Westchester,' I say. 'The looting is in North Oldeham,' I say. But still, she has me drive over to the par-ents in that storm with not one working traffic light." He waves his stethoscope in the air. "It's a minor miracle I didn't end up in a ditch. It took half an hour of dodging falling tree branches only to find the parents sitting happy as clams on their porch. They were listening to a tape of an evangelist on the End Times, waiting for the Rapture." He chuckles. "The things the better half makes you do can make you wonder how the Mormons manage with multiple wives. Surely, one is plenty."

"When can I get out of restraints, Doc?"

He looks over your chart. "No history of grand mals. Excellent. Both your temperature and blood pressure are normal. No swollen lymph glands. But we need to keep an eye on your kidneys as well as a slight swelling of your spleen." He forces a smile. "We'll check in tomorrow morning, then a determination will be made in conjunction with your medical team."

You look at your roommate also strapped in the bed next to you. He has a five-o'clock shadow; he is built like a farmhand with thick arms.

"What are you here for?" he asks.

"It's a mistake," you reply.

He says his name and you forget it. When you look at him, you see the left side of his face will not stop twitching.

"I don't belong here," you say.

"Others will decide when you are sufficiently polite to be accepted by society," he replies.

You're not one of him, you think. You can lie still on the edge of your mattress and the side of your face doesn't fidget.

12

**MISSION STATEMENT: Stay sober. Write for three hours.
Play community b-ball with Q.**

The morning is spent in my room at Colby Manor getting lots
of not-writing done, ironing out kinks on a MySpace page by
re-working my bio, and then taking a catnap around noon. Afterward, I build up the nerve and seek out the Rev in his study in
order to ask for a temporary loan.

Me: Do you have a moment?

Him: Surely, my Son.

Me: I have a huge favor to ask of you.

Him: It's about the Rings, right?

Me: Yes.

Him: Well, the Thing to remember is we're talking about a
Promissory Note that announces Intention.

Me: One of considerable expense.

Him: What are my Intentions? This is the Question to ask
yourself. And I'm not talking about Sentiment, mind you. There's
far too much emoting confused for Emotion. An Engagement is
more like planting a Stake in the Ground. One that says, this is
where we take our Stand.

Me: I'm looking at a buy in the five hundred range.

Him: Feelings are Ephemeral. They may never be as clear as that
Day you stake your Claim to mutual Fidelity. But this is neither
here nor there. Your Pledge should be like Sir Edmund Hillary

planting a Union Jack on top of Everest.[60] You've scaled the Summit. You've surveyed the View, and it is the Conquest of the surrounding Panorama that your Ring serves to remind you of when the difficult Days come.

Me: I should get her a diamond. At least this is what I found out online. If it were up to me, I'd skip the whole thing altogether. But Clementine will want to show it off to her girlfriends (insert chuckle).

Him: Say no more. I'd already decided on giving you an early Wedding Gift.

Me: Thanks, Rev. Six hundred is good. It'll be more than enough.

Him: One can't skimp on a Ring. It's much too valuable a Symbol.

Me: Maybe seven hundred to be on the safe side. Seven-fifty, if you think that's best.

(The Rev unlocks his desk drawer, hands over a folded handkerchief, and it isn't long before I find myself staring at a gold ring with a diamond setting.)

Him: It belonged to Meredith, God bless her, and I think Clementine is a worthy recipient of this Token of Conjugal Fidelity.

(Silence.)

Him: Jonah?

Me: I'm speechless.

Him: And so you should be when surveying the Himalayas from

---

60   Hillary is the first man reputed to have climbed Mount Everest, although it is believed a Tibetan was in fact the first to have done so. (I take no official position on the controversy; the latter seems more likely, but I withdraw any implication that might suggest this as a bias.)

the loftiest of Perches. *Ego sic argumentum.*[61]

I look to see if Elisha is kicking around. His visit may have been a ruse to get me as an audience for his nonsensical version of events around the corn scam that has the Rev on the verge of losing his church. Luckily, he's gone. Instead, I find Hurricane Elisha has left behind a nasty mess of dishes. Twenty aggravating minutes of cleaning later, I finally get out the front door.

Bingo, the contractor, sits on the front step rolling a joint and listening to a small transistor radio.

"How do?" I ask.

"I got the article." He reaches into a tin lunch box and presents me with a laminated page from a magazine. "Take your time, chief."

I can't get away from the house.

by Trip Hamilton
IN THE KNOW

BABYSITTING In town to promote the new season of the hit show, *Switcher*, **Tamala Exeter** and her beau, **Lance Itby**, spend a day with **Belinda Vernon** and her four-year-old daughter **Sylvia** (with actor **Rafe Curtis**). The foursome visited boutiques on Sharp Street and gorged on ice cream at Jermaines.

GRIST FOR THE RUMOR MILL Neil Kipper and **Desiree Boa** putting in some extra curricular activity on the set of **Alan Devlin**'s latest project, *Blue Summer*. While filming last weekend, the actors met at Wrack's, a private nightclub uptown where the costars danced together. Asked if his wife,

---

61   And this is what I argue (Latin).

Zazou Kipper would approve, Neil replied coolly, "What do you think?"

SPOTTED **Damien Knolls** and **Sasha** huddled together at a restaurant in the valley ... **Mary Zelmart** walking her Labrador through Flounders Park with **Jimmy Went** ... **Richard Yarrow** and his wife **Laura Carmen Lunsforth** threw a 100-episode anniversary party for the cast and crew of their hit show, *Tear It Up*, at Edwardians.

PERSONS TO WATCH **Bingo Jefferson**, the seventeen-year-old senior at Santori High, is 6'1" and runs the 40 in 4.2. He holds the Pennsylvania State record for most double-purpose yards by a high schooler (both rushing and kick-off returns). He's a threat as a receiver out of the backfield and as a top recruit at colleges is already being projected as a Heisman Trophy candidate.[62]

"It came out the week before I wuz hurt."

"That sucks."

"Yup. *Curranvale Style*. It don't get no better than that at seventeen."

"Life ain't fair."

"You got that right." He licks rolling paper. "Yezzir. It wuz rainin 'n' my right knee was shot up with cortisone. Yup. So when I cut on a L-slant, blam, the snap is all up in 'em cheap seats."

"Sorry for your loss," I mutter.

While Bingo retells his tale, I think of how the ex-con has huge balls. By that I mean, he blazes up a joint right there on the front step, and heartily inhales before expelling smoke from flared nostrils. After a series of puffs, he offers me a pull, and then gets into

---

62   *Curranvale Style & Society Magazine*, July 1994.

the nitty gritty of his failed attempt at rehabbing the knee, giving far too many details.

I find myself tuning in Da Stylus, who takes calls on 97.3 CKCU.

"Ka-ching ka-ching, baby girl," she exorts. "Ka-ching ka-ching. That's what y'all gotta listen for."

"Ka-ching ka-ching," the caller responds.

"Now tell me, what's your number-one station?"

"97.3 is my *only* station, ma."

Then it's back to Christian hip hop.

"I hear you fixin to marry her," Bingo says with a wink.

"The Rev's got a big mouth."

"Lucky dawg," he replies. "I'd looove to bang me some holay bootay."

"You've got a wife."

"And a couple of shorties," he says with pride. "But I'm like a African king, boss. I gotsta have me lotsa bitches."

"It's not like that anymore."

He's incensed. "What the motherfuck?" He shakes his head. "That ain't right."

"Nah, it's all good." I feel like I've failed him.

He explodes. "That ain't a'ight." He twists open a bottle of hooch in a brown paper bag, and helps himself to a couple of swigs. "A pimp's gotta have his bitches, chief."

∞

Under the spell of Bingo's combustibles, Jonah sits at the bus stop, alarmed by the great distance from coordinates in space named Curranvale City and the ones in space named Hoppa. Out of his wits, he watches folk drive past in cars that kill the planet, tearing a hole in the ozone layer and melting polar ice caps that will cause tsunamis. Instead of people surrounding him, Jonah sees Cro-Magnons,[63] Neanderthals,[64] and Australopithecines.[65] He stares at their oversized mandibles aware that everywhere violence crowds him. Warplanes bang in his inner ears, traffic straddles precariously upon his nervous system, and he sits on his hands, humming to keep hominids[66] from kicking the crap out of him for reasons known only to them.

Pressure builds in his bladder, presses on his ball sac, and he can smell his own sweat.

Thrown off center (without knowing it), he runs through a list of those who mean to do him harm. The Liwani Secret Police (LSP) assume he's been in cahoots with Gramps in his fight to bring an end to the ethnic cleansing around Hoppa. Concerned American Patriots (CAP) worry he's crossed the US border for purposes pursuant to terror, leprosy spreading, and/or gang banging in cars driven without a licence. At this moment, anyone who's ticked off about the existence of hypocrisy may be in a gun shop securing an automatic weapon without the necessary documentation, moving one step closer to a shooting spree that will end with Jonah's slaughter in the campus cafeteria.

---

63 Appeared in Europe 40,000 to 10,000 years ago.

64 Appeared in Europe and Asia as early as 350,000 years ago.

65 Appeared in Africa 4 million years ago.

66 The footnotes are in no way intended to draw attention to the fact that Africa is the birth place of human beings. This might suggest an Africanist bias. However, the inference would be false because the implied author isn't keen on ideas that appear inclined toward forging the conscience of races in the smithy of the soul *à la* Mr James Aloysius Joyce.

He can't stop shivering, and he really, really needs to pee.

Hominids gather around him at the bus stop, and he doesn't know what century he's in, and slavery doesn't seem that long ago, and the one with hairy knuckles looks at him, hateful, and intent on clapping on the chains as others move closer, hemming him in. Trapped, Jonah places his faith in God, holds out his arms in contrition and starts to sing.

Praise God from whom all blessings flow.

Praise …

First one hominid then another joins in with him. ★ ★ ★ ★ ★ ★
★ ★
★ ★
★ ★ ★ ★ ★ ★ ★ ★ ★ Outside the door of Q.'s apartment in Tilley Towers, Jonah jumps from foot to foot, clenching muscles in his lower abdomen. Bursting, he raps knuckles on Q.'s door as urine begins to slowly trickle from him.

Eliza May opens up.

"Washroom!"

"Nice to see you too."

She steps aside as Jonah flies past her, flings open the bathroom door, and painfully withholds the trickle of urine as he unzips.

What a relief when dark yellow pee gushes out of him.

Two minutes later, he checks to make certain there is no wet patch on the front of his jeans, and then returns to the living room where Eliza May sits on the couch in loud music. She wears a white sleep shirt and shower water drips from her wet shoulder-length weave to her bare legs.

"Are you okay?" she asks.

"The pipes needed draining," he replies.

"Glad to be of service."

He sits beside her and points to the sound system. "Who's playing?"

"*Meat is Murder.*"

"That's the group?"

"No. The CD. The group's the Smiths."[67]

"Never heard of 'em."

"You've never heard of Morrissey?"

"If you put it like that, sure. Course I have."

"Eighties rock. He was big into depression. You like?"

"Sounds whiny."

She clucks. "How's your story coming along?"

"It isn't. Yours?"

"The same."

"I can't focus."

"Looming nuptials will do that to a person," she says.

"It's not like that."

"So said Faust of his bargain with the devil."

"I didn't make the rules, Sherlock. I just live beyond them."

"*Thus spake Zarathustra,*" she replies.

"My point exactly."

"Well, Superman. I'm making margaritas, want one?"

Eliza May disappears into the kitchen, leaving me to drown in impressionist art by those whose names will one day be better known, and pine book shelves stocked with early edition

---

67   In what may or may not be a coincidence, the English rock band was formed in 1982 (the same year as Jonah's birth).

hardbacks in mint condition.

Quint C. is a minimalist in his tastes. Most everything is black and low to the floor; tables, large round cushions that substitute for sofas, surfaces of frosted glass that are hard and flat and look as if he just finished wiping them down with a toothbrush dipped in Windex.

Now that I'm among people, I know I'm doing better. The fear is gone and what remains is shame over my George Beverly Shea[68] impersonation at the bus stop. Odd, though, how a song from my errant Christian days gave me solace when I was at my wits' end. Yikes! As long as I have faculties in working order, I plan to never, ever, pull a weird stunt like that again.

Moving on.

I make out pal-of-mine through the door of his office. He's hunched over his desk looking windswept, as if he's been sailing in tennis whites with William F. Buckley Jr[69] all morning.

There is, it seems, a dispute over requested rewrites for several stories in his collection due out with Dilchester Press in the spring.[70]

"You don't get it," Quint C. complains. "The characters are what they are, frustrated by a system that gives them limited options. No! That's not what we talked about. Not even close. Excuse me. You're interrupting. Excuse me. Let me get a word in. I

---

68 This Canadian Gospel singer (b. 1909) is a favorite of the Rev.

69 An urban legend at DU still circulates that as a young man, Professor Iton made a name for himself with a rancorous appearance on this American conservative commentator's chat show, *Firing Line*.

70 *Gangrene & Other Stories*, winner of the Rushworthy First Book Prize (2004), the National Online Short Story Award (2004), and the Pennsylvania Heritage Prize (2004).

don't care if you think ... the people I write about ... puhleeeze! I'm not going to change a single word. Not a single ... freaking comma."

I wait for him to call for a duel, gats[71] optional.

Q.'s the real deal. Talented. Confident. He's had a foot in all that congeals in the tastier corners of our ailing, fucked globe. He's been stoned on a variety of combustibles on offer in far-flung lands: opium smoked in a brothel in Thailand, peyote ingested in a cave in Peru, hashish eaten in a crowded market in Morocco, and E popped at a rave in Germany. He's eaten roasted pigeon, grilled boa constrictor, and boiled ox testicles. As well, he's lounged on barges in Venice, done an ironical photo-op in boxers at the Taj Mahal, worn safari boots in the Transvaal, and used said footwear to climb ruins in Machu Picchu. There has been skateboarding and bungee jumping, sky gliding and downhill skiing. Also, Cuban cigars have been smoked while deep sea fishing at the Great Barrier Reef. As a result, the work he sends out into a world of complete strangers has them giddy over what they read about his perilous excursions on donkeys in war zones. Unlike Eliza May and I, he doesn't talk about the book he'll eventually write or the book he'll never finish. He isn't dependent on a well-turned anecdote whenever an interesting conversation is required at a public get-down. Even his crib looks as if it's owned by a fella in the bigs. He has LPs as opposed to CDs; PIL, The Cure, and the Violent Femmes instead of the Sex Pistols and Duran Duran. His shelves belong to the modernists with the men separate from the women, and arranged according to country of origin. Nothing like my *ad*

---

71   The original manuscript has the word gatling crossed out and pistol used in its place. However, the editor made the decision to go back to the slang as it seemed the better choice.

hoc discards picked up on the cheap in secondhand bookstores, strays abandoned by folk who've moved on.

∞

Quint C., writer, slumps onto a cushion.

"Is it a good idea to be so combative?" Jonah asks.

"The world is large and there are other publishers."

"Easy, dude," Jonah says. "Don't overplay your hand."

"I know what I'm doing. The stories they've got a problem with are still accessible to the well-populated, middle of the pack. We just have different ideas about what writing like that sounds like."

Jonah warns him not to forget that there are plenty of other writers "waiting in the wings if he stumbles." But Quint C. doesn't listen. Instead, he shuts down because what Jonah's saying doesn't track with the information that jams his transom.

"Heya, you're looking a bit chunky." He pokes a layer of fat on Jonah's belly. "Got to watch for that. An author photo influences whether a reader picks up your book."

"That's ridiculous."

"No," he replies. "It's realistic. You've got to be savvy enough to work on your look."

• "No. I meant it's ridiculous that I put on weight."

"Little known fact, the baby boomers, who run the shop, market fiction titles to book clubs, and the majority of those are run by older, mid to upperclass women." He scratches stubble at his chin. "Work on your look, boss."

Eliza May re-emerges to hand Jonah a margarita with a salted rim. Then, "You'll have to excuse me, boys," she says. "I'm off to

Rosemary's," as in Rosemary "the Bookworm" Levy. "We're taking our laptops to Ptolemy's to get some work done."

Quint C. pulls her into his lap. "Take a break, lamb chop." Pearl
white panties flash on her dark thighs. "Despite Professor Iton's
views to the contrary, practise is for those without pedigree."

Lawdy Lord, Q. has just rattled her with his snooty put-downs
for the third time today. Why? She's twenty-seven, four years Q.'s
senior, but unlike him she's not yet sold on the right to call herself a writer. She has taken only one summer with a Eurail pass
that took her from the Louvre to an astonishing three days with
Gaudi[72] in Barcelona. But there has been no hiking on Easter
Island and no train trip from Delhi to Nepal. She didn't get into
a writing residency in Bellagio and she only made it into DU
because three other students on the shortlist accepted invites to
better funded programs. In her estimation, she hasn't risen to
the mark. There are continents still to be traveled, and accoutre-
ments of the profession she has yet to procure; she hasn't published or successfully showcased her brand of cunning linguistics
to someone in the industry who can get her published. Sure, she
studies the minutiae of her craft with mentor-types known for
reconstituting genres, but she has yet to read with blue-chippers
at a literary festival of standing. Unlike Quint C., nobody has
sent her a questionnaire requesting what are her top three books,
and which of these is her biggest influence. Unlike him, she
hasn't been named as a writer under thirty to watch.[73] So, she

---

72 The unusual scaffolding of Eliza May's work has been compared favorably
with Antoni Gaudi, the Spanish modernist architect.

73 The *New Yorker* named Quint C. sixth on the strength of *Uvula*, a short
story published in the March '01 edition.

makes Jamesean[74] charts that start with a single female character around which she explores sets of relations in the gristle of the African diaspora, and she's sensitive to any comments that make light of her main strength, her work ethic.

"I don't look that heavy, do I?" Jonah asks Eliza May.

"What now?" she asks.

"Quint thinks women won't buy my book 'cause I'm too fat. Am I?"

Writers' symposium:

The trio trade choice invectives about the opportunistic Mayor of Curranvale City and his bullshit press conference with the chief of police about the shooting of Leroi Johnson. Official comments about the Blackout won't be made to the public while an investigation is underway. Get this, any officer found derelict in their duties will be prosecuted according to the strictest letter of the law. Thoughts and prayers go out to the Johnson family. Everyone is sorry for their loss. No, the department is not racist, nor does it condone racism. What bullcrap! Fascists! Where the hell do we live, Nazi Germany? The only thing those propagandists forgot to do was ask the good people of Curranvale to let the system run its course.

Enough.

After a brief silence, Jonah discourses on God.

Gather 'round.

Breaking his pledge to maintain a strict silence on "the incident," he gives a witty account of the partaking of Bingo's

---

74   Special thanks to noted literary scholar, Dr Arte Gjoes, who suggested that this allusion refers to the Preface of Henry James's *The Portrait of a Lady*.

combustibles (with an exaggerated take on the ex-con's views on harems), then he delivers a ramped-up version of his psychotic episode at the bus stop, and closes with a tale of the sing-along (adding a group hug for extra effect).

It bears mentioning that both Eliza May and Quint C. love Jonah like a sibling. However, in his absence, they're prone to spend their down time talking of the many ways he's not quite looped into reality. Once again, they love him to pieces and they show it by indulging his fits of whimsy, but it's difficult to know how well he separates fact from fiction. Often, it's impossible to know if what is actually going on for him has to do with his need to be in an interesting narrative, and as a result causes him to confuse character with an intriguing persona.

Eliza May kicks off the teasing.

"You were in the presence of the divine, Jonah," she says.

"I was stoned."

"Don't be such a skeptic, dude," Quint C. admonishes. "This is the way it is with most mystics. First there's an experience, then comes the understanding that it's a wake-up call from the numinous."

"I was stoned," Jonah says again with less vigor.

The couple suppresses a laugh. "I think you're pre-programmed to become a priest," Eliza May warns.

"You think?"

"Oh, yah. I mean, there's your grandfather and, of course, your mum was quite religious."

"Crap," Jonah says.

"Studies show that a predilection for that sort of propensity is built into the DNA," Quint says.

"He's right," Eliza Mays adds. "We have a friend who has three generations of clergy in her family."

"You mean Fanny?" Quint asks, pinching her thigh.

"Yah, silly." She won't let him distract her. "Fanny used to be proud of the fact she was a strict atheist, always saying things like Merry Xmas instead of Merry Christmas. But now she's in a seminary and three months away from ordination as a minister in the United Church."

"We're freaking him out, sweetie."

"Hey, if you've got the gift, you've got the gift."

"Crapcrap," Jonah says. "Crapcrap."

After Eliza May excuses herself to write (like those without pedigree), the boys switch to beer. Quint C., sage, takes another call about the book cover, and then returns to sermonize about the imminent dangers of Jonah's faux engagement.

"I'm just saying, don't put anything in writing," he advises. "Apart from the obvious legal ramifications, a writer needs to be careful about the paper trail posterity will pore over in the archives of the Harvard Library."

"Can we change the subject?"

"No problemo." Quint C. needs little encouragement to return to his favorite topic: himself. Blab, blab. He blabs about concern over his upcoming book tour and compares public readings to having "a jump-off leave you in bed—on the kitchen table, in the closet—right after the boning is done."

Jonah can't process information that doesn't concern him, apologizes in advance for what he's about to say, asks Q. for a loan, apologizes again, and then explains about Hiroko, the debacle over the ring, and how his inheritance will be coming through in three months, give or take.

"Whatever interest you want to charge is cool," he concludes.

"I've got cash coming in, but not for three days," Quint C. replies. "After that, you're welcome to whatever you need."

⌒

"There are twelve of us," one of the men announces. "First ten to make free throws get to scrimmage."

The shoot-around features those who talk to one another like men; nothing smarts that needs to be made public. There's nothing that can't be resolved with a decent night of rest.

I make the cut.

My team is made up of runts with the exception of Quint C., who is from the sub-category of rich runts. Another point of note, most of my teammates are covered in body hair.

No problem. Cool Hand Juke's in the hizzhouse, fashizzle izzle.

"The old man's got the kid," says a silver-haired fellow in high-tops who taps me on the chest before play gets underway.

His team is made up of those who barely missed out on being draft picks from '73 to the present, and they're all agility and speed.

For days, I run up and down the court, drunk and distracted by thoughts about my hard-wired Deoxyribo Nucleic Acid. I miss a mid-range jumper, then double-over to pant as the old man grabs the rebound and takes it coast to coast.

"Whose guy is that?" Quint C. barks.

"Sorry," I reply.

I run more. I can feel my thighs cramping. High Tops leans on me, pushes me out of the key, nowhere close to the ball that bounces off the rim.

"Get stuck in, Jonah," Quint C. says.

"Cool Hand Juke," I mumble back.

"What?"

"It's Cool Hand Juke." I'm not liking him much right now. Worse still, he's one of those dudes who makes every one of his long distance J's. Swish. All net. There's no way to defend him. I dribble up court. "Jonah!" Quint C.'s got his open shot. "Jonah! Jonah!"

Screw him!

I go to thread a pass to Hairy Bloke No. 1 under the hoop, but High Tops tips the ball away from me and breaks for a lay-up.

"I was open, Jonah," Quint C. admonishes.

"It's Cool Hand Juke."

The sound of feet are behind my ears, my team is down, and I couldn't give a rat's ass.

"Score?"

Nobody remembers.

"We're up at least seven," someone from the College All-Stars says.

I want a substitute to come in, but there isn't anyone on the sidelines.

As soon as play resumes, High Tops dunks on me. "Who's your daddy?" he says.

"You aren't going to let the old man speak on your dadda?" Quint C. chides.

"Ball," I demand.

Determined to shut them up, I dribble hard toward the basket. But High Tops, all over me, taps the ball away again.

"Your Mama," he says.

I re-up my effort, pushing against the silver-haired oldster who spins away and lays another in.

Fuuuck meee!

Quint C. pulls me aside, giving me an impromptu lesson in defense. I'm supposed to bend my knees. Keep my eye on the man, not the ball. Make sure he doesn't get between me and the basket.

"Do you think I'm being called to the ministry?" I ask him.

"What?"

"You think it's in my DNA?"

"Chazus H. Freud, dude. Focus!"

"Our next basket wins," High Tops interrupts.

The opposition does some clear out maneuver, leaving the old guy and I one-on-one.

I eye the brace on his right knee. If I let him in close enough, I can take his leg out. He crowds me—back turned and square. He's right where I want him. I block out distractions, execute a precisely timed leg sweep, and hit nothing but hardwood as he jukes left, laying it in behind me.

"Game, bitch," he says.

I barely get my toe over the threshold of the front door when I hear the Rev shout-talking at Bingo.

"Do you or do you not recognize your Name on this Traffic Ticket?"

Silence.

Like usual, Bingo will say as little as possible, and hope this tactic will make the latest conniption fit go away.

"One Hundred and Fifty Dollars!"

Nothing.

"If you think I'm swimming in Dollars, here, go through my

Pockets. I'll empty them out for you." Change clatters to the floor. "Help yourself!"

Good Lord!

The Rev's been moodier than usual of late. If he isn't on the phone trying to score cheap labor to do the electricity for the apartment he's got the sockless ex-con building downstairs, he's loudly arguing with customer service agents over cellphone charges he refuses to pay. He's taken to sitting in a chair while Bingo works, watching to make sure he isn't slacking off. He talks about how "Business isn't done with a Handshake." It's next to impossible "to talk to a live Person" when making a business call because "everything is automated." It used to be that one paid contractors for their services "after the Job was complete," but now you have to "put a Bundle down before they're willing to commit." His one respite appears to be Wednesday night bowling with Mrs Loretta Tucci. On his return, he is less hopped up on reasons why everything is wrong.

Shoot! One thing's for sure, he's not the greatest ambassador for the Holy Order.

I tiptoe into the kitchen and search for signs of a Post-it note about a call from Hiroko.

There's one from Da Stylus.

Shoot!

Before I can escape upstairs, the Rev limps into the room. "Where in Heaven's Name have you been?" he asks.

"What happened to your leg?" I reply.

Between Latin aphorisms and a review of basic rules regarding manners at Colby Manor, he explains that he sprained his ankle from a fall in the basement—the third one in the last six months.

"You need to sit, dude, and get the ankle elevated while I pack it in ice."

"Call Clementine."

"Sit!"

"Will you stop fussing?"

Da Stylus is right. We need to keep him on track and get him through his final sermon. After he's no longer under pressure, one hopes he'll be back to his old self.

I bargain. "I'll call her if you let me pack your foot in ice."

"*Peor es hurgarle*,"[75] he grumbles.

The Rev takes time to settle into a chair, and then painstakingly lifts his injured limb onto the seat opposite him.

It's swollen like a malnourished belly.

"Sheeesh." He squirms as I prod it with a finger. "Go easy on the old fella."

I open the fridge, shake cubes from the ice tray onto a dishtowel, drop onto a knee, and wrap the makeshift first-aid contraption around his ankle. Then I pick up the phone, dial, and don't let him see me hang up before it rings.

"Darn. I got voice ... *Allo, mademoiselle. C'est moi, Jonah. Reponds, s'il te plait*[76] ... uh, mail."

"That's strange." The Rev picks up a pen and stares at his crossword puzzle. "She was there fifteen minutes ago."

"She isn't there now."

I strategize. Should I offer to make him tea? No. If I ask if he needs anything, he might say yes. But if I say nothing, I risk coming across as rude. Jesus, how does Da Stylus manage to be nice all

---

75 It's better to let sleeping dogs lie (Spanish).

76 Hi miss. It's me, Jonah. Please call back (French).

the time? And why did she call again? We talked for an hour this morning, and even though she's hurting over Leroi, another call is too much. Much too much ... some people must just be nicer than others.

"Take a Picture, Son." I realize I've been staring at the Reverend's foot. "It lasts longer."

"Right."

The shift from daydream to unpacking Cool Hand Juke's sweaty gear into a laundry basket happens lickety boo. But before I can settle, I feel the need to transform into the Nubian James Bond, shaken not stirred, as I pull back the curtain on my bedroom window for a look-see down the street for evidence that God is communicating with me about plans to rush me off into the ministry: blinding lights, levitating mailboxes, all manner of weird batshit. *Nada.* There's nothing but familiar parked cars and piles of garbage bags left on the street for morning pickup.

I sidle like a world-class cat burglar over to my closet and fling open the door. *Nada* squared. Then I get down on all fours and search under the bed.

Unsuccessful in finding signs that categorically show I'm being called to serve the Lord, I sit down in front of my email.

Hi Baby, This must be Yuliya as you have guessed. Ha Ha. I see your reply is short because you are a surprise to hear me. I look for good man for to have for my life. I think that maybe you may be this man. Agency tell me I get good job in your city if you give me name, address and these things. They give me ticket in two weeks.

I am hard worker and having teaching certificate. If you look my picture, you see I am not supermodel. I know how

mans likes the looks. But if you will still like me, I can leave
my village to do big things in the world, and to meet with you
my special friend. I have sister who meet boyfriend in your
country. In three months they marry and come for to Russia to see my Mama. My Papa was going away when we were
small, so it is struggle for us. But this is not time for sad things.
I am happy to meet my special friend.

Let me tell you little of myself. I grow in Smolensk after
Papa go from us. We have little money but with my sister it is
like best of friends. I go to many walks for to be alone and see
it is sad for me in Russia. Then my Natasha, join agency and
they take her to meet a good man in your country. She work
there two jobs and she is happy for to leave Smolensk. Now I
will come for you.

I can be tolerate of many things but I cannot be tolerate of
you to look at other womens. Are you man who drinks and
who smokes. I sometimes do this little at party, so I'm not
perfect woman.

I have much of excitement for hearing of you. I go to Moscow soon. The agency will make a hotel for me to stay and
make my papers for the travel. I do not go to big city many
often and I must get used as I come to America.

Make an email to me for soon, my darling.

Yuliya

xoxoxox

Clicking onto her latest attached jpeg, I see that she's tanned
and delicious-looking in red Victoria's Secret lingerie on what
seems like a beach on a tropical island.

In response:

Hi loverly, I wish to curl on a couch with you and forget there was a time before Yuliya. I cannot imagine, the first snowfall of this winter without you in my arms.

Do not worry about your English, it's much better than my nonexistent Russian. Two weeks! This gives me time to prepare for our marriage :) Ha ha. I live in New York City, and while I can't put you up during your stay, I could look into a hotel for you at my expense. Of course, you would have a suite with a whirlpool and a delightful view of Central Park.

How long will you be here, babe?

To be honest, I'm quite intimidated by your beautiful photographs. The latest one where you lean on a coconut tree is especially sexy. Is there a beach near your village? As for me, I am a local bodybuilding champion, and what I lack in height is more than made up for in the bed, LOL. There's so much more to say, but I'm due in to work at the Aeronautical Institute. Yes, you guessed it, I'm in training as an astronaut. I hope this as well as my many muscles don't put you off.

If you are serious and send me a reply, I'll include a photo taken from my last bodybuilding competition.

Write me soon, my angel.

Ralph Ellison[77]

Time out!

I'm exhausted from my day's revelry of pre-Lentian[78] proportions. I pop two pills, bringing the grand total for the day to 650 milligrams, and clamber naked into bed.

---

77 Courtesy of the Ayot-Kolosha estate.

78 Once again, thanks to Dr Gjoes for unearthing this veiled reference to the Carnival and Mennipean Satire tradition.

First, I stare at Mum and Dad's leather Bible on my bedside table.

Tole lege. Tole lege.[79]

I don't feel St Augustine's compulsion to act.

I turn off the light, pull crisp sheets up to my chin, and pray to whomever is taking notes.

Dear Eternaleverything. Sorry for my sins, although I don't feel sorry right now, which must mean that I'm not. I did earlier, but I was stoned, which I'm sorry for. Or, at least I was sorry for it at the time. But not now. What else? Please be with those I love, and those I know, and those who suffer, and … darn, I can't pray for every damn person on the planet. I mean, how sincere is that?

---

79   Take it and read it. Take it and read it (Latin).

13

**Hegel says synthesis comes from the dialectic relationship
between a thesis and an antithesis**

However, this synthesis is constantly displaced by an anti-version
that creates another synthesis. It's a process that goes on and on,
until the end of linear time.

That says it all about my latest predicament.

Take my relationship with Gramps. Even though I was sickly
and prone to fevers, through the haze I was all manners; I put a
napkin on my lap at meal times, did not fart in public, held doors
open for "the laaadies," respected my elders, worshipped God, and
went to church. I obeyed the rule of law, was polite and well-spo-
ken, learned to play the piano, and always strove to be honorable.
It was a pure idea and, I ain't gonna lie to you, I worked it. To say
I was charming is to state the obvious. But … I got older, and
the damn idea kept shifting. The world I came to know wasn't
built for gentlemen. There seemed something absurd about the
well-mannered. As a ten-year-old, I watched Mr Charles Sebastian
Sibelius Collins, my piano teacher, during his weekly visits to our
home. He was tall, with a beak for a nose and bushels of hair for
eyebrows. He wore a top hat, a tie with a tie clip, and cufflinks.
He smoked a pipe. He belonged to a lily white country club fifty
miles away, in Dodama. Mr Charles Sebastian Sibelius Collins
came with books for me to read: Daniel Defoe's capitalist adventures, Jonathan Swift's flying continents, and quoted Coleridge's

druggie poetics. He corrected my grammar, and stunk of Old
Spice cologne.

"There are two types of people in the world, Jonah," he said.
"Those who have class and those who don't."

"Yes, sir," I replied, gagging on the smell of another century.

"Do you catch my meaning?"

"Yes, sir."

Our lessons ended with a "how do" before he stepped, in
full gear, into a wave of African heat. I'd walk him through the
pearless trees as he stiffly recoiled while local children crowded
him, bugging him for change. Sweat puddled around his beak
of a nose and he shooed them away with his pipe. All the while,
he talked of canals in Venice and of Rembrandts hanging in the
Louvre.

So, although I'm currently on the opposite end of the gentleman spectrum—consorting with a loose woman, indulging in
the cannabis, pleasuring myself with pornographic materials—the
experience at the bus stop may be a sign that I'm working my
way towards a synthesis. ★ ★ ★ ★ ★ ★ ★ ★ ★ ★ ★ ★ ★ ★ ★ ★ ★ ★ ★
★ ★
★ ★ ★ ★ I awake to the slap of water in my face and sputter back
into the Rev's agitated face.

"Get up!" he says.

"I'm up," I snap back.

He tugs the blankets off me and throws a bundle of clothes
onto my belly.

"You didn't take the Garbage out last Night," he says.

Horse crap. I forgot.

The Rev opens curtains and adjusts the bedside lamp to crank
the maximum amount of light into my eyes. "Do you also need a

Reminder about your Date with Clementine this Evening?"

"Course not."

He hobbles out the door.

Alone in the land of awake people, it all comes back with a dull rush: my ridiculous promise to come through with money for Hiroko, being double-booked with dates this evening, the submission for Iton's workshop I've yet to work on, and the resolve scrounged up in the midnight hour to be a better man, a gentleman's gentleman, a maestro of do-gooder derring-do.

Don't overthink.

On the way to the shower, the Rev nags from the bottom of the stairs. "Make certain you collect *all* the Garbage Bags from the Basement."

"Right."

Wrapped in a towel, I hurry down the steps.

"Not now." The Rev's exasperated. "Shower first."

"Right." I skip back upstairs, swallow 200 milligrams of government-approved anti-seizure pills and three aspirin. Then I jump into the shower, closing my eyes to allow the pelt of hot water trick me into being awake.

I scour myself with a pumice stone, rinse under the prickle of water, but cannot scrub clear.

On turning off the taps, I scram back to my room wrapped in a damp towel.

"Jonah!" the Rev yaps. "Hurry it up."

I ignore him, get down on my knees, and say the Lord's Prayer. *Forgive me for my trespasses as I forgive those who trespass against me ...* Nothing shifts.

Seated on the end of my bed, I lubricate my entire body with lotion, careful to moisten between chapped toes. Then I go

conservative chic with a three-button tweed jacket, beige trousers,
a thin black tie, a beige prayer cap, and black rubber Wellingtons.

8:10.

Again, he hollers about getting the garbage out on time.

I give myself a quick once-over in the bedroom mirror and take
a gander at the full kit from assorted distances: mid-room, from
the doorway, out in the hallway with a saintly, soft-focused pout.

"Jooonah!"

I sprint-walk over the carpeted stairs before making it to the
basement.

8:13.

Beside a pile of electrical wire and plywood is a huge mound of
Hefty bags filled with assorted junk. Lickety split, I haul two bags
upstairs with the Rev providing unsolicited commentary. "Check
the Twist Ties. There's nothing quite like Trash spilling out of a
carelessly closed Bag." He stops me at the front door. "Here. Let
me look." His furrows his brow. "Good Grief, this is precisely
what I'm talking about. Didn't you hear me tell you to check *all*
of them? Bingo doesn't twist them tight enough."

"I got to keep moving, Rev."

"Do you think it's Wise to wear your Prayer Cap?" he heckles.

"It's fine."

"Fine! Fine! Have you any Idea what happens to suspected Ter-
rorists? It is important to remember that, *non immunes ab illis malis
sumus.*"[80]

I refuse to rise to the bait. "It's no big deal."

"No big Deal?" He hovers above my shoulder, watching me
tighten each bag before inspecting them. "We'll see about what

---

80 We are not free of these faults (Latin).

kind of Deal it is." He walks onto the front step, and he glares at the Spielman's wrapped in blankets on their porch. "It will give those Christ-killing Jewish Spies more Ammunition to report to Homeland Security. Then you'll see what kind of Deal it is."

"They don't do that, Rev."

"McCarthyites!" he shouts at the old couple. "Informers!" Three houses away, the garbage truck idles to pick up a load of discarded furniture, and I hurriedly lug the garbage bags to the sidewalk. "Didn't you live through the Nixon Years? Have you People no Shame being in Cahoots with the American Gestapo?"

His voice bangs tinnily inside my skull.

14

The saintly side of Jonah moves uncomfortably where the money lives as he pedals a bike past homes with porches and twinkling perennials in flowerbeds

Cold breeze flattens his cheeks as the Right-leaning in the Senate have blocked the Left's latest attempt to learn what the Big Guy knew and when. Some in the House have begun to deliberate on how to make hay of State Department documents that say the Big Guy cherry-picked his evidence to make a case for an illegal war. However, if the Left in the House manages to see impeachment proceedings through to articles, the right of the Senate has already strategized to see that an up and down vote of yea or nay will ensure this investigation dies like the teen soldiers fighting in their cause.

Across many tolls that go state to state, Gammel Lane is the Pseudo-Black Freuds, the Super Rich-White Hardisons, the Spy-Christ-Killing Spielmans, the Cat-Happy Cuttlewots, and the Islamic-Jihadist Husseins.[81] St Jonah of Hoppa sees sin everywhere as folk stream into the driveways of prefab houses thrown together years ago in a spasm of expansion; every conceivable pigment of the fallen human species is on display—blush, mocha, midnight, paste. Children yawn while packing themselves into gas guzzlers, tired from roaming freely between "the appropriate houses" and

---

81   It has not been established as a point of fact that the Husseins belong to this militant group designated as terrorist by a number of nations.

playing in the "parentally approved" backyards—the creepy need not apply.

Who are these people?

Alistair Freud is a partner at Freud, Leaman, and Collins. He's gone from dawn till dusk, leaving the Mrs to organize their social schedule and to ensure he has a stress-free environment to come home to at day's end. The Hardisons are a Mrs in grey fur and a grey Jaguar and a Mr who owns a fleet of moving trucks. The Spielmans have a puppy that was sired by a movie dog. It noses open the refrigerator when it is left alone at home and eats cold cuts. Mr Cuttlewot left a life of landscaping to paint abstracts about war while his Mrs brings home paychecks from teaching kindergarten. The Husseins are a closed book and after a left on Eddings Street, St Jonah of Hoppa barrels downhill past the spot where Leroi took a bullet, barreling past a house of worship with a spire, a shopping mall with a supermarket, and an elementary school full of shrieking tykes.

Mrs Hardison is awfully chummy with Mr Cuttlewot. The Spielmans spread innuendo around the neighborhood as if it is fact ... and the zeitgeist is ... athletes take performance-enhancing drugs, politicos spread misinformation to stay ahead of scandal, and a percentage of priests diddle little boys.

Sin goes bumpbump against hedgerows, gas stations buzz with those who usher in the apocalypse by using credit cards to load up their tanks, and who knows what illicit acts are being contemplated by those leaving convenience stores blowing into hot cups of coffee. Among them, cops, tainted by the Blackout, sit in their cars, eager to bust the chops of anyone who rolls through stop signs.

Otherwise, all that's left is a sham, a shambles, a Shamela of epic proportions.

Hot from his latest pledge to be a vessel of all that's goodly, St Jonah of Hoppa slows for the drivers who carelessly back out of driveways. He passes those at bus stops who stand far apart from one another, their noses stuck in their copies of this season's mainstream media picks of top-notch page turners.

When he turns a corner onto Loch Lomond Lane, a materializing jogger suddenly curses.

"Wotcherfock!"

Jonah sharply veers and plunges into a hedge.

"Aaraabaschull!"

He leaps up, brushing himself off.

"Schtoopitchfock." The runner jogs away.

Pedestrians focus elsewhere, disinterested in disrupting their schedules to get involved.

St Jonah of Hoppa pulls his bike from the bushes, gives the handlebars a shake, and kicks a flat front tire. "Fuuuck meee!" It all pours out of him—Hiroko's money, Da Stylus's constant telephone messages, his writing sample for Iton's workshop, tonight's double booking with the gals, constantly having to remind himself to be goodly. "I'm so fuuucked!"

Stopped at an adjacent traffic light is a group of youngsters with their persons-of-a-colored-hue faces pressed against the windows of a yellow school bus.

"Oh, hi kids." Jonah's saintly mantle cracks. "You got to watch out for these Italian bikes." His status as a role model goes the way of the dodo. "The gears are a bit tricky." Bug-eyed, little brown girls with colorful ribbons braided in their hair and little brown boys with shiny faces gawk at him. "Yup, triiicky."

∞

Idiot! thinks Ingrid Ishigowa staring from the back seat of the bus at an Arab in a woollen cap taking swift kicks at a wheel on his bike. The world is full of idiots, she thinks before refocusing on her copy of *Beloved*.[82]

At thirteen, she's read twenty-seven of the top one-hundred novels of all time. Her goal is to finish them all by next summer. In her "humble opinion, this one is Morrison's best." She's read *Sula*,[83] "for fun," and *The Bluest Eye*,[84] as "preparation for the classic." And if only "the immature idiots" in the seats up front would stop "acting so obnoxious," she might get to the end of the chapter where Beloved shows up for the first time.

Idiots!

It bears mention that beneath Ingrid's determined grind through the great novels lurks another concern. First, she peace-marched with millions across the globe to say no to war. Now her MySpace pal, Ibrahim Khan—who likes to read books, fly kites, and collect stamps—may have been "blown to bits" (like Leroi).

"The planet is full of "imbeciles!" ★ ... A miracle.

"Need a ride?" It's the ex-con, Bingo Jefferson, driving by in the Rev's gas guzzler.

"What about my bike?" I ask.

"Come back for it."

I look around for a place to chain it up, and decide on a parking meter.

---

82 Veracity verified by the author.

83 Ibid.

84 Ibid.

∞

On the road, Jonah explains it'll be a temporary loan, and says how tomorrow he'll be getting the cash from Quint C. to pay Bingo back.

"You 'n' me is bidness men, right?"

Jonah nods.

"So, check it. I'll lend you the benjies until tomorra, if you help me with another job."

"Oh, no. No. I'm done with that."

"Jus' one more."

"Even if I wanted to, and I don't, I got class in two hours."

"We'll be right-quick."

"No. Thanks, but no."

"I'll throw in a dime bag of weed."

"I dunno, man." Jonah hedges.

"Didn't you dig the product we partook of yes'erday?"

Ganja is Jonah's weakness, and since the tantrum in front of the children has him far from the saintly person he managed to tap into during the bike ride, he really, really needs herbal assistance. Pot is one of the Creator's natural gifts, like flowers or the rain, so why not give a little over here for another shot at taking the green caboose express over there?

"What's the job?"

Bingo hits Jonah with it: a pickpocket scam they've both run before on the early morning supermarket crowd.

Danger. Danger.

Causes have effects. Whenever an instant of C happens, E eventually occurs. C and E are blood, so to speak.

"Are we good?" Bingo asks.

"Yezzir. We're good."

Bingo turns the gas guzzler around on Fifteenth and drives to Merry Cloud Supermarket.

Traffic thins on Cedar Avenue as the Buick makes tracks past high-end shops. Suits mingle with the casually dressed over breakfast at the Sheraton, the Holiday Inn. Glass is tinted. Statues of soldiers on horseback stand beside gushing water fountains. Banks and offices with tall, white columns are over two hundred years old, and wide sidewalks are safe for tourists.

There's trembling in Jonah's right paw that he steadies by holding it in his left armpit.

At a stoplight, Bingo points at a sidewalk that is eighty-plus percent white folk (give or take a margin of error around six percent).

"Look at 'em. Corrupt motherfuckers. It's jus' like with the toll-booth boy. See. Since they ain't no video, forget about it. Dang! Who cain't tell apart a toy gun from a reg'lar gun? Am I right? Tell you some'pin else. If Five-O get heat, then, like blaaazam, the shooter gets theyselves shit-hot representashun. Soon them cold fuckers is free as Willy." They slow at the back of a traffic jam. "Serious. Ain't no justice for po' folk up in this piece, yo."

Jonah has no real objections, so he nods.

"Mind if I turn on the radio, chief?" Bingo asks.

"Not at all, play-uh."

He laughs. "I ain't no playa, I'z a pimp. Yezzir. I takes care of all my bitches." He turns the dial to a deejay taking calls about Americans torturing locals in Iraqi prisons. This sets him off again; conspiracies have the biggest players in cahoots over monopolizing Arab oil, and torture goes hand in glove with raking in profits, just like the "whippin' of cotton pickers back in the day." If you look at a dollar bill, you can see the symbol of their secret order. It's a pyramid with an eye, and on 9-11 the government "did an inside job" knocking down the Twin Towers. "No way any higher-ups gonna see time for breakin' war laws, or I ain't Bingo 'Jackpot' Jefferson, smell me?"

Jonah thinks of how despite obvious drawbacks, at least Bingo is a man with a unifying idea; fuck being a gentleman, fuck making sense, do whatever the fuck.

Bingo changes stations until he's tuned into some hip hop. "Oh yah. Tha's wha' I'm talkin' about." He bobs and catches the flow. "Cutie put your boot, boot, booty in the freakin air. Dada will tap, tap, tap it till you wet in your Gucci underwear." He turns the car into a parking spot.

Hyped to get hype, I get out of the car, leave him in the get-away mobile, burn it through the lot, enter automatically opening doors, and slow enough to grab a hand basket before making a go for the aisle with the milk.

I don't check prices.

Quick, quick, quick. I race-walk to the section with the noodles, snag a bag of prepackaged lettuce, then jog-walk to the express line.

It takes four minutes.

The target, an upperclass dame thirty-five-ish, give or take, slaps her shopping wares onto the conveyor belt in front of a cashier with an indecipherable nametag on her white blouse.

"Yiiikes!" I'm in a hurry. "You've got too many goods for the express line."

"Say what?" she replies.

"You're only allowed eight. You've got, what, thirteen … fourteen items."

"Not true," she responds. "Count them. A toothbrush, tooth-paste, dental floss, chapstick, Q-tips, soap, lotion, shampoo, razor blades, cotton balls." Her straight black hair slinks way downward along the back of a business suit, and her open purse hangs off her shoulder. "Deodorant and a box of tissues. Okay, twelve." She talks to the indecipherable nametag. "Cancel whatever's been rung through."

Not what I planned. "Please, no. I …"

"I'll go to a different line," I say.

"I was just making conversation."

The wealthy target snatches items from the conveyor belt, and then slams them back into a hand basket.

Sighing, the cashier blows a bubble of gum. Then she fiddles with the register. Moments later, a blue light buzzes, and the contraption blows a gasket. "Santa Maria!" She cuts us both with a stare and then barks into a microphone. "Manager to eleben. Manager to eleben."

I've managed to draw too much attention to myself as the manager makes an appearance.

"Good evening, Clara." He wears a top-of-the-line navy tie. "What seems to be the problem here?"

"I start the lady in the mat-cheen. Then the *hombre* get, uh, *enfadado*."

"Speak English *por favor*."

"He shout—"

"I didn't shout."

"He shout at the lady. He say you got twelbe. You s'posed to uhve—"

"I didn't shout."

"The lady, she say *no mas, no mas*. Then the mat-cheen—"

"Thank you, Clara, I get the picture." The Tieman adjusts his tip-top tie. "Please bear with us, folks. If you'll give us a moment, we'll get the register up and running in no time." He lifts a flap on the register and tinkers with its machinery. "Ahhh, there's the problem. We'll need to put in another spool, Clara. Go ask Tonya. She's always well stocked."

I glumly stare at the express sign above our heads.

"Sorry for any inconvenience," the manager apologizes.

This is taking too long. "Listen, I'll be right back." I can't do this. "I have to check on my granddad waiting in the car." Hiroko will have to make do with an extra day wait for her cash.

I book it into the parking lot.

For the love of Jupiter!

Bingo is leaning against a wall beside a pay phone. The cobalt telephone receiver hangs downward and swings to (this way) and fro (that).

"Heeellooo, you're supposed to be waiting in the car," I snipe.

"Do you got it?"

"I called it off."

"Say whaaa?"

"Aren't you supposed to be in the car?"

"Get back in the huddle, playa." His voice is dry ice. "Run the pick and roll."

"It's too risky."

He reaches for the telephone receiver and smacks me across the chin.

Sharp pain pools in odd parts of my skull.

"Don't be a punk, Africa," he says. "We in the first quarter, and it's third 'n' long. Play or get played. That's how we roll, from the jail house to the mother-stabbin White House, ya heard?"

He picks up a plastic bag blowing around his feet and forces it into my hand.

"This is nothin personal, chief," he says. "It's jus bid'ness."

On my return to the cash register, my chin smarts, and the busted contraption is still busted.

Good grief! I should know better than to mix it up with a jailbird.

"Once again sorry for the inconvenience," the manager says. "We here at Merry Cloud work hard to see that you, the customer, are well served." I pick up an entertainment magazine and scan for celebrity hookups. "Oh good, Clara, that took an awfully long time. No matter. Watch carefully as I fix this because it will prove to be a good learning experience. Okay. First flip this up, like that—"

"Flip up," she repeats.

"Yes, then press this lever. Like so."

"Which leber?"

"This one here. You can identify it by the green cord right there. Then slip the spool over here, clap down the top, and feed the paper through like this."

"I see."

Once the register is back in working order, I spill my meager fare in front of the cashier.

"Bill that be eberything, sir?" she asks.

I rummage through my pockets. "You take bank cards, don't you?"

"No." She blows another Bubblelicious bubble and points to a sign on the register. "Cash, *por favor.*" She chews her gum with more chew. "Your card is not good here."

I can't control an onset of twitching in my upper lip as I make for the exit, and wait outside the automatic doors for the woman with the twelve items to show.

"I owe you an apology," I say. A male worker prods a long chain of shopping carts through the parking lot. "My mother, God bless her, would have been ashamed by my behavior."

She grunts.

"I'm not a good example," I continue. "It's not what Christ would have done."

"I really am in a hurry."

"We live in the End times." I follow her across a road, and toward a row of spanking clean SUVs. "In Revelations 3, verse ..."

"No, thanks."

I stop abruptly and grasp at the fleshy part of her upper arm. "God, no!"

Bingo rolls the gas guzzler smack dab into the buttocks of the line of shopping carts and keeps-a-moving until he smushes to a halt.

I run to him with the woman with twelve items hot on my tail. "Heey-ey-ay," I blather.

By the time we reach the car, Bingo is slumped against the steering wheel.

I hammer on the window.

"I'll call an ambulance," the woman says.

A healthy-sized crowd begins to gather around, eager to help. While the worker excitedly feeds them the tale of the tape, I take a step back to snip a couple of choice handbags from the shoulders of the distracted. Snipsnip, into the plastic bag.

15

Baked on a Molotov of herbals and prescribed chemicals, a sore-chinned Jonah walks through the stone pillars at the iron gate in front of Dingham U

He won't feel guilty about all that happened in the last hour. Access to the sacred is the end that justifies the dubious means to purchase him his current buzz. Jonah takes a cinder path that runs beside a cobbled road and steals glances behind him to see if suspicious figures dodge in and out of nearby bushes. *Get a grip!* To his left is an open field of dank grass and a sparse distribution of evergreens that crowds the banks of a small man-made lake. Ducks waddle among a bank of reeds while farther out, white swans dunk their necks into black water, aimlessly floating in pairs. To his right is a smaller field that borders buildings piled on top of one another in an awkward mix of old red brick and the latest experiments with huge glass panes randomly arranged in grey blocks of cement.

Conservative estimates place the student population at around 20,000, and a cross-section of them either populate the sidewalk or mill on the grass. Mature students and business majors are a study in conservative dress; they wear broad ties and black jackets with brass buttons on their sleeves. Out on the field, stubbly faced boys and jean-jacketed academics congregate in small, chatty clumps. Beside them, b-boys and wiggers decked in grey sweatshirts greet each other by bumping chests, and hotties with

booties busting out of faded jeans loudly dish dirt about the previous weekend.

As always, Jonah watches the art majors in dark greens who
hunch on stairs, sketching depth perception with newly acquired
supplies.

11:50 a.m.

At the path's end, he bypasses those who stand around ashtrays,
gulping on cigarettes. Then he boots up a short flight of stairs and
grandly swings open the glass doors of the Student Union.

Presto.

There are spacious rooms on either side of a hallway lined with
tables run by sunburnt frat rats, hungover sorority queens, shrill
masters of debate clubs, and anonymous addicts.

He keeps moving.

"Yo, *Salaam Alaikum.*" A brother wrapped bodily in *kente* stuffs a
cherry leaflet into his hands. "By all means necessary. Wooord."

Jonah grins, "*Alaikum Salaam,*" and keeps going.

The cherry piece of paper advertises, From the Margins
C★★★sucker, a rally to protest racist graffiti sprayed on the walls of
the African-American Studies Department.

Jonah slips the information into his back pocket, leaves the
building by way of the cafeteria, drags himself into the courtyard,
and takes a moment to pull himself together by sitting at the foot
of a ten-foot-high statue of the school's founder,[85] pigeon droppings dried on its head.

As he rubs the tender bump on his chin, he feels far from walking the groves of his inner sanctum with a former self that easily

---

85   See footnote 33.

communed with a higher beneficent power. Cut off from grace, he's morphed into one of those who spend their days unwilling to let go of a pull toward a darkness littered with best intentions.

A middle-aged black fellow with a handlebar mustachio, his arms loaded down with books, interrupts him. "Can you give me a hand?"

Jonah's had a long morning. "Sorry, chum." He's exhausted. "I'd prefer not to."

"I'm only going as far as the next building." Three books fall from the top of the pile to the paved courtyard. "It'll only take a minute."

Quick as spit, Jonah goes over his schedule in his head. "Sorry, fella." He's thirty-eight minutes behind the grand plan. "I'd prefer not to."

He leaves the fella with the handlebar mustachio stooping to pick up his fallen books, another batch precariously balanced in his arms.

Behind him, books topple to the ground.

Onward, Jonah passes the thirty floors of the Bob Cousins Library,[86] takes a left, and stops in front of the African-American Studies Building.

"Nigga Studies" is scrawled on the walls.

All business, Jonah climbs the stairs to the third floor of Desbelly Hall, turns right, walks through a set of swinging doors, and pops his head into the Creative Writing Department Office.

---

86   Bob Cousins taught at the school in the heyday of the counter-cultural revolution. During this period, he donated a sizable chunk of time, finances, and books to the library. On his retirement in the early seventies, a new, larger library building was renamed to honor him.

"Cheers," he says to the Silver Fox,[87] fixated on the computer screen in front of her.

She looks up, smiling. "Mr Ayot-Kolosha, what can I do you for?"

"Is Professor Iton in?"

"Hell's bells, Jonah!" she exclaims. "In all the years I've known him, he always gets here exactly two minutes before the workshop starts. Not a moment sooner."

"Can I leave a message?"

"You're better off talking to him, darling," she says. "The last time he checked his mail box was … darn, it was such a long time ago I couldn't tell you."

"Coolio."

Jonah leaves the Silver Fox to stare at her computer screen again.

---

87 Nickname for Fiona Markham, with origins that are obscure. She's been working at the school over twenty-five years, and the assumption is that the name took root soon after she started.

16

Fifteen minutes before Professor Iton's kick-ass writing
workshop, I sit in Ptolemy's Café across from pals of mine,
Quint C. and Eliza May

Today Quint C.'s weekend-at-the-Cape in a white V-neck and
beige khakis. Eliza May is woman-suffragette-glam in a white
flapper dress, three long, dangling pearl necklaces, and silver brace-
lets thick on both arms.

We drink from iced mugs of draft, and I give them a manic
rundown of *bona fide* excuses as to why I haven't been writing
much of late. Distractions, *mes amis*. The Rev has been obsessing
about the work Bingo is doing in the basement. Always, he's agitated by a quality of service which in no way compares to what
once was during the Golden Age of Elizabeth Taylor and her forty
grooms. Always, he goes on. Nonstop. And the *outre* weirdness
of living with a holy man in the middle of a Zelda Fitzgerald[88]
has this particular homie slightly off his a-game. Blab, blab, I blab
about Hirosita. Blab, blab. I think she's looking for a sugar daddy
and this makes me uncomfortable. "What to do?" I finally ask.

---

88   Reference to mental breakdown suffered by writer and wife of F. Scott
Fitzgerald (1900–48). Rosemary "the Bookworm" Levy theorizes that a pattern in Jonah's focalized sections reveals a "post Welt-Alltag fascination with
references to people who have suffered clinical breakdowns." There isn't room
to explore this Welt-Alltag term that was "coined by H. Broch, *Dichten und
Erkennen* (Zurich, 1955) to designate June 16, 1904" (or, Bloomsday, when
Leopold Bloom had his day of fracturing consciousness in Joyce's *Ulysses*).

"Talk to her," Eliza May says.

"Dude, do *not* do that," Quint C. says.

"Do you like this girl?" Eliza May asks.

"Dude," Quint C. says. "Call her, talk about the weather, talk TV. All she needs to know is whether you've come up with the money or not. Talking details to death makes you seem like a wuss."

Eliza May busts up laughing.

"You call that advice?" she says.

"Free of charge," Quint C. responds.

Two minutes early, in strolls Professor Iton, Man of Letters.

Today he's off the rack: casual jeans, a plain white t-shirt and generic running shoes. No notes. No introduction. He doesn't even sit down.

The usual suspects are gathered.

Cybil Harris, the Bostonian: "had a short story come out in the *Shipleigh Journal* over the summer." She "did a writing residency at Wing Gate Manor. No, not the one in Brooklyn, New York. The one affiliated with Oxford. Yes, the university as so named in the UK."

David Winch, the eldest son of a steel worker: "writes for his close friends" and uses the workshop to work on a blook. A Blook? "Yes, I'm writing a blog that's really a novel."

Eliza May Morton is there, as is Rosemary Levy, the self-avowed bookworm.

"I like the way the multiple narrative voices in *As I Lay Dying* form a colorful mosaic in the text," Rosemary famously said. As well, writing is the "thing I was born to do" and "a gift I feel compelled to share with the world." In sum, her writing style is "unapologetically pomo."

Quint C. sits between Jonah and Richard Spoils, the muttering Canuck from TO.[89]

Professor Iton looks over a list. "To see the past as the future, and the future as the past … the idea of backing into history has been on my mind of late. So, lets look back shall we, and see how next week's workshop with Eliza May, and the following one in which we read from Jonah, are a reversal. An inversion. A repetition in a sense. The experience will be … what it is. An expression I loathe. 'It is what it is.' 'It was so surreal.' 'We've all been there.' 'Don't go there!' 'He didn't just go there.' Going where? These are linguistic crimes by those who shouldn't confuse themselves when looking in a mirror for people who know what they're talking about. So, yes the workshops are to be what was as opposed to what will eventually occur. *Capiche*? Excellent." He picks up a stick of chalk, writes SCHRÖDINGER[90] on the board, and then draws a stick figure of a rodent and a box around it. "A live cat is placed in a steel chamber along with a device containing a vial of hydrocyanic acid and a small amount of a radioactive substance," he says. "If a single atom of the latter decays, a simple mechanism will break the vial and in turn kill the cat." Professor Iton checks his watch. "However, since the cat's inside the steel chamber, an observer doesn't know if the decay has taken place. Therefore, they don't know if the cat is dead or alive. You follow my meaning?" Everyone stares at their notebooks. "Nothing? Really? Should I

---

89 Toronto, Canada, neighbor to the United States.

90 Erwin Schrödinger (1887–1961), Nobel Prize-winning physicist whose ideas are a staple of the work produced during Professor Iton's middle period.

sit while you decide if this moment is occurring in virtual reality? On YouTube? Anyone? Listen, stop looking to the past for a response. Think, as I said before, of backing into the future. Don't try to find our answer in the *a priori* … in what Socrates would say we recollect from what's gone before."

The Bookworm volunteers a response. "Well, according to quantum law, the uncertainty about the status of the cat means it's simultaneously both 100 percent dead and 100 percent alive."

"Good." The Professor looks at his watch again. "Only by opening the chamber can we know with certainty whether the cat is in one state or the other. So, it is by way of observation, or at least through measurement, that the condition of the cat changes. It is by way of observation that we know single particles can be in multiple locations simultaneously. Are you with me here?"

Jonah puts up a hand.

"I was in the computer lab yesterday," Professor Iton continues, "and what struck me is how these are the museums of the twenty-first century. Computers are glass encased stores of human knowledge. And I began talking to this fellow, a janitor who supports three children on what he makes keeping this high tech site of speculation presentable to public traffic. And you know what he said, 'It's all there and not there at the same time.' That's how he described that metadiscursive ground of can-do ingenuity. 'It's all there and not there at the same time.'"

"Sir," Jonah interrupts.

"Yes."

"It doesn't matter whether I know if the cat's dead or not. If it's dead, it's dead. Right?"

"Not quite," he surmises. "If you think it's alive, it exists alive in your mind and dead in the chamber all at the same time. Much like a carefully parsed lie that can be both true or not depending on what knowledge the audience is privy to. Think oscillation. Vibrations. One receptor is signaling another one that isn't visible. It doesn't mean ..."

"But a theoretical cat isn't a real one," he protests. "If the real one is dead, it doesn't matter what I think."

"Work it through," Professor Iton says, sounding exasperated. "What we're really talking about is whether it's the reader who invokes the text or the writer, and my contention is that no matter what the writer does, none of it exists if the reader can't see it. Catch my meaning?"

"But it does exist," Jonah grumbles.

"What exists are squiggly lines on paper with the writer's meaning embedded in this code. With stories, what we're looking at is a shift that Julie Kristeva describes metaphorically as a dynamic process that is intuitively generated in the semiotic, passes through the thetic, and culminates in what Lacan refers to as the symbolic. Once narration emerges as the latter, there's an intertextual, or Bhaktinian double-voiced dialogic between a conventional language system and a new one. Thus meaning is utterly dependent on our ability to both identify as well as crack these conscious as well as unconscious codes. You follow?"

"That doesn't make sense."

"Listen, we can talk it over during my office hours." He sounds rushed. "We have a story to workshop before class ends, and I have to leave early today to meet with a former student visiting from Philly. As you can imagine, it's one of the great pleasures as well as biggest boons to watch the one's who keep writing grow. The direction is never ... What is that noise? Is that someone's cell?"

Quint C. launches into a long apology as he fumbles to shut down his phone.

"It would seem the number of calls that just can't wait to be answered is on the increase," Professor Iton continues. "It's an epidemic, like obesity. Stuffing our heads with too much talk. Correct me if I'm wrong, but one gets the sense that the species doesn't know what to do unless they're busily narrating the banal into a phone. Look around campus. I rarely see anyone walking around who isn't looking terribly important while updating a friend on their whereabouts. Oh, I'm five minutes from the library. Now it's three. I'm over near the staircase to the left of the trash cans. You see me. Good, good. Talk to you in a hot minute."

Richard Spoils, the muttering Canuck from TO, is today's lamb for slaughter.

His story takes place in rural Ontario, and there's a bounty of Canadian in-chuckles. The protagonist is a fan of Bobby Orr[91] and he gets through the story nursing a wonky knee. There are long discussions of Trudeaumania[92] and multiculturalism. A character from the Maritimes talks funny. There's a reference to a referendum for Quebec to split away from the rest of Canada and form a separate country. It's all quite impenetrable, really.

The Professor opens the smackdown with a short speech.

---

91 Famed hockey player; Boston Bruins defenceman (b. 1948). His jersey is available through an operation run by Bingo "Jackpot" Jefferson. Also available, jerseys of Pelé and Franz Beckenbauer, Björn Borg headbands, and boxing trunks signed by Thomas "the Hitman" Hearns and Sugar Ray Leonard.

92 Excitement generated in 1968 by political debut of Canadian Prime Minister Pierre Elliott Trudeau (1919–2000), politician, writer, constitutional lawyer. His biography, with an admission of hashish smoking during a youthful juncture, is required reading in the English Department's course, the Political Memoir 462 (T Th 1:30–3:00).

"Don't let anyone who reads fiction fool you," he says. "No matter what one says, we all have a theory about what writing is. Just listen for what someone says either failed or worked and you've begun to get a sense of what that theory is. Obviously, with the Internet anyone who can work a mouse is able to let one know, here's my theory. I may not have spent much time coming up with it, but here it is and what I have to say on the subject justifies the relevance of my opinion. But for me, writing is a conversation that exists between the writer and readers they have imagined." He writes this down on the board. "However, it takes a certain skill to render both so they simultaneously occur; think Schrödinger. The writer has to be aware that private knowledge—as specific to the writer—cannot always be accessed by the readership the writer has chosen to write to. Therefore, as one works, one has to decide whether to dip away from the intimacy of this relationship by providing a context to better enable an understanding of the former by the reader who hasn't been imagined. Richard's story is one that asks us to consider these types of questions. *Capiche?*"

Okay, pretty sensible.

Not so for the Canuck from TO. He breaks with both protocol and character by loudly defending his story before the roundtable can take a crack at it.

"What's with Americans?" He glowers accusingly around the room. "Nothing exists outside your borders. Nothing! What I'm doing is performing a basic function of literary fiction, that is to contribute to a national fiction. Joyce talked about being Irish. Hemingway was at times an American in Paris, as was Henry James in Venice." He clearly isn't muttering as he stands up. "My story deals with what it means to be a rural Canadian, and I'm not about to explain away every detail of the story to a bunch of … Americans." He gathers up his papers before rushing out the room with Professor Iton hot on his tail.

"Tell us what you really think," the Bookworm chuckles into Eliza May's ear.

"Is Canada its own country or another state?" she jokes back.

"Well," the Bookworm replies. "Whoever they are, we'd kick their asses in a war."

The Steelworker and Cybil the Bostonian chime in agreement.

Before Jonah can conveniently side with the group, Quint C. grabs onto his pal's forearm. "I can't take it," Q. says. "It's making me sick." He charges out the room with a hand over his mouth.

Eliza May shoots Jonah a look like, Go after him, you idiot.

So off he trots.

Out in the hallway, the Professor patiently listens to the muttering of the slouched Canuck while Jonah locates Q-Deezy gulping from a water fountain.

"Did you see that?" Q. asks.

"Couldn't miss it," Jonah replies. "Richard really took his anti-Americanisms out for a spin."

"No, not that," Q. says. "Didn't you see the way the Bookworm was all over Eliza May?"

"Must have missed it."

He slurps down additional fortifying liquids. "They went out for drinks last night, and Eliza May wasn't home until five this morning."

"Jeeezus!"

"You see why I'm upset?"

Actually, Jonah meant, Jeeezus, did the Canuck from TO just punch the wall?

"Did you ask Eliza about it?"

"Of course not," he replies.

Jonah decides to be agreeable. "Good thinking."

"I'm gonna have to fuck someone else," Quint C. says.

"Tonight?"

"Yes, tonight. Hit back, quick, and where it hurts."

"Good plan. Mind if I tag along? At least while you're shaking trees to see whether any kitty-cat falls out."

"Suit yourself."

After a long silence. "Eliza May could be seeing you and not seeing you simultaneously," Jonah says.

"Schrödinger's an asshole," he replies.

In all the afternoon's excitement I forgot about my banged-up chin, and only begin to notice it again as Q. and I commiserate over air hockey at Ptolemy's Café.

I'm up 12-0.

Q. weakly smacks the fluorescent puck at my net as I try to build his self-confidence by flubbing my redirect. Somehow I fail to score my own goal as the puck careens off edges and slides past his flailing defense.

13-0.

"C'mon, play-uh," I say. "Shrug it off."

He angrily swats at the puck that suddenly reverses field and caroms into his goal.

14-0.

Game.

To make up for the inadvertent thrashing, I buy the drinks and agree with everything a despondent Q-Deezy has to say. Yup, we really should ransack the Bookworm's apartment, find her diary, and flip through it for details of her liaison with Eliza May. No, no, no. That doesn't sound at all unreasonable. You want to be exclusive "friends *with* benefits?" That makes perfect sense. No ob-ligations, except if it involves sleeping with other people. Brilliant. How about another drink?

On and on Quint goes. Eliza May's a knockout in her faux leopard-skin coats, her flapper dresses, and she isn't about saying what she thinks people need to hear. What a classy dame. How completely at home in his Upper West Side clan. She doesn't sleep with a cache of automatic weapons under her bed, hold homo-phobic views, have trouble aborting fetuses in the first trimester, nor bear any opposition to cloning goats and sheep to geep.

Purr-fect, say I.

It turns out the Bookworm has an ace up her sleeve. Her par-ents own a home in the South of France. Somewhere near vine-yards and lots of dusty paths for hand-holding that conveniently descend into spots to "… I can't even think it."

"Do you mean to picnic?" I ask.

He sputters on. No. No. Don't be a dunce. Eliza May has a bug for traveling and the Bookworm has filled her mind with ideas about finding her voice in the fields Van Gogh did his best work in. "Her voice, dude. You know what that is code for. How am I to compete with that?"

"Listen, you're the one with a book coming out."

He's not listening to logic, and launches into a retrospective of better days with Eliza May. The first reading they took in to-gether is introduced as evidence; the way they laughed at the same places, how her smile made him realize "for the first time" why Gats changed his name to Gatsby and remade himself in an im-age pleasing to Daisy, why Colonel Dobbin stuck out the years as

Amelia Sedley's patsy until he finally won her hand.

Uh-huh, say I.

The only time I hedge slightly is when Q-Deezy, dribbling into his beer, gets dead solemn and reveals an insecurity about his inability to keep up with Eliza May sexually. It's been outstanding. Terrific. They do it hanging out the door of speeding vehicles or while dressed in hospital scrubs on the roof at Tilley Towers. Great, great, but he's running out of ideas, and the introduction of the Bookworm with "her honey pot" and her home in the South of France has left him creatively blocked.

I recommend crushed horn of the famous Liwani rhinoceros.

After two hours of this back and forth, Quint C. abandons the idea of fucking a stranger and trundles off to the library to see if Eliza May has sent him an email. ★ On his way to Hiroko's, Jonah passes a table with Professor Iton and the fellow with the handlebar mustachio from earlier.

"Jonah Ayot-Kolosha," the Professor says. "Meet one of my former students, Fish Coleman."

Fish Coleman, the infamous hack who Professor Iton always mentions! He's the author of *In the Cut*,[93] the best-selling trade paperback about a writer and his muse who rent a house that is built on a time zone. The writer's bedroom, at the rear, is located in Pacific Standard Time while his muse's room, located at the front, is in Eastern. The work gives an account of how each day the writer and the muse try to find literary techniques to capture the elusive hour at the meeting place between zones. Midway

---

93   200,000 books sold since its publication in 2001.

through the story, it morphs into a film-noiresque murder mystery. The locales shift to international urban centers—"Mee-lan, Paree, New Yawk."[94] A *femme fatale* emerges, briefcases full of money and secret documents change hands, spies materialize in the shadows, and sex scenes alternate with fight scenes.

They shake hands.

"Ah, yes," Fish says. "It's Bartleby in a prayer cap."

Jonah plays innocent. "Bartleby?"

"I'd prefer not to. I'd prefer not to."

He considers deflecting the attention with accusations about Fish's clunky, commercial prose (brought to Jonah's attention by Professor Iton).

"There's an explanation," Jonah says.

"We'd love to hear it," Professor Iton responds.

"I've always been somewhat fragile, health-wise. Asthma. Allergies. The lot." Jonah catches them up on his bike's flat tire, and makes up a tale about walking two hours to get to campus. Finally, "I have to be cautious about overdoing it, sir."

"Sir!" Fish scoffs. "Is he always so proper?"

"I've yet to see evidence to the contrary," Professor Iton responds.

"Please dispense with the formalities, and call me Fish."

"With all due respect, I much prefer, sir, sir."

They both laugh. "So what are you currently writing?" Fish asks.

"A novel in three volumes."[95]

"Well, you're working with the right man." He throws an arm

---

94 Spelling used in *In the Cut*.

95 As of this writing, Volumes Two and Three have not been written.

around the Professor's shoulder. "Three volumes of convoluted Proustian sentences that collapse in on one another sounds right up his alley."

"Don't corrupt him with your views about prostrating oneself to the open market." The Professor squirms out of his protégé's grasp. "He'll have time enough once he graduates to decide whether to follow in your compromised footsteps."

"Come now, Colin." Fish sounds hurt. "Don't be *so* old school. Readerships are changing, and it's important to keep an open mind about the importance of finding a wider audience for one's efforts."

"Cover your ears, Jonah."

Fish flicks a finger against his beer bottle. "What a crock!"

"Crock! Is that one of those words you've got your characters using these days?"

"Some of us have to make a living without a plum appointment at a university. We have to sell books."

"You still fall back on lazy rationalizations," Professor Iton chastises. "No amount of books sold can hide whether the writer has been willing to sift painfully through the swill in order to get their story told."

Jonah's hands go from his pockets, around his neck, and back into his pockets again.

"So you didn't like my novel," Fish snaps.

"I don't think it serves any purpose to say whether the work is good or bad. This isn't an interesting question. What is more appropriate is to consider what kind of integrity you brought to the process."

Fish turns to me. "Take what Colin here says with a grain of salt, Bartleby. Mark my words. Good writing is measured by what sells. That's how people decide what's relevant."

17

A little past nine, Hiroko sits next to a chatty Jonah, four hundred and fifty in crumpled bills spread out on the coffee table in front of them

Thank God, Ingrid has come and gone, so they're free to talk.

Hiroko's alarmed by the chin injury Jonah got while making her money, and she tells him how moved she is by his repeated insistence that she doesn't have to pay him back. His enthusiasm shows her he's where she wants him, so she waits for the right moment to ask the question that will put her final concern to rest. How much is he worth? The answer will determine how next she'll proceed. So, she waits for the perfect moment to make her move while tugging on frayed ends at a gaping hole at the knee of faded jeans.

"You're being paranoid," she says dismissively about his theory of getting stalked by the Liwani Secret Police.

"How can you be so sure?"

"This is America, hon. Sure we have our problems, but that isn't what happens here. We're the best damn country in the world."

"Try the fourth or fifth."

"Name one that's better."

"Denmark. The Danes have an excellent socialist *apparatchik*.[96]

---

96 A member of a state-controlled apparatus. Misuse of the term is found in all three major drafts of the manuscript.

One that's so much better than the oligarchy that passes for a democracy you got here."

"Commie."

"Capitalist."

"Forget the secret police, sweetheart," she says. "You need to worry about Curranvale City cops who'll bust you for looking at porn on the Internet."

"Really?"

Hiroko watches him interlace his fingers with hers as she runs through her list of what makes the total package. A fortune. Check. Can hold a conversation. Check. Looks. Double check. Loyal. Check. Quickly, she pounces, tightly grasping both his wrists before forcing him backward onto the couch and clambering onto his belly.

"Whose bitch are you?" she says.

Jonah flips her over, reversing their positions. "Not yours, that's f'ah sho." She thrashes against him as he pins her down, struggling until she's spent. "Who's the one with mad wrestling skills?"

"Me."

"On what evidence?"

"Can't you tell when you've been seduced?"

She watches him watch her as he lifts her t-shirt over her titties and stares at her mulberry nipples, then at her.

Check.

A note for the haters: Hiroko isn't about to apologize for who she is. She accepts that she needs a man who's got a nose for money; someone who reels in the kind of bank that makes the days pass in leisure. She sees herself owning a couple of homes; one will be functional while the other will be strictly for vacations. She'll have people to cook and do the chores. She'll take the Mercedes to the spa, to shop for clothes or groceries, and to workout at the gym. On occasion, she'll host parties for those who are movers and shakers in the entertainment industry. She'll have a room to do her sketches and another to develop photographs. She'll have a vegetable garden, and get dirt beneath her fingernails. She won't need to know what to do with her life because she'll be free to fill out a schedule based on how she feels. When she has children, she'll take them in the Benz to ballet and to soccer practice. She's got to be realistic. There are only a few more years left in which she'll be able to turn the heads of the rich boys and be able to fetch herself a high return on their investment in her.

"I need a smoke." she says.

"*Moi aussi?*"

"Couldn't you just say that in English?"

"*Je m'appelle Jonah. Et toi?*"[97]

"Translation?"

"I can only loosely translate it because obviously the registers of the different languages aren't copacetic, if you will. I said, the new moon in the harshest winters echoes with your name, Hirositasan. Hirositasan sounds among woodsmen chopping timber that falls incessantly, unceasingly. Hirositisan."

"Knob. There's no way you get a whole paragraph out of five or six words. Especially when one of them was your name."

"Who's the one that speaks French here?"

"Not you. That's f'ah sho."

Jonah lets her up, and she leads him by the hand into the kitchen.

---

97 My name is Jonah. And you? (French).

Her sink is piled with plates fur-layered with grey mold. Countertops provide clues as to what she's eaten of late: an open jar of mayonnaise with a bread knife in it, a rock hard slab of cheese, perforated bags of flour, dried orange peels, and busted egg shells. She rummages through cupboards while Jonah turns on the tap and begins to wash her plates.

"Stop cleaning!"

"I don't mind."

She opens up a can filled with coffee beans. "I do." Digs around for a joint.[98] "So don't be a fuzzpot."

He laughs. "It's fusspot, luv."

"That's what I said."

"You said fuzzpot."

She playfully punches his arm. "Fuzz. Fuss. You know what I mean." She sits on a cluttered counter in front of the kitchen window and sparks up.

"Cheers."

They trade puffs before Hiroko grabs Jonah's lapels, roughly pulls him between her legs, and frenches with him. She can feel his fingers find her anklet before tracing the outlay of cartilage and shaving bumps on her shin.

"Jonah."

"Yah."

"I gotta question for you."

"Shoot."

"What's up with your inheritance?"

"Later, baby girl," he mutters.

---

98   Jonah seems to have forgotten he has Bingo's pot on his person. Therefore, it's unlikely Hiroko would have had to get some from her stash.

She pushes him away. "You say you wanna hang, but you won't be real."

He has another toke.

"How long will it take?" she badgers.

He explains about the Rev having power of attorney over his estate, and how he has to show he's responsible if he's to get monthly payouts starting on his birthday. Then he makes a calculation on his fingers, and comes up with "700,000 jwakas, or about 80,000 US dollars, per year for the considerable future."

She whistles, twirling strands of her hair around a finger. The numbers are impressive. Enough for both of them to live on comfortably.

"Are you sure the Rev has a right to meddle?" she asks. "There's something not right about that guy. I wouldn't put it past him to be bullshitting about his power of attorney."

"My God!" Jonah yelps. "It's snowing."

Hiroko swivels to look out the window.

He grabs her hands, pulls her off the counter, and rushes her downstairs.

Outside, they stand arms akimbo, heads thrown back, and mouths wide open. Thick snowflakes lethargically trickle down onto their tongues.

It's gotta be a sign.

Pleased with her vision of the future, she pushes Jonah onto a thin layer of snow dusting a bank of grass and anoints him with a face wash in terse light.

dear reveend,
　　jonah was a no-show. please, please talk to him.
love c.

Dear Clementine,
　　I'm delighted you'll be going out with Jonah tomorrow
night. He has a surprise for you, something that belonged to
Meredith. Let me know how it goes.
　　God Bless,
Love Reverend Tusker

dear reverend,
　　we're on for nine tomorrow. pray for me.
love c.[99]

On the couch, Hiroko strokes one of my earlobes.

"They're freezing," she says.

I take her by the wrists, lower her hands to my belt, then lift her
tube top over her head.

Should I tell her that I'm not supposed to see her?

She claws open my buckle, my fly, and her hand disappears
inside my boxers. I trail my fingers down past the ring on her
belly button and slide it into her thong. She's soft, wet nether hair
as our hips move toward one another. Swiftly, she takes me inside
her and I feel myself entering deeper. Her breath catching, sharp.

I look down—her legs open wide, her hips lifting as unable to

---

99　Emails courtesy of Clementine Pinkston's private collection (spelling
error in the original).

stop, everything gathers and moves us forward.

"God."

"Fuck."

Winded, we're attached at the belly.

"You dig me a little?" she asks.

I pant. "Uh-huh. You save me from a lifetime of looking."

"Yah?"

Wet snow taps hard against the windowpane.

"Yah."

Hiroko looks at me, the hardened edges lining her brow softening as the telephone rings in the other room.

"I've made a decision, daah-link." She leans forward, touching her lips to mine.

On the answering machine, Randall gives the room number of a hotel where they'll meet Thursday night.

I pull back and sit up. "You see customers outside the club?"

"He's my agent."

"Why meet in a hotel room?"

"Grow up," Hiroko says.

"What you're doing isn't what people do."

"It's who I am."

"It's wrong."

"Fuck, Jonah! Is there an us or isn't there?"

"Sex for ... that's morally wrong."

"You think I'm immoral."

"Not you. What you're doing."

She punches back. "Isn't it a little hypocritical for you to suddenly have a conscience. Especially considering I've always been straight with you about what I do."

"There are better ways to go about this."

"You know *I'm* right."

"C'mon, Cakes. We're better than this."

"You mean, you're better than this. Why not say it? You're too pure to be messing with the help."

"That's unfair."

"You got money coming in and, all of a sudden, your shit don't stink."

I gather my clothes. "I got to get back for curfew."

"Snob!"

Once outside her building, I tear a business card with her phone number on it and drop it in a papery trail in the snow.

Back at Colby Manor, Reverend Tusker works on a "Goodbye to the Hopes" he harbored with Meredith for their son. Goodbye to how they worked to see him study the piano so he would be immortalized in the canons that decide these matters. Meredith passed away, and then Dorothea with her blond wigs happened, and soon it was one excuse after another explanation before Elisha retired from twangling in prestigious halls, his pedal smug with attitude as …

"Howdy, Rev," Jonah interrupts. "Are those documents about my inheritance?"

The cleric is startled and stuffs papers into a drawer.

"Curfew is Eleven O'Clock," he says.

"Can I see them?"

"You were supposed to be here an Hour ago."

"I had a seizure." Jonah points to the Bingo-bump on his chin. "I smashed my jaw against a cement floor."

"Good Lord. We better get you to the Hospital."

"No need." He toughs out a smile. "I've been to the emergency, and they said I'm fine."

The Rev's brow twitches. "For Heaven's Sake, why didn't you call?"

"I couldn't remember where I was."

"Right." He locks the drawer with a key on the bundle looped to his belt. "You need to go straight to Bed. I'll call Clementine to tell her what happened."

"Oh, no! No! I forgot about our date." Stupid Schrödinger! It isn't possible to be in two places at once. "She'll never forgive me. Never."

"Don't mind all that, Son. You're unwell. Get some Rest. I'll explain it to her. She understands that Life happens."

I go online, and call a major summit in a chat room run by pickup specialists.

I wouldn't be doing this if it wasn't for the ringing testimonials on the homepage: a varied collection of the uncoordinated, the nearsighted, the tone deaf, and those who still live at home with Mama. Also, the head pickup artist is a black man with a PhD.

I open a thread succinctly presenting the question at issue: is it or is it not a good idea to date a woman in the sex trade? All best, Ralph Ellison.

> From Sleepless in Seattle—Loser.
> From chucky cheese—She'll never be that into you.
> From Boner—Stay on message, focus on your sets, slide in
> a neg or two, and move the target to an alternate location. Do
> this, and you're in.
> From Out to Stud—Stay on message? Where the fuck are
> the WMD's, Repug asswipe?
> From Boner—All tin foil hat-wearing left wing conspirasists

need to get a life.

From Out to Stud—That's conspiracists not conspiriasists. Illiterate Reichwing moron.

From Out to Stud—Bump

From Sleepless in Seattle—Loser

From Nicknames—Sitting around responding to asinine remarks on a message board qualifies you all as big losers.

From Boner—What does that make you? That's right, a fucking idiot. Loser.[100]

My jaw starts to hurt somewhat awful. I drag myself to the bathroom, lean over the sink, turn the taps on with my elbows, and scrub myself clean. A long time passes as I soap my forearms and between my fingers. There's soil trapped in the lifelines on my palms as I rinse in lukewarm water and repeat, rinse and repeat.

Much better.

I go to the kitchen, lodge my head in the crisper of the fridge, and search for fixins to make a sandwich.

The telephone rings.

"Hello," I answer.

"Hey, asshole."

"Who is this?"

"It's me, fucker. Quint."

"It's one o'clock in the morning, dude."

"Good news."

"Eliza May's back in the picture?"

"Not it. She's still with the Bookworm."

---

100   Many thanks to Bobby Johnson, whose efforts through the American Civil Liberties Union and the Freedom of Information Act made this information available.

"Do you have to talk so loud?"

"Listen, Professor Iton won't write a blurb for the back cover."

"This is why you're calling at one in the morning?"

"I don't get the black establishment," he says. "I didn't think I'd have to fight with them for a little love. I mean, I'm not saying that he has to like my work, but … c'mon."

It's taking me a moment to get a handle on what he's saying. Okayokay. The Iton blurb. The kitchen light flicks on and a flannel-jammied Rev stands in the doorway, tufts of his hair standing on end.

"Is that Clementine?"

"It's Quint."

"No phone Calls after Eleven," he grunts before turning off the light and disappearing upstairs.

"I got to go, dude," I say.

"Listen," Q. replies. "There's another reason why I called."

"Shoot."

"I ended up splurging on two tickets to Amsterdam over the Christmas break. You understand, right? Eliza May's always wanted to see Anne Frank's closet and wear a pair of wooden clogs, so I pulled the trigger on the purchase. This means I can't get your money for at least a week."

This is awful news. "Don't do this. I promised to pay that psycho Bingo back tomorrow."

"A week. I promise."

The light turns on again.

"Gimmie a second," I say to the Rev.

He snatches the phone out of my hand, and shout-talks into the receiver. "No phone Calls after Eleven." Then hangs up.

I stare at him, dumbfounded, as he launches into a diatribe

about "Cause and Effect," about how I need to "distance myself from that Octoroon," about how "light-skinned Blacks have it easier," about how "Noses need to be held to Grindstones. *Dictum sapienti sat est*.[101] No, it's not Prejudice, it's a sad Fact."

Disgusted, I brush past him.

Hiroko may have a point about the power of attorney business. Why the hell won't the Rev just show me the dang papers? If he's doing nothing wrong, there should be nothing to hide.

I stalk off to my room and listen to a dead rock legend play the drum kit on a CD recorded in a day-long session.

How dare he ... shit, what the fuck did he just do again?

I dump the dime bag of weed into the can and flush it into the sewers. Then I rinse my face with tap water, scrub wet soap onto my arms from fingertips to elbows, and stare for lost minutes at yellow eyeballs in the mirror.

Tickets to Amsterdam. What a dick move.

Sleeping children from Mexico City to Aix-en-Provence toss on bedsprings that are crammed with their brothers and sisters. Others curl tight in rooms of their own with views of man-made lakes or snooze with teddy bears on mattresses of queen-sized fluffiness. In cities and towns hung with sleep, predators earn bucks on the sale of body organs or trafficked flesh. There are runaways displaced by disagreements they were born into, and those who will be awoken in a matter of hours to practice double axles at the local rink. Some are purebloods like the Rev, others

---

101 A word to the wise (Latin).

are mixed like Quint C., like me. Some will be boys who grow to like other boys while some will be girls who cut both ways like Eliza May. Ingrid may or may not become a camgirl like her sister, or she may turn into a Bible thumper like Da Stylus.

It reeks of the apocalypse, and I fight a cramp building in my neck.

BOOK III

Analepsis

On me, hail belts tin roofs, muck roads is muck and shacks wobble-topple off.
Wind goes off and clouds go off. Up is a big lump of grey moon and flying ant-
animals. Tadpole-froglegs go open in ditches as giant Mama always is on time to
give the ache inside of me to milk. She makes a change of my wraps of cloth, and
rocks me in her giant chests until I am not anymore. When I am back, giant Baba
flings me in sky, we fly, and I drop back to giant hands.

Everything is me forever and I'm going where the giants stop the sky from dripping water on us.

It is dark, Baba brings to us a fire, small-like-me, that he blows and it goes off.
Water comes to us from where Mama twists hands.

During the loud times, orange bright moves hotly around that is me. White
paper that sits in Baba's giant hands is mine, and Mama's giant fingers make sweet
noise from pressing down on a white and black plonk-plonk that is mine. **Outside
of me, the God that was jealous sends to me two serpent-snakes that I squeeze
to death.**

Then plonk-plonk is no more. There is hiss-hiss noise, there is many much
shapes coming and going, going and coming. Baba is stuck to a shape that makes
him not to move, and Mama is the sound I make when I tell her of how nothing is
inside of me and it must go off. She goes to talking-sound to me and I crawl to the
hiss-hiss noise around the wall that comes from where Mama and Baba go away
to.

Quick-quick I reach for the big hissing machine where water is made hot, I tip
it to me, and am made to see only sharp-sharp as I maked me to be fire.

"Oh, Lord!"

Mama picks me up by her fingers. She gives to me in a blanket, and I bump
inside her hands while they quick-walk me to where the many giants live.

Baba has no voice.

It's a long time of ouch, and they took me in black light that goes twinkle-twinkle, yellow moonstone that is only part itself.

Mama makes the song that brings quiet to us, and she can't make the ouch better itself.

At the big house with big lights, big voices move fast. Baba is one of them and the other one comes from a big face with a white coat. Then I'm pin-pricked with an ouch. I do not feel myself and I go to the dark place.

In there I look all over for the big light to come back for me. When I find it, I see again and I have a huge, huge machine that puts itself in me.

"Praise God!" Mama sounds. "He's awake."

"God has nothing to do with it."

My chest is fire and I pull on my new skin.

"Hold his hands," Mama sounds. "He's tearing the bandages."

Baba makes me not to move till I feel another pin prick in me, before I go more to the dark.

Many times I move in and out of the room of big light. Sometimes I can touch things that do not go away and sometimes not. Sometimes I make it for the sky to drip water. Sometimes Mama talks to the pain in my side, and at some times Baba talks to a big paper in his hands. **One time I must go to a valley for where the lion has done bad. I am to bring its skin to the light. I take it onto the ground, make it dead, and when I come off the valley, the nice big man in green skin changes my skin, and feeds to me water by machine.**

I make many tries to open my eyes. Then I says to Mama that I do not want the big room of moving in and out. I do not want the dark where the lion from the valley had a home. She holds me on my sides and they bring another pin-prick to me.

I looks to Mama who says her soft song to me. I looks to Baba.

Take me off take me off.

Mama and Baba look with wet moon eyes, but they do not say to stop, or to take me off to where everything is mine.

So I go where it is hard to open up my eyes.

⁀

Much is made for me to be done. I must go to the swamp with the one who has nine heads and one in the middle of it that was living for all time. I must use a stick and when I knock its head, then two more come to the same place. It is only with the fire that must come and go that I stop its heads from coming again and only with the big stone that I use to bury the head to death that cannot die. Then I must take the river and make it clean the stable full of oxes for the king.

On the bestest time, I'm taken by Mama on the vroombus that has many smells and keeps not tipping over like it wants when it rounds one bend and then to the next. I am speedy past big walls with broken glass on top. Big hills of dirt sit in front of big houses with long chimneys that smoke. There are many cars around me that then go stop. Then the vroombus goes into much of cement houses like my house. Outside of them, the big people ride bicycles, or lie on the ground to sleep, or they give out vegetables from wooden places that lean on one another like everyone in the vroombus.

We go jerk. We stop.

The giants on the bus squeeze on all my sides. I have no breath, and I lose touching Mama's hand.

It's a big, big noise and hot. My face presses into a leg and I fall to the door and land on the outside in the land of all women.

I blink onto big sun that is making a place in a space between tall houses. It fills up my whole eyes.

A woof-woof dog comes from the land where the sun is from and it sniffs beside me. When I go to say hello to its head with my hand, it goes grrr, and runs off inside the many big women-people. I look to the faces of all them women which all look to the ground. They go fast around me and do not make talk.

I'm afraid they will see the mark on me from the bad thing what I did.

"Jonah!" It's Mama.

I hide out myself in her arms. Then I tell her about the non-breathing place and the woof-woof dog that comes from the sun and the land of women-people, but her voice is not being my friend. It is sharp, like I'm again in trouble.

"We'll walk the rest of the way," she says.

I do not do the right things, I tell me to myself. It's like if you eat a thing that makes your tummy ache but it pains in the chest and you do not know the medicine for taking it off. If I can only get the girdle of the queen of here, I will be kept well.

Mama goes fast and faster. If I do not run to keep next to her feet, she makes a sharp pull on me until the pain comes in my shoulder where the mark is.

"Heavenly Father," she says. "Give me strength."

In the woman's land outside of the big sun I sees everything that is big from around me. I sees chicken. I sees dove birds. I sees crates with maize till the top of it. I sees goats and more chickens. I sees motorcars that make black smoke from out of the back of them.

I looks to women on mats. They talk to small giraffes, zebras, and elephants made from wood that sit with them.

Sounds say different words I do not know. I go fast to hold to Mama's feet. The voices say to me noise that hits me in the ears.

After we go to many roads, Mama stops to talk with a bent giant-queen woman who is on a stool and has a stick to hold for her hand. They say different words I do not know from Mama's mouth, then the giant-woman pinches on my cheek.

I pull on Mama's skirt to say she is it who has the girdle.

"One minute, dearie," Mama says.

The giant-queen woman with the stick looks over me with round eyes—one of them is a grey plate, one is a brown plate. The sun makes a big splash behind her head. She says words, and Mama shakes her head down and down. **Then she gives to me the girdle.**

When Mama and I go away again, I do not make more trouble with sticking to her feet. I want to sleep, but I want to stay where Mama goes to. I do not want the land of the sun with the two-one-plate-eyed queen woman who can see inside of the bad thing I done.

Soon we are on the steps that go up to the glass door where Baba goes off to. On all the sides of the door are big white pillars going up and up. We go on the steps, go inside where the pillars is, and stand on the floor with scribbles on it.

I run.

"Walk!" Mama says.

I go to the end of it, and open a door. A big-up woman with glass eyes for her face looks to me from a click-clacking machine on her fingers.

"Phineas's boy," she says.

"Jonah," I reply.

"I'm Mary."

Mama does not talk a hello back to the Mrs and pulls on me go to where Baba is.

Inside the door is a room full of boxes. Baba puts rubber bands round piles of small money-papers, then makes of them piles in the floor.

"Baba!"

"How's my boy?" He puts me to the lights.

"Why is she still here?" Mama says in sharp words.

"Don't start, Rahab."

Baba puts me to the floor.

"As you can see there's a lot to do around here. It doesn't make sense to bring in someone new right now."

"Liar."

I look from Mama to Baba and want them to have a good voice for talking to one other. I do not know which is the best way for my thinking to go.

∽

In the time after Baba brings the yellow car to us, we move to Kiregwa Estates.
We get a big garden with grass for cutting and a garage for putting the car in it. I
**make one mountain to become two of them, defeat the giant and his two-
headed dog, and bring to the three-bodied monster some oxen to the land of
the red.**

I am myself and I watch everything between the open spots in the fence. Today
whirlywind spins up dust in a field on the other side. Big people, with brown skin
like my Dr from when I burnt my chest, play field hockey like yesterday, and the
day before, and the day before. Some have white turbans on, and their beard nets on.
They run and run, making dust fly while chasing the white ball. They have sweet
food and hot food, Mama says.

After I see the playing, I go inside for lemon drink made from lemons and sugar.
When some of my lemon drink is finished, I'm full up. I jump from my chair, go
to the sitting room, and sit down with Lego pieces all around on the floor. Around
me on the walls are pictures of us and pictures of Babu. I build Mama a house
with sloped pieces on its roof, then it's time for Baba to come to me from the office.

I hear the car go to the inside of the garage, and I go to the door to tell Baba
about my Lego house for Mama.

Baba's steps go clomp outside, and when I open the door, he has a big surprise
box in his hands.

"It's a television," Baba says.

Mama wipes a wooden spoon on her apron. "Phineas!"

Baba gives a kiss to Mama. "We can afford it, sweetheart."

Mama frowns from her forehead. "Is there nothing you won't buy?"

"Investments are paying off." Baba smiles to us. "C'mon, son. Give me a hand
assembling this thing."

I'm good with making things, but not good like Baba who puts out everything
from the box, plugs in wires from the TV's back. While he does the fixing he tells

me of his advice. "Names, my boy. Always remember names. If you go to shake a man's hand and you remember his name, he'll be your friend for life." He puts an antenna that looks like whiskers on the top of it. Then he shows to me which switch to turn for it to go on. "Your turn," he says.

I pull on the button.

The face of a giant talking man who wears the same suits like Baba's comes onto the front. I put my face close to where the voice comes from.

"Not so close," Mama calls from the doorway of the kitchen.

"You heard your mother." Baba sweeps me off where my feet were, and I giggle as I'm thrown on the sofa.

Mama moves to us and all of us sit on the sofa and watch the giant wearing a tie inside the television talk about serious words. After, he shows a picture with a man in it that is sleeping in a bush. He has one shoe not there.

"Why does he have one shooze?" I ask.

"Shhh," Baba says.

Mama and Baba make a holding of their hands like when a bad thing comes to their ears.

I want to have a talk with the people inside the television. I want to tell them I'm Jonah and I live on Kiregwa Estates and how old are you. I want to know how they can be inside everyone's television when they go to mine also.

Baba stands and goes out and comes back with his drinks that's only for Baba, Mama makes lots of quiet, Baba drinks his drinks and his talking is sharp to Mama about the man with one shoe.

∞

Baba's car horn beeps in the garage. I run to there to get my surprise that he comes home to me early from work. When I see inside the garage, Baba has his head on top of the steering wheel and the car horn beeps.

"Baba." I knock on the window. "You can stop the horn now."

He does not look to me.

The bad thing is happening.

"Mama!" I shout.

She comes fast and opens the door to get Baba. She shakes him up and he opens up his eyes to us.

"Hello," he says. "I must have dozed off there."

She helps him out from the car and carries him to the bed where he sleeps until supper time. After Mama gives him soup in bed, he goes to sleep again. I kneel down beside my bed and I tell Jesus the Sun of my sorriness for the bad things I did to make something go wrong inside Baba. He tells me to get the golden apples that I do not know how to find. So I go to the tall man who holds the world on his shoulders. I take the world to my shoulders and he goes to get them. When he comes back he does not want to switch again. It takes good talking and then I give to him the world back for the golden apples I take to Jesus.

∞

Baba must go to the airplane for business.

"Look after your mother," he says.

He is not big now, and he has a sleeping sickness that comes and goes. So Mama does not like that he is going on the airplane to do his business.

After breakfast, Baba does not do a prayer with Mama and me for his safety. Mama makes a fuss for it, but Baba just looks to his newspapers.

We go inside the car with his suitcase in the boot. Mama drives and we go to the road that has thorn hedges going beside it. There is sweat on Baba's face, even though it is cold in the car from the wind.

Mama looks to the road.

I'm jumbled up in my thinking. I look to the houses going past outside the window and make a long talk to God for him to make Baba not take the plane away from us.

After we go to the airport, I wait for Baba's mind to be changed up. I keep waiting when he gives his ticket to the airhostess at the counter. I wait when we walk to where the x-ray machines is for checking to see if you have a gun.

"No clowning around," Baba says and puts me in a hug. "You're big now, so take care of things till I come back."

Him and Mama give a kiss to each other, then he goes inside glass doors that close on him from behind.

I keep waiting for him to change up his mind, and come from behind the doors.

"We can watch him board his plane from the waving pad," Mama says.

I want to tell her Baba will come back to us and we must wait. But she takes me on the hand and makes it for us to walk on an escalator and stand in the waving pad where we can see all of the planes.

There is a plane taking off from the runway while another one is landing. I do not want to look at them make an accident.

We watch Baba with his sleeping sickness walk on the tarmac with other passengers to an Air France. He carries a walking stick on his hand and the wind makes his tie flap around about his chest. I wave for him to come back to us, but he does not look back. Instead, he slowly climbs stairs that take him inside the plane.

"He did not see us," I say.

"He will, darling," she replies. "When he's seated, he'll look for us from his window."

I count till twenty, then I wave for Baba again.

Some men take away the blocks from the wheels of the plane. Another man stands in front of the plane with a paddle in his hands and he shows the pilots in the cockpit where to drive. The plane stops at the beginning of the landing strip, then it starts moving again. I wave with all my heart for it to stop as it goes fast and faster. The noise is big. Mama covers her ears. Finally, the front of the plane lifts up before the whole thing goes into the air to take Baba away to the Eiffel Tower.

On the way home, I am mad with Mama. Why can she not make it so Baba stays in his bed for his sleeping sickness? I cross up my arms and make my mouth hard. I will not talk with God inside my head. I will make him sorry that I am not being his friend.

∽

Each of the crossed-out days has a name. Monday. **On Tuesday, I make a wrestling match with the man who if he falls on the earth he becomes stronger. So I must hold him over my head until I am a winner.** Wednesday. Thursday. Friday.

On Saturday the watchman to stop robbers at the gate brings his boy, Keti, to live where the servants have home. I look from the window to him and he looks from his window to me. His head is shaved off of hair and he is black all over. After many times pass, it is Sunday, so Mama's hands go quick-quick on my laces. I can't control my thinking on how she can make the loops go round. Then she ties my tie and gives to me the family Bible, and I go to it in my hand to the car. Keti sits there in its back and he has blue for a shirt. I sit where the grownups go in the front to not sit where he is.

Mama takes a road which goes down, down, down, then up, up, up. On the sides is a green hedge, then a big black gate, then a hedge, then a white gate. She says to Keti, how is you and if he likes to be in the city. He says, yes, madam, and no, madam. On them gates is signs which Mama says they mean to watch for the dog that eats you if you do not have permission to go on the inside of the hedge.

We go to a sign that says how the church is at this place. Mama turns the steering wheel, and we go inside where cars have found places to stop. We must drive around the other cars until we see a free place for us to stop.

We stop inside of it.

I wait for Mama to open my door where I sit. She takes me out of it and pats my clothes to make them smooth. She takes Keti from the back, and then she takes from me the family Bible, holds our hands on both sides, and we go to the house next to the back of the church where there are small people like me.

"Be good," Mama says.

Keti and I go inside to a room of serious talking. It has many, many books on the sides, other children sit with crossed legs on the floor and grownups stand at the front of everyone.

Mama says the grownups are for our safety, and I sit with Keti on the floor close to them at the front when they tell us the story of Jesus the Sun. They make to show his picture and the sun is round over his head. We give a prayer to say sorry about our bad things like when I made my skin on fire and we ask him to be good. Then the grownups give us' plastic buckets for the sandbox.

I poke the ground and put it in my bucket.

On my side is Keti. He puts his tongue out at me in rudeness, so I pinch his arm. He bites my leg. I hit his head with my full bucket. He jumps on where my mark from when I did the bad thing is, and we roll in the sand that goes all over our good Sunday clothes.

"Stop it," Mrs McClintock, the grownup, says.

She pulls us on our ears, and we must squat in the corner of the talking room until our legs are rubber bands.

"I want you to say you're sorry to each other," the grownup, Mrs McClintock says.

"Sorry," I say to Keti.

"Sorry," he replies.

"Now go play on the slide together," says the grownup, Mrs McClintock.

Me and Keti swoosh down the slide, then run back to the ladder for another one. Our breath is going in puffs. We go one time with me on the front, and Keti on my back. The bestest time is when we go womp-womp in a big pile on the feet place of the slide.

Then me and Keti go back and forth on the swings. He goes high, then I go high, but we cannot reach the white clouds. After we are tired, we do not see the grownups watching over us.

Keti walks outside the fence and runs to a tree.

I go quiet and stay where the gate is.

Baba and Mama will make a spanking of me because WaSimbi are not allowed outside the fence.

Keti goes higher and higher into the sun where Jesus is from and I do not want to be made to be left back. So I go on the outside and climb slowly to him. I put my knee where two branches go together and lift my body closer to where Keti and the sun is.

"Help!" My knee is stuck. "Help."

Keti climbs down from the sunny place. He pulls on my arms. He pushes on my knee. But even if he tries his best, I don't move.

I start to cry.

He jumps to the ground and runs to find the grownup, Mrs McClintock.

Inside, I have the tummy ache in my chest where the mark from the bad thing I done is. My thinking cannot stop itself.

∞

Baba goes for two weeks on the calendar system, and then when he comes from the airplane, he goes back to his bed and he stays there and does not come from it.

The days go away too fast and it's hard to remember my mind. I start to think of a thing, then I forget the thing I was thinking. Afterward, I go over what it was and I can't remember right.

Anytime I let my brain go to think of Baba burning in the lake of hell's fire, I'm sad. If I do not stop the thinking, I go to the place like when I burnt myself. It's hard to wake up from it, and if I cannot leave it, then I cannot help Mama who is starting to have the sleeping sickness.

In the morning, it is me who makes her to wake up. I open her curtains to bring the sun. I make a cup of tea like she likes with two scoops of sugar and no milk that I bring for her. If I do not let the thoughts of being followed by bad things come, no bad things will happen to Mama.

Sometimes the pain from Baba is all in me. I do not know how to make it better that he did not go to church, and I do not know how to make a change to this. I sit beside the fence with Keti, and we look at ants eating the wood.We follow them with our eyes.They live in a big hill of red dirt on the other side of the fence. Keti says they have a queen, and if you go into the middle of the hill, she is lying there bossing everyone. I want to knock it down and stop her meanness. I want happy things, all the time. I do not see any more adventures. ★ Babu arranges a trip for Mama and me at his house in Hoppa before my school time starts. He says Keti can come as my friend.

The night before the trip I cannot sleep until I can.

Hold on.

The sky in front of the car goes soft and there is a lake of silver fire that Mama drives us to with Keti and me in the backseat.

"A mirage," she says.

It disappears and is replaced by another, and another, and another that we chase all day in the car. In front of and behind of us, buses tip sideways under the heaviness of suitcases piled onto their roofs. Mini-buses are also full up and overtake us. They are the best drivers.They can go fast all day and all night, just like the winners of the car rally in the rainy season. Sometimes petrol tankers go by zip-zip in the other lane.They can explode like a bomb if we make an accident with them.

Soon we see cars stopped in a lineup ahead.

"Must be a road block," Mama says.

She stops at the back of all the cars before we slowly go again.

"Looks like an accident," Mama says.

Keti and I pop up, and look around where the danger is. A white car is overturned beside the road. Its roof is flat, and blood comes out from its doors.

I am buzzing in my tummy, but I do not look away.

Huge flies go next to the blood and two army men that smoke cigarettes.

We go again forward.

Butterflies bump against the windscreen and leave splotches of blood on the glass.

Up ahead is a row of spikes on the tarmac. We must go slow where army men stand with shiny rifles tied with straps on their shoulders.

We all get quiet. Nobody wants trouble.

"There must have been a robbery," Mama says.

She rolls down her window when we get closer to the roadblock.

A soldier's head pops into the open window. He sweats, and swats at flies with his hand.

"Where to?" he asks.

"St Andrew's Anglican Church in Hoppa," Mama presses money into his palm-hand. "My father is the pastor there."

We are waved to go through.

Once safely on the other side, I do not say a prayer of thanks to Jesus the Good Sun of Christ. If I do, it does not matter.

No one talks about the squished car. Nor about who made the accident. I want to ask Mama, but it is rude to talk.

The car must have bad people in it. They must have gone on the spikes and got shot and had an accident.

We drive to where the tea plantations cover hills. Women put leaves in big baskets they carry on their backs. They have no shoes on.

Mama turns around to us. "Babu has a nice field behind the house. I'm sure you boys will love playing in it."

"Can we play rally cars there, Mama?"

"I don't see why not," she says.

Me and Keti smile to each other. Cars is our favorite and we can have a real rally race at Babu's.

It is dark when we get to the dirt road that goes to Babu's house. It has only one lane, and there are big bushes of sugar cane crowding us on both sides that scrape against the car. The bumps make us jolt around in our seats like dolls.

We stay on this road with big holes in it until we enter a clear place with a tall black fence at the end. Mama honks the horn, and a watchman comes out from the dark place to let us in. He has a dog that runs round-around the car with a tongue that hangs from where it only has a half-mouth. Mama drives us into the garden and we follow a road to Babu's home at the end of it. The whole time, the dog with a half-mouth runs around the car, barking like a madman.

I don't like that dog, so everyone gets out the car except me.

"Come along, Jonah," Babu says.

The half-mouth dog stands on back legs and has paws on my door.

"Baraka!" Babu says. "Down!"

Babu opens my door. He takes me on my hand and I press against his legs.

"He won't hurt you," Babu says. "He just wants to play." He picks up a stick and throws it into the dark.

The dog runs for it, and I go fast to the front door.

Inside is mostly dark.

"The generator is down so kerosene lamps will have to do tonight," Babu says.

I walk into the room for sitting where there are a circle of wooden chairs. There are photographs all over the walls. Mine is there when I was at the photograph man's studio with bright lamps that make you hot all over. In the middle of the chairs is a table with one plate of usolali, one plate of boiled chicken, and one plate of cabbage. There's a black piano at the back by the fire.

I run to the piano, sit down on a stool, and bang away on the keys. Plonk-plonk.

"Pipe down, Jonah" Mama says with a sharp voice.

"Let the boy live a little," Babu replies.

I look back to them, and Mama has a hard face on.

"Why don't you show us how it's done, Rahab?" Babu says. "You haven't touched your organ since the boy was in the hospital."

Mama shrugs and goes to the kitchen. When she comes back she has a basin of water so we can wash our hands before eating. This is the rule at the home of Babu. Everyone must wash up before they share the food by taking it from the plates straight to their hands. ★.★ ★ ★ ★ ★ ★ ★ ★

★ At lights out, I lie in the bed on one side of the bedroom and Keti is on the other side. We have many thoughts to think about. At supper, Mama was making Babu hush about the army soldiers on the road.

"Jonah," Keti says.

"Uh-huh."

"Are you scared of the soldiers?"

"No," I lie.

"Me either," he says. "The army is for our protection from enemies to Liwani."

"I need to go to the toilet." I climb from bed and go to the toilet. On going back, I hear Mama and Babu having a serious talk. I look from the corner. Babu has his hand around her shoulders and she is crying gulpy, hard sobs.

"God didn't desert Phineas," he says. "He deserted God. If it was too much for him to be marry to WaSimbi, he should have stayed with the Jinjabi. Going to prostitutes was no solution. Now Jonah's going to grow up without a father, and you are sick." His voice becomes big. "Let him rot in hell for what he's done."

I go back to the room, pull the covers over me, wriggle my feet, and hate Babu.

∞

In the morning, we get up the first of anyone, lie on top of the covers, and talk of our rally that we'll go for before breakfast.

"I brung my Renault," Keti says.

He leaps up, goes to his suitcase, and throws all his clothes to the floor.

I look out of the window. The half-mouth dog runs all over the front of the house sniff-sniffing the grass.

"We'll have to go to the field from the back door," I say.

We put on our scruffy clothes of jeans.

"Do you know how to tie a tie?" I ask of him.

"No."

"Me either."

We go to the mirror and take turns making our hair nice with a brush.

"Kayo," he says.

"Kayo. Okay," I reply.

Keti and me go to the back door. I look for the half-mouth dog, then we make a dash for it to the gate that goes to the back field. We hear barking, and go fast and faster without looking behind until we open then close the gate.

The field has so much maize in it. We go to the side where there is a walking path beside a barbed-wire fence. We put our rally cars down and start to pull them on their strings on the bumpy ground that has stones sticking up from it. We go slow so the cars do not overturn on us, we do not want to have penalty points put on us.

I look to the other side of the fence where there is a watering hole that has moo-cow footprints and moo-cow dung all around it. Dragonflies hit against reeds that stick up from inside the water and in the back of there is a crane standing on one leg. Its beak is long, sharp, and thin.

Keti picks a stone and throws it to the crane which flies up and away to the sky.

"Bad luck for you," I say.

"Ha, ha. That's so funny I forgot to laugh."

We go back to rally driving. I pull my Ferrari onto a patchy place with short grass. The route stays like this way till we go to the end of the fence. Outside of it is a dirt road that runs all the way along it. On the other side of it is a place of sugarcane.

"Let's drive on the road," Keti says.

I step on the lowest barbed-wire and lift up the second wire from the bottom. Keti crawls through the hole, then he makes a way for me to go through as well.

We drive some more. This time, we stay on the flat part that was made by people. We go fast and faster and make red dust go whirling up. On the sides there is more sugar cane. The road goes for a long time before it makes a turn into grass that goes into some woods. We can hear water rushing around inside the trees. We drive our cars through the grass, over twigs, and push tree branches from our eyes as we go to the woods. It's hard to see in front, but we stay going straight until the trees become thorny bushes. Our jeans are snapped up by prickles, and we kick them off of the way.

The sun is hot on my neck as we stand next to the brown river. We leave our cars beside the water, take off our shoes and socks, then go to stand on slippery rocks.

The water bubbles warm around on our ankles.

"Do you like your Babu?" I ask.

"Mine's dead."

"I wish mine was too."

We walk back to the muddy side place of the river. My fingers pick up a dead yellow butterfly that I put it in my pocket.

Our jean bottoms lick on the mucky ground, and we go to a corner bend where the woods become a clear place with huts in it.

Nobody is there, so we go near them to look better at it.

Outside the first hut is a pile of burnt firewood. Around it are stones to sit on. I pick up a stick and poke around where the ashes is while Keti pulls on the thatched roof of the hut.

There is a loud shouting noise.

When we turn I can see a boy run toward us, waving around his arms. Then other boys come running from the bush. They all shout and point to us.

I'm scared.

I look to Keti to know what to do. Over his shoulder is bees coming to us. I jump on Keti, knock him on the ground, and we lie flat on our bellies.

I shut my eyes.

The noise is a tractor that goes close to the ears.

After the noise stops Keti jumps on his feet, screams, and slaps his arms and legs. "Safari ants," he howls.

The boy from out of the bush tackles him to the ground, and they go away from sight in a big puff of red dust.

For the first time, I see that we're been surrounded by boys in big green army clothes. Some of them have shiny rifles that are as big as them.

We need to go home for breakfast, I think.

The two boys talk in WaSimbi language to Keti and hold him on the legs and arms. When Keti keeps still, one of the boys throws water on his legs. Then he picks ants, one by one at a time, from him.

I do not know what to do, and I sit down on a rock.

After Keti is calm, a different boy soldier brings a calabash of medicine for him to take it. Keti has a sip and coughs.

All the boys laugh.

I too laugh.

Keti starts to laugh.

The boy soldier who is really a girl drinks some medicine from a calabash, then she passes it for me to take it like her. It is bitter when I have it. She motions for me to have more. So, I keep taking it until it makes the inside of my head go round-around. I can count to ten boys and six girls next to a big pile of watches, shoes, bullets, rifles, uniforms, and cigarettes. The girl soldier folds leaves in half, eats some, and gives to me the rest.

It is bitter.

My head goes heavy inside of it. The sound of WaSimbi language clangs into me. I can't stop from watching some boy soldiers have made Keti to put on a baggy soldier uniform.

He stands and gives to our friends a salute.

We laugh, and I must pee. So, I walk in zig-zags off to the long grass.

It is heavy in my head, I hear loud car engines. I walk from the grass and see men soldiers jump from Land Cruisers.

I go down inside the thorns.

Guns shoot, and I cover up my ears with my hands.

I do not move, even though I'll be in trouble for missing breakfast without telling Mama where I've gone. ★ Under bright stars, boy-girl-soldiers lie among burnt huts. Keti is sticky blood and flies that buzz on him.

I do not know how much time passes.

Yellow weavers scram from the trees into the sun, bees come from a circle of rocks, and hum on steaming grass. ★ Sorry. ★ ★ ★ ★ ★ ★ ★ ★ ★ ★ ★ ★ ★ ★ ★ ★ ★ I am found dead by Babu beside the dry riverbed leaning on cracked bark.[102]

---

102 *The Notebooks*, June 24, 2006.

BOOK IV

———◆———

Floating in a Porcelain Bowl

I

Ms. Rachel Dalgleish, Agent
134 60th Street
New York, NY
10011

Dear Ms. Dalgleish,
I have two parts of the history written. At present, the work is
shaping up to be a kunstleroman, a development that makes
sense considering the subject matter. As you will see in my
footnotes, I've gone through journal entries and gathered
other research material from pertinent private collections at
a considerable personal expense. Therefore, money is increasingly an issue. If you think there's enough material here to go
on for a submission to various publishers, I'd greatly appreciate
it.[103]

STRUCTURE
There's a frame narrative that takes place in a mental institution, and a number of embedded ones that look at the events
leading up to Jonah's hospitalization. The story shifts between
first, second, and third person in an attempt to reflect the various degrees of distance between original documents and re-
constructions based on the thousands of pages of notes. As you
will gather, much of the story is based on material written in

---

103   The list of four publishers considered for submission would only accept
completed manuscripts. Thus there was a one-year delay before work com-
menced on the latter part of this project. During the interim, the writer didn't
live in a car, or in a hammock on a beach, as speculated.

Jonah's hand (cleaned up considerably from his untidy scrawl).

SYNOPSIS (of embedded narrative)

The story begins at a strip club where Jonah talks to Hiroko, a dancer, after a long absence from her scene. After they retire to the VIP room, he has a seizure. Hiroko takes him back to Colby Manor, Reverend Tusker's home, where she takes care of him until he falls asleep. Once he's woken up, Jonah goes to the kitchen to find her with the Reverend. A heated argument takes place between the man of God and the stripper, and, in support of his love interest, Jonah leaves with her.

The following evening, Hiroko lets Jonah know she needs to raise four hundred bucks in two days. He's coming into a sizable inheritance, but not until he turns twenty-one (in three months). So he doesn't think he'll have much of a problem getting a loan that he'll pay back when he gets access to his fortune. A complication arises when the Reverend, displeased with Jonah's consorting with Hiroko, decides against signing off on the inheritance until his charge shows himself to be more responsible. An unexpected solution presents itself when Da Stylus, on the Reverend's surreptitious prodding, convinces Jonah to get engaged to her. He agrees to the plan with the thought of both proving his mettle to his guardian, and asking the Reverend for more money than he needs to buy Da Stylus a ring in order to pay Hiroko. Unfortunately for Jonah, the Reverend gives him a ring that belonged to his late wife, so Jonah is stuck with both an engagement as well as no immediate prospects for raising Hiroko's cash.

Soon after this, Jonah gets stoned on some killer weed and has an experience that leads him to seriously ponder his moribund relationship with God. He embarks on a quest to live a blemish-free life with mixed results, an enterprise that is scuttled when he decides to help in a scam in order to get the money from Bingo, a contractor hired by the Rev to build a room in the basement. After doing the job, Jonah spends the rest of his day at school. During a writing workshop with Professor Iton, Jonah's good friend Quint C. is upset over the fact that Eliza May, his friend with benefits, is flirting with another student. Quint C. tears out of the class, and Jonah ends up commiserating with him over drinks. Later that same evening he delivers his hard won money to Hiroko, and in doing so forgets that at that time he's supposed to be on a date with Da Stylus. At the tail end of their visit, Hiroko and Jonah get in an argument over the morality of her lifestyle. He leaves, and that part of the narrative ends with Jonah committing to a drug-free life while on the verge of having another seizure.

I plan to continue wading through his notes as I piece the rest of the manuscript together. Hopefully, a flashback to childhood will be used in Book III, but I'm not entirely certain this is where it belongs. Please let me know your thoughts on what has come together so far. I'm open to any input you see as relevant.

All best,
Eliza May Morton

Slowed from hurting, you hobble on feet of frostbite to the nurse's station to ask to go home. On the way, you pass a girlygirl who stands at her door in red fishnet stockings, pointing to a yellow line of tape on the floor inside the doorway.

"Where are my democratic rights," she says.

Ignoring her, you tell Nurse Shelley it's time for you to go to school and that you must talk about an assignment with Professor Iton. She says, "Sure." She's preoccupied in conversation with other healthcare personnel.

You're pointed to the cafeteria. It's the size of a squash court with tables, chairs in the center, and grey sofas against the walls. At the opposite end from the door is a tiny kitchen with a fridge.

Ending your fast, you sit alone at a table with your first solid meal in days. You do not look up at the nuthousers. Warm oatmeal with raisins goes down in solid chunks that slither past your uvula into piping that runs to your rectum. It feels like a miracle that you have a circulatory system that goes to work day in and day out on your behalf. You think about where this miracle got started; you break apart an atom and look at electrons and such. You cannot break it down enough to find a source. The only out for you is that-which-a-greater-cannot-be-thought. Yes, an imperfect copy of that-which-a-greater-cannot-be-thought exists as the universe with its many possible siblings as well as the prime mover who did the deed. As such, the workings of your inner piping is a copy of a part of this impossible thought endlessly reproduced in multiple formats; pie charts with hyperlinks, maps in three dimensions, abstract conceptualizations that take cranks to crack, sketched attempts at realism that suck the marrow out of teats, formulas in fonts which …

Before you finish your introductory *pensée* on cosmic inner linings, you're interrupted by a pint-sized, bowling pin-shaped sister.

"They call me Lady G.," she says. "Wooord."

You grunt.

"Listen up, yo, got smokes?"

You take a packet from your pocket, and give her two singles.

Her face erupts with tics and her hands fly into the air as she speaks in a voice that is much, much too big for the back of your mind. Tidbits about Nurse Shelley and the Doc enter your inner ear, and vibrate among hard, waxy hairs; there's a wife with a "shorty" in her tummy, "belie' dat," as well as a firm "get outta here" denial by the "fat cat" Doc (and an inability for him to remember details that occurred in the smoke room, in room 412, and on the linoleum tile upon which you sit), and as you listen to a history that won't make books. You think that later, maybe before noon, the caseworker will be coming to pronounce when you can get back to your assignments for school that await at home.

After breakfast, you're quieted with routines of medicine before meeting for Group on time.

Tainted, you sit in a circle of collapsible chairs slung around the room. You wait in a purgatory where original sinners, heretics, and rabblerousers have gathered to assess and decide what remedy will best take us past mistakes habitually practised for seconds on top of months that have stretched back over years. None of us know how we can return to our duties on the outside, and you don't know whether you will ever again sit at a computer sputtering with the ambition to be well regarded. You've been chained to metal, medicines have been crushed and mixed in your juice, and still your skin crawls at thoughts of cleaning up, and as pure as the robin's whistle you realize you haven't heard since late summer.

Group.

It's led by the specialist in charge of the encouragement of in-patients who do not have a history of receiving it. He looks scrubbed, his white shirt and beige khakis laundered and pressed, and his brains appear to have tackled the difficult inner workings of superegos that bargain with ids.

"Thereza leaves today," he announces.

Our team of the despicably sinful clap.

"How do you feel today, Thereza?"

Theresa, wizened beyond repair, has managed to survive the in-side. However, she doesn't know if she will make it in her crack-addicted house on the outside.

The specialist recommends that she make "a new set of friends" and that "she go to meetings" with addicts who will high-five one another like the victorious who take on days divided into quar-ters. Round and round the room they go. Each person announces what it is they will do today for the common good. Some choose kitchen duty. Others volunteer to clean the dining room before and after meals. One has made a list that she will follow through one task at a go.

You are still an individual, so again, you worry that there are no thoughts you think that the powers who have secured your signature on green paper will not search. Again, you suspect that talking to strangers about your failings is uncouth.

When it's your turn to say what sacrament you will observe to attain absolution, you announce that "by noon, I'll see the case-worker and he'll tell me I do not belong here."

The specialist notes it on a white pad.

When his case load is manageable, he'll tell your team of caregivers that in his professional assessment you present with symptoms of bi-polar disorder, that your unconscious is repressing primal urges to pluck out your eyes after sleeping with imperfect copies of Jocasta, that your anxiety level can be charted on bar graphs according to imbalanced chemicals inhabiting your genes, and he will recommend the bazooka-strength meds that have helped Thereza with her schizophrenia.

You hobble past the nurse station and listen to the sane study gossip. They take sides, cliquing up as it were, in the latest drama obtaining between Nurse Shelley and the fat cat Doc with his big-shot corporate buddies in the pharmaceutical reach-around. To some, she was duped by an offer of marriage, but not to others, who say she duped him with the offer of favors his wife was less comfortable giving him, all of them angered by the loosening impressions that fall out of those with whom they do not agree. Camps form, coalesce, and congeal as the ward divides into the ones who get it (re: Nurse Shelley) and the ones who get it (re: the Doc). In the meantime, three new patients sign the green form and are shown to inhospitable bedrooms that they'll later discover will cost them four figures for the day.

"Join the campaign for Nurse Shelley," the boyCEO shouts in your face, offering you a card. "We're always looking to hire those with leadership potential." He whispers about a willingness to exchange three cigarettes for a peek at his smutty stash of porn. "T-shirts are forthcoming. Bumper stickers. Hats. Give me a call."

"Settle down," the Doc faction at the nurse station barks in response.

They must settle down. All of them. Everyone, the world over.

At last, you meet with the caseworker whose arms are crossed, her face saying I'm unconditional friendship.

"What happened?" she asks.

It's uncomfortable finding a way to sit without pain from your legs. When you reply, the assemblage of your words is random, and the nib of your tongue will not be still.

"I don't recall," you say.

The case worker, overtired after using the weekend to patch

together a coalition that won't take sides in matters of internal hospital policy, readies for your counter-arguments. You watch her choose the adjectives to determine the story of your first encounter.

"You were found in a snow bank. Your blood alcohol level was four times the accepted level, your kidneys are leaking poison into your system, *and* you came within a hairsbreadth of having your legs amputated. Does this tell you anything?"

You stare at a wall.

You have learned to be strategic in your silence and how not to recollect details until you know the code that'll get you the fuck out the c(k)link. You have learned that whatever you say will incriminate you in the write-up that will go in your confidential record, the one that will be accessed if you are brought before a judge for a future infraction that can only be discerned in entrails. You will not make incriminating admissions in order to beef up her unpublished study that tracks instances of bi-polar among blacks between the ages of eighteen to twenty-four, or to give her evidence that progress on their terms is being made.

In the hallway, Lady G. nips at your heels. "Did'cha hear? Did'cha hear?"

"Hear what?

"Nurse Shelley got suspended."

"Yeah."

"Heya, can you hook a sister up with a cigarette, dada?" she replies. "Just a single."

"Sure."

"Just one."

"No prob."

"I'll pay you back right quick."

"Sure."

"I'll git you on the outside."

"Don't worry about it."

"We cool?"

"Yup."

"See ya." She splits.

Slouched against a wall, the Island girl is sad with fat. She doesn't know how to stand up when it's time for a change in the daily routine. She will continue to sit, in her lime-green dress, until a shaman appears.

Do your duty, you think. Find something to focus on that keeps the shit straight.

For a moment, alone, you hide in the bathroom behind a door that doesn't lock. You fill the sink with water and get to work scrubbing soap all over your face, the back of your neck, between your fingers, and over your forearms. You are smeared in white bubbly suds as you tell yourself the things that keep you sane. *You* can say the alphabet backward. *You* are not at all like the Islander sunken in sadness. *You* have writing assignments to get back to. If needed, *you* can lean on the parts of yourself that talk to a Many-Named God.

2

BREAKING NEWS:

"Aristotle[104] believed it took seventy-two Years for a one-degree shift in the fixed Star that first rises over the Earth's Horizon at the Equinox," the Rev says over breakfast. "After 2,160 Years, or seventy-two times thirty-one-degree shifts, he calculated that a new Age would begin."

Vaulting from spring board to pommel horse to Byronic hero,[105] Jonah focuses elsewhere:

In matters metaphysical, he ponders reasons for his latest round of questionable doings, and asks himself where to draw the line that says this is the beginning, the prolegomenon, the whence of where it all went south. On the socio-economic frontier, he's in deep *kaka* with Bingo; the street has a way of handling folk who don't pay off their loans, and he anticipates ways to handle him. Also, he has a nagging suspicion that the Rev is screwing him with the inheritance, but he hasn't settled yet on a course of action. On the domestic agenda, he may have made a mistake in getting sanctimonious on Hiroko, *and* he most certainly screwed up by destroying her phone number. He needs to get his ass down to Club Carnival where her tush will need to be kissed and, in

---

104   It should be the Greek philosopher, Plato (429–347 BCE).

105   In this case, an idealized, but flawed, character originating in the life and writings of Lord Byron (one who is moody, proud, cynical, and defiant). Rosemary "the Bookworm" Levy finds the parallel forced, and she suggests it is only the moodiness that applies to Jonah.

this way, he'll initiate the re-harmonization of the cosmic universe by rectifying the ongoing conflict with his testy romantic lead. As for doings germane to the haloed halls o' learning, Jonah has twelve days to pull together at least twenty competent pages for a dry run of a story for Professor Iton's workshop.

Whew!

Let's take a short break with our corporate sponsors and, when we return, we'll talk with an expert panel of perverts to ascertain if there's truth to rumors that indeed the wicked get no rest?

This just in:

"After twelve such transitions, or 25,920 years, or the Period it takes for each of the twelve Constellations to appear for the thirty-degree duration of its Age, the Stars and Planets will return to the original Point from which they first began their Journey; thirty Degrees times twelve equals 360 Degrees, making a complete Circle. You see what this means? See? There's an Order to the Universe on a macro Scale that we can see in micro at work in our DNA."

Jonah is far from the Rev's analysis of inner workings of the larger cosmic order as he pokes a spoon in oatmeal and contemplates whether there's a unifying thrust beneath the many activities that need his attention. Watching the Rev's facial features buckle and torque, he thinks of how his own salvation, at least on the physical plane, rests among the many fine, material features evident in Hiroko Ishigowa, his kinky lady love. In sum, he's tempted to heed primal urges to sally forth among her mulberry nipples, armed only with her name emblazoned on his chest plate and his mind furnished with her simulacra-like-Playboy-bootay-bunnyness.

The bleeding telephone again.

The Rev picks up and proceeds to jibber-jabber at speeds un-detectable to the human ear.

"What kind of Racket are you running over there?" He shout-talks. "This is the third Time I've talked to Someone about this Service Charge. Of course, I don't know who I spoke to. Mar-tha. Marilyn. Who knows? No, no. You listen. Have you heard of categorical Imperatives? ... The Point is this: if Everyone went around shirking his Responsibilities like you do, Society would be absolute Chaos. Wouldn't it? No, no. I will not calm down. No one there is the least bit interested in doing their Job." He pats down a protruding tuft of hair. "Yelling? You want to hear what yelling sounds like. DO YOUR JOB."

While ropey veins bulge at the Rev's neck, Jonah visualizes his Loverly Lady Hiroko, the vessal that stirs in him the powerful inclination to reject *prudentia,* and its sweetest of companions, the Golden Mean.

My first responsibility is to get the Rev ready in timely fash-ion to be picked up by Loretta Tucci for an outing at the C.C. Contemporary Art Gallery. An undertaking that involves talking him off the heights of perilous Aristotelean[106] abstractions while he limps on his bum ankle, in and out of his bedroom, in various states of undress.

First he appears in oversized white undies in the middle of one thought (he prefers to think "*Mimesis* is a form of Counterfeit as opposed to an act of Imitation," although it's "fascinating" to con-sider how "Mimicry dovetails with Artifice to create that which is *Contra-fetus,* or against breeding"). Then he disappears, only to return to finish the confusing analogy with a black sock on his

---

106   Should be Platonic.

left foot, a dark blue one on his right hand, and a finger poking through a hole where the big toe normally lives. Talk, talk, talk, Old Norse and Saxon is evoked and it takes forty-five minutes before he's ready for the art gallery's new exhibit of West African artifacts from 93 CE to the present.

Right on time, Mrs Tucci shows up at the front door of the manor looking grand with her mane of brown Barbie doll hair, her bright red televangelist wife lipstick, and a beige pantsuit, all the rage among female politicos. It's a look that goes a long way to abet the voodoo-that-she-do, which untangles the Rev from the increasing bouts with what he describes as "anomie."

"Congratulations on your engagement, Jonah," she says.

I grunt.

"There's nothing quite as difficult as committing to set aside the fantasy that something unexpected is supposed to be waiting around every corner," she continues. "So you've done well to choose one person, Jonah. Very, very well."

The Rev makes a surprisingly sane entrance. "It's not like you to be on Time," he says to her.

"A lady's schedule is never truly accounted for by a man." They peck cheeks. "We take our time to decide on what we wear while you've been wearing the same thing out of habit every day this month."

I worry he'll find a way to derail the outing as I watch them walk with looped arms to her car.

Danger! Danger!

Once inside, they get into a debate over what seems to be the adjustment of side mirrors, one that ends after Loretta Tucci lays into him with a fierce mane shaking rebuttal. Then she grimly backs her station wagon out of the driveway as he stares out the window muttering to himself.

When they're out of sight, I bound upstairs, enter his study, and go straight for the desk with my documents for the inheritance. It's locked, so I go on a treasure hunt throughout the house for his spare keys. Flower pots, soap dishes, and books upturned and strewn about. Then I return to the scene of the ongoing crime in order to attack the lock with a letter opener.

Three minutes later, I'm certain that my gambit won't work.

Yawning, I repair to the bathroom mirror to pluck nose hair until I'm satisfied no protruding uglies exist. Then, groomed and slathered in body lotion, I put the morning's frustration behind me by luxuriating in front of the TV, surfing a smörgåsbord of talk shows, news programs, and sports recaps.

ORDER NOW FOR THE LOW LOW PRICE OF 34.99

COMING THIS SEASON.

COMING TO A THEATER NEAR YOU

Buy One get One Free

Quickly, I call Da Stylus with an update on my health, and to apologize for my absence at the roller rink. How is *she* doing? Half an hour passes as we talk Leroi, and then I dodge every which way to avoid making plans to make plans once I'm well enough to get together during a mutually available block of time.

How the heck did we get to this point?

Here I am, responsible for attending to every one of her emotions and for giving her updates on my every move so that she can determine which activities belong to us. When did I agree to being tracked by her like a UPS package?

Okay, I gather myself for the activity ahead by hunkering down with the smartly dressed panel of female hosts on *Pillow Talk* who dash through the main topics of the day.[107] Each panelist has a story to tell that begins, "The funniest thing happened on the weekend." One ran out of laundry soap in the middle of loading the family's clothes into the washer. Another visited with in-laws and ate wild rice with a Virginia ham and homemade cranberries. Leroi's death goes national as the hosts refer to the event by its current handle, the Blackout. Three are horrified, one defends the *status quo*. "A cop is the enemy until you need one," is said. Then a minute-long debate takes place on the question of whether the Commander-In-Chief is truly a Born Again, the audience loudly applauding each opposing view. Finally, Tamala Exeter, the first guest, appears. The season opener of her Emmy Award-winning show, *Switcher*, led the Nielsen ratings last week, and conversation focuses on allegations that she's romancing costar, Rafe Curtis. There's a firm denial followed by a seemingly rehearsed tirade against the stalkarazzi. A camera pans to her tycoon hubby, Lance Itby, who wears a big-ass grin in the front seat of the audience.

"We'll be right back after another break."

America's Number-One Warranty.

---

107   A successful TV format with women from different generations, races, and political stripes talking about matters important to the sisterhood. The first shows were conducted in pajamas, but this was changed after the second week because of a deluge of inappropriate email from young males in the eighteen-to-twenty-four age demographic.

Hot local single action.
Call now.

Join THE BRAVE, THE PROUD, THE MARINES.

Free consultation. No cash down, money back guarantee.

I turn my attention to hip hop videos.

Man, oh man!

It's quality soft porn: lots of blokes with bejeweled teeth swimming in a horny swill of bosoms and butts, the women inexplica-
bly begging for it while hustlers rub hands together and chew on
toothpicks.

Enchanted, I take medication that grogs me out with a sledge-
hammer of a buzz.

After I wake well into the morning, I'm boiling. The dang
heater is cranked and I don't have a clue as to how to adjust it. I
go upstairs to cool off in the shower before making a wardrobe
change; dressing classical with hints of rapper chic, my dark cords
and two-button tweed jacket with high constructed shoulders are
offset by an untucked turquoise turtleneck.

Me: Q., sorry about the blurb, man.

Him: What?

Me: The call last night about not getting the Iton blurb. I'm
sorry it didn't work out.

Him: Oh, that. It's forgotten.

Me: Beg your pardon?

Him: Do you think I should go over to the Bookworm's and
give Eliza May the plane ticket?

Me: Chazus and Mary Jones, dude! Are you doing okay?

Him: Should I?

Me: How would I know?

Him: Should I?

Me: Of course not.

Him: Are you sure?

Me: Yup.

Him: You're probably right.

Me: Am right, son. Am right.

Him: She's got to come to me?

Me: Be a man's man. Remember?

I get on the horn and goad Eliza May into telling me whether she and the Bookworm are an item.

Her: Is that what Quint thinks?

Me: Well, I don't know what he thinks. We haven't really talked about it.

Her: Not that it's any of your business, but there's nothing going on between Rosemary and I.

Me: Rosemary and me. Really?

Her: Rosemary and me. Christ, can't women just be friends without everyone thinking they're sleeping together.

Me: So you're not sleeping with her.

Her: Well, we've slept together. But not slept together, slept together.

Me: I'm confused.

Her: Like friends. Don't you and Quint ever just fall asleep in each other's arms?

Me: In the bed?

Her: The couch. The bed. Wherever.

Me: The answer to that would have to be no.

Her: Guys are so uptight. Yes, Rosemary and I sleep together.

Me: Are sleeping or slept?

Her: The progressive, hon. But it's no big deal. Anyway, Quint was the one who pushed for us to have a friendship with benefits. No strings attached. Come and go as we please. So I don't see what he's getting upset about now.

Me: Like I said, I don't know if he's upset.

I hang up and call Quint C. who's waiting with his cell in hand.

Me: So we touched on the topic of the Bookworm and she's fairly emphatic they're just friends.

Him: Do you believe her?

Me: Like I said, we talked about a lot of other things. But, it sounds fairly harmless.

Him: You think I should tell her what I'm feeling?

Me: No!

Him: No?

Me: Hell no. Wait her out. Act aloof. She'll come around.

The air itches in my throat.

I stare into the fridge, wishing I was less sober, more cut loose. *Nothing I want.* So I call Elisha and give him a rundown of the Rev's greatest misses. He cracks jokes about marriage and it takes a concerted effort to rein him in enough to convince the lazy ass to get his head out of his *keister*, stop by asap, and check up on his father (whom he's quite possibly ruined).

At noon, I try the desk drawer once again, stupidly wishing for a miracle. After unsuccessfully jimmying the lock with a wire coat hanger, I drag my butt off to see Ma Petra-Freud about a paying gig to put toward the money I owe Bingo.

∞

Next door, the Spielmans sit in their wicker rocking chairs
between two huge American flags on either side of their porch.
They watch the happenings that pass before them on a street de-
nuded of leaves as if this were the vocation they'd saved for years
to secure. We stare at each other, say nothing, and I move on.

The Black Republican answers a knock at her front door; she's
wearing a painter's smock and boy shorts.

She's alone, and grateful for company as she listens to the university student ask if there's any part-time work he can do for her.
Shoveling? House cleaning? Anything?

"Come in, come in," she says with gusto. "Alistair's been away
for a few days, and I've been painting up a storm." She's drunker
than she realized. "Come and take a look."

She grabs his hand and leads him into her basement studio.

Four pieces hang on the walls, and one sits on an easel. They're
all of the Cuttlewot's house in the light of different times of day.

"They remind me of Manet's Cathedrals,[108] ma'am," Jonah says.
"Are you with me here?"

She loops a hand around his upper arm and leans her head
against his shoulder. "That's exactly what I had in mind," she
muses. "Do you think they're any good?"

"Good! They're the suburbs as a monument to an ever-shift-
ing present." He bungles, like a swatted fly, toward a more sym-
metrically aligned definition of what he means. "Have you read
The Waves? No. Well, each section begins at a specific time of
day to mark the different stages of the character's life. Morning
is childhood and so on. Anyhow, what Woolf does is to invoke a

---

108   Jonah makes an error. He meant the French Impressionist, Claude
Monet (1849–1926), not Edouard Manet, French Realist and Impressionist
painter (1832–83).

transcendental consciousness, if you will. One that performs in a number of interwoven inner monologues. It can be confusing at times, but reminds me of what you're doing with your representation of an eternal present ... follow my meaning?"

"So you don't like them."

"No, no," he protests. "I love them, ma'am."

She sits in the middle of the couch and sips white wine, moved by Jonah's startled rush toward ideas like a calf staggering to its feet. It reminds her of before Alistair, and their manic nights that ended at dawn. It's been ages since she felt anything more than the frumpiness of her daily routine.

Bored? It isn't that. Numb? Not it, either. More that she didn't account for the sacrifice involved in marrying a man educated at a public university, "one who values culture by its price tag." Alistair can't seem to help but "embarrass her with his constant boasting" about the expense of his latest purchase. The vacation to Tahiti coast such and such—"including meals *and* the whale watching." The new extension at the back of the house costs so and so. "Frankly, it's vulgar."

"Come, Jonah." She pats the spot beside her. "Tell me more about how wonderful you find my work."

He scooches down next to her.

"I hope you don't mind me saying so," he says. "But I detect a tentativeness in your brush strokes, a self-consciousness, if you will."

"Really?"

"Yes, but the Pollock-influenced dribbles you substitute for sky indicate the emergence of a different animal. A carnivore rather than a herbivore. Someone of voracious appetites. You follow my meaning?"

Ma Petra-Freud reaches toward the coffee table for her handbag
and removes two crisp hundred-dollar bills from a wallet. "What
say you to being paid for your stimulating company?"

"Can you afford me?" I joke.

"One hundred per hour."

"One hundred!"

"Okay, one-fifty."

"When can I start?"

Her hand rests on my knee.

"I like you," she confesses. "I like your energy, and I enjoy
spending time with someone who can keep pace." She's surprisingly gentle as her fingertips travel up my thigh. "No strings attached and discretion is a must. Are you with me?"

Time out!

Learned reader, let us examine our hearts and see what stuff we
are made of.

Effects are causes that produce other effects.

What to do?

We can throw in our lot with those whose *modus operandi* is to
feel one's feelings in order to make the sentimental choice? Or,
we can rationalize this potential infusion of cash as a miracle from
the Prime Mover who makes everything happen for a reason? Or,
we could throw in our lot with those who think poorly of the
ones who believe in feeling every damn feeling, and so they opt
to take the pragmatic option?

"Of course, ma'am," I reply. "I'm with you on this."

"Infidelity isn't nearly as vulgar a thing as the mind that cannot
appreciate art," she philosophizes.

"Yes, ma'am."

I feel her trace the outline of my hip bone, losing myself in being felt up by someone of social standing, someone who dines with heavyweights whose investments make a profit while they sleep, someone who pledged at an all-brown-paper-bag-skinned sorority,[109] a skimpily clad cheerleader of the free market who belongs to a world that is disciplined in the ways it arranges itself around money.

I turn her, pull aside her boy shorts, and fuck her beneath a freshly painted Cuttlewot colored in the yellows of the mid-afternoon.

Are you with me here?

∞

The air kicks with soft snow flurries as Jonah heads into Africa America for his work shift at the People's Laundromat (the job Da Stylus got for him). He has most of Bingo's money, courtesy of Ma Petra-Freud, and he gleefully skip-steps through tumbling white fluff near a barricade of bedsprings.

His gut tells him that her Ladyship Hirositasan would approve. Sex in itself is neither right nor wrong, but one element in a species of acts that belong to the *genus* of intimacy. Come to think of it, under the right circumstances, truth is variable. Anything goes. Well, almost everything. Not murder, obviously. Although, there are circumstances where a mercy killing might be appropriate. But this romp against the Cuttlewots with Ma Petra-Freud wasn't the

---

109 The "brown paper bag test" was a ritual once practised by certain African-American and Creole fraternities and sororities who discriminated against people who were "too dark." That is, these groups would not let anyone into the sorority or fraternity whose skin tone was darker than a paper lunch bag.

same as taking a human life. Not even close. It was a consensual sticky tickle, a sub species in the *familia* of touch.

"Grow up."

The good ship Hiroko has a point: sex providers perform a service done by those who look reality dead on, and stare down hard truths. In fact, the argument can be made that it's downright saint-like—St Francis of Assisi-like, if you will—to donate one's spare time to acts of charitable intimacy.

Two cottony blocks later, Jonah's out of the cushy bougieness of North Oldeham and inside one of the other Americas. Brothers and sisters sit on or mill about snow-flecked brick stairwells. Men wear baseball caps, oversized parkas, and spanking clean Timberlands. Women sport bright-rose track pants, and walk around bundled in knitted caps, scarves and mitts. Small groups of boys yap and blow into their hands while girls play hopscotch on the slushy sidewalk.

"What'up?" Jonah says.

"Whazzaaa?" a sharp fedora replies.

Our sex provider stares at the ground, nervous, and presses forward.

In a salon, women get their hair tweezed, and Jonah passes a fella selling an assortment of electronic goods from the back of his van.

"You like rap, boss?" he's asked.

Don't get involved.

"Five bucks," he continues.

"I don't have any money."

"You ain't gonna do the black bidnessman like that?"

"Like what?"

"Hatin," he says. "On the real, this here's the first release on my label."

"No, really," Jonah reiterates. "I'm not hating." *Shit, it's hatin.* "I don't have any money."

The black bidnessman brushes both shoulders off with fingers, then quickly moves on to another hustle.

Once at the laundromat, Jonah spells off Mama Foreman, Da Stylus's sixty-eight-year-old aunt who can't afford to retire. She's flecked grey hair, red rivulets in her eyes, and rows of worry implanted in dark-dark leathery skin.

They trade edited accounts of personal happenings over recent days. Today's main topic: a visit from her son from Jersey resulted in a telephone bill with charges to 1-800 numbers. She and Da Stylus are 200 dollars short, and their line is about to be disconnected.

"Here." Jonah, sex provider, forces his man-whore pay-out into her hands.

She hedges, he insists. She refuses, he coaxes.

Finally, "God Bless you, chile." She hugs him, long and tight. "Clementine is surely a lucky gal."

"Could you please not mention this to her, mama?" he says. "She'll make you give it back. She's like that."

She breaks the hug. "Shoot, boy. You an angel." She loads a rayon shopping bag with knitting. "You need ta go on ahead 'n' marry my Clementine 'fore I get too old."

"I'm working on it." He helps her waddle off into the afternoon with a hand to her elbow.

Apart from the company of Martha, the crackhead, huddled on a plastic chair among her plastic bags and the presence of my marked-up copy of *Jane Eyre*, I'm pretty much alone.

Martha talks to herself. "No, honey, don't pick up the little boy."

She strokes her chin with her fingers. "You're a real sweetheart, thank you." She sucks on a ring on her finger. "Charles is coming early." Then she removes a makeup kit from her bag and powders her chin. "Roger, I'm not trying to get into the little boy's pants." She throws her head back, laughing. "It's best we take a minute. Just a minute. Honey, you keep asking if it's the original song. It isn't. It's the cover." She smacks dust from her clothes. "No, no, honey. Don't do that. I don't want you to touch my molecular structure. I'm a very peaceful person. No, I'm not that beautiful. Stop it. I've got something not right I've got to get rid of." She scratch attacks a difficult to reach spot on her lower spine, then giggles before glimpsing into her compact mirror.

Holy batcrap! I'm stuck without Bingo's money between a fidgeting crackhead someplace/nowhere-Africa America and Brontë's world of antique furnishings, windy heaths, and sprightly diplomatic discourse.

3

Without my man-whore money, I head deep into the Heights to man-up to Bingo

There are post-mod hieroglyphs on the walls of buildings with glassless windows. Metal screens are pulled down over storefronts. Yusuf and Ibrahim, bald Muslims in white robes, sit beside tables where they sell bottles of homemade massage oil.

"Brutha," they say in unison.

"Brothers," I reply.

I turn left near the Methodist church[110] with a cross at its apex, walk past boarded buildings that tilt in shrubbery-filled lots, and look for Bingo in front of the liquor store (where regulars slur together sentences and the pace of their language is swift, incomprehensible). I spot him playing dice with "his niggas"; a couple of them occasionally breaking away to swap dime bags for crumpled bills with white folk in cars that slow as if inching past Burger King's drive-thru window.

"Yo, supafly," Bingo says on spotting me. "Where my money?"

"I had complications."

"How much?"

"Four hundred."

"That's a lot complicated." He turns to one of his boys. "Did I say one day?"

---

110   Previously written as a Baptist church, but here it is corrected as a Methodist church.

"Yezzir."

"One ain't two."

"Nozzir."

"He fuckin with my money?"

"Sho is."

Bingo stands up and clamps an arm around my shoulders. "Listen up, yo." He squeezes me close. "See, Bingo got this bootay call who wears them nipple clamps while I fuck her. She takes 'em rubber bands, puts 'em on my Johnson, and ping. It get so, if she even look at me, I get a hard-on."

"Yezzir."

"Yup. So I sees her last night. Yup. We tapped it funky. Yup. Now I'ze in a generous mood." He spits. "So you got ten days, smell me?"

"Ten days to get the money?"

"'N' it ain't gonna be kosher if you short."

"I'll have it," I reply.

He smiles. "Serious. Y'all better do right by a nigga, nigga."

Drained, I hurry away, and only slow when I approach Drake Street—the border between Santori Heights and North Oldeham. Overhead, warplanes jiggle wind that swirls grit around the crucifix on top of the storefront church.

My feet take me up the church's pathway and I stand in front of its forest-green door. A sign indicates they'll be open for another hour and guests are welcome. After looking behind me to make certain there are no witnesses, I fiddle with a latch that sticks before the door squeaks open. *Make haste slowly.* I tiptoe onto a red carpet, pass pews dotted with Bibles and hymn books, and deposit myself onto my knees at an altar draped in a crimson cloth.

Stained-glass windows refract shards of white light around me, and I wait to be told what to do in this hollow crypt.

I can't think of a quick fix for transgressions too numerous to itemize. I can't find my way back to being a blank slate. I can't draw inspiration from otherworldly sources to supply me with the will to change my ways.

Am I too proud to beg?

I cross myself.

4

On some nights, there's nothing to be done when one has yet to settle on a subject

Jonah shuffles yellow index cards and considers how far he is from an affordable one-bedroom of his own above a coin-operated laundromat, one with an east-facing window that looks out onto an independent cinema. Dankness fells the city as he gets distracted from trouble by re-reading Eliza May's story.[111] He hates it. Maybe.

Yes, the grammar is sound; she makes good use of the compound sentence. But she refuses to help her reader through the unfamiliar and the unrecognizable. The tone is impersonal, and the gentle reader has no idea which situation calls for what emotional response. Characters don't speak in completed thoughts. There are footnotes, and endnotes, and no unifying consciousness. As for the style, the figurative language performs in ways that say, Hey folks, look at me, I'm a writer.

He turns to his own work, firing up the computer and typing out a segment for his submission to the workshop.

 beads chuckle, truly as he licks and laps and tastes the borders
 of freaky scents. as she trembles in his mouth, the slight hitch

---

111 Slated for publication in the fall of 2008, pending the resolution of legal issues.

of her hips rises up to meet the cleave of him tonguing deep in her.

She's the one place where he's sure what the core of him feels. Not as clarity. Nor passion. Not even as a suitable match (she's mostly wrong for him). It's more, she's what he wants to explore. All of it. Who she was. What she's becoming. How she looks stuffing potato chips into her gob while luxuriating in front of the telly. He wants what they do in the bed chambers, and what it brings out in him.

Spurred to action, Jonah rings directory assistance for her information. When he finally hears a live voice, he offers the coordinates.

"We have many listings under Ishigowa."

"What about H. Ishigowa?" he asks.

"We have three listings for Ishigowa, sir."

"No H's?"

"No, sir."

"Give me all three."

"I can only give out one listing at a time, sir."

"Okay, what's the first one?"

"747-9851."

"Thanks."

"Thank you, sir."

He calls the number.

"Hello?"

"Hiroko?"

"My God, it's eleven forty-five."

"Is Hiroko there?"

Click.

It's the time of no-time, and Hiroko is a sullied something-or-other who has gone over the details of her choices so many times, a headache has come on. Her belly feels bloated. She wishes for a holiday.

Club Carnival's customers enter and exit her as if she were a toll booth. They trash-talk and rampage their way through as she sucks on her teeth while servicing them; those dressed as if they're on their way to future prospects, those bankrolled by insider information, those with attitude wedged up their asses. They come and go. Jonah and his cash-money came and went. No one stays.

Her condition has no entertainment value.

Tonight, she and her on-again-off-again buddy, Monay, work the car dealership angle: if they don't come up with one grand by tomorrow morning, they're fucked. Then they work the irregular heartbeat story: bad news from the doctor, and without health coverage, they're screwed. Finally, they work the back rent is due tale: the ex-boyfriend left, and since their name is on the lease, they're up shit creek.

Girlfriend's leaned on by circumstances, and doesn't know how much longer she can toil without a guarantee that will multiply her worth.

Hiroko's trashed, but smiles because the hours move fast when there are no pauses in the fluid, kinetic motion of human traffic. Multi-tasking, she simultaneously answers a question about the whereabouts of the cheapest gasoline in town and studies the imperfection of her own gestures.

Should she tilt her head, like so? Undo her top button, more like that? Grasp at his belt buckle?

Yes, her skin is dark, but she refuses to be rattled (there isn't time to indulge this luxury). Instead, she reminds herself that she's embedded—one of them—trying to figure out how *not* to be on the public record as one of those who get left behind.

Da Stylus fetches to fix herself a happy ending, so she spends the evening shouldering Mama Foreman off the phone. Whenever her aunt is on the line for more than a couple of minutes, Da Stylus bumbles around in the general vicinity until Mama hangs up.

"Did the Rev really say Jonah was going to ask me to marry him?" she asks her aunt again.

Technically, he didn't ask the first time. He just agreed to go through with it. So it's good news that he's going to make it official, as Reverend Tusker told her, with a ring.

"He sho' did."

"What exactly did he say?"

"He workin on it."

"On a proposal?"

"On *it*, Clementine." She takes another phone call. "Don't be ornery, chile. Have faith."

Alone in the kitchen, Da Stylus wipes down countertops and travels into a future with Jonah as her husband—besieged at his ankles by pages of his latest manuscript—and imagines herself in support with a trickle of teas and soups and encouragements as needed. Reverend Tusker has told her Jonah's story, and as a result she sees him in the ways he refuses to see himself. Unlovable. Unloved.

She puts together an equation. Since God is love and sex is love, she imagines God's desire for her is that she give herself bodily to him. Abraham was willing to sacrifice Isaac. The heavenly Father sacrificed his one and only son. So she must act, love more fully and show her willingness to obey more readily. A community that prays together stays together, and in time she'll go with or without her husband from village to village leading prayers morning and night. As Christ wills, she'll raise the necessary funds to provide entire districts with mosquito nets. Yes, as soon as Jonah returns her call, she'll tell him that this time she's ready for wherever the spirit leads him. No more looking for a ram caught in a thicket. No more fuss.

No longer at loose ends, and not far from her happy ending, she stares out the kitchen window at a new moon edging its way above the Heights.

Outside along the main drag, cars peel across tarmac in high-end squeaks. Propped up on pillows in the marital bed, Dorothea watches her taped rerun of the season starter of *Switcher,* where the Rafe Curtis character manages to thwart the Tamala Exeter character's ambitions for him. There are few reasons left to justify Tamala's choice to stay, but she doesn't say any of this to him. Instead, she's wild with thoughts of another suggestion for Rafe that is respectably white collar: an opening for a mid-level management position at RTU Industries, another opportunity with the upside of a promotion to upper management within the calendar year. In today's episode, Tamala has the courage to recommend the name of a person who'll make the introductions that would elevate their social position. She waits through breakfast, then lunch, and finally gives up when he goes to spend the evening working the Stairmaster at the gym.

Dorothea craves a tranquilizer. Her prescription for Vicodin wasn't refillable, so she has no remedy for the latest discomfort. She eats fat-free potato chips and, as crumbs mount around her, thinks about how Rafe and Tamala always enter into polite conversations in which they end up circling around each other: she never confronts his failure to say what he thinks, and she never quite manages to tell him what she feels.

In another room, Elisha mumbles into the phone.

Entrenched in her own pain, Dorothea can't see any wiggle room for either Rafe or Tamala. In the past when Tamala tried to push Rafe in order to get something to change, nothing worked. Instead, much like Dorothea, she was weighed down with anticipated criticism that was as inevitable as the light dust of snow in Curranvale City over the weekend. Like Tamala, Dorothea doesn't love being married to a man who isn't how he presents himself to others. For instance, when she met Elisha, there were childhood stories about trips to Africa that never materialized, and how he'd sit alone in his room with bags his mother had packed for him as his parents argued over God's punishments for those who broke their word. At the time, Dorothea'd wished to be one person Elisha could rely on, but now she can see how just about anything he ever says is a plea for empathy. So all that remains in her is resentment over the gullibility that left her open to the suggestions that got her to walk away from a career in retail for him. She left her family of blue collar Baptists and became an Episcopalian for him. As the years progressed, she convinced herself he knew where he was going, so she followed him. But twelve years later, he's changed the direction of his chosen vocation so often that it has soured her irreversible decision to share her future with him.

As the headlights of station wagons flare yellow through the curtains of her window, Dorothea twists her fists into balls and curses the weakness in Elisha that has cast her in the role of a person who specializes in being difficult.

"I used to think love meant sacrifice, Clem," Elisha whispers over the phone. "Eventually something gives and everyone agrees that the struggle is worth it. But that day just never seems to arrive with Dorothea."

"I know what you mean," Da Stylus responds, thinking of Jonah. "I know."

Eliza May pats her belly, full from a stack of pancakes two days ago (Saturday), and refuses to feel guilty. Both Quint C. and Jonah say they love her story and offer her compelling evidence for it, but she's stared so long at her pages that she no longer knows what she's looking at.

She tells herself that she won't be in Curranvale City for the duration, and that she's a shoo-in to move to a quicker city with television studios that make celebrities. She'll present industry insiders with letters of introduction from respected mentors—Iton definitely, Fish Coleman if they maintain a correspondence, and Quint C., the rising star with Rachel Dalgleish,[112] his agent, and her enviable author list.

But who is she kidding?

How will she support herself while she waits in cafés with wireless access to the Internet trying to find her own thoughts? How long will she be able to wait before she realizes she cannot do this on her own?"

"What is enough?"

Quint C. recalls a night he cleaned a puddle on Eliza May's bathroom floor with her favorite bath towel. They argued over who was more imperfect, indulging this drama until the Book-

---

112   Head honcho of the Dalgleish Agency.

worm said Eliza May was good and he was bad, just as suspected.
Dude!

He's got an agent, *he's* got a deal, *and* he's only twenty-three.

But … of late he's been taking a pummeling. The editor won't
budge on a demand for changes to his collection. Professor Iton
didn't write a blurb, and everything is conspiring to tell him he
has no mo in his jo.

Once again, he reviews Eliza May's latest effort, and is irritated
with her plotless narratives, and does not care if randomness has a
purpose. When a sentence doesn't comply with his expectations
of the medium, he writes down his findings (too purple) and is
pleased his assessment is fair. The outcome is established, she may
or may not choose to join him in Amsterdam, but if he makes the
changes to his stories as asked, he'll be published long before she
finds anyone to take her work seriously.

O Lachrima Christi.[113]

Reverend Tusker stares at the title of the sermon that's a week
away, but he's all out of crucial thoughts. He misses his dear Meredith and after he's trolled his depths without her, the only solution
he comes up with is another reason to telephone Loretta.

He talks about retiring. "Whenever I tell the Flock that there's
no certainty in this Life, many are displeased," he says. "They think
I mock them with my talk of living without Hope as a reliable
Companion. Why do I even want to continue preaching to these
People?"

"Don't give up," she replies. "The moment will pass and you
will come out of it stronger than before."

---

113   Christ's Holy Tears (Latin).

On he goes. *Sermo datur cunctis, animi Sapienta paucis.*[114] What hasn't he tried? He's presented himself in blacker suits to convince them of his seriousness. He's told himself, there will be misunderstandings while constructing sermons enlivened with entertainment to a degree. But in response they always ask, "How will our Story end?"

"None of us knows the true impact of our labors for the Lord," Loretta responds. "You of all people should know this."

The Reverend talks, talks, and talks until she can no longer stay on the phone.

Alone again, his mind runs amuck with evaluations of him made by his flock over the years. "Your demeanor isn't happy enough." "Your Sermons need more precise Outlines as to how you measure our progress." "More personal Story. Please."

Reverend Tusker is tired of their input. For years, he's worn blacker ties, and given them tools to enable the making of Money. *Beatius est magis dare quam accipere,*[115] he has told them. But, what are the results? They want to throw him out on his ear.

Good Lord!

At bedtime, he lies in the dark unable to ignore the pain in his ankle, near his kidneys, and above his heart. He cannot move beyond fatigue, as once again, he cannot dispel an image of Nehemiah prodded from behind by the bumper of an army cruiser filled with a gaggle of JinJabi[116] teen boys weighed down by baggy uniforms, oversized boots, and wristwatches stolen from the dead.

---

114 Everyone knows how to talk, but not many are wise (Latin).

115 It is better to give than to receive (Latin).

116 Largest ethnic group in Liwani with a population of 340,000. See footnote 19.

They giggle and toy with prey who resembles a petrified rabbit caught by its paw in the teeth of a large, toothy trap.

Nehemiah stumbles, fasterfaster as the teen boys fire one shot after another into the sky. Jammed sharply behind the knee with a bumper, he drops to his haunches. His eyes bulge in confusion, his bones strain the limit of sockets.

Passed down from a generation of fathers to a generation of sons.

There's numbness in Nehemiah's feet that doesn't stop at the ankles as he cracks absolutely and topples forward beside a field of maize. His forehead taps down against the blunt edge of a stone, taptap taptap.

Red earth is stacked against an eye that, despite great effort, he cannot open. A pang jumps him sharp and quick, then numbs the base of his neck.

Deepersleeping, his nose deeperstill in muck.

A slant of light flickers huge and bright. It goes dark.

5

The following morning, Jonah watches Reverend Tusker
walk around in baggy flannel pajamas, and with a tensor bandage wrapped tightly around an ankle that won't heal

"My my, is it eight-thirty already?" The Reverend plucks a canvas
shopping bag from a hook behind the front door, and slings it
over his shoulder. "I've got to get to the recycling Bottles before
it's too late." He wobbles as he makes his way onto the first step,
contemptuous of weakness.

"Shouldn't you take it easy on your leg?" Jonah calls out after
him.

"That, my Boy, is neither here nor there," he replies. "Contrary
to premature speculation, I'm not as yet an Invalid." He sucks in
his belly, doesn't grimace, and creakily picks away at stairs that descend to the street, a bundle of keys jangling on a loop at his belt.

Jonah pursues him to the pathway. "What's the rush?"

"I must remember to check the Odometer when Bingo gets
back from his Errands," the Reverend announces. "One can never
be too certain with the ones one hires from Santori Heights. It's a
Gamble. Old-fashioned though it is, I still believe a Man's sense of
Purpose comes with making an honest Wage."

"Slow down, Rev. You're not doing your ankle any favors."

"Keep up, Son, and don't be such a Nag."

As they walk toward the recycling bins, Jonah listens with
skepticism as Reverend Tusker talks in glowing terms about
Elisha. The boy "has a good Sense of Humor," his marriage with

Dorothea has lasted "well beyond that of many of his Peers," and his business ideas "show real Talent." It's unfortunate that "he lost his Mother at such a difficult point in his Adolescence." Jonah listens, aware that this speech is a sign that the Rev will never admit that Elisha is a world-class fuck-up.

Before the Reverend is done itemizing his son's fictional virtues, they stand on the uneven earth where cinders separate grass from tarmac. Horse flies angle for snacks of flesh. They swarm in circles, they plunge. He slaps the air, missing the hairy, bug-eyed buggers before honing in on Mrs Petra-Freud's recycling bin.

"By the bye, Jonah, Clementine told me what you did." The Reverend thinks of the money given to her aunt.

"Uh-oh!" Jonah thinks he's referring to how absent he's been in her life of late. Especially now with what happened to Leroi. This isn't who he wants to be, an a-hole who makes the people who care about him suffer. "I had hoped to explain myself before you talked to her."

"Faith, Hope, and Charity." He's proud of the boy. "And the greatest of these is Charity."[117]

Ashamed, Jonah gets silent. Throwing St Paul at him is the ultimate diss. Guilt. Suddenly, whatever Jonah thought about Hiroko last night makes little sense in the light of this deserved scolding. There are no decent counter arguments to be made. He can't afford her, not for at least two and a half months, and he's fairly certain this pressure to be financially solvent doesn't bode well for building a relationship with her. Da Stylus likes him with or without his fortune. The Rev likes her. So, Jonah needs to stop

---

117   1 Corinthians 13:13. The entire chapter was recited at Reverend Tusker's wedding, and was a favorite of his wife, Meredith.

being such a hurtful douche bag and fantasizing about what isn't
real. Chasing after Hiroko is like hustling after a mirage on the
road to Hoppa. She'll always be one run of good luck away from
losing interest in him, and as soon as he's no longer useful to her,
she'll avoid the places he regularly goes. What he needs is someone stable. He needs to get the Rev's ring onto Da Stylus's finger
and make a long-term promise to work on "them."

"Gosh. You'd think People would peel the Labels off their
Bottles," Reverend Tusker continues. "All it takes is a quick soak."
He scrutinizes each of Mrs Petra-Freud's bottles before he care-
fully deposits them into his canvas shopping bag.

"Did Clementine … ohhh, someone's coming."

The Reverend straightens up out of the bin. "He-lllooo, Mrs
Petra-Freud."

The Black Republican bustles toward them in a skirt much
too tight for a person whose personal fortune ought to make her
more considerate of the influence she has on other black folk. "I'd
love to stop for a chat Reverend," she says. "But I'm in hurry. The
book club is holding its monthly meeting at Senator _____'s
home tonight, and I'm running late."

"You should hold onto these tin Cans, Rita," Reverend Tusker
replies. "They're Money in the Bank."

"Busy, busy." Mrs Petra-Freud keeps walking. "We'll get together soonish. The wife of the _____ Ambassador will be joining
us to discuss a most important slave narrative." She taps a paperback under her armpit. "I really must skedaddle."

"There's a veritable gold Mine in here, Rita," Reverend Tusker
says as he places tin cans into his shoulder bag. "A veritable gold
Mine."

"I must toot-e-loo," Mrs Petra-Freud says, rushing off to her

Chevy van with a petite black handbag banging against her hip.

Reverend Tusker patrols the street for more bottles. "Just between you, me, and the Lamppost, I don't think the Freuds know what Conservative means." He pats down a mess of protruding hair. "Take her, for instance. For a Mother of advancing Years, she certainly pushes the Limits on what is appropriate Attire. Hardly a Family Value, wouldn't you agree?"

Before Jonah can respond, chunks of hail begin to fall.

I could hear the clump of keys looped to the Rev's belt. Clumpclump. Fuckin clump. The stank of fennel punched me in the nostrils and I fumbled a recycled bottle to the pavement.

Sorry, sorry.[118] ★You sit in the smoke room with a scrum full of miscreants who draw on deep pulls of tobacco, and with each passing moment, your ability to keep it straight among them diminishes.

Lady G. can't stick to a work schedule and she will stay here as long as possible because she doesn't like to sleep in the streets. The Islander will stay because the speed of the language is disorienting on the outside. The Straight Shooter, who studied gender politics at the university, will stay till he understands why he no longer wants to live. From another life, the boyCEO quotes exquisite reasons for war, and bargains over what other nuthousers are willing to exchange for a private fifteen-minute shower with the girlygirl in red fishnets who cannot cross the yellow line. Visiting

---

118   *The Notebooks*, September, 2005.

hours are well into the future, and the Single Ma speaks quicker than speed, lickety split.

"The bitch neighbor dropped a bicycle on my daughter's head," she says. "From the top of the stairwell she did, and just missed too. So I smacked her good, and then the cops came and I told them about the bicycle, now I'm here." Her stories are too large for her petite form. "They won't let me see my kids unless I keep it straight, gotta keep it straight to see my kids again."

The boyCEO's fist clamps into the wall.

"Don't tell me the free market is crass!" he yells. "Not being able to supply a demand is crass." He wants the world to be quiet so he can form his sentences. "Fifteen minutes for fifteen cigarettes isn't crass. That's a minute a cigarette. A deal. A basement price bargain. An unbeatable price. I could get twice as much if I charged according to demand."

The man on the outside of the door opens up, clamps his hand on the boyCEO's shoulder, and banishes him to his boardroom for the day.

Lady G. is in a state. She refuses to believe in consequences. She will get what she wants, and she will behave as she chooses.

When the Single Ma announces, lickety split, that tonight she will be permitted a visit with her children, Lady G. begs her for cigarettes until a flustered Ma breaks off a fist into G.'s belly, ensuring Ma won't see her children for another three days.

For a moment, Lady G. is genuinely happy and to celebrate she sings a spot-on rendition of "Stop in the Name of Love" by The Supremes.

You hobble back to bed and prop up your hurt places with pillows.

On the inside, there is little room to ponder the outside because in fifteen minutes you must be ready for Group.

Group.
We talk medicine.
The Straight Shooter can't get it up anymore. The Islander's tongue cramps around her vowels. We don't know the name of the day. But still we must take yellow pills, even if we cannot seem to wake from their sleep.

At visiting hours. The families come. Upbeat. Tired from carrying the filthy secret of our incarceration. They have assembled teams of support on the outside because their loved ones have taken irritability and deplorable sadness to an extreme. The visitors move among our tribe of the sequestered, and they learn the anomalous ways of our species.

We can't have visitors until the team made up of the specialist, the caregiver, the doc, and the occupational therapist agree that we're stable (even though they can't agree on whether they can sit together in a room after all that has passed between the fat cat Doc and poor Nurse Shelley).

We swallow five scored pills, hide our dizziness and don't know what tense we're in. ★ In the Heights, black folk hustle to or from their daily grind. Some sit on steps, legs stretched out. Others wait at bus stops, or laugh and talk about baby daddas who should feel free to kiss their "en-tire" black asses. Still more are bored, and bored senseless with the company they keep. They yawn in hair weaves and glance around for big shots who, in a moment of grandiosity, will be easy to part from their money.

Enter Jonah Ayot-Kolosha, ring bearer, furtively looking left to
right as he ambles past iron shutters drawn down over store windows, and huge chains looped around door handles.

Men who've fucked up royally in life stand on street corners
and teach others lessons about pitfalls to avoid; others wear dark
suits and lecture passers by as to how to be the right sort of black
woman or man. Go to work, they say. Get an education and
marry, they say. Do not forget where you came from. Do not, they
repeat, do not pass Park Avenue on the way to the Big House.

Circling around it all are cops who search for b-boys who
resemble suspected looters in grainy videos collected from the
Blackout. They are more intent than usual on making examples of
the bad guys since the incident has been mentioned by the Commander-In-Chief at the tail end of a radio address that reaffirmed
the importance of the rule of law (after reframing the current
mission in Iraq as well, it's difficult to decipher).

Exit Jonah Ayot-Kolosha, avoiding any and all eye contact with
a world that is … off-track and futile in ways that don't technically exist.

"Yo, yo," a small group of preteens call out to him. "Wait up, yo."

They wear black bandannas on their heads, and their oversized
jeans hang low enough to showcase logos on the waistbands of
designer undies.

"What up?" Jonah asks.

The fella with one pant leg rolled up to his knee does the talking. "You work the laundry? Yup."

"Yezzir."

"Dat true you from Africa?"

"True dat," Jonah replies.

"Then speak some click language."[119]

"Sorry?"

"Click language, cuz."

"Oh." I cluck at them a few times to get them off my back.

"Wooord," the preteen replies. ★ ★ ★ ★ ★ ★ ★ ★ ★ ★ ★ ★ ★ ★ ★ ★
★ ★
★ ★

★ Da Stylus runs through the parking lot wrapped in a red scarf, a handmade Guatemalan backpack bobbing on her shoulders.

The door is locked.

She kicks the wall, then sinks to the ground with her back against the door and pulls her scarf over her face.

"Alloallo," Jonah interrupts her.

She lowers the bundle of knitted material to eye level.

Jonah launches into a prepped speech. "I'm so, so sorry ..." he begins.

"Don't be," she insists. "You've been sick."

"Yes, yes. But Leroi happened, and this isn't the time to go AWOL."

"No need to apologize. I totally understand."

"You're a saint," he observes.

"A pinhead, more like."

"Huh?"

"It's my turn to set things up for a meeting, and I stupidly forgot my key."

He sits down beside her. "Do you need someone to pick the lock?" She flushes when their shoulders touch. "Not me, of

---

119 WaSimbi is not based on clicks like the Xhosa language of South Africa or the language of the Kalahari Bushmen.

course. I'm against that sort of thing. Unless you want me to set
all that aside for the higher good."

She giggles. "I've missed you a lot."

"A little a lot or a bunch a lot?"

"A bunch a lot."

Overhead, warplanes zip-zip from base to base while conduct-
ing a war without televisual images of atrocities.

"Listen, you want to get a coffee at Ptolemy's? Not like you
need one since obviously I'm not saying you look like you just
woke up. No. More that we, persons in general, could use a hot
beverage now and again. You know, brilliant for the complexion,
that sort of thing. Which isn't to say you need to work on yours,
which is great, by the way. Although not in a racial sense, like I'm
objectifying you as a dark Hottentot Venus."

"Are you okay?"

"Redbone. High Yella. Taupe. You guys are into all that."

"Us guys? African Americans, you mean?"

"Not all of you, but yah. You're a bunch of tribalists. The divi-
sions just aren't what they were two hundred years ago. It's no
longer Ashanti and Yoruba, or House and Field. But East Coast.
Left Coast. White Lite or Ghetto. Taupe ..."

She loops her arm into his. "Taupe isn't one of the colors, dear."
Then she leans her head on his shoulder and stares with him
at members of the Santori tribe—rushing around no place in
particular—to whom those who got out return less and less to
reminisce with.

I finger the ring in my pocket. "Remember how I said my mum
was a good woman," I say, "but my dad constantly cheated on
her?" She nods. "I don't want to be like that."

"Ask. I'll say yes if you ask."

"We're a good match. So … here." I hand her the ring.

"Yes.Yes," she blurts. "I love you."

"Da Stylus …"

"Can I say something?"

"Go 'head."

"Since we're officially engaged," she gushes. "There's no reason why we shouldn't make love."

I'm dumbfounded.

"I prayed about it, and I want this for us." She speed-talks. "Come to Leroi's memorial tonight and if you get the Rev's car, we'll go to the park afterward."

As she speaks, I feel like a calf roped at the rodeo. She's already scheduling me for activities I hadn't allocated time for and I already feel I've lost the right to say no. So, as she makes plans to make her plans happen, all I can think about is a way to gracefully back out.

"A memorial?" I try to get my bearings.

"I'm so happy."

"Slow down, babe. What's this about a memorial?"

"It's for Leroi. I'm gonna broadcast it on the radio show. Hopefully with enough attention, it'll prevent this type of thing from happening again."

I try for a response that'll upset her plans for us. "You think it'll make a difference?"

"Are you joking?"

"No. Not at all." I speak compulsively. "I mean, what's it going to change? Conditions in the Heights are systemic. It's part Machiavellian, dick around the black folk cause they don't respect you otherwise, and part Hobbessian, police the hell out of the

Heights as a way of showing the larger community you're acting
in their common self-interest."[120] She flinches at the edge in my
voice. "Then when a tragedy like Leroi happens, the messiness
that wasn't advertised about the system gets kicked under a rug. A
few junior cops are sent to do desk jobs for a couple of months,
and the illusion is created that something significant was done. In
the meantime, we get to make speeches, go on marches, and ...
nothing changes." I stop, overheated.

Da Stylus battles the weaker parts of herself by reciting 1 Corinthians 13:1. "Though I spake with tongues of men and angels,
and have not charity, I am become as sounding brass, or a tinkling
cymbal." If she's patient, if she's consistent in showing Jonah that
he's loved, if she comes through for him where others have been
a disappointment, there is a wonder-working power in modeling
the one who walks with the Christ.

Finally when she speaks, her voice sounds much more con-
stricted than she meant. "Do you wanna come to the memorial,
or no?"

I recollect sitting alone against a wall in an art gallery crowded
with neo-expressionist graffiti and cartoons with persons of a
colored hue featured as superheroes.

On stage, in front of a huge black-and-white photograph of
Leroi Johnson, Da Stylus thanks everyone for coming.

"Many of us knew Leroi," she says. "He was a son, and a brother, and would one day be a father. But now, alls that's left is the

---

120   An unacknowledged quotation from Professor Iton.

memories we got." She talks of his generosity, the kind words
he had for everyone at work. Then she talks on behalf of mothers in the Heights and about the genocide of the children in the
community—gang violence, AIDS, institutional indifference. She
doesn't want to dwell on it, but she takes a shot at the Commander-in-Chief's War. "How can a fella whose daddy pulled strings
to get out of military service send other people's families to war?"
After the applause subsides, she ties her social commentary back
to a plea for the reunification of the black family under the ban-
ner of our Lord and Savior, "as a way to honor Leroi's legacy."

After a long applause, Da Stylus lightens up. She jokes with the
audience about how we started on colored folks' time. Late. Then
she lets us know of hand creams for the black man and woman
for sale at a table in the back. She also alerts everyone to flyers
by the door for the sisters who opened a new hair salon in the
neighborhood. "We gotta support each other." Finally, she reminds
us to tune in to her radio show on 93.7 FM for updates on the
community fashion show next week.

"Now, I want y'all to put your hands together for our first
poet," she shouts. "Sister Deidre. Wooord."

Loud whoops mix with clapping.

Sister Deidre does a bit about how Leroi made her feel comfortable about being overweight. Then she strips down to a one-
piece leotard and says, "I am not what I ain't, but I am what I is,
Queen of Nubia, daughter of the Sphinx."

The younger folk holler in approval while the old fella beside
me appears confused.

"Queen of Nubia," he snorts. "She ain't nothin but Deidre
Simpson."

Next up, an indigenous woman burns sweet grass and leads a healing ceremony. Her people have been fucked over, like our people. She finishes with a prayer for Leroi.

A short break to fix the microphone is followed by ... pink-sweatered Hiroko Ishigowa, who reads a poem that compares L.J. to square miles of wheat.

I'm nauseous.

An intermission is announced to work out glitches with the sound system.

Some folk go outside for a smoke. Others take the opportunity to flee to bars. Hiroko stands in a group at the refreshment table, styrofoam cup in hand.

Always, she scratches her legs, her watch is of the old style (with hands), and in mid-speech, she rubs balm on her lips.

When she's alone, I push up on her as she bends with a potato chip over a bowl of dip. Her long hair is plaited in a braid that hangs off her left shoulder.

"Good, isn't it?" I comment.

"Did you bring it?"

"Bring what?"

"The dip."

"I meant the slam is good."

"You think?"

Before I can muster a response, Bingo barges in between us.

"Yo, nigga," he says. "Why you talkin to my girl?"

I'm shocked to see him. "Your girl?"

"Ping ping," Bingo says at her.

"Stop it!" Hiroko snaps.

"My rubber band gal."

"Stop!"

Bingo wears a bright yellow suit with huge lapels and a match-ing silk shirt undone to his belly button that reveals a million thick gold necklaces—a look that says I'm up for a good screw, any place, any time.

"Ready to roll?" he asks Hiroko.

His hand is on her ass.

"In a minute," she replies.

"Hurry it up, babe." He winks at me. "I'll be outside."

He leaves.

My head swims with heat: *See, Bingo got this bootay call who wears them nipple clamps while I fuck her. She takes 'em rubber bands, puts 'em on my Johnson, and ping. It get so, if she even look at me, I get a hard-on.*

"Bingo!" I'm doing a terrible job of sounding unaffected. "Bingo!"

"You split, honey."

"That was a mistake."

"You got that right."

"Let me make this better," I beg.

"I can't believe you split on me."

"Name it. A trip to the Poconos? Jools?"

"You think I can be bought?"

"No. Maybe. I don't know." I'm lost. "Hirosita, I'm sorry. Nix Bingo, and let me make it up to you. Please."

She dips a chip, then nibbles on it.

"You'll spring for a haircut?" she asks.

"Sure, Cakes. Whatever you want."

"I'll call you."

She hotfoots it after Bingo.

Without a moment's hesitation, I find Da Stylus and backpedal; feel my forehead, love. You don't feel that? I'm burning up. No, I'll stay. No, no, this is a big night for you. You think I should go? Really? It's not too far for me to walk home and you still have MC'ing to do. What say I call after I've had some sleep? Oh, honey. I'm disappointed too. But this way we can make our first time special. Dinner with candles. A movie. Nothing too scary, unless you're willing to hold my hand. Ha ha. We'll get a room in a hotel, and jump in the whirlpool afterward, or before. Whichever. Darn, I reaaally looked forward to spending time with you tonight. God speed. Mwuah mwuah.

The Rev is slouched over a hardback in the kitchen, fixating on the words in front of him. I help myself to a bowl of choco cereal, sit down opposite him hell-bent on finally confronting him about the power of attorney hogwash. I start slow by pointing at the ratty book sleeve of the book he's reading, St Anselm of Canterbury's *Proslogion.* "Obviously, you realize that he got it wrong." The Rev licks fingers and turns a page. "Following his twisted logic, I could go around claiming the ideal woman I can't conceive exists because I can't conceive her."

The Rev perks up. "You've read Anselm?"

"Sure. Why not?"

"Then you should know his point is that God's a Being who transcends Thought, a necessary Being. He's not talking about contingent Ones like the Ideal Woman you use as an example."

I'm still upset about Bingo and Hiroko, so I'm more contrary

than warranted. "That-which-a-greater-cannot-be-thought to exist in the mind isn't a necessary Being just cause it isn't dependent
on our minds to exist," I say. "That's a … tautology, if you will.
As far as I'm concerned, the Almighty *is* an edgy sense of what's
funny. Scumbags bank big dollars and do to others as they please.
Goody-goodies are mild with their meekness and inevitably finish
in the arrears. So, beyond good and evil, the Deity is full of jokes,
ironical yuk-yuks, gut-busting rip roars."

He dogears the corner of a page and puts the *Proslogion* onto
the table. "I'm curious, Son. Did your Grandfather ever talk to
you about Concerns with his Work?"

"I don't follow."

"He had his Doubts, you know. He wasn't certain he'd made
the right Decision to build a Life around teaching Nonviolence."
I still don't follow. "I'd remind him he hadn't committed to the
Vision because it felt Good, but because it was Right." He wells
up with tears, and takes a couple of minutes to compose himself.
"Good Heavens, look at me. Despite all my Talk, the Reason I'm
sitting here is because I'm terrified my Legs will give out if I try
walking up the Stairs. Funny, isn't it? An ironical Yuk-Yuk, even.
A Man of Faith searching for Answers in a worn-out Copy of
Anselm because the simplest of Things are suddenly out of his
Control, *and* because I can't get past a Sense of Meredith's disap-
proval over how I failed Elisha."

He gives over to loud, heaving sobs.

Overwhelmed, I give his arm a pat down.

∞

on another night that won't sleep, i sit at the computer, unable to explain a universe much larger than i'm able to tame with my imaginings.

i think of hiroko ishigowa with her ass-length tress of hair pinging elastics on bingo's johnson.[121]

---

121   *The Notebooks*, November 19, 2003.

6

Urgent

My darling, It is some problems I meet to come for you in
America. I come to Moscow for to get my ticket. But crime
is big and I have been stolen of my money. I want to come to
you. But please if we must be together you will please to send
to me $600.00. Pay to Western Union this money for us to be
married and to make family. I'm impatient for you my love,
Yuliya
xoxoxox

Yuliya,
I was warned by my friends about this. How disappointing. I
thought you were serious, but now I see you're only interested
in my money. Now I must cancel the horse carriage ride, and
the tickets to see Wynton Marsalis at Carnegie Hall. How
could you do this to us? I'm not a spook or a Hollywood
ectoplasm. I'm a man of substance, of flesh and bone, fiber and
liquids.
    Please excuse the sharp prose, I'm very upset right now.
Regards,
Ralph[122]

"Where is it?" the Rev towers over my desk.
    "*Guten morgen.*"

---

122   See footnote 77.

"Whenever you tidy up, I can't find my way out of the Mess you create of my Things."

"Now what?"

"My Shampoo? Where's my Shampoo?"

I have a nice cocktail of booze and meds sloshing about in my system. "I'll look for it later," I let him know. "I'm busy checking email."

The Rev comes at me with a got-to-start-something frown in fine got-to-rumble form. "These Things don't up and walk away."

"Give me like half an hour." Submerged in a porridge of hot thistles, anger rises in my gullet and gobbles beneath my clavicles. "After that, I'll schlep around looking for as long as it takes."

"Schlep around!" Oh, baby! "Schlep around!" Sense data clacks into place. "Don't touch my Things."

I stand up, mistakenly bump into his shoulder, and knock him for a spill.

Sha-bang, sha-bang.

"Oh, God. I'm sorry." I extend a hand. "So sorry."

"I can manage," he growls.

The Rev's hand balances on the dresser as he hoists himself, slow as sloth, to his knees, his breath coming in piffles. Then he oh, ohs his way to his feet, dignified but still oh, oh. Nerves in his body quibble with their transmitters, and he collapses back onto the floor.

When I try to lift him off the hard wood, he pushes me away.

"Leave me alone!"

My brain jerks and jounces as his hands curl around the leg of the dresser. His entire body quivers and he tries to lift himself off the floor once again. Frustrated, he pounds his weakened legs.

I can't watch.

"Come on, Rev." I lift him by his underarms.

"Hey! Hey! Take it easy!"

When I prop his hip against mine, I can feel the delicate lightness of his bones.

I gently help him collapse onto a bed covered in documents. When I start to arrange them in a neat pile, he snatches at my hand. "Leave those alone," he orders. "Those are *my* Papers," he says. "Not yours. *Mine.*"

"What's the big deal?"

"Get out," he says.

I leave him staring red-eyed at the realization that he's no longer fully human.

Unable to get the image of the Rev thumping on his legs out my head, I call Q-Deezy.

Eliza May answers, which must mean they've made up. "He stepped out to get rolling papers. But he'll be back in a moment." She waits a beat. "Listen, can I ask you something in the strictest confidence?"

"Shoot."

"Do you think I should go with Q. to Amsterdam?"

"How would I know?"

"I mean, on the one hand it would be just what I need for my writing, but I only want to go if I'm into being with him."

She stops, hesitant to go on.

"There's more, right?" I say.

"Did you know he made all the changes to the stories his editor wanted him to?"

"So."

"I can't respect that."

"What is this really about, Liza?"

She hesitates again. "Traveling with a white guy through Europe is a lot complicated."

"You're not serious."

"We might as well take a trip to the Deep South."

"But he's not white."

"Having a great-great grandmother who was one fifty-seventh black doesn't ... hold on a sec. I think ..."

I hear a muffled bang, and Eliza May giggles before Quint C. gets on the line. "We can't talk, right now. We're going to drop Ecstasy and listen to the ..."

"... *White Album*," Eliza May yells in the background.

"Her idea," Quint C. says.

"Not true," she shouts.

"Oh, and don't forget, next week you're speaking to my writing class," he continues.

I retire to my room and sit on my bed with curtains drawn.

Hard as it is to admit, the inheritance is the reason I haven't been writing of late. It's given me a perspective, a new point of view that is clamped tightly to my ventricles. Now, what I seem most aware of is a writing scene deficient in good manners. Anything goes in the name of "just business." Eliza May as good as said she's using Q. to get a leg up with Rachel Dalgleish, supra agent. He can holler at persons on the other end of telephone lines as long as the topic of disagreement is in the interest of what's best for his book sales. Fish Coleman, with all his units sold, and Professor Iton, with all his awards, batter each other with their ideas about who is more deserving of being awarded toys. I'm too busy working on my career to make the time to get to the bottom of what ails the Rev. At the end of the day, it's all "just business," the emotional need not apply.

∞

I slink over to the Rev's bedroom at lunch time with an olive branch·in hand. But he's no longer there. I make a beeline to the kitchen, calling out his name.

No response.

I open the refrigerator.

!!!!!

There's a bottle of herbal shampoo beside a container of leftover gravy.

Count down from ten.

Try not to think.

I spot the Rev's big-ass loop of keys on the table.

12:50 p.m.

If I'm quick, I should be able to get into his desk drawer. No worries. It's just business.

I peer out the windows onto the street for signs of his car, then make for the stairs.

The rest of my trip to the dark side is of tippy toes and startled crouches whenever the wind suddenly whips against the windows of Colby Manor. So far so good as I skillfully maneuver onto bended knees before unlocking the drawer.

I slide the key into the lock.

Open sesame.

Therein lies a treasure trove of papers simply labeled, "Obit by

Reverend James Lewisham Tusker."[123]

Good God!

I'm shaken by the documented trail of gibberish. Part of it is work on a comprehensive theory of everything. There are mathematical equations partially calculated then abandoned, words are defined to their etymological cousins six times removed, Anselm is paraphrased with inverted re-formulations of That-which-a-greater-cannot-be-thought, Egyptian hieroglyphys are traced in a variety of blue crayon around pasted copies of thick-lipped cartoons of Sambo's in the *New York Times* from 1880-1928. Tiny, slanted scrawl documents arguments both for and against Booker T. Washington's view of the races being as segregated in the way fingers are separate on the hand. To be fair, there are stretches in the past weeks where clarity peeps through. He's considering the most effective way to off himself. Carbon monoxide takes a while, but it isn't painful. Sleeping pills may cause stomach cramps. Hanging is violent, but quick. And why not? There isn't a part of his body that doesn't ache. At the end of his career he's being defined by a scandal he did nothing to create. All of this taking place as a lifetime of savings has dwindled down to nil (budgetary projections are intercalated with times and dates). Improvements in the basement have been costly. Receipts show an overpriced electrician fucked up the wiring, and Bingo is the last of three contractors whose work had to be re-done.

I startle when the telephone rings, and reflexively pick up.

"Tusker's residence, Jonah speaking."

"It's Rita here."

Ah, the Black Republican.

---

123   From the private collection of Reverend James Lewisham Tusker.

"Hi, Mrs Petra-Freud."

"I'm glad I caught you," she says. "I haven't had much luck for several days."

"I didn't get a message."

"I didn't leave one."

"No message?"

She talks fast. "I have a new painting for you to see."

"Wow. That's prolific."

"The old gal still has kick in her yet."

"Did you say old?" I reply. "A gal, yes, but certainly not old."

"You're sweet." She pauses. "Listen, I have some time this evening. We can celebrate over dinner after you've taken a look at the painting. Do you like French? There's a terrific menu at La Fleure's, with a good selection of wines."

"I'd love to, but …"

"Alistair gets back tomorrow. It has to be tonight."

"It's just …"

"A girlfriend?"

"No, a friend."

"Jonah, immature girls are always making unpleasant demands. To hell with her. Tell her you're busy. Come by at seven." She laughs high, and in the nasals. "And promise to make certain I don't get too drunk."

"I promise to make certain you *do* get drunk."

She giggles. "Toot-a-loo, then."

I hang up, suddenly nervous.

Focus!

The front door slaps against a wall. "Anyone home?"

It's the Rev.

I push the pages back into the drawer, take a dive into his closet, and curl into a ball.

I can hear the Rev and his alarmingly disappointing son talk in the living room.

"You took Vows in front of Witnesses," the Rev says. "Till Death do us part."

"I know what I said, Pop," Elisha replies. "But all her badgering isn't what I signed up for."

"She has a Right to want to move to New York. Her Family is there, and you'll find more opportunities for Work than in Curranvale City."

"Pop, lets just stick to my business proposal," Elisha says. "All we need is your signature as a co-signer to get the financing."

"Have you seen my Keys?"

"Dad!"

"I'm sure I left them on the kitchen Table."

The Rev gingerly makes his way upstairs, enters the office, and starts searching through piles on his desk.

"Where are they?"

He walks toward the closet and reaches for the handle.

The telephone rings.

"Not again." The Rev backtracks. "Hello, I know it's you, Mrs Petra-Freud. You should be ashamed. A married Woman prancing around in hot Pants and chasing after a young Boy."

Irritated, he hangs up, forgets why he came into his office, and goes back downstairs to his disappointing son.

∞

Elisha wipes sweat from his hairy upper lip with a shirt sleeve while his father lectures him: "Waves create an optical Illusion of lateral Movement in the Ocean because, in actuality, water Particles rotate in three-dimensional Spirals." Frankly, his old man seems to be becoming more and more like the oddball who stands in the middle of rush-hour traffic spouting apocalyptic. "How is this applicable to our Conversation about having Children? Before I met your Mother, I envisaged a scrawny Girl in a yellow Dress. I fasted in my Apartment and meditated on how our Relationship would not easily be forgotten. The following Day I saw her in an Elevator, dressed as I'd imagined. In the rush of Conversation between us, private Understandings made collective Sense, and explained how it's possible to generate wave Patterns that enable the Mind to influence Outcomes." Elisha isn't interested in the old fella's abstract nostalgia about Meredith. None of it resembles what actually happened. What he remembers are the arguments, and his only escape from it all was at the piano. Then after his mum died, he's been plodding along, waiting for the unexpected to occur in his own marriage to Dorothea, a squeaky, frail woman with a weakness for jeans that are much too tight for her and blond wigs that she's much too old to pull off wearing. At first, she suited him. However, with time, he grew uncomfortable with the independent spirit her tight pants and wigs symbolized. Take six months ago, when she went behind his back and called one of his potential investors with her concerns about the wisdom of throwing cash at research and development in corn as an oil substitute. And so Elisha was forced to forge his father's signature and borrow the cash from the church. He planned to pay it back, but Dorothea couldn't keep her mouth shut, and Mrs Torvil was quick to spread the news. Her disloyalty made him think about how more often than not Dorothea stays home taping afternoon chat shows. She chews gum with her mouth open, and as such is much too *gauche* for what he envisions for himself. He wishes for a fresh start and a life in which he isn't constantly

thwarted by his wife in his designs to be a millionaire by the time
he's fifty. "… Don't be such a Negative Nelly, Son …" Elisha's
losing Clem to Jonah, the *poseur,* the A-1 clown. "Are you paying Attention, Son? Son! Good, I thought I lost you for a Minute
there …" The affordable corn-based fuel enthusiast is dreaming of
venturing with Clem among tourist traps. Waterfalls. Then, over
meals with side dishes of baba ganouj, listening to her hickory-
smoked voice until the day arrives when the money is enough so
they can marry. "… Meredith's Mother, a jazz Singer, went into
Labor while performing at a Concert featuring Clifford Jones and
his Orchestra. The Band was in the Midst of "Lollipop Trot"[124]
when her Contractions began. Among the Musicians performing that Evening were Jimmy Shore, Vocals, Clifford Jones, Piano,
Clayton Himes, Trumpet, Troll Dawkins, tenor Saxophone, and
Jo Jo Smith, Drums …" As the old man speaks, Elisha says diddly
squat. He's bored, and his only respite is the hope that Clem will
make one of her scheduled visits to Colby Manor. If so, he'll take
the opportunity to enjoy how she doesn't wear a bra, speculate
about her in ways that he never does with Dorothea, and envision
his darling with ice cubes as well as battery-operated gadgets he'll
employ to service both her vulva and clitoris. "… I bought her
red Roses, led her to a black Motorcar, and drove her to a Home
with a plum Tree. When I received a job Offer to preach at St
Peter's Episcopalian, we took up Residence in Housing provided
by the Church …"

---

124   Recorded live at Hooligans in New York in 1963. It was Troll Dawkins'
final concert before his unfortunate death by drowning while snorkeling in the
Indian Ocean on Christmas Day that year.

"Send me one idea a day," the boyCEO shouts to usher in the morning. "Don't backpedal. Figure out what will sell. Bumper stickers. Mugs. We need a slogan to bring back Nurse Shelley. One that's punchy. Memorable. Catchy."

In the kitchen, you clean a sugar bowl and scour mold from the kettle to do your bit for the common good. It's difficult to stand for long, so you sit at a table with the Straight Shooter and eat a bowl of snap, crackle, and pop.

The Straight Shooter cannot easily get his spoon of cereal to make the trip from bowl to mouth. He's lost control of his motor skills; the spoon travels in a shaky wave pattern and strikes his cheek before his other hand helps to guide remnants of cereal into his mouth.

Troubled, you pace the hallway with a cane and won't acknowledge the involuntary twitching in your own neck or the desire to have a drink.

7:30.

The clock says it's too early to go back to bed, and you don't know if it's chilly outside (like last Tuesday). You don't see what on your list of commitments can keep you from going under. If you read a book (the caseworker recommends biographies) there will still be more to read. You can write (it has been what habit recommends), but doing so for moments of public adulation seems like vanity and "chasing after the wind."

Inside this echo chamber, there's a nothingsilence that says everything and nothing. You are left only with the nonsensical part of you that converses with the other nonsensical part that wants to make you whole.

∽

Tree boughs bend in stiff breeze, and the sidewalk bristles with melting salt as I walk away from Ma Petra-Freud's with more man-whore money in my pocket.

Everywhere I see entropy. In the house across the street, time is running out on Mr Cuttlewot, the artist who wants nothing but to paint abstracts and leave his wife. But one day she will leave him while he walks with their cats among his canvases and on his return from a collage, he will find his home ransacked of all she's given him. Over near the playground, Mr Cuttlewot takes a break from his unconventional passions to argue his anti-views with the man who makes paper napkins in a factory and lives for the day he'll retire (his home is full of enough canning to see him through at least two acts of God). Mr Hardison pretends to ignore them as he plows his driveway with a snow blower. He thinks of his satellite dish on which he will watch the Playboy Channel, and then he will fantasize about his virtual mistress who emails that she's getting a book of shots together for a top modeling agency. The man who wishes to retire defends a Commander-In-Chief he did not vote for because of an even stronger dislike of the cat-happy Cuttlewot. Over by a stop sign, nobody plays with a boy whose best friend is his bicycle helmet. A little girl jumps off her front step and hates the boy with the bicycle helmet, and her friends are Belinda, Caroline, and Francis as a grey cat hunts birds it will drag to the front door where the girl who hates the boy with the bicycle helmet will cry and bury the bird in her snowy garden while a warplane pilot cruises overhead without a clear idea of what it is he has been asked to die for.

I think the world must shutupshutupshutup.

7

Due dates: my workshop in eight, Bingo's money in six, sex
with Da Stylus and the Rev's sermon in three, and Eliza
May's workshop in one

Juiced on meds, I return to my strategic location behind the large
fern in Vickers Hall and wait for Hirosita *über* babe to show up at
her Contemporary Women's Art class. Today, all reading material
stays in my briefcase as I'm not interested in trying to crack the
code in Eliza May's story.

I fixate on the classroom door.

Campus lists with students overwhelmed with bags filled with
library books and the pressure of student loans that won't be paid
until 2050.

Eventually, Hiroko appears.

I'm uncharacteristically macho and push between her and the
door.

"Good of you to make it," I say.

I sound testier than I did during this afternoon's dress rehearsal
in front of my bedroom mirror.

"Can we do this later?" She reaches around me for the door-
knob. "I'm finally on time for class."

I move aside to let her pass before barging in after her.

"You said you'd call," I say accusingly. "You promised to get
back to me."

"Can we talk about this later?"

I get Rev-Tusker-loud. "I've been waiting to hear from you."

Four rows of Contemporary Women's Art women reach into their bags for pepper spray.

"Can you act anymore like a psychopath?" Hiroko counters.

"Why didn't you call?"

"I did call." We stand in front of the blackboard. "But that hypocrite of a Reverend started screaming at me about chasing young boys in hot pants."

"Mother fuckingfuck." I probably shouldn't say motherfuck in front of this crowd. "He's always spouting crazy drivel like that on the phone. Okay, it always is a bit strong. Whatever. Okay, what's my point? Can we forget the last five rather embarrassing minutes and try this conversation again?"

"After your freakout, I'm not sure."

"Sorrysorry. The Rev's been—" I'm rushing in case her professor walks in. "—While looking though his drawers, I found a suicide note he's been writing. That's the reason he's been acting more deranged of late. Yah, so yakity yak yak, and I just really want another shot at setting things right with you. No, not shot. That's a bit on the violent side. More like … an opportunity."

"He's trying to kill himself?"

"Long story," I reply. "Meet with me, and I'll fill you in."

She glances over at her sisters in the front row. Then, "How's eight tonight?"

"At Ptolemy's?"

"Yah."

"Is Bingo gonna be there?"

She giggles. "Of course not, freak. I'm done with him."

8

The thoroughness of my preparation for an evening of adult entertainments isn't to be imitated by the faint of heart

I skip my classes and lock myself in my bedroom to do a cramp-inducing regimen of sit-ups (I read in a gossip rag that *Switcher's* Rafe Curtis preps for his love scenes with Tamala Exeter in this way). Unfortunately, my effort doesn't result in the much-anticipated six-pack—although there are subtle hints of a potential two-pack.

Afterward, I soak in the tub with sprigs of lavender from the Rev's garden. For one and a half hours, the scent yummily suffuses my pores.

I groom in the tub: shave my face, pluck nose hair, and clip fingernails as well as toenails. Then I douse myself in my go-to cologne, pheromone-laced AquaZar, top choice of one Mr Rafe Curtis.

In the bedroom, shining with aloe vera body lotion, I slide on sexy crimson boxers. Four outfits later, I settle on a baggy beige blazer and forest-green chords, Dad's thin red tie, ankle-high leather boots, and a black woolen cap.

I look … delish, a Thor-like God of straight-up fucking, if the truth must be told.

Good to go, I feed the Rev my alibi, a faux reading event that will have me back home by my eleven o'clock curfew. I call Da Stylus to make another excuse to delay our next get-together, only to end up cornered into firming up plans for a sex date in her friend's apartment after the Rev's farewell sermon. Then I spend the rest of the day given over to popping pills for the right level of buzz.

Superbe.

On the way out, Bingo waves me down despite also blabbing on a cell. "Tell the shorties Dadda misses his little girls," he says. "Yah. I love you too, shuga." He makes kiss noises into the receiver. Kiss. Kiss. Then he hangs up and leads me outside by an elbow.

I'm quick to cover my ass about the loan. "I've still got six days, big pimpin."

"I ain't sweatin it," he replies.

"Honest to God. I'll have it by then."

"Easy, chief," he says. "Alls I wanna know is if the rumor has it right that you seein your fiancée from the radio tonight."

"Huh?"

"Da Da Stylus on Da Da Wireless." I don't get a chance to reply. "A brutha needs to be with a sista, for real. Like me and the wifey, kn'a mean. That's somethin special right there."

I nod to avoid disappointing him.

He hands me a balled-up white sock. "Here."

"I'm cool." I point to my feet. "See, two socks."

He takes a deep breath. "No, stuff it in your pants." I'm not following. "A pimp's gotta have a bangin package."

A bangin package ... oh, "No, no," I object. "I'm not padding my crotch." He looks insulted. Shit. "Okay, okay," I say, and stuff the sock in my pants as he steps back to make sure I got it well placed.

Bingo smiles. "Good. Now get out there 'n' show the sista you got game."

∞

I get to campus at seven, one hour early.

Unfortunately, I must have pushed too high with the meds because my hands give over to uncontrollable shakes, and I feel a tickle of cobwebs straddled athwart my brain matter. Va-voom; I spend a good chunk of time in the rest room with my head under a faucet of cold running water.

As soon as I'm sufficiently steady, I hide out in the library reading an article in *Writer's Digest* on what agents of the finer writers are looking for—a manuscript written for a target audience, the addition of a sentimental hook. In other words, nothing I currently possess.

By eight o'clock, I managed to down three gin-and-juices as I sit in Ptolemy's, far from speakers that blare hippity hop from the Dirty Dirty.

I haven't eaten in two days, and the drinks do nothing to quell rumbling in my stomach.

Hiroko's late.

What the hell does she take me for? I'm not some random guy she can just blow off like some random guy. In my village, I was known as *d'naganaa isse vahtu na nqcluck*, he who has stared in the eye of the python during the time of No-Time, then spat between its teeth. (There's no English equivalent for *d'naganna* as the WaSimbi have seventeen words for the concept of time, but *nqcluck* is similar to the word stare—even though we don't have a word for to stare *per se*. To be held in the gaze is the closest in meaning.)

Half an hour after the appointed time she shows up in a fetching yellow chemise. Her long hair is tucked into a matching silk kerchief and she wears tall black fuck boots.

Hot diggity damn.

I'm tipsy and I've lost all feeling around my nose as she sits, pointing to a glass of brew.

"Is that for me?" she asks.

I nod.

"Score." She takes a swig.

"About my freakout earlier ..."

"Never mind. We've moved on, yah."

"You sure?"

"Uh-huh. You?"

I'm a twit, and alcohol mixed with my meds is like truth serum. What comes out is more like vomit than a coherent breakdown. I give a wordy assessment of feelings that are wild. I want to know her, not control her. I'll do whatever she needs me to do. Although, I can't stand that I feel this way. After all, a man still has to function. Ha ha. "The Rev? Yes, my big fear is his sermon will be his last hurrah. His work is the only thing that's keeping him alive. Yup. Take evening last, I was looking for tacks to put up a poster of Picasso's *Don Quixote*. The stick figurish one that's like Giacometti's stick-like existential sculptures. 1926? '36? Sorry, I'm getting off track. Where was I? Tacks. I was looking for tacks in a cupboard under the kitchen sink when I found a box of rat poison. We don't even have rats, never have. So I ask him about it, and he fudges. He says it's for his friend, Loretta Tucci. They've known each other for donkey's ages. Since '72? '74? Something like that. Anyway, nice woman. Great smile. Big laugh."

"Jonah!"

"Right. So I look at him like, say what? And he's getting into a whole deal about how he was over at her place, eating pasta marinara, when a rat walked onto the kitchen countertop where she prepares her food. Rat city, and Loretta doesn't even blink cause she's into animal rights and doesn't believe in harming rodents. But he flips, and can't finish his meal. Fast-forward to later that night, he goes to Home Depot and buys rat poison to put in her cupboards once he's made her see reason. I'm listening to him, and the thing is I don't know what to believe because I saw the note."

She reaches over our drinks and squeezes my quaking hands, her face crinkling with affection.

In order to snap me out of it, she orders another round of brews before suggesting we try the dartboard.

Jim and Jan, a couple of Barbie and Ken-like brunettes who look more like siblings than lovers, are about to play a game. They ask if we want to join them.

Booyah!

Hiroko gets competitive, challenges them to a battle of the titans, and ups the stakes by throwing down twenty-five bucks. Fueled by my cocktail of numbing, self-administered medicinals, I up the ante to fifty.

Jim and Jan put their perversely alike features together for a consult.

"Okay," they agree.

Hiroko and I proceed with a severe drubbing, throwing darts that miss the board by a country mile while the sibling-alikes clean up with one triple-twenty after another. As the obscenely similar lovers whup us, I note how different Hiroko and I are from people who work together like well-matched accessories. In short, these differences add up to what's happening to us at the dart board. Together, we're losers, and we post the lowest scores in Ptolemy's dart history.

Well and truly humiliated, we return to our table for more focused drinking.

Troubled by concerns about whether we're cosmically fucked, I ply Hiroko with questions geared to unlocking the mystery of who she is, her reddish-orange contacts locking with my eyes in a gaze that's difficult to read.

"I was brought up on a pineapple plantation on Oahu, yah."

"You don't look …"

"What?"

" … plantationish." I try again. "I mean, I can't imagine you walking around with machetes underarm as you quote *The Communist Manifesto*."

She punches my shoulder.

Her parents moved to the Mainland when she was ten. They lived in Oldeham Proper until her dad gambled away their loot. Then they moved to the Heights where the folks got jobs at a supermarket; her mum as a cashier, her dad as a grocery bagger. She tries to visit once a week because she loves Ingrid, who has a bizarre ability to focus her attention for inhumanly long time-spans.

What else?

I ask her about her fiancé, Ito.

"His parents were close to mine on the Island, and we've been together on and off since I moved here. He lived with us through high school, so he's like another member of the family." She runs a finger along the rim of an ashtray. "But he hates the Mainland."

I slurp the dregs of my warm beer. "Does that mean you're eventually moving back to Hawaii with him?"

"Fuck, no. No. The Island is where he's most at home, but can we talk about something else, yah?"

I decide to clearly mark the differences between me and soldier
boy by diving into a risky but calculated tirade about the War. The
usual. The Commander-In-Chief is a moron, and anyone who
thinks he's a genius is also a moron, and anyone who thinks I'm a
moron for thinking they are morons are both dicks and morons.
"I can't understand why Ito would put his life on the line for
reasons that change according to what advertisers think will sell to
the public," I say.

"Ito's from a military family," she says. "It isn't a choice for him."

She looks hazy through the booze and the numbness in my
face, the effect of my government-sanctioned happy pills.

"Jonah." She places a hand on my arm. "I've been meaning to
ask, are you taking penis enlargement supplements?"

??????

Oh, no. No. "No, no." (Bingo's sock is still in my crotch.) ★ ★ ★
★ Once
again, it's colder than the day before, and, unencumbered by the
run of the mill, Hiroko and I lounge on her couch. Next to me,
she puckers her lips against my bare stomach and nibbles.

We watch a rerun of the pilot episode of *Switcher* on the telly,
the one that has Tamala and Rafe as corporate types attracted
to one another despite the fact that she's a cougar, ten years his
senior, and he's ruthlessly ambitious. There are predictable misunderstandings—at first, her friends think he's her young intern;
his friends think she's his older aunty. Then her friends think he's
with her to social climb, and his friends think she's robbing him
of his youth. Hilarity ensues. The bedroom scene is played as a
farce for laughs, beginning with a crane shot that zooms into the
window and stops for a closeup of a freckle above the cougar's lip.
Niiice. Then, at the point where the orgasm is had, there's a cut-

away with documentary footage of missiles firing and an explosion of fireworks. Near the episode's end, they each make a speech at a company dinner about how age is nothing but a number. The men in attendance are all smiles and the women weep. Credits.

"That was mindless," Hiroko says.

"Just what I needed."

We snuggle, making the occasional endearing remark.

Me: "The way the nape of your neck meets your collarbone is like a valley bordered by a tease of subtle hills."

Hiroko: "Hills are bumpy. Lumpy."

Me: "Not these ones, these are like rumpled silk."

Hiroko: "Rumpled?"

At the moment before the world decides it's time for adults to sleep, eleven or so, Hirosita plies herself with face creams, flosses, and brushes her tongue. Then she curls up beside me in bed.

"Tired?" I ask.

"Getting there," she replies.

I cradle her head in my hands and stare at the cushy roundness of her cheeks.

"Do you mind if we don't mess around tonight?" she asks.

"No. Nope." I'm disappointed. "It's been a long day."

"Good," she murmurs. "I like that there's no pressure between us to jump into the sack."

"Me too."

"Sometimes with guys it's like, you do one thing and there's this expectation you'll do it all the time."

"Totally."

"It isn't sex that makes me feel closer, y'know." She twirls a finger in a strand of hair. "In fact, sex makes me feel numb most of the time, like I'm squeezing out pleasure that I could just as easily do alone, to myself."

"Right."

"Not with you, though. We can play darts. For God's sake, we connect in other ways." She smiles, closing her eyes. "You're a saint."

I don't get it. I don't.

... her tiny fingers tug fast, and slow, whatever she wants, and i reel and whirl and toss and i am hers, and her, my busy hummingbird, my wet, freaking, fucking angel. guttural she is as she takes me in the buttery light of the moon and the freaking, fucking headlights of cars that flare and go out as we fuck, slow, steady, hard as we just plain fuck, my dick in her pussy ...

I'm losing my grasp on what's real between us. How much of *that* experience had anything to do with *this* person who doesn't feel anything? How much of *that* night was shape-shifting surfaces and *not* a submersion at depths?

Beside me, this stranger who thinks I'm a saint sighs in her sleep. Abandoned in the land of awake people, insomniacs, I wait for fatigue. First, the left side of my body is against the wall. Then I stuff a pillow between crooked knees and relax my shoulders. Minutes later, I'm on my back, staring at the ceiling. Boisterous and despairing, the sleeping stranger who thinks I'm a saint mutters an indecipherable litany of complaints.

She then sits up and pays a visit to the toilet she will not remember in the morning. Her hair is willy-nilly as she clambers back between the sheets.

She returns to snoring.

Nothing dispels the fret that accompanies the moment after it's odd not to be asleep. Lack of sleep is in my temples, it's in the arches of my feet. The night realigns around pop songs that say how compromised my life has become. What exactly is real about my presence with this person, with an alias, in a foreign room?

The less rest I get, the less writing I'll be able to manage in the morning.

I'm a retracting person, sliding backwards into dullness.

Her eyes open, take me in, and then close.

Child soldiers do not repair in dreams, I think. They don't know this relief.

BOOK V

Analepsis Revisited

I

1931

When The Self-Not-Self knew the un-time, the eye of the greater light doused the tilapia-filled waters in the east. The looming bright ascended to its height, bearing the flint-bladed assegai, while the lesser light waited in the boma trees for the appointed hour when she guarded the dark.

In front of the high priest's kraal among the smaller sub-clans, the Knowledge Holders drink stale beer through straws and talk the talk that makes elders shake their heads.

"Not even the roots of the boma tree will cure us of this latest disease," says the one whose father died, leaving his mother pregnant. "The Idol Worshippers have begun to settle in the east. Now sickness has spread to the homesteads beside the ancestral river."

"Mark the signs," replies the one whose mother experienced considerable bleeding while carrying him in her womb. "The lioness cannot trust the lion when it lies down among the cubs."

While the greater light walks the early sky, Akoth, the daughter of the bull, balances an ochre jug on her head before setting out from her father's kraal. She passes through an opening in the fence of thorn bushes and presses out along the dusty path that leads into the banana trees. Copper bells at her ankles trick the air with music. As she passes beneath the many-fingered leaves, she doesn't notice Ayot, the storyteller, who dreams the tale of his people hidden in the cool of the shade. On seeing the daughter of the bull, he forgets himself as her tinklebells tickle stiffness out of the northeasterly breeze.

As the greater light walks the sky, Ayot watches her giraffe-tail necklace swing from her neck smeared with the sticky juice of the gum trees, her bosoms jiggle with the promise of milk, and her bead skirt gets tangled in a current that delights her hips while she dunks her clay jug beneath the river's brown skin.

Bewitched, Ayot does not return to his kraal to eat his black porridge as is the custom. Instead, he desires to claim her as his bride.

Ayot enters his hut, moistens his skin with sim sim oil, and dons the colobus monkey hide. After consulting with the cowrie shells, he hunts in the yellow plains for the climber plant, searching among purple catacombs and red anthills. He wanders plains cracked by the great bright until his mouth is dry as the brush before the rains.

The bells remember him, the day becomes night, and he walks the outer curve of the thorn bush where the egret laid with the un-time.

Carrying the climber plant, Ayot approaches the riverbank where the one with a tattoo around her belly button rests among clothes that dry on rocks. He rubs his palms together and an oval eye rises from his groin, passes through the center of her forehead, and levitates above her head.

In awe, Akoth stares into the pupil of fire and is charmed by its spell. She forgets the hour to grind the millet, and her memory is trapped in a gourd.

Before the greater bright steals away to meet the twilight, Akoth gives Ayot a copper bangle from her upper arm and shows Ayot the way to her father's kraal.

A dowry of ten calves and eight goats is offered, and their marriage is followed by a period of great affluence for the clan. People from places as far as the distant waterfalls seek out the couple for counsel, and after the month in which the fish are plenty, Akoth announces her pregnancy. Light passes into the void, the void passes into the light. The dry season follows the rains and the granary is tied with rings. Then, on the shortest day after the harvesting of millet, Akoth gives birth to a girl as Ayot makes a sacrifice of twelve bulls at a shrine on Umala Hill.

That night, before the dew stays on the grass after the appointed hour, the comet scatters the darkness with its tail of fire. Akoth knows without knowing that she is half of herself, and she forgets her way to the dawn.

Ayot attempts to rekindle Akoth's wisdom by pouring water from a calabash into her mouth. But her mind grows heavy in his hands and her head drops among the beetles on the dung floor.

Dark descends onto the deep, the deep gives way to mist, and Ayot drags his wife's body in among the banana trees. He breaks the dust with the tough skin of his heel, and returns her to the ground in and out of time.

While the lesser bright ascends to its height, the storyteller rattles his headgear, flings ashes over his shoulders, then cites the precedents—on the day after the last comet broke the night with fire, the mother who died at the settlement in the hills brought locusts, and the mother who died near the waterfalls brought the end of the rains.

He listens for the voice of the Lively Tempered One for guidance.

The remedy is extreme. To protect the village, tufts of hair are to be taken from the newborn and buried in the ancestral riverbank. Then the child is to be abandoned by her father in the Saroto Forest, where the People first knew the un-time.

Ayot doesn't eat his porridge, the world rots, and the air rattles with disquiet.

He walks among the foothills to the north, and the wide-open plains in the east, and stops beside the swamp where the river reeds once lived. After the wind has skinned the baobab trees, he removes a pouch from his neck, drops herbs onto a tuft of dry elephant grass, and lights the sacred herbs.

Third sight.

Scarlet soil shudders in this everlasting-always moment as vibrations divide song into the sound that knows itself.

Before the lesser light descends into the dawn, Ayot takes Hono, his daughter, away from the WaSimbi stronghold. They linger on the open plain, and walk through a patch of spiked thorn bushes that leads them into the western horizon. They do not stop in the desert pan until they see the everglade of purple flowers. They do not sleep until he sees the Idol Worshipper, who has talcum powder for skin, who wears a white frock that modestly covers flesh from her ankles to the top of her neck, and teaches a Bible lesson beneath an overhang of bush.

So it is here that Ayot converts to Nehemiah, the girl is baptized Rahab, and they move to the Mission.

In the time it takes for the food to cool, Nehemiah learns from Reverend James and Elizabeth Simpkins about medicine in a book. He must wear a crucifix that bounces at his chest; the long black fabric that makes him sweat.

In the morning, Nehemiah and Reverend Simpkins change meaning, and push Bibles among those who speak in tongues that are not their own. Hauling gold-gilded Bibles, they bustle back and forth in the surrounding country, swatting at flies. As they walk, Reverend Simpkins hoists his trousers at the belt and explains to Nehemiah the necessity of a foundation of rock.

"A home that is built on sand will not withstand the heavy rains. But one that is built on rock …"

Ushered patiently on by the steadying hand of Elizabeth Simpkins, Rahab plants rosebushes next to a small plot with cabbages and carrots.

"Who was King David's best friend?" Elizabeth quizzes.

"Jonathan," Rahab replies.

"What was the name of Abel's brother?"

"Cain?"

And in this way the old ways are left behind.

The shooting star lights the dark.

The generators arrive and electricity follows.

Malaria appears.

First, Reverend Simpkins dies, then Elizabeth. After the installation of a telephone line, Nehemiah takes Rahab and joins the tea pickers.

They pluck tea leaves from the plantation in the valley, toiling beneath fat pellets of rain with mud squeezing between their toes. They haul wicker baskets on their backs and carefully select tea leaves by separating stems from branches.

One morning during a season of plenty, Nehemiah's hand feels its way deep, and deeperstill into a shrubbery for tea leaves. He tugs. A pang jumps him sharp and quick, then numbs the base of his neck. Electricity surges through him, and he slumbers deepersleeping his nose deeperstill in the muck.

His spirit dreams him back among his kin, the WaSimbi, whose killers near the swamplands dragged the survivors onto the plantations of the ones who dispensed suitcases full of Bibles. Deep in the interior, below the stone hills, Nehemiah's spirit lingers and observes them lulled with presents of tobacco, brought to heel by horses and muskets, and then sold to till parched grass near water points below splintered crags.

The one who comes for Rahab is a Jinjabi with hair of dark charcoal and works as a clerk at the Liwani National Bank.

The days gurgle hot, the wind kicks whorls, and Phineas not-not grins. Always, his arms are full of lumpy parcels, and in the time it takes to spit, the couple hold hands at sunset in forever-un-time waiting.

Nehemiah indulges the wishes of his daughter, and does not object when they marry.

BOOK VI

———◆———

Petite Mort

Leroi Johnson's death is no longer news

He's had his moment in the news cycle, and now Curranvale City is busy with the mundane details of the day to day, and his immediate family no longer receives the condolences of well-wishers. New episodes of *Switcher* are slated for broadcast during Sweeps Week, and the talk of the town is whether Tamala Exeter will be back for another season. Contract negotiations have stalled over residuals on the back end, but interest in her off-screen romance with the Rafe Curtis character continues to generate all-time Nielsen ratings highs. Speculation at various watering holes in the city is that Tamala is big enough to make a successful leap to the movies. However, she's been adamant on nightly entertainment telecasts about wanting to return to the show because of letters and emails she receives "from younger women whose lives have been saved by the eating-disorder issues the show hasn't shied away from confronting."

Will she, or won't she?

What evening dress did she wear to dinner at Julio's on the night when talks with the network broke down? What percentage of folk polled online thought the shimmery, gold backless number she wore that night was a thumbs-up success? Who wears the outfit better, Tamala Exeter or Carolyn Hoffman (star VJ on a rival network)? Is the photograph evidence that Tamala got an eye job? Folk are asked to go online at www-dot--------dot-com to compare her current eyes with a shot taken at the Golden Globes last January, and to say whether they see a difference. Also welcome are emailed comments on the question, Who is to blame for the increase in eye jobs among women between the ages of eighteen and thirty-five?

These are the central concerns uppermost in the minds of Curranvale City's citizens. Therefore, although there are still loose ends to tie up regarding grief, racial profiling, and the adverse effect of this tragic event on African-America, out of respect for the polled data of our readers (with a plus or minus margin of error at five percent), we bid adieu to Leroi Johnson and move on to some of our other breaking news.★ "Eliza May's story takes the kind of risks that turn the style of critique one finds in the book-review section of the weekend paper on its head," Professor Iton says. "Her work subverts market forces that call for duplication of the norm. Ultimately, it disrupts notions of conformity in ways that reflect the kind of work I'd like to see more of." He closes his eyes. "Simply stated, it's a splendid exploration of associationalism. You follow?"

Huh?

I like Eliza May. Sure I do. She's kind, thoughtful, and the story is a decent piece of writing. But anointing her the messiah of the form, what bull crap. There's no real plot, no story, just a whole lotta beautiful words, spurious episodes, and coy high-mod diction. In fact, it seems to be all gimmick, like an asthmatic rabbit riding a unicycle.

Friggin-frack!

What the hell is she saying anyway? I mean, the thing has an unreliable narrator and the writing's a *tour de force* of poetic curlicues. But the main character, a female writer from Zambia, does nothing but have sex with other women, or muse about sex with other women in an arbitrary splatter-fest of abstractions.

Why doesn't Eliza May just simply come out and say precisely what she means?

"How is a story made?" the Professor continues. "This is the kind of question the author poses to the reader. The telling, or narration, suggests that the story is an omnivorous medium, one that is bound only by the imagination. Here on page nine, the dense language gives way to a moment of clarity. The narrative voice momentarily shifts from third to first, then back to the third. In this moment, the frame of the story is broken and we are thrust into an unbounded universe. Or, to put it another way, the implied author, the one whose attitudes inform the work, sets up the subsequent surprise, a fully conscious protagonist. This momentary stabilization quickly disappears and we, the reader, do not know when or if the "I" will return. Are you with me here? By playfully putting off its re-emergence, the organizing intelligence stokes an underlying tension, one that rewards those of us who are willing to sit in the swill of the unknowable, much like in life. Look at the neutral, undramatized language at the top of page three: 'It's a cold day in November.' Compare here to page ten, 'GoodGoddamn it's cold.' How much does this emotive shift reflect the views of the narrator? And how is the norm, or the reader's values, challenged by these subtle departures from objective ways of speaking?"

I take a quick look at the two sentences.

GoodGoddamn, how could I have missed all that?

Without further ado, the Bookworm kicks off the roundtable

discussion. She prods her eyeglasses at her nose, then reads from a prepared statement. "The term 'an important story' is bandied around far too loosely," she says. "In effect, one is left with the impression that this term has morphed into a not-so-subtle put-down. By this, I mean the work described as important self-consciously tackles concerns that 'compel' one to take it seriously. So, when *I* say that Eliza May's story is important work, *I* want to be clear that *I* mean it in its purest sense. Eliza May Morton, or I should say Eliza May Faulkner" (insert nervous laughter) "has touched on what can only be described as the fundamental constants: birth, death, and the feminine in exile from the mainstream. And she's done so with élan, courage, and insight."

Moved, the Bookworm pulls examples from pages seven, thirteen, and twenty-one to illustrate her point. But before she can remove her lips from whence they are planted adoringly upon Eliza May Faulkner's *derrière*, her voice cracks a little bit.

"Well said, Rosemary," the Professor interjects. "Well said."

I'm queasy as the discussion reads much like the selected raves on a one-page newspaper advertisement for an award-winning foreign flick.

"Gripping! A must read."—Cybil Harris, *Boston Herald*.

I look over at Q. who appears to have an image of Eliza May's number-one fan munching on her whatnots as she compared Liza to the modernists. Sadly, the pressure gets to him and he's underwhelming in response. "If there is one story that should be read this year, this is it. Brilliant!"—Quint C., *New York Times*.

The rest of the comments get back on track.

"Quintessentially post-ironist. The inter chapters within the footnotes make for a hyper textual feel that is revelatory."—Richard "the Canuck" Spoils, *Globe and Mail*.

"It's not the kind of story I normally like to read, but I dug it, dude."—the Steelworker, *Trotskyite Press*.

The enthusiasm is infectious. Eliza May *is* God masquerading as Eliza May Morton, and we've all witnessed the setting of the gold standard.

"It takes you by the lapels in the opening sentence, and you remain in its grip long after you've finished reading it. There's a textural quality that cajoles the reader, ever so slightly and quite against one's will, like a shout borne by a gust of wind and carried into a river that flows to the sea."—Jonah Ayot-Kolosha, *Liwani Standard*.

Too much?

Once class ends, everyone files out the door slightly dazed. Everyone, that is, except yours truly, who shamelessly gloms onto Professor Iton's jock.

"Excuse me, sir," I say.

"Yes, Jonah."

"I'm having trouble finding my way into the story I want to tell." I'm quietly campaigning for an extension, a commuting of my sentence, a reprieve. "I have ideas, but nothing that holds my interest." I launch into it about Eliza May's daring exploration and finish by saying that I need more time to match her standard. More, sir. Please, sir.

He puts up his hand, enough already. "Always tell the truth in your writing," he says. "Do that, think Schrödinger, and you'll be fine."

"I don't understand," I reply. "I mean, I understand the concept of truth *per se*, but assembling a bunch of facts on paper as I recall them doesn't necessarily add up to a well-told story. Life isn't organized around narrative structures. Facts don't necessarily make for the best version of a particular tale."

"Tell the truth," he repeats as he makes for the door.

I join the recently crowned literary sensation and her boy-toy *du jour* at our weekly post-workshop scrum at Ptolemy's.

Quint C. jabbers at light speed. "See, babe. Didn't I tell you it was good? Just wait till my agent reads it. Fiction is a tough sell, but there's always a niche for the next great thing."

"In my case, the next great black thing," she corrects. "That's as much attention as I'm liable to get."

"No, babe," he replies. "No limits. You're coming through."

Eliza May is glum. "Sure, the workshop liked it, but a bunch of MFAs don't represent the average reader." Her bangles jangle. "People want slave narratives, but that ain't me, Q. The only people who'll read the story are other writers with comps to the obscure journal it'll be published in."

"Eliza May Morton," I interrupt, heated. "Professor Iton called it work he'd like to see more of. He doesn't get much more effusive than that."

"She needs us to say something negative," Quint C. comments. "It's the only way she'll think we're being objective."

"It's a bleeding masterpiece, boss," I reiterate. "Deal with it."

"Yah, deal with it, babe," Quint C. chimes in.

Eliza May smiles.

Over her shoulder in Ptolemy's doorway stands Hiroko, the first guest at our weekly bull sessions.

"There she is," I sparkle.

Both Quint C. and Eliza May watch *über* babe dodge bodies with an unlit smoke dangling from the corner of her mouth. She makes her way toward us in baggy black trousers, a wife beater, bright red suspenders, and bright white clown shoes.

"Isn't she great?"

"Settle down, dude," Quint C. says.

I leap up, knocking the table with a knee and spilling drinks.

"Hey, hey." I hug Babycakes before making introductions. Bla de bla. She's an Aquarius. Such and so. Loves solitary walks. Then we sit, Hiroko on my left, Quint C. to my right, and Eliza May across the way.

Quint C. flags down a waitress and orders a fresh round of beers.

"I can't stick around long." Hiroko empties the contents of a handbag onto the table and rummages around until she finds a lighter. "I'm having a shit day, and I'm not putting you'all through the drama."

"You're not going anywhere," I respond. "You *will* get comfy and you *will* give us a blow by blow of why you're such a miserable …"

"I will?" Hiroko lights up.

"We insist," Eliza May assures her. "And please don't worry about how you come off. Bad days happen to Jonah all the time. So, Q. and I are used to whining."

I ignore the ribbing. "Feeling piled on?" I ask Hiroko.

"Yah." She fidgets in her seat. "I'm bogged down in high-maintenance relationships, and …" I must look startled. "Not you, Jonah. You're a sweetheart."

"He's a darling," Eliza May says.

"A regular tug on the heartstrings," Quint C. adds.

"Did something happen?" I ask.

She stabs out her smoke in an ashtray and lights another. "I've had it up to my titties with Ito."

"Ito's the fiancé," I announce.

"This morning we had one of *those* fights over the phone." Hiroko swirls a finger in her beer. "He's been emailing Monay."

"She's a dancer from the club," I explain.

"Yah, and I don't mean to be nasty, but …"

"She's a skank," Eliza May contributes.

"Yes. And whatever the skank said got him chewing me out over time I've spent with …"

"Jonah," Q. offers.

"Who's also a skank, by the way," I add.

"Jonah and I've barely seen each other, and even if we had, I wasn't into listening to Ito list all the reasons why both he and Monay think I should change," Hiroko explains. "And I got angrier and angrier at how sensible he was being and hated that my only response was to lose it. All the while I know he can't wait to get off the phone and email Monay about the latest crazy bitch thing I just said."

We get quiet.

Eliza May breaks the silence. "I lived with my girlfriend up until a year ago," she confesses. "Yah, and we fought all the time about silly things. If I left clothes on the bedroom floor, she saw it as indifference to her feelings. If she didn't clear her place at the table, I got twisted over how little work she put into our relationship." She glances at Q. "One day, she accused me of being selfish. But just as I was about to yell back, I saw how it would play itself out. There'd be a drama that would end up discussed among our friends, her friends really. You know, they'd say she was good and I was bad, just like it always happened. So I got into my car and smashed it into a tree at fifty miles an hour."

"Good God, Liza," I mutter.

"She spent two weeks in a coma," Quint C. says.

"Gelsie and I had been together about three years," she continues. "Three years of running ourselves ragged trying to stay one step ahead of criticism. And even though I was miserable I thought at least we were taking it to another level." Q. reaches for her hand and squeezes her fingers. "But the coma made one thing clear: I knew that if I didn't leave her, I'd try to kill myself again. I just couldn't live with her anymore." We stare at her as if she's on *Pillow Talk*. "Don't worry. I'm doing better now and I can see what appeared fucked was just about sorting through a difficult transition."

It takes a good while before the conversation stutters back into motion.

"Leaving is a gamble, isn't it?" Hiroko says. "Like you think, maybe if I move on I can actually find someone who'll climb Mount Fuji with me. You think it's going to be right the next time if you follow your heart, but there's always something. You want a dog and he's a cat person, and still you go ahead and try to make it work. Then when you have a child, it suddenly occurs that you've both made a huge mistake."

"I disagree," Quint C. says. "It takes patience to find a person who's compatible."

"Spoken like someone who's always bought whatever he needed," Hiroko says, shakily lighting up another smoke.

"Q. isn't like that," I say in his defense. "Eliza May yes, but not Q."

"I didn't mean ..." Hiroko says.

"No explanation required," Quint C. replies. "My family has money. My parents aren't divorced. I've never felt as if I don't have options. But, I still think it's a mistake to assume a stable relationship with another human being is impossible."

"Lately, alls I've known are cash flow issues." Hiroko reveals. "So whenever the squeeze got too tight, I traded in on my independence to improve my circumstances." She crushes her cigarette in the ashtray again. "Ito has money, and he's always taken care of me whenever I needed it. So, I don't feel I can leave him ... especially not now." She places another smoke between her lips. "God, I must sound like a freaking bitch."

"No, it sounds more like you've had to grow up fast," Eliza May surmises. "But the thing to remember is that *feeling* trapped isn't the same as *being* trapped. It may not look like it, but there's life after Ito."

"To freedom," I say.

Quint C. raises his drink. "To new beginnings."

We clink glasses.★ Hiroko: Can we *not* have sex tonight? I'm too tired, hon.

Me: No sweat.

Hiroko: You're a saint.

Me: That's me.

Hiroko: You're mad.

Me: You're the mad one.

Hiroko: How so?

Me: Mad like a fox.

Hiroko: FYI. It's crazy like a fox.

Me: FYI?

Hiroko: Mad like a fox makes no sense.

Me: LOL, Babycakes. LOL.
Hiroko: Mwuah mwuah.
Me: Smiley face.

2

My throat is thick, and I'm feeling rushed into a day of
scheduled activity I wouldn't under normal circumstances
have chosen for myself

Last night, Hiroko and I decided that we should spend time apart.
No, not like a separation. Instead, we decided, like a team, that
I should use the coming days to tend the home fires at Colby
Manor and keep the Rev on a short hook. Today, he preaches his
anticipated sermon, and who knows what he'll get up to once it's
over. If he acts erratic, my gentlemanly duty will be to get him
into a psych ward without access to sharp objects.

At least this is the plan.

In practice, I lie in bed with the covers over my head, failing
terribly to block out the Rev's latest attempt to get me to join
him for the drive to church. Charley Pride makes a country-fied
ruckus on the record player while in the kitchen the Rev drops
pans from a height sufficient enough to add to the racket.

I can't make myself budge.

Compounding my difficulties is Da Stylus's absurd attachment
to the Rev. Since I didn't want to upset her by mentioning the
obit, or the rat poison (which I threw away), I've quietly gone
along with her plans to consummate our prenuptials on a day that
is finally here. So, let horns be sounded, battlements be shored
up, and ramparts drawn ... asunder. Let the spawn of Cronus mix
with the four oceans, and produce from Neptune's loins a genera-

tion to *posthaste* form a bipartisan committee to slow my upcoming afternoon of boot-knocking, premarital rump-shaking, and make-a-da-luv-making.

Shitdamn. I wish retrospectively to book passage on the *Titanic;* a good smack with an iceberg would relieve me of my civil service to the higher good.

After fifteen minutes of a thorough contemplation of simpler days—rustic walks in Hoppa's cow-dung pastures, gulping fresh air unblemished with toxic exculpations, the merry laughter of children not yet plagued with cancer from the Feltway Dam—the Rev unleashes the nuclear option. He batters on my door like it's a gong.

I squeeze a pillow down over my ears.

"We're pressed for Time," the Rev bellows.

"I'm on it."

"Hurry it up, Son. I'll wait in the Car."

Once I hear the front door clank shut, I take a look out the window and see where the Rev's a forehead on the steering wheel.

It looks like he's telling on me to God.

I go into pre-game mode. Not liking what stares back at me in the bathroom mirror, I wash gunk out of eyes, attack plaque with bristles to teeth, and then extinguish naturally occurring scents with a new razzle-dazzle aerosol product whose latest ad has over 680,000 hits on the 'net. Before squeezing into a tight-fitting charcoal suit, I make a quick pit stop in the Rev's office to turn off a desk lamp he's left on (an act that shows blatant disregard for the tin-hat wearing, radical-left flim flam who go on about the perils of wasted energy during a time of global warming).

Sound the alarum!

On his desk is a pile of tell-all print-outs of emails from Elisha. The Rev's covered many years' worth of his son's accumulating debt with money taken out of my inheritance.[125] Names are named, approximate estimates of money spent are given, and I'm revolted.★ ★At St Peter's Episcopalian, the Very Reverend James Tusker delivers his sermon from his pulpit (and into a video camera lens), with a still, quiet voice. "We seek out the Advice of Columns in Magazines." He all but disappears in a white robe with puffy sleeves. "Without Answers, we hurry to reach Pinnacles of Achievement so that we might say that the suffering was worth it. Everywhere we see the Ones who grow old, having ceased to believe they will lose thirty Pounds and keep it off. There are Obstacles. Our Acquaintances sum us up; they say if only we chose to spend our Time this way instead of that, all would be well. Who among us has not met important Personages, shared similar Obsessions with Detail, and learned to resent those who do not think we too are extraordinary? Yes, older and wearier and full of Resentment over the good Fortune of Others, we fear that any Day we will die from an inability to swallow."

The Sunday crowd is a cross-section of Curranvale City's aging, diminishing church-attending set; of note, Mrs Rita Petra-Freud sits beside Alistair Freud one pew in front of—from left to right—Jonah Ayot-Kolosha, Elisha Tusker Jr, and his tight-panted wife,

---

125   A sizable chunk of the inheritance is slated to be seized by Collins & Williams Loan Consolidation Co., and therefore Jonah can expect to receive a significantly reduced sum on his twenty-first birthday (specifics unavailable).

Dorothea. All of them processing concerns they've yet to come to terms with in full view of Clementine "Da Stylus" Pinkston, who sits in the choir behind the thieving Reverend, waiting for the conductor's cue to sing the Offertory Hymn.

"In this way we are like Children. In nothing is Childhood more strongly distinguished from Adulthood than in this, that the Child has no true Purpose, no divine Plan of Life by which their Energies are directed. The Child lives, in great Measure, to enjoy the passing Scene, and to find Happiness in that agreeable Consciousness which from Hour to Hour comes to them by chance. If their Life is governed by a Plan, a Purpose, it is the Purpose of Another, not their own. By contrast, Adults have their own Purpose, their own Life and Aim. But the sorrowful Experience of Multitudes in this respect is that they are never Men or Women, but Children all their Days."

Mrs Petra-Freud fondly recalls her last play date with Jonah and draws up tentative plans for when she'll bump lovelies with him again; perhaps later today after she manages to send Alistair on a fool's errand (yet to be determined). At her elbow, her husband calculates the amount of money it will cost to upgrade his real estate portfolio, and how much he will profit from a return on his investment. Since the past weeks have been spent working in relative isolation on arguments and briefs, he's enthusiastic about sharing his musings with adult members of the post-church community who will stick around for a refreshing post-service beverage and snack. On stage, Da Stylus worries that the Reverend won't get through the sermon without a glitch, and she goes over a list of possible booby traps, trip wires, and lapses of logic he might yet stumble into. Once she emerges from her daydream, she's shocked to note she's been staring into the eyes of Elisha, the fuck-up, who, unbeknownst to her, ignores discomfort over what people in the congregation must think of him and focuses on how to ditch his tight-panted wife in order to get a close-up, post-service looksy at whether Clem is attending church bra-less. Beside him, the one he plans to give the slip burns with shame over their public humiliation and distracts herself by retracing her steps earlier in the morning to ascertain if she turned on the timer of her VCR. On the docket is a seminar on stratagems for success-ful living that she'll add to her expanding video library.

"In Youth, Life is a fairy Tale unfolding, but with Age we see that our Tale ends in Death. Therefore, the Adult must be oriented in Service to a higher Good and that, in short, is the Work I've tried to do at St Peter's. In my Years as your Pastor, I've learned greater Worth exists in the giving of Oneself to Another, a Lesson taught by St Augustine when he refers to our inner Teacher. And through the application of this Teaching, I've made it my Plan and guiding Principle to live by the basic Tenet that over one's moral and intellectual Being, one's sway is complete. As such, I take full Responsibility for the Breach of your collective Sense of Trust in my Stewardship of this spiritual Community, and with grave Humility I place my Fate in your Hands with a Belief that my Exit will be a premature Intervention of Work still to be done. I am but a flawed Vessel who reflects daily on the ways in which I can serve the Lord better. So know this and let there be in your Bosoms a calm, decided, and all-pervasive Compassion in your Deliberations. Look first and last to God to aid you in determin-ing the most suitable Shepherd in the great Task still lying before us. Look to Him for the Wisdom to choose the most Prudent way to walk uncorrupted in both our Deeds, our innermost Thoughts and Feelings. If you find my continued Presence at St Peter's useful, together we will continue to evolve as the Instruments of God's Compassion expressed through the Example of his Son, Jesus Christ."

Jonah can't decide whether the Rev is better described as a turncoat, a backstabber, a Judas, or a Benedict Arnold. Each word seems a suitable fit, so it's impossible to settle on just one.

℃

The Rev holds out his arms in contrition.

"Now let us confess our Sins against God and our Neighbor," he says.

After a brief silence, aged churchgoers read the Confession and Absolution along with him. "Most merciful God, we have sinned against you in Thought, Word, and Deed, by what we have done, and by what we have left undone. We have not loved you with all our Hearts; we have not loved our Neighbors as ourselves. We are truly sorry and we humbly repent. For the Sake of your Son, Jesus Christ, have Mercy on us and forgive us; that we may delight in your Will, and walk in your footsteps, to the Glory of your Name. Amen."

Reverend Tusker continues alone. "Almighty God have Mercy on you, forgive you all your Sins through our Lord Jesus, strengthen you in Goodness, and by the Power of the Holy Spirit keep you in Eternal Life. Amen.

"The peace of Christ be always with you."

"And also with you," they reply.

"May God bless you, my Children."

After the choir sings the Offertory Anthem, the Reverend leads a presentation hymn. Then he breaks a wafer of bread and fills the silver chalice with wine. "This is the Lord's Supper. God's Feast for all of God's People. There is always an Abundance here and there is a Place for you. You are invited and encouraged to feast at God's Table."

The choir lifts their voices in a communion anthem, and the penitent step into the aisle, waiting to kneel at the altar for the receipt of the holy sacrament. One by one, they move toward the wine that substitutes for Christ's blood and the bread that substitutes for his flesh. Steadily they march, an army of common folk, rich folk, poor folk, unemployed folk, would-be-saints, inveterate sinners, back-stabbing back-stabbers, calculating cheats, sex-addicted crazies, pill-popping miscreants, player-hating misanthropes, top-notch execs in the corporate ass-wipe, daydreamy do-nothings, fascistic fascists, world-class whiny hineys, sheisterly spin-meisters, power grubbers, and knobs, and after they've drank and eaten, crossed themselves and returned to their seats, a post-communion prayer is offered to the heavenly host by Reverend James "Judas" Tusker, their leader, before a closing hymn.

Then, "Thanks be to God! Alleluia! Alleluia!" he praises.

For what might be the last time, the Rev walks down the aisle behind the cross-carrying acolyte before he greets the faithful at the front door.

⊂⊃

Jonah dawdles in a scrum made up of Alistair Freud, Mrs Petra-Freud, Elisha Tusker Jr, Dorothea Tusker, and Clementine "Da Stylus" Pinkston. Consensus appears to be that the Reverend will live to preach other sermons.

Then Alistair talks Dow Jones's and IPOs, pleased to be *incom-*

municado with persons other than his secretary about something other than his caseload. "There's one apartment in Oldeham Proper that's listed at half a mill', and a conservative estimate has it fetching in the neighborhood of three-quarters of a mill' on the back end." He talks in Jonah's general direction. "It's an offer that's much too tempting to pass up."

Still scattered after the untimely discovery of the questionable behavior by the fuck-up's dad, Jonah wonders whether Alistair speaks in code. Too tempting to pass up! Jonah sees subterfuge everywhere. Is the legal eagle on to what he's been up to with his wife against the Cuttlewots? Is he plotting tortures that include, but aren't restricted to, hot wax dripped onto the genital zone?

"Wasn't my dad inspired today, Clem?" Elisha wonders if the bra-less Sunday School teacher currently flies panty-less. "He seemed in good spirits during the service, didn't he?"

"That isn't necessarily a good sign," Dorothea cuts in, habitually and without malicious intent undermining her hubby at every turn. "It is most likely an indication that he's not dealing with his true feelings about this crisis. So what, in fact, we're looking at is the first phase of the grieving process, the denial phase."

Da Stylus gets defensive. "I like to think he managed as well as can be expected under the circumstances." She's irritated by the stream of perpetual nonsense, which she hates herself for noticing in the Reverend's daughter-in-law. "Not only does he deserve our praise for a job well done, but I think we ought to keep our inflammatory assessments to ourselves."

Mrs Petra-Freud touches Jonah's arm. "I was hoping you could come by this afternoon to pick up the book I told you about."

Jonah flinches, afraid she's being much too familiar for this venue. "This afternoon isn't going to work, ma'am," he says.

"Clementine and I have plans."

"It's going to be difficult for him to adjust to what has happened without some form of talk therapy," Dorothea continues. "And just so you know, I'm expressing a fact, not an opinion. The seven stages he'll go through are denial, anger … shoot, I can't remember the rest."

His tight-panted wife compounds Elisha's dangerously high levels of anxiety, so in order to spare himself the bother, he immerses himself in a conversation with Alistair about his own plans to market his corn-based gasoline product. "I've got my eyes on land in South Dakota. Two hundred acres, more or less." He speaks loud enough for Clem to overhear, thinking of the toll it's taking to publicly maintain an illusion of Dorothea's sanity. "All I'm waiting for is a go-ahead from investors."

Mrs Petra-Freud tugs on Jonah's shirt sleeve. "How's a little later? Say, five o'clock?"

Da Stylus can't bear to listen to Dorothea anymore. How does Elisha put up with her? The guy's a sweetheart while the tight-panted blow-hard clearly hasn't a clue. She certainly hasn't taken into account how awkward it must have been for Elisha to be at the service. Knowing how this selfishness feels in her relationship with Jonah, she empathizes with Elisha.

"Denial, anger, acceptance, sadness, and … shoot, why can't I remember this?" Dorothea is distracted by how Elisha is an A-one classic example of what's wrong with people. In public, he never gets his facts right and despite all that has happened, he's still bringing up his latest pipe dream about corn-based oil for the population at large. How much more embarrassment can a person take? "Anger, denial, crying, no, not crying … shoot, shoot."

"You can't go wrong with real estate, Elisha." Alistair is pleased to be talking with other persons keen on high finance. "Land is dirt cheap in the Midwest since no one of consequence chooses to live there. Hardy har har. Don't shoot the messenger. Hardy har har. Yes, so it might just be an offer that's too tempting to pass up, despite the short-term damage it'll do to your pocketbook."

Jonah thinks about throttlings. He'd like nothing more than to throttle Elisha. Also, he wonders if Alistair's continued reference to temptation means the legal beagle would like nothing better than to throttle him.

"No matter what happens now, I'm Free," Reverend Tusker interrupts. "*Non bene pro toto Libertas venditur Auro.*"[126]

Loretta Tucci, silver-haired and alabaster-skinned, stands beside him. "Wasn't he terrific?" she asks.

The gang of five, minus Jonah, erupts into a frenzy of panegyrics, encomiums, and congratulations for a service that was "truly inspired." ★

★ What Reverend Tusker needs is solitude to pray—an all-nighter, a hair-puller, a clasped-hander—on bended knees. Instead, Jonah, Elisha, Dorothea, Clementine, and Loretta help him to find his missing car.

He limps on an arthritic development emanating from somewhere near his sprained ankle.

"I think I parked on Plum Street," the Reverend muses out loud. "Weren't you paying Attention, Jonah?"

"I had other things on my mind," Jonah replies.

---

126   Liberty is not for sale for any amount of gold (Latin).

"Go back over your steps, James," Loretta say. "What landmarks can you remember?"

"I parked on Plum Street," the Rev responds. "I'm certain of it."

The gang of six travels the length and breadth of the block; Elisha has his father by one elbow, Clementine has him by the other, two steps behind them Dorothea says nothing while Loretta leans against Jonah's arm.

"I remember walking past a Bus Stop," Reverend Tusker mumbles.

"There is a bus stop on the Corner of Trent and Plum," Clementine offers.

"That's most likely where it is," Elisha encourages. "Good call, Clem."

"Yes, I'm parked on the Intersection of Trent and Plum."

"Are you certain?" Loretta asks, out of breath.

"Of course. Yes."

They undertake another slow trudge west before searching among Subarus, Toyotas, Hyundais, and Hondas. "This can't be it," Reverend Tusker deduces. "These Cars are parked on a diagonal. I'm fairly certain I parallel parked."

"Why don't we try looking on Trent Street?" Clementine suggests.

"Fantastic idea, Clem," Elisha responds.

"Absolutely top notch," Jonah mocks.

"I left a Box of Tissues in the back Window," the Reverend says. "I distinctly remember passing a Bus Stop."

"Don't worry, Reverend," Clementine assures him. "We'll find it."

"Unless it's been stolen," Dorothea pipes up. "One out of every five car owners will have a vehicle stolen this year. Or, is that one out of twenty-five? No, it's five. One out of five."

"Some of us shouldn't be such alarmists," Clementine scolds.

Reverend Tusker begins to pray to the Holy Father. He needs this one. He needs his memory to correspond with measurable realities. He's suffered dizzy spells of late, and he needs to find the car if only to convince himself there's nothing whatsoever to worry about. He used to be able to manage most situations, but he can't recollect the moment he changed. It's as if the present is all that he ever was and everything he'll ever become.

"There it is!" Clementine exclaims.

"Praise the Lord," the Reverend yelps. "I told you it was parallel parked."

"That you did," Elisha exhorts.

"Does he have to be so condescending?" Jonah mutters.

Elisha pivots on his heels. "What the hell crawled up your butt, Jonah! You've been a pill all day. Why not be a man and just say what's eating you."

"Splendiforous! Stupendacular!" Jonah snipes. "Your hyperbole is my problem."

"You're such a negative," Elisha responds.

"Cut it out, boys!" Loretta intervenes. "It's Sunday."

Once daggers are reluctantly returned to sheaths, the Reverend apologizes to everyone for mis-remembering the location of his vehicle.

"I'm sorry for putting you through all that."

"Puh-leez," Clementine and Elisha respond simultaneously.

"Jinx," they say in tandem.

"I said it first," Clementine laughs.

"No. I did," Elisha responds.

"Puh-leez," Jonah mutters.

Dorothea shudders with giggles.

Whatever fueled Reverend Tusker with insights earlier in the day is spent. He's deflated of charm as the youngsters delay final goodbyes by taking an interest in his health.

"How's your stool?" Clementine asks the Rev.

"Never better."

"Always check the color of your stool," Elisha advises.

"It's fine. Really."

"When my mother experienced internal bleeding, hers was black," Clementine says, then fiddles in a bag, and produces a bottle of spring water. "Drink this. It did wonders for her."

"Thanks. But I'm fine."

"Take it, Dad," Elisha says.

Loretta intervenes. "Enough badgering. I'm taking him home, making him a bowl of soup, and getting him into bed." Everyone laughs except Jonah. "I meant, to make sure he has an afternoon nap." She turns crimson. "Nothing else."

3

Late afternoon, Jonah kicks at a Coke can as he leaves the downtown core with Da Stylus

Several hours ago, he plotted ways he could crush both the Rev and the douche bag's spirits. Waterboarding. Electric cathodes attached to testicles. Stress positions. Hot cattle prods applied to butt cheeks. But he's had to put this on hold while he pictures an unhappy end to his upcoming assignation with the choir member, one that can't be avoided after they've "whacked away at making the beast with two backs, happily whipping their lard together."[127] He envisions himself in the harsh light of the mid-afternoon as he lies next to her, sticky with their collective juices, feeling guilt-tripped into engaging her latest set of expectations about what these new developments in their relationship ought to mean.

This won't be good. No, sir.

Why exactly?

To the material point, the couple have talked this dalliance through so often that there's no way either one of them will be able to relax. Or, at least matters will be more difficult between them since it's going to be a day game, one played without the aid of intoxicating mental lubricants. A night game would have provided the cover of darkness, allowing him to avoid looking the moment dead-on by giving him a built-in excuse to take a *post-coital* snooze. Instead, daylight will force him to go over the final

---

127   Rabelais, François. *Gargantua and Pantagruel*. See footnote 29.

returns with her; assessments of whether the practice of jumping bones was equal to how it appeared in the pre-game plan, and an accounting of requisite duties spurred by the principles that must now exist between them. Consequently, he's scared witless, and all he really wants is to be left alone, out of reach of anything that requires an obligation from him.

His conscience tells him that if he doesn't listen to his intuitive desire to leave, he'll look back in the years to come at this definitive moment as the one he chose as the easy way to a fortune, an immoral act that would leave him as helpless as an adult elephant who'd been tied by a rope to a wooden stake during its formative years. From here on out, he'll be on a precipitous decline that'll eventually find him shirtless, and endlessly smoking fruit-flavored hashish from a hookah in a seedy bar in Marrakesh.

They pass through parts of the city's grubby underbelly and enter the red brick of Oldeham Proper. Passing a Cineplex where quality sound massages inner ears, Da Stylus beats herself up over what she must have done to put Jonah in such a foul mood. Is he upset that she didn't pretty up with makeup, or could it be that she looks too casual wearing jeans? As they pass cafés, she nervously launches into a meandering take on the War.

"I don't want to say *this* is wrong and *that* is the way to fix it," she remarks. "But the threat of terror is the current idiom for facilitating social change."

"I'm tired, honey," Jonah says, responding to matters of national security. "Let's not talk about all that."

Over beside the cheapest bagels in town, she loses confidence in her own grasp of populist rhetoric as well as of her own goal to reduce suffering in the world by half. Amber tints of sun spark

high above distant flatlands and, as they walk, she surmises that
her time with Jonah is no better than the many ways she tiptoes
through her aunt's orderly home (replacing the toilet paper roll
just so, wiping stray puddles of water off any exposed surfaces).
Like always, she worries that she isn't doing enough and, like
usual, she falls back on the habit of trying to lighten the tension
with chatter.

"Wanna elope?" she jokes.

"Don't be silly."

"I'm not doing anything next Saturday."

Sidewalks are plugged full with people moving toward tasks
assigned to relieve the humdrums—dinner reservations at six,
movies on the quarter hour, nightclubs with music sorted by
taste. Customs are observed in the way orderly cues spontane-
ously form outside of doorways, or else at intersections where
the young belligerently no longer aid the elderly who tap canes
against icy crosswalks before painstakingly trying to beat ped-
estrian lights. Skyscrapers are rooted in land that once was an
Indigenous People's hunting ground, and Da Stylus gives herself
over to prayer as they turn into a dark tunnel that descends along
an incline. Downward they go into subterranean darkness, and she
begins to understand why she's hesitated to go the distance with
Jonah. Biblical injunctions aside, she simply doesn't feel close to
him. Beneath the Earth's surface, she feels compromised by all that
she's done to make her sense of alienation disappear. She stopped
wearing brassieres, let him put his hands in her panties, and ig-
nored Elisha's warnings that Jonah was seeing another woman. If
he was, it would be a stage on his way to spiritual maturity, like
with Malcolm X. However, nothing is changing, not a jot, leaving
her dependent on a miracle to cut through a barrier that prevents

her from taking the steps necessary to get close to him.

Once inside her friend's apartment, she directs me to a couch.
"Orange juice? Coke?"

"Bathroom?"

Oops. I've yet to rid myself of the habit of assuming people
are attuned to my thoughts, something I catch moments after
my mind has already changed tracks. Coke, I think, but out slips
"bathroom."

"First door to the left."

I splash my face with water, notice a green bottle of cologne,
unscrew the lid. It smells of Gramps.

I reach into my jacket pocket and sip from a flask of scotch
before swirling mouthwash between my gums. Then I leave the
door as ajar as I found it before sitting on the couch in front of a
side plate of creamy cheeses and salted crackers.

Da Stylus slips off her heels, rests the back of her head on my
lap, and stares up into my face.

After a long silence, she asks, "Have you been drinking?"

"Sorry?"

"You smell of alcohol."

I turn the tables. "Have *you* been drinking?"

"Huh?"

"You must be drinking to accuse me of doing that."

"I don't drink."

"So, because I've tied one on in the past, you assume ... what?"

"Let's not do this," she pleads. "Not today."

"Have I been drinking?" I snort. "What kind of attack dog ...
attacking is that?"

On the spot, Da Stylus places barricades around the parts of herself she wants hidden. She apologizes, flush with flaws she can't forgive. Stupid. How stupid of her to bring up his boozing (that's a subject to deal with after the wedding). Today's supposed to be special, and now it's ruined. If only she was a better Christian. If only she got out of her own way, and focused her efforts on supporting him. If only she could somehow manage to stop this reflexive habit of trying to be worthy of him.

Angrily, she sits up with her arms folded across her bra-less chest, and tacks left.

"You've never done anything to earn my respect," she says. "A big nothing. A big, fat zilch. All you do is make me feel bad about myself."

She cracks at her edges, and the mean-spirited person I suspected was there all along appears.

I'm like Steve who does the church's billing, she says, snot pooling at her nostrils. I'm like George who does the church's computer programming. I'm "lazy" and refuse "to accept responsibility for my lack of effort." All I think about is what works for me and I never consider how "my behavior might affect others."

I stand.

"What about Hiroko?" she asks.

I sit. And like that, I learn I never will give a shit-damn about her desire to reduce suffering in the world by half. I want to go back to the Rev's, fire up the computer, and write freely on my surprising findings about how human beings are intuitively immoral.

"Be straight with me for once," she says. "At least respect yourself that much, or I'll never be able to respect you." I've got to stop getting her by vulnerable parts, clamping down hard, and not letting go until I've punished her for acting like a person I don't believe exists. "Answer the question, or go."

4

The Ayot-Kolosha Diet © copyright 2003

Jonah's been at it for three days. He's been either buck nude, writing and re-writing at the computer, instant-messaging with Hiroko, or else slipping on boxers before checking on the Rev, who must wait at least a week to learn the outcome of the church's response to his sermon. The tension between them has been at an all time high. Jonah has avoided confrontation, but made his resentments clear by openly acknowledging Hiroko as the woman he will marry by his twenty-first birthday. The point is non-negotiable. What to do about the money isn't an issue he can take on until after presenting his short story to the workshop. Consequently, this latest venture into stoicism has been augmented by a low-carb, high-protein deal that involves the denial of food for as long as possible in an effort to keep his mind pure. Then once undue hardship can no longer be borne, the dieting party scarfs down anything that happens upon his path—discarded pieces of crusty bread, the yellowing pages of literary books, slow-off-the-mark pigeons, the aged out for a vigorous lunch-time stroll.

In addition to fasting starkers, surreptitiously planning to ask Hiroko to get hitched for real, and mollycoddling the anxious man of God, Jonah's been deliciously unsteady at 700 milligrams of anti-seizures. The majority of the time he's been sloppy with the giddies, the hours passing in immensely tedious swathes filled with his latest writing experiments or his heart-melting engagement speech for Hiroko. It's been one sentence at a time, revisited one word at a pop. It's been cigarettes smoked out the window and shots of coffee spiked with whiskey. It's been keeping his bedroom door slightly ajar, at the ready to leap into motion and call in the paramedics if the Rev appears to be going *loco*.

As expected, the cleric is upset about Jonah's booze-fueled breakup with Da Stylus and his intention to make "the Succubus" his bride; so much so that it appears to have revived his sagging emotional reserves by giving him more than the construction in the basement on which to fixate. He's risen like Lazarus, definitive executive decisions have been made, he's called for a summit with Jonah, mediated by Loretta Tucci, and has made it clear the inheritance is off the table until he agrees to an independently administered "psych Eval" and a stint in rehab.

Over the past days, the only breaks Jonah and the Reverend got from each other's tyranny of mutually perceived incompetence were when Loretta Tucci accompanied the cleric to Curranvale City's museums for doses of arcane culture. Against the odds, Jonah still squeezed out a story that's thirty-four double-spaced pages (with ten-point font); definitive tics of the characters have been noted, the sky has been colored in its various shades according to its season, and the narratives have been organized around a chronology that starts at the end, returns to the beginning, and works its way forward. Done, Jonah stares out of his window at the light grey-green of the a.m., stretches his arms above his head, and watches the sun welcome in the morning by edging its way slowly behind a luminescent patch of clouds as it ascends above the iced rooftops of North Oldeham.

A stiff breeze slaps loose bits and hanging bits against the flat surfaces of Colby Manor. Explosions of snow swirl, rattling the windows. Lulled into complacence by the force of vehement beauty, Jonah falls asleep for the first time in days.

5

6:37 a.m.

Hanging on a makeshift hook in the bathroom is the Rev, a designer belt strapped around his neck, the designer leather whistling, stupid with strain, troubled by his weight.

Jonah bungles with the strap at his throat, his nails scritchscratching for a hold. Fuckfuck. He can't unclasp the buckle. Jeezusfuck. He lifts the Rev by the underarms, but cannot loosen the designer grip saddled beneath his chin. Jonah hoists him by the ass onto one of his shoulders. He fiddles. Bobbles. Jimmies. Swears. But it's impossible to get his fingers between the windpipe and the clasp of tanned hide.

Shit dribbles down 'tween the Rev's legs.

Jonah tries the buckle again, tugging and tugging until it gives, and the Rev pitches loose, free-falling forward, cuffing him in the head.

He retreats a step and rubs the welt blowing up above his eye.

Regroup. Regroup. He regroups and hauls the Rev to his bed, a trail of feces marking the way.

Jonah slaps his cheeks. Pap. Pap. Pap. No reason or rationale behind the reason. Pap. Pap. Pap.

Seven galaxies away at a black hole, radioactive decay collapses in on itself.

Jonah shrieks, then is shaken awake by both the Rev, and Loretta Tucci, his overnight cuddle buddy.

9:05 a.m.

"Where my money?" Bingo asks.

"In the bank," I lie. "But I'll have it for you by the end of the business day."

"Let me school you on a little somep'in." Bingo blazes up a spliff. "A man ain't shit if he don't keep his word. Don't matter what you does in this worl. Collect garbage. Be president of these United States. You ain't a man if you don't keep your word."

He hands me the *ganja*.

I take a hit and cough up the inner walls of my abdomen.

"Five o'clock. No 'scuses, son. Smell me?"

10:55 a.m.

Groggy, Jonah makes for the crapper in Desbelly Hall and washes his hands in the sink—an exercise he's been repeating on the hour, every hour, since he woke up. Fueled in large measure by the nightmare, he can't shake perpetual nervousness in all the obvious places: an itch at the back of his neck, crawly creepies down the spine, a tingling sensation beneath the ball sac.

"Goodness gracious, Jonah," Mrs Markham, the Silver Fox, interrupts. "Whatever are you doing in the women's toilet?"

"Say what?"

"You're in the women's toilet."

Sorry. He bombards her with apologies. Sorry. Sorry.

"Are you drunk?" she asks.

"God, no. Are you?"

Jonah totters on his way to the door. "Whoa there," she says. To steady him, she clutches onto the flesh of his upper arm. "Are you sure you're alright?"

Yes. Certainly. He goes on at length about all-nighters, the Rev's fragile state of being, and sputters into the crucially important lecture of the Transit Lit movement he'll be giving in Q-Deezy's class in a few. Then he changes the subject. "Is that new lipgloss? It looks splendid on you. Yummm. Well, good chatting, but I gotta get ... scram, skedaddle ..."

She steps aside to watch Jonah bang around like Abbott and Costello into every possible blunt object in the women's can. He stops, concentrates hard, and manages not to buckle at the knees as he takes another crack at veering off in the general direction of the door.

I sit behind a table at the front of the classroom, waiting for sky to crumble into seas.

Q. announced my visit to his class of twenty-four, but only eight have bothered to show up. Three girls sit in a corner at the back, defiantly doing homework for another course. In the back corner on the other side of the room, four boys slouch in chairs, staring me down.

Baba's car horn beeps in the garage. I run to there to get my surprise that he comes home to me early from work. When I see inside the garage, Baba has his head on top of the steering wheel and the car horn beeps.

"Baba." I knock on the window. "You can stop the horn now."

He does not look to me.

The bad thing is happening. The bad thing is happening.[128]

"I guess we'll get this party started," Quint C. says after a good

---

128   *The Notebooks* (undated). Events occur in approximately November 1988.

wait. "Any stragglers will just have to get caught up after class."

He kicks off the proceedings with a masterful intro; I'm a young up-and-comer from Liwani. An odd comparison is made to blaxploitation writer Donald Goines, the fellow who gave big pimping its handle.

A kid with a mustachio puts up a hand.

"Yes, Gregory," Quint C. says.

"We getting tested on this?"

"Of course," he replies. "So take notes."

Without further ado, I, Jonah Ayot-Kolosha, novelist, take center stage.

To describe the following forty-five minutes as a catastrophe is to put it mildly. My left eye twitches as I write the name of my movement on the board. TRANSIT LIT.[129] Then I launch into what can only be described kindly as an incomprehensible muddle. First, I go for the laugh. "Have any of you heard the one about the priest, the rabbi, and the medicine man?" One of the girls looks up from her homework. "Probably not, right?" She gets back into her assignment. "What I mean by that is this construction is an old convention in joke-telling that our generation doesn't bother with, kn'a mean?" No takers. "So this in miniature is the reason for Transit Lit"; I meant to say, this in miniature is the pressing reason for Transit Lit, but chickened out at the last minute. "We shouldn't be writing books that are modeled on eighteenth- or nineteenth-century literary traditions. The whole point of a novel is to be new. Original. Novel. That's what all those writers managed to do at a time the word, novel, didn't exist. They parodied what came before with a ... bevy, as it were,

---

129   Copyright with the Jonah Ayot-Kolosha estate.

of unprecedented narratological structures. Take for instance, the proto-pomo satire of Laurence Sterne, or the epistolary stories of Samuel Richardson, or the ironical observations in the domestic dramas of Jane Austen, and so on. Our generation needs to find its own J.D. Salingers, our own ways of telling our stories by parodying previous literary works within a multi-genre format. You with me here?"

A hand goes up. It's one of the boys.

"Yes," I say.

"Can I go to the toilet?"

I look over at Quint C. He nods.

While the toilet-bound bloke scrapes and sha-bangs his way out the door, I re-check my notes. I'll skip the manifesto and go straight to the exercises. "Rather than bore you with a laundry list of do's and don'ts, I thought it might be fun to work on some of the techniques required to open up your writing instrument." The remaining boys perk up. "In this way you'll more readily be able to access the basic tenets of Transit Lit. Crisp sentences. Flights of fancy. Parody as *para*, or comparison, not as an object of ridicule. And so on and so forth."

"I'd like to see Lori's writing instrument," Gregory chuckles.

"Pig," one of the girls replies.

"Settle down, you two," Quint C. admonishes.

I walk to the middle of the room, tell them to get out pen and paper, and then I begin in earnest. "Write a short sentence," I bark. "Now write a long sentence." On and on. Link "two compounds with a colon." Be "ironic as opposed to sarcastic." Start with "an image, extend it into a metaphor, but don't think." Take "an archetype and juxtapose it with a contemporaneous deviation of said type." Put one foot behind your ear and the other one at a hundred-and-twenty-degree angle adjacent to it. Walk and chew tabaccy at the same time.

As I walk around the classroom while they write, I look over their shoulders: one of the boys draws circles, a girl doesn't try to hide the fact she's ogling the beautiful in her *People* magazine, Gregory asks to go to the washroom to join the one who hasn't returned.

The bell sounds.

In the run-up to the class, I pictured students crowding me afterward, full of questions, and girls slipping me notes with their cell numbers as well as their IM addresses. The reality is a mad scramble for the door.

"I thought that went well," Quint C. says.

"You can't be serious?"

"This is a shy bunch," he continues. "They may not have had any questions at the end there, but the material was new."

I don't feel so good. "I need the can before Professor Iton's class."

"By the way, just so you know ..." He doesn't finish the sentence.

"What?" I'm impatient. "What? What?"

"Liza signed with Rachel Dalgleish."

"Really?"

"Yup, she found out this morning. Pretty good, huh?"

"Good for her. Good. For. Her."

I excuse myself to give my hands, the back of my neck, and my inner ears a hose down and scrub (in the men's room this time). Then, cursing Eliza May's skill at working her Q.-connection, I reach into my bag for an itty-bitty sip of a refreshing whiskey beverage.

12:55 p.m.

Jonah walks toward Desbelly Hall on scattered salt that has cor-
roded the remnants of ice on the path. From a distance, opposition to the Nigga Studies graffiti has grown outside the chancellor's office, and the methodology is fierce as picketers stand
ankle-deep in snow.

He walks toward their taunts.

"DU is racist," they shout.

He tries to push through a group of kerchief-wearing folk of
color who block the way to the door, but fingers hook onto his
upper arm.

"You ain't hangin?" a brother asks.

"I would," Jonah replies. "But I've gotta workshop a story two
minutes ago."

The brother shakes his head, disgusted. "You ain't never gonna
be white enough for all that milquetoasts you trying to impress."

"I gotta go."

"Get black, my brutha," he shouts after him. "Get black."

*I sit at a long table with other fourth formers and am distracted by walls laden
with photographs of an illustrious past. On my left, white-skinned former head-
masters and headboys mug for posterity. It starts on the far left with cotton side-
burns and bald heads from the late 20s, progresses to short combovers in the 60s,
and finishes with contemporary versions of the shoulder-length variety. To my right
are those who've been listed on the honor roll in capital letters on large wooden
panels. Behind me, on either side of the entrance, are glass cabinets crammed full of
engraved plaques and sports trophies.*

Everyone stands to sing a processional hymn.

Afterward, we remain on our feet while the white-skinned headmaster, Reverend

Father Griffin, offers up the salutation from a golden lectern at the front of the room. He sports a throwback comb-over and wears a black robe with a cleric's collar.

"Blessed be God. The Father, Son, and Holy Spirit." He crosses himself.

"And blessed be God's kingdom, now and for ever. Amen." We read from a prayer book.

"The Lord be with you," he says.

"And also with you."

"Let us pray," he continues. "O God, who before the passion of your only-begotten Son revealed his glory upon the holy mountain: grant to us that we, beholding by faith the light of his countenance, may be strengthened to bear our cross, and be changed into his likeness from glory to glory; through Jesus Christ our Lord, who lives and reigns with you and the Holy Spirit, one God, for ever and ever. Amen."

"Amen," we respond.

Then he makes way for the white-skinned headgirl, Fiona Collins, to read the lesson of the day from Exodus 24:12–18.

We sit.

Over the shoulders of Reverend Father and those of the white-skinned teaching staff seated on wooden chairs behind the lectern are panels with the years and names of awards the various Houses have managed to win. I belong to the yellow-colored Hildegaard House. Dominant in eight out of the last ten years.

"Hear what the Spirit is saying to God's people," Fiona concludes.

"Thanks be to God," we reply.

The Reverend Father returns to the lectern and explains the school motto, Summa Voluntate. Cicero is invoked, and we are asked to embody the utmost of goodwill. Then he introduces each member of white-skinned staff before the white-skinned headboy, Timothy Wells, stands to introduce the white-skinned prefects.

"I'd like to welcome all the new students to Scottsdale Anglican Academy," he says "If any of you have questions or concerns, please feel free to seek anyone of us out. Summa Voluntate."

"Summa Voluntate," we reply.

The Reverend Father returns to the lectern.

"The peace of God be always with you," he says.

"And also with you," we reply.

We wait for the procession of staff and prefects to follow the Reverend Father out of the dining hall before we stand and disperse to our first class. [130]

Jonah locks himself in a bathroom stall and wishes he could clamber into bed with Hiroko, then disentangle like a wave unraveled and pooling wherever he finds a hollow. He doesn't want to face the workshop, he doesn't want to face Bingo, and he doesn't want to go back to Colby Manor to face the Rev. What he wants is to go back to a home that no longer exists.

1:03 p.m.

Professor Iton starts off with an anecdote. At a party over the weekend, he had a conversation with Fish Coleman beside a restored mahogany dresser once owned by Gertrude Stein. At that time, the Professor learned that Fish received five hundred grand for his current manuscript-in-progress. "I've had the fortune of reading the accepted draft and, on an up note, it's quite cinematic. But you should see the prose. Predictable. At turns clunky, the overly determined reason for the protagonist's descent into mean-spiritedness is never adequately addressed. The only reason I see for Coleman's huge payday is the commercial value that comes with writing a slave narrative from a fresh perspective, that is, a relationship between a Negro boy who develops a secret friend-

---

130   *The Notebooks*, September 4, 1996.

ship with a pack of his slave owner's hounds. It's an absurd enough idea to appeal to an equally absurd industry. You follow?"

A tremble goes up my leg into my hands, and I feel like I'm about to pass out.

Switching gears, the class plows ahead with the sound of protesters' chants clanking against the window.

The room seems cramped, everyone in it appears to own disproportionately large heads, and voices amplify inside-out as I stare down at my notebook, unwilling to make eye contact with anyone.

"Chancellor Madison is a fascist," they shout.

Professor Iton proceeds to describe my story as a work of creative nonfiction and says a few nice words, none of which I take in. Instead, I focus on his comment about unevenness in the narrative voice. Cybil Harris, the Bostonian, takes this up. She finds "it has a cloying, off-putting, performative quality." Others chime in in agreement. The Steel Worker is disturbed by its "lack of an emotional center," as well as "the ending that doesn't work." The Bookworm feels "the writer has hidden behind virtuoso literary techniques."

Eliza May mounts a bit of a comeback for the pro-Jonah faction; she quotes several passages she found both moving and well-written. Quint C. brings up Donald Goines again and suggests the characters are something new. Not for long, as the Canuck recounts the horror of his experience with the work. "I was sick," he says. "Literally. Good God, the excess of adverbs. I couldn't finish it." The Bookworm agrees, pulls three examples of the cliché from the text, and wishes the whole thing would "read more African, like Chinua Achebe."

No one says what they think of the story, or what they think of what it is about.

After the shellacking is over, I'm invited to respond.

"Thank you for your input," I start. Then I compete with a speech outside shouted into a bullhorn as I attempt a redacted ramble cribbed from my lecture on Transit Lit. I muddle my perfect tenses with my pluperfect ones, I mix my metaphors and in this manner I cease to be other than what Da Stylus imagines: white lite—a copy of the same-but-not-exactly.

Settle down, mate.

Professor Iton teaches attentiveness to the sentence. "There is no such thing as a globule of rain, Jonah. Do not be so imprecise with your images."

When I disagree, he removes his spectacles and wipes the lenses with a white handkerchief.

I learn from his patient correction. I must prepare in isolation, then return with paragraphs of considered phrases.

After class, no one looks me in the eye as they hand me their copies of my story, complete with editorial notes and a letter with a summation of their blood-curdling commentary.

I avoid Professor Iton and beat a hasty exit to the men's bath-room for another full body wash.

3:42 p.m.

Jonah won't return to the Rev's because of what he expects to find there. Physical pain. The onset of dying. A corpse. So he gath-ers with a green salad in the writers' lounge. Opposite him, Quint C.'s legs are crossed and one hand is squeezed between his legs. Next to him, Eliza May swallows aspirin to stave off a low-grade migraine from too much caffeine.

"Listen," Quint C. says. "Take the comments that are useful and ignore the rest."

"I don't believe how rude some of those people are," Eliza May rubs her temples. "'It made me sick.' What does that have to do with literary criticism?"

"'Most people treat stories like a ride on a cruise ship,'" Quint C. says. "'I felt comfortable here.' 'I wasn't enjoying myself there.' Who cares?"

"'It needs to read more like Chinua Achebe,'" Eliza May says. "What does that have to do with anything?"

Jonah wouldn't normally take their spirited defense seriously. After all, Quint C.'s contradicting himself with that crap about not caring about the reader. He changed his work because of pressure from his editor, *and* it's the first time Jonah's heard him say anything remotely in sync with a position taken by Professor Iton. As for Eliza May, well, she's always kind.

Jonah imagined it all going so differently. All of it. The presentation. His writing. His freaking love life. Being in Curranvale City. Endings.

"Wakey, wakey, Jonah," Quint C. says.

"Huh?"

"What do you think?"

"About what?"

"About us moving in together after we get back from Amsterdam, numb nuts?"

He thinks of Eliza May snagging Q.'s big-shot agent. "Bottoms up," he mumbles. "Quint gets the one thing he can't have, and Eliza May has her meal ticket."

"Dude!"

"What the fuck?" Eliza May says.

He gets up. "Then congratulations are in order." He bumps the table, jostling soda cans. "Brilliant! Fantastic really! I've got to go. But we'll celebrate soonish. Cheers."

They both stare at him as if he's just trampled on a spanking new litter of Labrador pups.

3:48 p.m.

I sit in tweeds in the Creative Writing office, waiting for the great man to make an entrance. I'm still uncertain what to say to him. Am I any good? Should I quit? On my own, I'm all blurry edges. I want so much to be told what to do.

The phone rings for the umpteenth time. Mrs Markham, the Silver Fox, answers before providing an address where an application can be sent along with a check of seventy-five dollars. Behind her, through a window, is a courtyard where students in puffy parkas trudge through snow.

I pick up a brochure from the coffee table in front of me and fold it into a paper airplane.

"Jonah." Professor Iton stands in the portal of the door in jeans and a white t-shirt. "I can see you now."

I follow him through the hallway and into room 340.

Cramped into the small windowless room are a desk, two chairs, an empty bookshelf, and a black rotary telephone. He sits behind his desk while I get comfy in a wooden seat.

"I must apologize." He lights a cigarette. "Some days, coffee's the only way to endure the vagaries of an institution run by blue bloods whose lives are spent bickering over who left the shed door open." He stubs the cigarette out in an ashtray and hands me an article. "Have you seen this?" It's a review of Professor Iton's own soon-to-be released novel, *Bodice Ripper*,[131] written by, of all twits, Fish Coleman. "The article's due to appear in the *Village Voice* tomorrow."

I take a gander.

The opening paragraph begins with an oh, how sad to see the great ones fall. Then Fish summarizes the plot, revealing secrets that lend the story its tension. Nothing new here, he writes, before segueing into a begrudging acknowledgment of merits: the nice font, the choice of paper. In paragraph two, he returns to content. Boredom set in at page ten. Unremitting. Unrelenting. On page thirteen, four sentences from the bottom, the great writer didn't exercise control with his adjectives. The side story is voyeuristic, too cutesy; nothing is at stake and Fish wishes for a different direction in the narrative. To conclude, he quotes Homer, and apologizes that sons inevitably must castrate fathers.

"Jeezus," I remark.

"The motherfucker is going to make the publication of my book about him," Professor Iton muses.

Despite a hypothesis to the contrary, my latest bingey smear of writing, pills, and booze suddenly arranges a moment of clarity. The great man is like Midas, perpetually alienated from anything he comes in contact with. I mean, he's actually telling me something real about himself, and all I can do is sit, blankity fuckity blank. Even if I'm given days to come up with a better response, it'd still fall short of speaking to whatever it means for him to be a person of considered literary repute beaten behind the woodshed by his commercially successful protégé.

---

131   His twelfth novel, published in the fall of 2004; well-received by the critical press, but low sales did not augur well for a second printing.

Professor Iton lights another smoke, laughing. "Okay, back to more important matters, I hate to say this about your story, but there are parts of this that look an awful lot like something else I've read."

"You mean the style."

He clears his throat. "No. Word for word."

I'm stunned. "You think it's plagiarized?"

"Yes."

Mrs Markham opens his door. "It's time," she interrupts.

"Already?"

"It's time," she repeats.

"We're going to have to wind this up." Professor Iton has a committee meeting to chair on the question of whether the term nigga constitutes a slur. "I'll get back to you on this after I've done a bit more research. But, suffice it to say that if I find it's plagiarized, you'll get an F for the course. You follow?"

10:40 p.m.

Nowhere left to turn, I bang on Hiroko's door, wait, and bang again. Eventually, Ingrid answers. She stands with one foot on top of the other, cradles a bulky copy of the juvenalian hijinks of *Tom Jones* under an armpit, and chews on a strand of her long hair.

"Is Hiroko in?" I ask.

"No. She got called to work."

"So you're alone?"

"Did you figure that out on your own?"

I backpedal. "Bye, then."

"Wait," she says. "Can I ask a question?"

"Shoot."

"Do you love my sister?"

"Sure," I reply.

"So why haven't you come to see her?"

"I had to … wait, why the hell am I explaining this to you?"

"Are you going to help her, or not?" she asks.

"I beg your pardon."

"Imbecile," Ingrid scoffs. "You love her, right? So are you going to help or not?"

"What's going on, Ingrid?"

"I don't like the people she's with," she says. "I think they're going to hurt her."

"Right now."

"Yes now, idiot. What meds are you on?"

I take a breath. "Could you take the insults down a notch, and just tell me what's going on?"

"Mum's bipolar, and sometimes she makes a huge mess of things. She wracked up big debts on her credit cards, and Hiroko had to go to work to take care of it. Then you didn't call and …"

"I'm not getting any of this."

"You have epilepsy, right?" she asks. "Is that why you can't understand?"

"You want me to bring her home?"

"No, dummy. I want you to leave her at work until something bad happens. That's why I'm telling you this, so we can sit and do nothing. Jeeepers!"

"Hold your fire, Ingrid. I got it."

She smiles. "You know, you're not as bad as that bore Bingo. That's for sure."

"You mean, Ito."

"Who?"

"Ito. Her boyfriend."

"Bingo's her boyfriend."

"What?"

"What do you mean, what? Bingo. B–I–N…"

12:40 a.m.

Shutupshutup, Hiroko tells Hiroko to tell Hiroko.

She needs to preen in the mirror of the ladies' toilet, then earn back the lost cash.

She applies a spritz of ylang ylang.

Get this over with. Half an hour, tops. After I've clocked enough paper. After. I'll slide into sweats, ignore the girls jabbering about assholes and whooping coughs, then flee this hell-hole before another customer latches onto me for my number.

Her first move is to work the main room. She hits up the aged relic who's been into the white girls all night. Five minutes of chitchat pass before it's clear they're going nowhere. Then she sits down with a square-jaw determined not to spend more than he has for three drinks. She loses ten minutes on him.

Time!

She can't seem to produce it. No matter which way she manipulates time, it is indeed a fugitive, in flight, from her.

She plunks herself down in front of Bingo.

"You been ignorin me?" she asks.

"Nah! I been hustlin."

"With Monay, right?"

"Don't get in my bidness, girl."

"Okay, are you gonna buy me a drink or no?" She isn't about to waste her time, pad his ego by showing her jealousy. Right now, she wants to be home, flaked-out under her poster of the one whose mantra is oommmmmmm. "A Grey Goose would be nice."

"Slow down there, baby girl," Bingo yells into the side of her face. "Where we at with Jonah?"

"C'mon. One drink."

"Jonah?"

"It's all good."

"That's alls I need to hear." He slaps a folded wad of cash onto the table. "Five 'un'red if you party with me in the bathroom."

She hesitates. "You're shitting me."

"Your call, baby girl."

Five hundred. Damn. "Let's go."

"A'aight." He taps his nostril. "I could use a quick toot. You?"

"Lead the way." Hiroko divides five hundred by six dances at three minutes a pop, twice coming up with the same answer: time well spent.

She follows after Bingo, and then waits outside the door while he pays off the shitter's attendant.

Bingo grabs her by the hand, and pulls her into a stank stall.

The tuxedoed toilet attendant sits on a stool, guarding towels beside a small wicker basket.

"En-joy," he stammers at them.

Bingo drops more bills. "Thanks, brah."

"Pleasure, sir." He looks the other way.

Minutes later, thirty more than she planned, Hiroko is bent over the dirty lid of the porcelain tank in the shitter, a rolled-up twenty in her nostril. Three lines and her smacked-up sinuses itch, the light collapsing in on her as she turns to face Bingo in the locked stall.

"How zhat?" he asks.

"Fine."

She listens to traffic at urinals; the drag of feet repeating a muffled, boozy trek to the head.

Her fingers fidget in a shank of hair, then adjust the slinky dress at a slit at her flank.

Her mouth is dry.

Thinking is difficult.

"No condom?" she asks.

"Not for big Poppa," he replies.

"No condom and you don't get tuned."

"Seven-fifty up front?"

She thinks it through. *Seven-fifty on top of everything else. Damn, girl.*

"Don't punk out on me," he adds.

"No. It's not that."

"You punkin out on me, baby girl."

Her brain churns words to the surface, piled up and bullying with an insistence, she lashes back. Haggle for space. "I'm no punk."

She steadies herself with a hand against graffiti on the wall. Her mind going over the rationale—time well spent.

"So, what'up?" he asks.

Okay, if she gets a bit higher, a little more of that out-of-kilter, run-on feeling.

Why not?

"First, let's do a few more lines," she replies.

"Whoa there, sweetheart."

He tucks fingers into the back of Hiroko's dress and scratches his nails along the ridges of her spine. She feels his hand cup a tit.

She tries to remember … what?

He pushes his cock up against her thong, his hips shark back and forth, his cock pushing the silk, bit by bit, inward as he tries to find a rhythm.

"Stop!"

His head slumps forward.

"You ripped my dress."

"Fuck, that's a Versace, ain't it?"

"Sorry?"

"The dress."

She takes her slinky number off, drapes it over the toilet paper holder, and leans back against the shitter's porcelain tank. She lets the grip of Bingo's fingers on her arms block the flow of blood to her wrists.

1:57 a.m.

Jonah pushes open the door to the men's can. The toilet attendant sits to the right on his stool, chewing on the fingers of one of his white gloves. "Good morning, sir," he says.

Jonah ignores him, his attention focused on the row of three stalls to the left of him. He marches to the spacious wheelchair-accessible one where the porcelain bangs against the wall, Hiroko's familiar sighs mixing with a steady stammer of grunts.

Jonah tugs a wool cap over his ears before he kicks the door. Three whacks later the door gives and Jonah stares at Hiroko on the toilet seat clutching her dress to her chest, covering her buck-nudity. Bingo stands, watching Jonah, grinning as he calmly zips up his fly.

Jonah launches himself at Bingo the asswipe, swinging.

"Stop!" Hiroko exclaims. The attendant runs inside the stall and grabs Jonah by the shoulders.

When he's finally pulled away by the attendant, blood streams from Bingo's nose.

"What the fuck?" Bingo drops into a crouch with the dexterity of a welterweight and dances on toes before popping off a series of quick jabs. Jonah's feet slip on the linoleum tile as his adversary closes in with a crunching hook. Fluorescent light is bright, the writing candidate buckles at the knees and his head snaps back, first slamming against the toilet attendant's wicker basket and then the porcelain sink.

2:40 a.m.

I wake up on Hiroko's sofa with my head resting in her lap. She wears dark mascara on her bottom lids and is pressing a soaked cloth onto a lump at the back of my skull.

I piece significant events together.

All she's done is tell me lies, and then I find her fucking Bingo in the can.

I sit up sharply, pushing her hand away. "What the hell, Hiroko?"

"I've never pretended to be anything but who I am," she responds.

The back of my head friggin hurts. "He's married."

"Jeezus," Hiroko flings unwashed clothes from the sofa to the floor. "Your idealism isn't cute anymore." She stands, walks to the doorway of the kitchen, returns to sit down on the farthest edge of the love seat, then stands up again with a lit cigarette. "It's getting old."

I finger an engagement ring in my pocket. "All you are is a parade of clever responses." I think of her farfetched story about growing up on a pineapple plantation. "Can't you say something that is real for once?"

Smoke fumes from her nostrils. "Okay, so what the fuck is a relationship with me going to cost *you*? What the fuck are *you* giving up?" She sits again, stands again. "You're no different. You just hide behind clichés you actually believe in."

"You're changing the subject."

She points her cigarette at me. "That's exactly what I'm talking about. I may as well stop talking because you've already got this conversation pegged." A long ash dangles from a cigarette, threatening at any moment to drop to the floor. "Right now, I'm just gums flapping at you."

"Don't be ridiculous."

"Now *I'm* ridiculous!" she exclaims.

"I didn't mean *you* are ridiculous." I try to sound contained. "I meant, like you're inhabiting the space of the ridiculous. Like one who's in a swimming pool, but not the water in the pool. You know? One is wet, not the water, not ridiculousness in itself."

"You're the one who's ridiculous," she says. "You're the one who's been holding out about being engaged."

Shitshit. "Say what?"

"Well?"

I'm flabbergasted. "Who told you that? Bingo?"

Smoke blows out of her mouth. "Ah, what the hell do I care?"

"Okay, I was engaged," I blurt out. "But it doesn't mean what you think. It wasn't real. We did it to so I could get my inheritance."

She abandons one cigarette, lights another. "You go around saying this is right and that is wrong, but none of it applies to you."

"Fine. Stop the freaking presses." I think of the Rev. "I'm as much of a hypocrite as the next guy." I strangle a scream. "But you ought to listen to yourself sometime. All you ever do is take easy ways out and get angry whenever anyone contradicts you in a mad rush to defend your lazy habits."

"Fuck you, bougie asshole!"

"Case in point."

"I have to talk to you like you're a teenager," she says. "Grow up!"

"I'm sick of this."

"Look, I'm a booty call. Your fiancée is a way to get your hands on money. You can't stand the Rev even though you pretend you're worried that he'll kill himself. No wonder you can't write worth a damn. There ain't a thing you'll pay a real price for."

"Christ Jeezus and Mary Jones, babe!"

"Don't shout!"

"I suppose you'd respect me more if I asked you to put rubber bands on my cock."

She slaps a glass of water out of my hand and sends it shattering against the floor. "Get out."

I stand. "What else did you do with Bingo? Crap on his chest?"

She grabs hold of my leg and we tumble over each other onto the hardwood floor. First she's on top of me, clawing at my face, then I'm on top of her, squeezing her in a bear hug. Out of control, we spit curses as we roll near a closet door that jams open against my knee.

Hidden among jackets and shoes, Ingrid is curled in a tight ball. Hiroko and I fall away from one another.

Sorrysorry, I mutter. I can't get my thoughts straight and scramble backwards toward the door. I ... I'm sorry. Unable to find my shoes. I stumble in socks down the icy staircase and tip-toe onto the slick sidewalk.

a botched cartography is stale grey, the earth is snot rags and
pigeon dumps, the evening terse with a frustration that rots

like bad fish. in my pocket, an engagement ring scratches
cotton against my thigh as i walk between this ethnic block
and that: white to black to brown to yellow in seventy-three
steps. ticktocks tick something fierce as i bend into gusts of
nor'easterly wind contorted by blowing plagues without a
cure—cancers, bird flu. toxic gases are exports that career this-
away in falling snow as cement, imported from the orient on
the cheap, is bruised, cracked. everyplace i turn multiheaded-
media rises up to dismantle borders, and there are arguments
over left wing hoaxes, right of center phantasmagoria, and
loose nukes. as i walk a paper thin edge, an atom bomb named
rita hayworth was dropped fifty-five plus years ago and its
effects cannot be seen in curranvalean folk who think themselves in and out of ideas unsupported by evidence. they wear
mitts the size of melons, and don't look my way, and don't care
in the slightest that we speak garborated nonsense that cannot pass the smell test (churned rubbish that doesn't change
a belief in superstitions one nanometer). once more, a fella
sleeps on a steaming manhole, another on a cardboard box
beneath a causeway, another beneath a blanket beside a shopping cart. and once again, newspapers from kilimanjaro peaks
to wide canadian prairies are plied with editorials whose edges
shiver as they say this has more to do with those who say their
story would make a great novel. not a one notices my head is
down and the balls of my wasimbi-jinjabi feet are ice. i am in
and out of questions about what it takes to let go of my own
rubbish that hangs on me like the smell of a summer barbecue
clings to a turkish rug airing out on a banister. i too have been
paid sheckles to buy my ascent. shut up and love anthems, and
dulce decorum est pro patria mori because how sweet it is to die
for energy policy hammered out in a secret room, it is better
to be sweetly killed as accountability glances off the well-con-

nected who spread cheer despite evidence to the contrary. words are entertainers. they perform in australasia, in the marketplaces of kathmandu as death mounts among sons and daughters of those who grind in car factories in motown, in garment manufacturers in bombay and mönchengladbach. up ahead, a foreclosure sign sits in a glass doorway. is there service that i can render to that-which-a-greater-cannot-be-thought? i have yet to genuflect before *solar rex* or the oscillating elec-tromagnetic big bang, or before persons who give off high frequencies of attitude and are convinced of the correctness of narratives that say how they hate one another without know-ing one another. beside me shoes slush in melting puddles as i hear plagiarized quotations of plagiarized quotes everywhere. head drowned, i walk voices that aren't paid the scantest at-tention as they swing low between shadows from trees that cling to muddy snow banks from the industrial edges of curranvale city to the wide wyoming plain. i'm oafish among paper wrappers from beijing that blow roundaround my naked ankles, and i can't arrange my thoughts to mark an occasion i don't yet understand.

how sweet it is when there is nowhere left to go.

i feel a twitch in my left cheek, skin tugs away from bone and prickles near my upper lip. my tongue thickens at the base of my throat, and my mind grows old. ★ ★ ★ ★
★ ★
★ ★
★ ★ ★ ★ ★ ★ ★ ★ ★ ★ ★ ★ ★ ★ ★ after all these years, you arrive in the smoke room. they have taken your matches and left you with a device that looks as if it was invented for those who are easily discouraged. there is a line in front of a silver bowl that is three inches in diameter and screwed to the wall three feet above the

ground. there is a hole in it large enough for the insertion of a cigarette. there are coils inside the bowl that light up when you press a small red button, two inches to its right. you wait among those who are like you. it won't be long as you wait your turn holding firm to your place in line. minutes later, you stand before the silver-plated chalice. you press the button on the wall, wait for the coils inside to get red-hot, place your marlboro inside the hole, bend down, and suck on the filter until the cigarette catches light. smoke burns in your lungs. you inhale, cough, and then sit beside the other nuthousers in this room that is locked and has an orderly who looks into a small window to make sure there's no tomfoolery going on.

this is where it ends.

this is where your list of reasons has dwindled to one.

this where you abandon your dwindling supply of smokes and find meaning in the need to give the utmost to ...

BOOK VII

———

Return

I

One-and-a-half years earlier at the red brick home in Hoppa, we meet Reverend Nehemiah Ayot, who preps for the after-effects of a heavy famine

In a mirror, we see him measure the deterioration in his daily battle with shaving paraphernalia—fulminating shaving lotion, drooping bristles of a brush, a blunt razor blade. We see him clear away grey stubble, itching beneath his chin, for what he knows is the final time.

To watch him is to witness the decline of a man who doesn't know easy distinctions between *terra firma* and the up-yonder nestled in the empty canopy of sky. It's to see this man, an older man, creep around in dark shadows, avoiding the sun that punches its way through open cracks between drawn curtains. It's to witness him, bloated from a diet of too much salt, lean over a sink and cough blood into a drain. It's to stand by as he works stubby fingers into a kink above the kidneys.

As we watch Nehemiah stare into a mirror at the curved cartography of his eyeballs mapped with crimson blood vessels, he tries to imagine what his grandson, who said little and watched others a great deal, imagined him to be in his pile of spiral-bound notebooks. Whatever it is he knows, the boy gets it wrong. Under his stewardship, his chapel has attracted the attention of other great people of God, and they have worked to bring running water, hopes. But that notebook … no. Jonah is from a generation that has abandoned communal responsibilities to pack themselves into the cities with the belief that new means improved. They see men of the cloth like him as dictatorial generals in Christ's fascistic army. Like Jonah, they don't understand that he's one of the few who still follows visions that come to him at night, visions he faithfully acts upon once sleep no longer enchants him.

Standing at the mirror, resentments reawaken that Nehemiah's become less inclined, over the years, to address; since the death of his daughter, Rahab, the unpredictability of living is a bother; to get rolling each day, he likens himself to Abraham and painstakingly slaps mortar on crabbed nooks in his character he hadn't noticed until they showed up in his grandson's glances, the ones that tell him he's no longer formidable, the quick once-overs that say, yes, his judgment is suspect, and it's only right that he relinquish the responsibilities that give his character shape.

If we look closer, we can see tremors erupt at Nehemiah's wrists that disappear right before he splashes boot polish-strength cologne against skin the texture of burnt deciduous bark. Afterward, we watch him pad toward the refrigerator in bedroom slippers, bluffing his way through the rites of another morning. He wears himself out scrubbing burnt rice from a pan, boiling water for tea, and slicing a mango before settling at the dining table, alone, recollecting the vision that told him today is to be his last.

This day is also the one Jonah leaves for grad school abroad and Nehemiah disciplines himself by distancing himself from his own emotions. As required, he reins in all feelings, deepened by aging, as if bridled to a galloping horse. As a result, he's difficult to read while he watches the peculiar boy prop a scuffed suitcase on top of his head before they walk together to meet Reverend Tusker at the chapel. Silently, they traverse the footpath shaded by fruitless guava trees. Beside them, squadrons of swallows swoop low to the stubbly grass, and sweat spreads like an inkblot over Nehemiah's cassock, a second, thin coat of skin.

"Sorry I'm getting away a little late," Jonah apologizes.

"You let yourself off too easily," Nehemiah returns. "The rains are a little late. Christmas takes place late in the year, but you …"

"I know, Babu. I know."

They lapse into yet another silence.

As far as Nehemiah is concerned, Jonah is too much like the boy's father. Lax. Slow. Interested only in hiding whatever secretive thoughts run through his head, always something on the side; a girlfriend that's never introduced, walking the neighborhood at the most dangerous time of night, selfish in his single-minded pursuits, and unable to see how these behaviors inevitably lead him into his various frustrations.

Side by side, they walk into an opening of prickly beige grass where slabs of limestone mark the graves of his daughter and her unfaithful husband, Phineas. They pass sheets of corrugated iron that obscure the pits in which WaSimbi children often hide from the local Jinjabi recruits hired to protect the ongoing construction of the Feltway Dam.[132] In time, they make their way onto a dirt road that winds through sugarcane, the air filling with the rustle of frogs leaping among stalks that block a view of an untidy sprawl of bullet-riddled buildings.

At five past nine, they meet Reverend James Tusker behind the chapel.

---

132 Construction began in 1999 with financial aid from the World Bank, although it was stipulated all working contracts were to be awarded to Western companies. As of this writing, the dam has yet to be completed and international funding was cut due to reports of human rights abuses in Liwani.

As far as Nehemiah can tell, his old friend looks chubbier than he appeared fifteen years ago during a stint doing missionary work at Hoppa. His cheeks are rounder, his khaki shirt and his rumpled trousers are tighter. Also, as always, his nose is smeared with white sun block, and flakes of dandruff decorate his shoulders.

"How long has it been, my brother?" Nehemiah asks.

"Too long," Reverend Tusker says, squeezing his friend's arm before turning to Jonah. "And how's our scholarship Boy doing?"

"Fine."

"Nervous?"

"Nope. No, sir."

Reverend Tusker points to a mess of tents in a field behind the chapel. "That's quite the collection of Refugees."

Nehemiah clears his throat as they observe a small cluster of volunteers and aid workers stoking fires and stirring wooden ladles in boiling pots. Among them, barefooted boys and girls walk in and out of tent flaps as well as run in and out of black smoke (much like their lives haven't been interrupted by the Feltway Dam Relocation Project).

"Blessed are the Peacemakers, for they will be called the Children of God," Reverend Tusker says.

Nehemiah reaches quickly for his handkerchief and has a coughing fit, lasting half a minute, and then the handkerchief comes away red from his mouth. "Sometimes I wonder whether we're the forsaken ones, abandoned like Job's first family in that bet between God and the Devil," he responds.

"Buck up, Nehemiah. You don't teach nonviolent Protest because it feels good. You do it because it's Right."

"Is it so?"

"Blessed are the Merciful, for they will obtain Mercy."

"Amen," Jonah interrupts.

Nehemiah's lips curl into a faint smile: the boy's sarcasm reminds him of his daughter. He wonders if he should tell him about the dream he had the night she died. Instead, Nehemiah swivels to look again at the world that fuels Jonah's cynicism. An amputee with nubs for knees leans against a tree trunk while another with stumps for arms lays in the shade of a eucalyptus tree on sun-baked soil. In the distance, a steady roar of motors cuts through hot breeze and scarlet dust clouds billow as armed convoys crowd onto a newly built army base near Hoppa.

"We've got to go." Reverend Tusker hurries toward his Toyota.

"It's time, son," Nehemiah says.

He shakes Jonah's hand, then watches as his perplexing grandson wipes down the passenger seat with a face cloth before getting into the car.

"God bless," he says.

Reverend Tusker starts the Toyota, Jonah's response is lost in the din, and Nehemiah lets go of the boy he'd been entrusted by his daughter to prepare for the sacrament of Holy Orders for what will be the last time. ★
★ ★
★ ★ ★ ★ ★ ★ ★ ★ ★ ★ ★ ★ ★ ★ *Get in, get out, get in, get out.*

As a safety measure, Reverend Tusker left for Curranvale City two days ahead of me, so I stand alone in the clotted heat of the departure lounge at the Liwani Airport. I stare at eyelids swollen by a lack of sleep, *rigor mortis* settling in at the cheeks of those who shove one another aside, and say fuck-damn.

Get in, get out, get in, get out.

I turn, step onto an escalator, and merge with once click-happy tourists turgid with worries not soon to be forgotten, their holidays brought to a sudden halt by the bombing of a tour bus by the WaSimbi Freedom Party (WFP) in the popular game reserve near the Saroto Forest. As I jostle en route to Gate 6, the shoulder strap of a bag full of papers digs into my collarbone, and I bump against others also migrating to packed exits. Some gawk quizzically at their boarding passes, the rest quickstep blind over those in sleeping bags as they hustle toward arrows to follow: this way to the baggage carousel, that way to Customs.

Momentarily stalled by a rampaging herd shuffling along in orderly panic, I wait behind a cattle breeder; burly, ruddy-faced, brusque.

"Getting out for good?" he asks.

Bitter like burnt treacle, I manage a smile. "No. I'm off to study in the States. Yourself?"

"Good Lord, yes," he mutters. "I've learned the hard way that one can take the cannibal out of the jungle. But not the jungle out of the cannibal. Take my meaning?"

I'm uncomfortable, and look away.

"Oh, God. Not you. You sound like one of us. It's the rest of them, one bloody step removed from boiling each other in a pot of stew. Tribalists! It starts with killing tourists and ends with bleeding warlords squabbling over the capital city." He takes a deep breath. "Say what you want about British rule, at least we knew how to run the shop."

Bodies make way before us, and with a "right then," the cattle breeder clears out, mumbling about how the natives are letting it "all go to hell in a hand basket with their condom-less fucking like bunny rabbits."

I wait for distance to open up between us before I push on toward the security checks, hastening past the working stiffs—spit-polish black to boot—who cart luggage and sweep up the interminable terminal for a lifetime.

"Excuse me," I say. "Coming through."

Like presto, I weave through khaki-clad settlers sun burned at the edges of collars and freckled at the nose. Then once again I stall in a long line occupied by a generation of men and women emancipated by a proclamation (May 6, 1971).

Chloe, the name offered, is jittery with nervousness. "Are you Liwanian, hon?" Others similarly infected speed-talk around us. "Liwanian? Is that right? It sounds suu-per weird to say it. Liwani sounds better." Luggage toppling from a cart distracts her. "I'm on my way to Windhoek. Did I pronounce that okay? It's such a mouthful. Wow. You try say it. Wind-oh-eck." She makes a pistol with her fingers and puts it against her temple. "Poof. I'm making a mess of that one too."

"You're doing fine," I say.

She strokes my arm. "That's awesome of you to say, hon."

We arrive at the counter and I hand over my documents to an official of the Republic.

The woman, with a bleach birthmark on her cheek, takes her sweet time.

"So you abandon your people," she says.

"I'm only going for a few years to study."

"Heh, heh, you go to become a big doctor in America, and you think you will remember home?"

"Yesyes," I insist. "Course. Yes."

She laughs to herself. "He thinks he's going to enjoy his Hollywood, and then come back with his big degrees and go straight to the village."

"I'm coming back." I thrust my hands deep in the pockets of charcoal trousers, hints of stubble itching at razor bumps beneath my chin. "I am."

She squints, studying my passport photo. "Who is your family?" she finally asks.

At all costs, I must avoid drawing attention to my WaSimbi mother. "I'm alone."

"Eh-hem. You do not have people you come from?"

"I'm alone," I repeat.

Lickity split, she beckons a guard saddled at his waist by a pistol shooter. He struts over, trigger-happy and schoolboy-thin in a baggy, forest-green uniform.

"He's going to America," she says. "And he does not think he will enjoy his Disneyland and forget home." They both bust up laughing about insights privy to in-groups.

"Is it?" he asks me.

The smell of blood tickles in my nose hair, and my skull threatens to blow like an over-inflated balloon.

"My papers are in order," I respond.

"WaSimbi dung beetle!" he says to me. "You are all born speaking with a lizard's tongue."

"I've done nothing wrong."

"That is for us to decide," the woman corrects.

"Follow me." The guard points to a closed door behind them. "There we settle questions about papers."

It's decided: bruises will be tattooed onto my legs, stripes drawn with serrated edges into my skin, and my bones popped at sockets until I admit I'm a dung beetle of WaSimbi pedigree.

As I gather myself, Chloe intercedes by placing hard, Western currency on the counter before us.

"Is there a problem?" she asks.

The woman with the bleach mark is quick to cover the pile of bills with her hand before sliding them to the pistol packer. He licks his fingers, then turns his back to count them.

"Is there still a problem?" Chloe asks again.

"No problem," he replies.

"Good." Chloe helps me gather my papers. "Thanks a million."

Humiliated and giddy, I follow after her as we're directed through x-ray machines to a lobby.

"What gate are you leaving from, hon?" she asks.

She gently reaches into my jacket pocket and looks at my ticket. Then her hand slides beneath my elbow, and she delivers me to the gate where I am to board a flight that will stopover in a European city famous for its white chocolate.[133]

We hug.

Cheers.

Much too late, I think, *I didn't thank her.* ★ I watch my reflection in the window for signs that I might cry as the plane pitches forward, lifts for minutes, and escapes the latest talk of a *coup d'état*. High above the thatched huts where Gramps lays hands upon the anointed, my ears crackle and pop. I ding the dinger for aid and comfort from the stewards of the sky, but there's no response. There are carts to load with aperitifs; there are babies to coddle in preferred seating.

The plane shudders before it cruises above an African wilderness that has surrendered to red and browns, and recedes into

---

133   Zürich. See also footnote 39.

darkness that once played with cumulus clouds. Flight attendants in navy blue make their way down the aisle, making small-talk with each other as they push carts ahead of them. I recline in my seat above the wing, anticipating turbulence. Meanings shift and undetermined parts of myself displace while the plane moves, adroitly, through international airspace. ★ Shortly after 3:30 p.m., eighteen hours after the initial take-off, the aircraft begins its penultimate descent toward rectangular plots and square houses crammed against blue swimming pools, slung around the banks of a winding river.

The plane drops onto its haunches on a cement strip and taxies to a halt.

Seat belts can now be unfastened while the attendants perform official rituals of arrival. Welcome to Curranvale City, stay to the left.

I disembark to follow signs that lead to uniforms who take my papers, ask my legal name, my country of birth.

Where exactly am I?

Approximately 4:05 p.m., I'm stalled at Customs.

I sit at a distance of about one-hundred-and-ten feet away from a bank of coin-operated television sets with folks watching a talk show. Today, blood tests will be revealed, and the guilt of an unsympathetic guest (according to sixty percent of those polled in the studio audience) is to be determined after a paid announcement by a corporate sponsor.

"Follow me, Mr Ayachtt-Kolosha," a black man in a white short-sleeve shirt says.

"Ayot-Kolosha," I correct.

"Ayut."

"No. Uh-yot as in Uh-not. Ayot."

"How's Jonah?"

"Good enough."

In an office, at a desk, we sit opposite one other. Behind the short-sleeve shirt, positioned to the left of his shoulder, is a picture of the leader of the land whose smile retains a well-coached swagger that reassures with cocksure alpha manliness.

The brother enters security codes into his computer, joggles down the screen, and flushes with pragmatic reasons for his employ. He's not to be confused with the ones who will not hesitate to insult your mother.

I'm asked to drop my belt and remove my shoes.

The uniformed brother taps information into a computer's hard drive, and then digitally scans my index finger and takes digital mug shots to update my biometric data.

I avoid eye contact with the lens of a surveillance camera.

I'm asked to be exact in the explanation of the nature of our motives.

Six hours later, I hobble toward the baggage section.★ ★ ★ ★ ★
★ ★
★ ★
★ ★

★ ★ Bingo Jefferson rushes the young African seated in Reverend Tusker's Buick through tiny openings in lanes of swift-moving traffic. He's thinking ahead, calculating his next hustle.

"The Rev sends remonstrances for not coming hisself," he says. "He twisted up his ankle, so I'm the DH."

"DH?"

"Designated hitter," he replies. "The Rev ain't what he wuz." He waggles a finger in circles next to his temple. "He crazy. *Loco*. But you ain't heard that from Bingo. Whaaat."

"He's crazy?"

"You gonna need all your African voodoo, witch doctor shit to keep 'im from clampin negativity into your game."

Outside, the sun melts into an orange smudge dropping west of a ragged jut of skycrapers, bubbled domes, and interwoven freeways. Bumper to bumper traffic sputters along, carrying Curranvalean folk plugged into iPods or listening to their voice mail before speed-dialing business associates and booty calls.

"Good Goddamn." Bingo still has to stop by the hardware store for a new brake light before doing the Rev's weekly shopping. "Ain't traffic a bitch."

He inches left until a white Porsche in the lane beside him makes way for him.

"Sorry for taking so long at Customs," Jonah says. "I hate being late."

"Chill, brah. I got in a little late myself," he says. "I hadta go see my PO, 'n' they wuz paperwork to fill if I want to get the shorties signed up for health insurance. It's all a wholelotta whutwhut. A release for this, a release for that. Bullshit that has you runnin around tryna figure words that mean a big heap of nuthin. Then I hadta pony up cash money to file the dang papers. Hidden taxes, yo!" He lights a spliff. "The government be robbin po' folk blind by chargin this 'n' that jus so they can keep bombin Eye-Raq. True dat. 'N' alls the time politicals has us fightin terror over there, a nigga's rights ain't jackshit right this here."

Jonah rolls down his window.

"Yup. The world full of motherfuckers. 'N' that's why I gotta get me a little coochie, and smoke a little of this here killer weed now 'n' again. Yup. Jiggawhat? Jiggawho?"

Bingo checks the rear view.

Whitebread sits pretty in a yellow Porsche, riding smack-dab-close to the Buick's bumper. Vexed, Bingo pumps his brakes and slows up, itching for Whitebread to swallow hook, line 'n' bohos. Success. The fella hammers his horn, disappearing from the rear view before pulling up beside them.

"Get that piece of shit off the fuckin road, asshole," Whitebread jaws.

"You want what I got," Bingo yells back.

"Porch monkey."

"Cracker."

The Porsche turns left, accelerates down a side street, and the two of them flip each other off.

Bingo turns to Jonah. "That there's Curranvale City. Rich bitches from Oldeham Proper with no love for a nigga."

Once the Buick inches forward a couple a blocks, they pass peace marchers crowding the sidewalk, slipping between multi-generational all-sorts with red and black targets on their faces, twirling flags and waving placards. "Check it, yo. This here business in Eye-Raq is an argument between white folk." The army of protesters link arms, singing. "We got no say in nuthin what matters."

Near a hospital, cops with gas masks and plastic shields sit on brown horses in front of paddy wagons.

"This is a lot like Liwani," Jonah says. "Riot police. Tear gas."

"Absolute power corrupts absofuckinlutely, brah," Bingo replies.

After the traffic clears, the Buick follows a loop to the right on to Gammel Lane before driving among homes with manicured

hedges and children who pedal their bikes on the sidewalk. ★ ★ ★
★ ★
★ ★
★ After the
first day of class, I force myself to pop in for a quick meet-and-
greet with the other writing candidates in the writers' lounge.

To settle myself, I chug back three bottles of ale in under ten
minutes.

Good to go, I mingle.

Quint C., from New York City, is there with his pink mouth
and green eyes, blinking in tennis whites with a tennis racket
tucked into an underarm. He's in the third semester of his graduate degree, and he has a sandy crown of hair.

"I think it's all about finding a compatible bang buddy," he says.

"Bang buddy?" I ask.

"A jump off," he replies. "The rest is bourgeois bullcrap."

"What about human nature?" I ask. "Your methododology …"

"Method," Quint C. corrects.

"Your methodology encourages people to get trapped in a
relationship with a faux egalitarian they didn't realize was a proto-
Stalinist."

"No, no. I'm talking on a higher plane," he says. "More …
Nietzsche. Straight-up banging for the strong, no weaklings need
apply."

Eliza May Morton, returning to school after five years working
at a desk job in San Francisco, interrupts us. She wears a leopard
skin hat with a matching overcoat. Her shoes are some sort of
purplish half boot.

"Love is a series of associations that add up to the desire for
unconditional surrender," she says.

Quint C. and I both groan.

"For real," she continues. "You get to a point where the only sane option seems to unconditionally accept everything about the other person, and vice versa."

"Now *that's* how you end up married to a Stalinist," Quint C. says.

"Herehere," I say.

After the clinking of glasses, I look around the room at students from the English program. They stand in small clumps near a long table furnished with wine, cheese, cold cuts, and grapes. Behind the fixings is an Asian woman in a tight pink sweater, with waist-length jet black hair braided into a tail that runs parallel to her spine. She fishes a bottle of beer from an ice-filled cooler, fumbles with a bottle opener, and curses when foam cascades all over a plate of cold cuts.

"Who's your agent?" Quint C. asks Eliza May.

"Don't have one."

"I'm with Rachel Dalgleish."

"Who?"

"Her list includes three National Book Award winners."

"Doesn't she represent the porn star?" I ask. Luanne Damme's well-known for her transition from skank to respected Internet porn entrepreneur.

"Yah," he sighs. "To make it in the biz you can't depend on the writing anymore. Not many people will say it, but these days you pretty much need a personal trainer who'll recommend the best colonoscopy to get you prepped for your close up."

"I'm thinking about writing my next story on amphetamines," Eliza May says.

"Writing on amphetamines, or about amphetamines?" I ask.

"After ingesting them," she replies. "Know where I can get some?"

"Ask him," I say.

"Why me?" Quint C. asks.

"You've got an agent with a hookup in the porn industry."

Quint C. smiles.

"Are you writing anything?" Eliza May says to me.

I'm unprepared. "Yup. A novel." I've taken Professor Iton's words to heart and plan to take more unconventional risks. "The hope is to write it in eighteen parts. Eighteen. Sort of like infinity, if you know anything about sacred numbers. Anyway, the point is I'm crafting something that is evolving ... organically. From the gut."

"You don't have an outline?" Quint C. asks.

"Why should he?" Eliza May says.

"'Cause he probably writes twenty pages for every one he keeps," he says.

I ignore him. "I'm not interested in knowing where it's going," I say. "I'd rather make discoveries as I go along."

"Dude, the last thing you need ..."

"Should we sit for this?" Eliza May interrupts.

"The last thing you need is to listen to Professor Iton," Quint C. continues. "The guy's published more than ten books, so it's easy for him to talk about the meaninglessness of publication and the sanctity of the craft." He shifts his racket from one armpit to the other. "Don't get me wrong, I like the highbrow stuff as much as the next elitist. But publishers aren't philanthropists, and that, my friends, means that editors with sales quotas are looking for what's accessible to the well-populated, middle of the pack. Forget experimental drivel for an ideal reader. Make a plan. Write something for the person who'll wear brown cardigans in the fall, 'cause a recognizable personality says it's what's done."

"Forget all that reader-response bullshit," Eliza May replies. "What's needed is a return to the days the public intellectual influenced the culture."

"Like who?" Quint C. asks.

"The Beats, for one."

"Let me get this straight," Quint C. interjects. "You have no interest whatsoever in *any* interaction between the reader and the text?"

"Catering to the reader has gone too far," Eliza May says. "It's become about marketing to an idea of the informed reader. So a book's meaning has more to with the work's potential demand than the quality of a writer's thinking."

"That's just a whole lotta text-as-object wind-baggery." Quint puts a hand on my shoulder. "Dude! Make an outline of your story. Maps help."

Mrs Markham, the Silver Fox, interrupts.

"Jonah! You've got a call about your grandfather. It sounds important."

My stomach begins to churn.

Quickly, I leave a beer bottle on the table in front of the pink sweater with the long braid of hair. Terrified.

She winks at me, and then continues to dab spilled beer suds from the table.

BOOK VIII

The Plimsoll Line

I

Realigning himself, Jonah works his way toward an ending, one task at a time, until visiting hours. He arranges the tables for lunch, mops the linoleum floor, then dusts behind the radiators

He's one good choice after the next, one good decision followed by another:

Health and strength and vitamin water.

Nuts and fruit and salad after soup.

Turns of exercise of up and down the hallway between three square meals.

A fresh reboot at foundational ethics.

Flossing and brushing.

Conversation that is sensible and meditation that is prayer.

Relationships that are like a tortoise shell carried around as a complementary part of the whole.

Promises made that can be kept.

Cream on the bottom of the feet.

Doing laundry once a week.

Taking care of others in equal if not greater proportion to taking care of oneself, and work through the day before resting at night.

On the outside, he will plant a garden in the summer, feed the robins sunflower seeds, and out of respect for his grandfather make peace with the Rev.

He will live modestly on what's left of the inheritance, pay off debts, and give a ten-percent tithe to charities in Liwani at each month's end.

He'll scratch rows into notepads, and he will learn to practise a dependence on a necessary other that is within. ★ I push the door that does not close but always swings open, collect my belongings from a storage locker, retrieve my belt and my wallet, clutch tightly onto my keys (the first metal objects I've had in my hands for days).

For the final time, I limp through the hallway, passing the girly girl who sits at her door waiting for the man who makes action films to take her away to a place with a fabulous pool. Then I stop at the nurse's station to sign a yellow paper before I'm buzzed through the locked door.

It's cold.

I make my way to an elevator, take it down to the main floor, and walk through an emergency-filled room with those who twist in an overflow of beds lining a hallway that smells of camphor. Breathing slow, I hobble toward revolving glass doors that twirl me into the sun's blinding glare. Drawn to solids, I steady myself against a wall beside a sidewalk lightly dusted with snow.

THE END[134]

---

134   So ends Volume One of our brief history. A second volume is in the works despite disputes with certain well-regarded critics over questions about plotting, the lack of adequate closure at the story's end, arguments over the representation of gender as well as race, lack of agreement over the realism of the dialog, and chatter about disturbing shifts in the narrative voice. In addition, legal matters regarding Reverend Tusker are pending. Currently without a title, an early draft of the subsequent volume deals with a number of outstanding issues: Jonah Ayot-Kolosha sightings in the Graduate Department of Theology at the University of Pennsylania, the subsequent fate of his inheritance, concerns pursuant to Hiroko Ishigowa and Clementine "Da Stylus" Pinkston that may or may not result in marriage, the meteoric rise and fall and rise again of certain characters in prominent literary circles, and finally an accounting of business matters in regards to book sales of Volume One in the US, Italian, French, Indian, and English markets. —ELIZA MAY MORTON

David N. Odhiambo is a novelist, poet, and playwright, and the author of two previous novels, *Kipligat's Chance* (St Martin's Press) and *diss/ed banded nation* (Polestar). Born in Nairobi, Kenya, he moved to Canada in 1977, where he lived in Winnipeg, Montreal, and Vancouver. He subsequently studied writing in Amherst, MA, and now lives in Honolulu.